THE
SERPENT'S
FANG

THE SERPENT'S FANG

An Everett Carr Mystery

Matthew Booth

To David,
In memory of a mentor, a colleague, and a dear friend

Praise for the Everett Carr Mysteries

"Everett Carr makes an excellent detective. He has his own sufferings, which make him compassionate as well as a shrewd judge of human nature, and he's observant of every unexplained detail. ...*The Serpent's Fang* is everything you want in a 'Golden Age' mystery: a country house, stolen poison, a missing will, and the denouement in the library where Carr reveals the final shocking twist. I couldn't put it down and such is the dastardly ingenuity of Matthew Booth that I didn't guess whodunnit."—Jean Briggs, author of the Charles Dickens Mysteries

"...an engrossing mystery, with a despised murder victim and a group of suspects, each of whom has a strong motive to kill the victim. The description of each character is finely drawn, the setting atmospheric, and the conclusion to the mystery eminently satisfying. So many secrets. So many suspects. So many twists and turns. *The Serpent's Fang* offers a sting in the tail."—Laraine Stephens, author of The Reggie da Costa Mysteries

"...a macabre but satisfyingly cosy crime. Booth handles the introduction of his quite significant cast with grace and ease...the opening scenes flow so beautifully together and the murder itself does not disappoint."—Mairi Chong, author of the Dr Cathy Moreland Mysteries, Amazon

"Everett Carr is...a marvellous protagonist. This is a descriptive, well-paced mystery...a recommended read for mystery lovers."—Fiona Alison, The Historical Novel Society

"Booth's work is about as good as it gets. We see the master craftsman at work. His characters not only behave in a believable fashion, they speak in a believable fashion. Echoes of Christie and Sayers here, and the plot, characters, and dialogue are all of the best and all fit together perfectly."—John Hall, author of *Death of a Collector*: A Freddie Darnborough Mystery\

"A classic locked room mystery in the finest tradition which will delight old and new readers alike"—Dr M Jones, Amazon

"A classic page-turner and must-read for all fans of Christie, Sayers, James and the country house murder mystery genre"—Ms M Powell, Amazon

"An Everett Carr Mystery is not to be missed. The sense of time and place is there on every page, and author Matthew Booth knows how to spin a tangled web of people, murder and blackmail in a fashion reminiscent of the best 'Golden Age' mysteries."—Helen (helenfrominyocounty), Goodreads

"Enter the marvellous and enigmatic Everett Carr, who sees beyond the seemingly impossible …a wonderful homage to the Golden Age of crime"—intheamazone, Amazon reviewer

I

PART ONE: PREMONITION OF DEATH

Chapter One

"I'm so frightened, because I think one of them is going to kill her."

Everett Carr had been in the cemetery for perhaps half an hour when he heard the voice. He had not been aware of anyone else in his immediate vicinity until the words, shrill and desperate, were borne on the breeze towards him. Looking back, it seemed almost to be a question of fate that he should overhear this particular fear being uttered at that particular time. A moment of time either earlier or later, and he might never have come into contact with the Kettering family, and the whole truth about a murder and an attempted suicide might never have been brought to light.

Carr was a regular visitor to the cemetery, since it was here that his wife, Miranda, was buried. He felt no compunction about sitting in the particular peace which religious surroundings offer, but to claim any devout faith would be an act of hypocrisy. He had believed in the Scriptures as a young man and had attended services accordingly from a young age, but his experiences in life had been such that his belief now was more cautious than it once had been. It was not simply the human wickedness that Carr had witnessed personally that raised those questions in his mind, but it was also larger issues that strived to twist faith beyond endurance: the consequences of the recent German elections, Stalin's Bolshevik purges, civil wars across the world, and economic disasters. The world was changing, too quickly for the tide to be turned, and Everett Carr felt it keenly and faced it with trepidation, searching in vain for any sensible argument that it was part of any plan of a tolerant, forgiving, and loving God. These thoughts prevented Carr from entering the church to worship, but he had no qualms about visiting the resting place of Miranda, and, while he was there, he knew that the only matter of importance was that he felt as close as possible to his wife.

The shattered knee began to ache. Doctors told him it was the cold affecting the wound, and he had never argued the point, but in his private moments, he felt it had less to do with the weather and more to do with guilt. The bullet in his knee was one of many that had found a target on that fateful day. They had all been meant for him, retribution for a sentence he had delivered on a dangerous and violent criminal, but only this one, now embedded in his knee, had hit him. The others had all gone into Miranda. Carr had survived, his wife had not. Another piece of what people said was God's plan, which seemed to Carr to be not only cruel but insane, and another reason to question what he had been brought up to believe. The dull pain in his leg, the lameness which he had suffered since that day, was a permanent reminder of what had happened and what he had lost, a physical memento of the fact that she had died in his place.

The headstone, which bore Miranda's name, was obviously no substitute for her, but it was strangely comforting. There had been times when he had spoken to it, called it by her name, which had seemed ridiculous to him initially, but which had become increasingly natural as time passed. Comfort, he supposed, had to be found wherever possible. On that day, he had said nothing, however. He had simply stared at the engraved letters, the dates, and the Shakespearean quotation, simple but suitable:

> *"Fear no more the heat o' the sun,*
> *Nor the furious winter's rage."*

Miranda had always loved the sonnets, and it had seemed to Carr at the time that the choice of epithet had been made for him. He had taken the lurid, crimson handkerchief from the top pocket of his black jacket and dabbed at the corner of his eye. Something must have blown into it, he thought, as there was the slightest trace of water running from it.

And then, without warning, the words had floated through the air to him. They had seemed almost intrusive in the solemn tranquillity of the cemetery, and Carr had been instinctively startled by them. The voice had been a young girl's, strident and laced with suppressed fear, so that it was evident that it had been louder than the girl had intended, and the words themselves surely suggested that it was hardly appropriate for them to be so casually overheard.

"I'm so frightened, because I think one of them is going to kill her."

Carr kissed two of his gloved fingers and pressed them against Miranda's stone, offering brief words of love and farewell. Then, stiffly and slowly, his leg resisting the effort, he walked in the direction from which he fancied the voice had come. He did not have to walk far before he saw the girl. She was kneeling in front of a headstone and, as he drew nearer, he saw that she was younger than he had imagined, perhaps not much over majority. The skin was naturally pale, but the chillness of the breeze had stained the cheeks pink so that they glowed like small, delicate apples. She was dressed in a long, dark coat, with a pillbox hat, similarly funereal in colour, as if the girl had thought that her presence in a graveyard demanded a morbid formality of dress. Blooming from under the confines of the hat was a cloud of curled, platinum hair and, behind the short lace veil, there was a pair of grey eyes, two large discs of slate, which now stared at Carr as he approached. He held up his hand and gave her a smile of reassurance.

"Forgive me, my child, I do not mean to intrude."

"Who are you?" Her voice was alert, refined, but held within itself a blade of defence against this stranger.

"A fellow mourner, only. I'm sorry to say that I have good reason to come here regularly. My name is Carr." He gave a small bow.

"I come here often, as well," the girl confessed. She pointed to the headstone before her. "My grandmother. I miss her terribly."

Carr lowered his head. "My wife lies only a few yards from here. I miss her terribly, too."

"How did your wife die?"

The question was unexpected and abruptly direct, and Carr was caught off guard by it. He flushed a little, stammering the beginnings of a response, and gave an embarrassed gasp of a laugh. The girl was immediately aware of her tactlessness and rose to her feet, shaking her head in apology.

"I am so sorry," she bleated, "that was stupidly intrusive of me, and it is really none of my business. I'm afraid I can be a bit of a raging bull sometimes. You must think me awfully rude."

Carr had recovered himself, and he shook his head against this effusive apology. "Think nothing of it, my child."

The girl seemed hardly to have heard him. "Of course, you don't have to answer me. In fact, I won't let you answer me."

"She was killed." It was a statement of fact, spoken softly but with no demand for sympathy or comfort, and without any suggestion of an invitation to probe further.

The girl stared at him, her grey eyes fixed in shock on him. She seemed to be seeing him for the first time, and she found herself strangely captivated by the darkness of his eyes, the calm authority of his expression, and the polite humility of his manner. The luxurious moustache and Imperial beard, as bone white as the swept-back hair, were startlingly impressive, but she felt that his face without them would lack something of its obvious kindliness. Like her, he was dressed in black, but there was an incongruously gaudy handkerchief and necktie, both in the same deep scarlet colour which contrasted severely with the solemnity of the rest of his attire. And now she saw for the first time the silver-handled walking stick he used and, as he shifted his weight, she recognised the obvious lameness from which he suffered. His age was uncertain, but she had the impression of a man who might look older than he was, perhaps because of the white hair and the sadness lurking behind those otherwise kindly eyes. In some ways, he reminded her of her grandfather, also deceased, and the memory sparked in her an immediate assurance of trust.

She held out her hand, which he took with another small, courteous bow. "My name is Josephine Kettering. I'm pleased to meet you, Mr Carr."

"The honour, my child, is mine. Forgive me," he added, after a short but diplomatic pause, "but I came over to see you because, by chance, I heard you say something which, I confess, startled me."

Josephine bit her lower lip, and Carr noticed now that the teeth, though kept in perfect condition, were slightly too large. He wondered if she had sucked her thumb as a child. "I didn't realise I'd said it so loudly."

"You sounded distressed, perhaps with just cause, and I wondered if you might wish to discuss it."

"With you?" She was surprised rather than alarmed by the suggestion.

Carr shrugged. "If what I heard is a genuine fear of yours, you must do something about it, my child. If it is not a genuine fear, perhaps the unbiased opinion of a stranger might help you to see it. And, if I may be so bold, Miss Kettering, it seems to me that if a person must resort to voicing such fears to a gravestone, it suggests that there may not be too many living people whom that person feels able to trust."

Josephine smiled at his gentle candour. "I would always seek solace in my grandmother, Mr Carr. Confide in her and ask her advice. After she died, whenever I felt I needed her, I'd come here. She never replies, though." The joke was well-intentioned, but it deserved neither a response from Carr nor the false laugh with which Josephine rewarded it.

"But I can reply, my dear," Carr said with a smile, "if you'll permit me."

Josephine had begun to weep silently. "I would like that, I think."

Carr nodded and offered her his arm. "Then let us find a tea shop nearby, out of the cold, and see what we can do. Yes?" The deal was struck with an increase in the flow of tears and a relieved nod of her head.

They went to a small café off the Edgware Road. It was not busy, and Carr asked for a table in a corner, near the window, to ensure as much privacy as they could expect. Josephine, while not at ease, was still convinced in her ability to trust this man who had drifted into her life, and if there had been any doubt about it, the warmth of the tea rooms and the prospect of hot, sweet tea would have been sufficient to dispel it. They placed their order, and Carr held out the small wooden chair for Josephine before seating himself opposite her. She watched him as he removed his coat and hat, placing them on the stand behind him, before easing himself into the seat and resting his cane gently against the tip of the table. She found herself mesmerised by his precise, feline movements, as he carefully, almost fussily, unfolded the napkin and placed it across his lap. She could see now the silver skull, which he wore as a lapel pin, and whose ruby eyes were, along with the lurid red of the handkerchief and necktie, the only colour in his appearance. He was, she thought, a fascinating little man, but whether he actively set out to be or not, she couldn't be sure. She doubted it. She suspected that this was simply how he was, that he gave no special thought to it, and she supposed that any fascination he prompted in others was more a result of their own eccentricities rather than his. Involuntarily, a gentle smile of unsuspected and unwarranted affection flickered across her lips.

He made amiable but inconsequential talk until the tea arrived and had been poured, and the small plate of scones and jam placed between them. He offered her the plate, but she declined, and likewise, for the moment, he resisted. Instead, he latticed his fingers together on the table and smiled at her.

"Now, my dear," he said, "let us talk."

"I don't know where to begin," Josephine said softly. "I'm afraid it will all sound so foolish if I say it out loud to another person."

Carr quoted Josephine's words to her. "*I'm so frightened, because I think one of them is going to kill her.*' Let's start with that. Who do you think might be killed?"

Josephine sipped some of the tea. "My mother. You may know of her. She was once the actress Rowena Steele."

Carr's eyebrows raised slightly, and his dark eyes widened in surprise. "Not only an actress, but a great one. I saw her once as Lady Macbeth. A captivating performance."

"She'll be glad to hear you say so. She does so love to be admired."

"I have not heard of her for some time."

Josephine shook her head. "She retired from the stage, Mr Carr. Almost three years ago now."

"May I ask why?"

"She says that when a woman reaches a certain age, the stage is no longer interested in her, even if she remains in love with the stage."

Carr had the impression that the excuse, created by Rowena Steele, had only been repeated by her daughter. "There is more to her decision than that, surely."

The girl nodded. "Her eyesight began to fail her. Reading the lines became too difficult. It's beastly, isn't it? Hard to imagine."

"A tragedy indeed," said Carr. "She is not altogether blind?"

"No, but the doctors say they can't rule it out."

Carr shook his head and clasped his hands in his lap. "Life can be very cruel."

Josephine nodded her agreement but had no desire to prolong the conversation. "Then, of course, there's Daddy."

Carr raised his eyebrows. "He surely didn't force your mother into abandoning her career?"

"He's never said so, but he's Ivor Kettering." She said it as if it explained everything. "You'll know his name, too, I suppose, from the newspapers."

Carr bowed his head. "Indeed, I do."

"Well, he's had to work his way up to where he is in the government now, and I daresay he thought his career wouldn't be helped very much if he had an actress for a wife." The tone of voice was sufficient to suggest her personal views on the matter, even without the additional comment that followed, delivered in a hushed, bitter voice. "He's never said it. I just get the feeling. You must think me very cruel."

"Not at all," said Carr, with a smile.

"Daddy's lost interest in Mummy, anyway, and found somebody else. Daphne Clements, much younger than Daddy, of course, which I suppose is the point. Mummy is furious, as you might expect, and simply refuses to grant Daddy a divorce."

"I see." There was a gravity to Carr's tone of voice. "Your father and this lady…are they who you fear might harm your mother?"

Josephine nodded, her eyes starting to brim with tears. "Daddy is so used to getting his own way, you see. I just wish Mummy would let him go because I'm frightened of what he might do otherwise."

Carr's voice was solemn. "Do you think your father is capable of doing what you fear?"

Josephine Kettering looked into his eyes and her lips parted slightly, as if an answer was about to be given, but something about its nature prevented her from uttering it. Her uncertainty hung across her expression like a frost over hillsides on a winter's morning. For Carr, it was answer enough, and the sudden aversion of her gaze showed that she knew it.

"And then, there's Felix," she said.

"Felix?"

She dabbed at her eyes with a lace handkerchief. "My step-brother, Daddy's son by his first marriage."

"And what part does he play in your troubles?"

"I don't know really, but I saw him and Mummy having a terrible row a few days ago. Felix looked as if the Devil had got hold of him. He was barking in Mummy's face, pointing angrily at her with one hand and the other balled into a fist. I was frightened for her, Mr Carr, I truly was. When I asked him about it, he was terribly rude, even hurtful. He told me to disappear and mind my own business."

"Did you ask your mother about it?"

A nod of the head. "She told me not to worry. Felix would get his comeuppance, she said, and she was not afraid of him, so nor should I be. And I'm not afraid of Felix, not really, but when I saw him being so threatening to my mother, I do find myself afraid of what he might do. Can you understand that, Mr Carr?"

He smiled, and the slight nod of the head assured her of it. "You have no idea what this argument between your mother and step-brother was about, though?"

"No. I asked Adele about it, too, but she said something very similar to Felix. I'm afraid she's never really liked me."

"And Adele is…?"

"Felix's fiancée. And the looks I've seen her giving Mummy, Mr Carr…"

She looked out of the window at the traffic on the Edgware Road, wondering briefly about all those people in the city who didn't have to confess their fears to a stranger. None of them, she assumed, were living in the shadow of murder. Carr allowed the silence to pass, knowing that there was more she had to say and that it must be said in her own time.

At last, she broke free from her reverie and looked back across the table at him. "Do you believe you can read murder in someone's eyes?"

"Oh yes, my child."

Josephine wiped another tear away from her eye. "Well, then, I've read it in Adele's."

Slowly, Carr sipped his tea. "And is there anything else, Miss Kettering?"

She hesitated, as if unsure whether to say any more, and she disguised her uncertainty by taking a gulp of tea. When she replaced the cup, it rattled against the saucer, as if it were an audible manifestation of her anxiety. "Only Dr Jarratt, but the situation with him is rather complicated."

Carr gave a small smile. "He has feelings for you?"

Josephine nodded slowly and lowered her head, embarrassed by the confession. "He's asked me to marry him."

"You have refused?"

"Definitely, on each occasion."

"How did Dr Jarratt handle your rejections?"

She shuffled in her chair. "With typical arrogance. He assumed I simply wasn't ready, but that it was only a matter of time. But then Mummy spoke to him."

"She warned him off." It was not a question, as there could be no doubt about it.

Josephine nodded. "I don't know what was said, exactly, but whatever it was, they were both furious. Mummy told me not to be alone with Edwin for a moment, and when I asked her why, she said he was a monster. That was the word she used, Mr Carr—monster."

"She did not elaborate?"

Now, Josephine shook her head. "And I didn't ask. Mother doesn't always encourage further discussion. Sometimes, you know not to say anymore."

"And Dr Jarratt?"

A sudden coldness seemed to come over the girl. Her skin seemed to blanche, her fingers clasped together, and Carr might have been certain that a shiver passed through her. "He called mother all sorts of wicked things, which were shocking in themselves, but he ended by saying that it would be better for everyone if she just…" But the final, inevitable, terrible word would not come to her. It was cut off by a curt, choking sob.

Everett Carr sat in silence for a few moments, his lips pursed beneath the luxurious moustache, and his dark eyes almost hidden by the brows which were drawn forward in concentration. Josephine Kettering also fell silent, but she did not emulate Carr's intense stillness. Instead, she sipped at the tea, now almost cold, and dabbed at her eyes, now almost dry, with the lace handkerchief. The scones remained untouched.

"Now, Miss Kettering," said Carr at last, "I wonder if it would be possible for me to speak to your mother myself."

Josephine was reluctant. "But then she would know that…"

Carr held up a silencing hand. "It is very important that I speak to her, my child, and I will be discreet, I assure you."

And then, in that moment, Josephine understood. "You don't think my fears are unfounded, do you?"

Carr shook his head. "No."

Her hands began to tremble, and she could feel her stomach quivering with anxiety, a feeling of nausea rising to her throat. But she refused to succumb to it and, even more fervently, she refused to cry. "Can you help us?"

Carr smiled. "I hope so."

A sudden sense of hope, of relief, sprang into Josephine's spirit. "I'm so very glad I met you, Mr Carr. Are you free this weekend?"

The question seemed to surprise him. "I believe so."

"Daddy is having some sort of weekend party at Marsden Grange, our place in Longhampton, on the Norfolk coast. I didn't think I could face it, with everything going on in my head, but if you could come, then I would feel so much better about it, somehow. And everyone will be there."

Carr reached into his inside pocket and pulled out a small, black leather diary, which he consulted. "I am free," he said, taking out a pencil from his pocket and making a note of the engagement. "I shall be there. You will be good enough, perhaps, to send me some instructions on how to get there?" He handed her a business card. "To that address, if you would."

Josephine heaved a sigh of relief and, instinctively, threw her hands onto his. "Thank you, Mr Carr. You're so very kind."

"Not at all." Carr pulled his watch from his waistcoat pocket and glanced down at it. "Now, alas, I must go."

"Yes, of course. I should, too."

He paid for the tea, put on his hat and coat, and made a gesture to her that he would follow her to the door. It was not until they were outside, the air now colder than it had been earlier, that Josephine spoke once more. "Mr Carr, may I ask you a question?"

"Of course."

"Are you some sort of detective?"

Carr smiled and gave a shake of his head. "No, my child. I am not a detective. But I am, if you will permit it, a friend," he said, resting his hand on her arm. Then, with a bow and a tip of his hat, he turned on his heel and she watched him disappear into the crowds.

Chapter Two

Rowena Kettering had not noticed the rain begin to fall. How long she had been sitting there, staring out of the window of the house in Campden Hill Square, was impossible to say, but it seemed to her now that it must have been raining for some time. The streaks of water down the windowpane, like the tracks of tears down the palest of cheeks, suggested a prolonged period of rainfall, but Rowena was sure that there had been no suggestion of it when she had sat down at the window for a quiet moment of privacy. Now that she was aware of it, Rowena focused on the patterns of the water on the glass, taking in their detail and beauty, both curious and random, before looking out over the park to see them replicated on the leaves of the trees, and in the glistening sleekness of the streets and pavements. She had never before realised quite how entrancing and strangely soothing heavy rain could be when experienced in isolation and silence, away from the noise of traffic and the bustle of people trying to avoid the wet and the cold. From here, Rowena found it mesmerising, almost intoxicating, and she felt suddenly as if she could sit there forever, staring into the incessant, perpetual rain.

She had come to her bedroom for peace, an escape from the constant talk about the impending weekend in Longhampton. Now, and not for the first time, she contemplated refusing to go. How many people would be sorry if she were absent? Josephine, at least, and Tilly Royce, of course; but beyond those two, Rowena doubted anybody would care. Certainly not Edwin Jarratt, and now, after the argument of the other day, she suspected Felix and Adele would resent her presence. She did not care about Jarratt, of course, not knowing what he was, but she could convince herself that she regretted Felix's dislike of her. He was not an easy man to like, and Rowena knew that stepmothers were very often perceived as wicked and malicious, but she had tried so hard not to live up to the cliché. She flattered herself that she might have succeeded, had it not been for Adele Mills. If Rowena's suspicions were correct, Felix was better off without her, if she could only make him see it. He had accused her of interfering in his personal affairs, and Rowena supposed that it was true, but her motives were pure. And yet, Rowena could not lie to herself. She did not like Felix Kettering, and if he wanted to marry a dangerous woman like Adele Mills, then it was not up to Rowena to stop it. Let Felix marry the harlot and be damned to him. But there was always Ivor, and if Felix came to harm, it would bring a much crueller harm to his father. Rowena wiped away an unconsciously shed tear.

Ivor…

Rowena knew that it had taken courage for him to request her company for tea one afternoon. He had not been entirely convivial on that first engagement, but over the course of a few more, Rowena had begun to find a charming and thoughtful man under the frosted veneer. When he had explained that he had been married before, with a son, Felix, to show for it, Rowena had been surprised but not shocked. Every living person had a background, a past that brought to any new relationship or acquaintance the memories and scars of those that had gone before. It was what made a human being and Rowena, despite her dramatic inclinations, was not so fanciful as to be unaware of the fact. If she had been shocked, it would have been the worst type of hypocrisy, since she had hardly lived a life of purity. If Ivor's childhood went some way to explain his austere manner, the news that his first wife had died seemed to complete her understanding.

And yet, despite his reticence and repressions, she had always known that Ivor Kettering had been captivated by Rowena Steele from the moment he had met her. There had been a flicker of devotion in his curiously grey eyes which had betrayed his immediate feelings towards her. It had been so slight that she might easily have missed it, like the gentle vibration of a needle that serves as a precursor to an earthquake, but she had seen it for certain. Only later did Rowena realise that Ivor Kettering had fallen for her as soon as he had looked at her because of a flaw in his character. The truth was that Ivor was one of those men who, starved of love as a child, fell deeply into it too readily as an adult. Rowena knew it now, but she would never have suspected it if she had not seen that same almost imperceptible flicker of immediate infatuation in Ivor's eyes when he had been introduced to Daphne Clements.

It had been only a few months earlier, at one of the dinner parties that a government minister and his wife were expected to attend. In her own way, Rowena enjoyed them: the spectacle of the evening gowns, the sparkle of the chandelier lights on the champagne flutes, the politely artificial conversations with strangers, so unlike the discussions held in private, and the equally mannered movements around the room, all seeming so very like the world of the theatre which she so sorely missed. Ivor claimed never to enjoy those dinners, although Rowena never believed him. She suspected he indulged himself in the formality of the occasions, just as she did in their theatricality, but both their attitudes to them were to change, once Daphne Clements entered their lives. Wiping away another tear, Rowena reflected on just how much had changed since that moment, and it was much more than their mutual enjoyment of political dinners.

At first, Rowena had deceived herself, pretending that there was nothing about her marriage that needed to worry her until she had almost convinced herself of it. After all, if she had detected something in Ivor's demeanour that suggested the worst, Rowena had seen none of it reciprocated in Daphne Clements. And there was the girl's age, of course. She was perhaps some years older than Josephine, but she could not have been very much younger than Felix. It was scarcely credible, then, that she could be attracted to Ivor, a man old enough to be her father. Such things did happen, of course, and Rowena had witnessed it in her years as an actress, but there was still nothing in Daphne's conduct around Ivor to suggest anything approaching love. Fondness, perhaps, but not that smoke raised with the fume of sighs.

Rowena's personal denials, inevitably, came home to her soon enough. It was not long before she noticed the prolonged glances between her husband and this younger woman, increasingly regular invitations for her to come to dine at Campden Hill Square, and her barely hidden desire that Ivor should walk her home. If Rowena had tried to persuade herself that there was innocence in these factors, she had failed. Her suspicions deepened, her reluctance to believe any of it began to erode, and her determination to keep her husband intensified. Until, at last, he had confronted her with her worst fear.

He had said it without preamble, and without any emotion, as if he were commenting on the weather. They had suffered a silent dinner alone, neither of them eating very much, and both of them aware that there was a malignant spectre over their feast, something which had to be said but which neither of them seemed able to address. As it was, Ivor was silent because he was biding his time, waiting for the moment, and Rowena said nothing because she didn't want to discuss it. So, the question of divorce hung between them like a silent, unspoken cancer.

"Rowena, I want a divorce."

Once spoken, it had momentarily seemed anticlimactic. Rowena had feared it so much that to hear the words spoken seemed to diminish their effect and their meaning, as if their power over her had been in her mind rather than in the words themselves. She was conscious of the notion, but it only briefly flashed across her mind, and once it had passed, she felt the nausea of betrayal consume her.

"So that you can marry a girl young enough to be your daughter?" she had said. "Do you realise how stupid that makes you sound, Ivor?"

"I don't want a scene, Rowena."

"No, I'm sure you don't. I'm sure you want your own way, like you always have. I'm sure you want me to allow you to trample all over my feelings so that you can look after your own. Well, I won't allow it, Ivor."

"It isn't a question of allowing me to do anything, Rowena."

"Isn't it? You need my consent to divorce, Ivor, and I won't give it." She had looked away from him. "How can you do this to me? After everything we've been through, everything we've faced together. And with what's happening now."

"You can't hold that against me."

She had glared back at him now, the tears flowing. "I'm going blind, Ivor! How can you possibly think of leaving me to deal with it on my own?"

Ivor was not so selfish or cruel as not to be moved by the words, but he had known that any reply would seem unwittingly callous. "I can't help how I feel, Rowena. And a divorce doesn't mean total isolation from each other," he had added. "I can still give you any help you need."

She had sneered. "Must you be so idealistic? Or is it simple naivety? You don't know much about people, Ivor, if you think Daphne Clements will allow you to nursemaid me while she sits at home."

"She's not vindictive."

Rowena's eyes had hardened. "Are you sure about that, Ivor? What do they say about scorned women?"

"You're being ridiculous."

Rowena had spat in his face, a satisfying but oddly pitiable response. "If you leave me, Ivor, I'll kill myself."

For a moment, he had stared into her eyes, trying desperately to find a trace either of bluff or, more frighteningly, truth. At last, he had seen what had come as no surprise. It was a familiar glimmer of one of her more frustrating qualities. "Must you always be so melodramatic?"

"I mean it."

He had shaken his head. "No, you don't. You don't have the courage."

And, in the end, she had lowered her head. "You can't blame me. I don't think fighting to save a marriage and one's own happiness can be classed as being melodramatic. You're only saying it to make me sound unreasonable, hysterical, as if it will give you some more validation for walking away. You think people will sympathise with you for leaving a histrionic woman. You think they'll wonder how you managed to put up with it for so long."

"I don't think anything of the sort," he had replied. "This is really very simple, Rowena. I don't love you anymore, I love Daphne. These things happen. We have to be sensible about them."

She had risen from the table. "How long do you think Daphne Clements will tolerate that sort of cynical arrogance? Or will you not give her long enough to discover it, Ivor? Maybe the next one will come along sooner than even you expect."

"There won't be any others," he had said. "I love Daphne, and that is all there is to it."

"You loved me when you first met me."

"Things change."

"Things will change with Daphne."

He had shaken his head. "They won't. I want a divorce, Rowena. Will you grant it or not?"

Her answer had been immediate. "No, Ivor. I won't."

The discussion, request, and refusal, or a variation on them, had been repeated several times over the subsequent days and weeks, but the outcome of it had never altered. The atmosphere between them had soured, but Rowena refused to buckle under its bitter pressure. Ivor went about his business, only speaking to her when necessary, and his tones brisk and efficient, as if she were his secretary rather than his wife. They had moved into separate bedrooms, blaming the incompatibility of her occasional bouts of insomnia and his need for early starts in the mornings when he was expected at the House. She doubted any of them cared if the lie was believed or not, except perhaps for Josephine. Whatever else divided them, whoever else came between them, Josephine was a bond between them that could not be shaken, corroded, or soiled. In that, at least, Rowena felt sure they were in agreement. Especially after what had happened to Peter…

Her thoughts were broken by the sound of a knock at the door. Somehow, even before she gave consent to enter, she knew it would be Ivor. He stepped into the room, not as if it were a room in the house they owned, but as if it were an intrusion into a stranger's privacy.

"May I come in?"

Rowena gave a short, tired sigh. Surely, they were not yet so distant that he needed such permission. If they were, she thought, perhaps it was time to end it after all. "Of course, you can come in."

He closed the door behind him and walked slowly towards her, joining her at the window. "Dreadful weather."

"You didn't come to talk about the rain, Ivor."

She looked up at him, finding him looking down on her with an expression which she might otherwise have mistaken for compassion, but which seemed to her altogether more like pity. Age had not withered him, but somehow had improved him. He had grown into his face, so that what had once appeared to be aloofness now came across as a dignified authority. The hair, once brown, had turned an iron grey and both the colour and style suited him, being brushed back over his slightly too prominent forehead, with its now permanent crease at the bridge of the nose. The hair was the same shade of grey that the eyes had always been, a biological trait that Josephine had inherited, and the simple, horn-rimmed spectacles, which he was compelled to wear, emphasised the intelligence of his features. Despite everything, Rowena still found him an attractive, desirable man, even if now she almost hated herself for it.

"I wanted to have a word," he said, although she did not respond. "The fact is that I've changed my mind."

For a moment, her heart seemed as if it was about to fall out of her breast. "About wanting a divorce?"

He was embarrassed by the presumption, the cheeks flushing briefly, and the mouth stammering silently for a moment. "No, not about that."

Rowena felt instantly foolish and despised herself for the naïve display of optimism. "Of course not."

"I meant about Daphne and this weekend."

She glared up at him, her eyes fierce with livid fury, and, in that moment, she hated him more than ever. But the anger quickly gave way, submitting itself to a much more profound sense of hurt and sadness. He had made her a pledge, a vow that he would not allow Daphne Clements to attend the weekend gathering at Longhampton, and now he was here, in her private solitude, retracting his word. Of all his betrayals, somehow, this seemed to Rowena to be the cruellest of all.

"You promised me," she hissed, the tears breaking her voice. "You promised me you wouldn't do this."

"I know, I'm sorry." If he meant it, his face was unaware of the fact. "But this weekend is important to me, Rowena, and I want her there."

"You can't," she barked, "and I won't allow it."

Calmly, almost cruelly, he shook his head. "It is my party, Rowena, to celebrate my appointment to government. Who attends, who I invite, is a matter entirely for me."

"You cruel, arrogant bastard!" Rowena got up from her seat and pushed past him. "Well, if she is there, I won't be."

As a threat, even as an ultimatum, it was worthless, and Ivor knew it as well as Rowena. "Very well. It is your choice."

He walked past her, ignoring the desperate but futile slap of her hand across his shoulder and her hissed declaration of hate. He walked out of the room and closed the door quietly and coldly behind him. Rowena wailed in agony, throwing herself onto the bed and screaming almost inhuman sobs into her pillow. Her head pounded with a dull pain, her eyes burned with tears, and her throat soon began to coarsen with the strain of her weeping. She seemed to be screaming with despair, making as much noise as the most tempestuous storm, but nobody came to her. No enquiry about her anguish, no consolation, and no assurances that life would improve.

Eventually, Rowena Kettering cried herself to an uneasy slumber, but she was not aware of it until she awoke an hour or so later. By then, her tears had stopped, and the rain outside had ceased to fall.

Chapter Three

Felix Kettering had not swallowed the contents of one glass of whisky before he was filling it again for a second. It was too early even for the first, but Felix was hardly in the mood for social convention. There was a time and a place for it, he was willing to admit, but the here and now were neither. It was unlikely that drinking heavily in the afternoon would become a habit for him, in any event, so when the occasion or his mood, even both, demanded it, he was damned if he wasn't going to satisfy the need. Besides, he thought, Rowena and her malice were sufficient justification for any amount of alcohol.

If Felix had ever considered his father's marriage to Rowena Steele to be a betrayal of his mother, he had never said so. He had asked himself the question many times, and he had never thought it was true. He supposed it was because he had barely known his mother, who had died of tuberculosis before he was ten years old, so there was insufficient memory and experience into which Rowena could intrude. She had not played a significant part in his childhood, and he could never accuse her of trying to replace his mother or even act like one to him. If anything, during his later teenage years, Felix had come to suspect that Rowena disliked him. She never said so, but the feeling was impossible to resist. He couldn't say that it troubled him. It might have been different if he had been fond of her, even loved her, but all his teenage self could feel about his stepmother was indifference. She was part of his existence, but she played no part in his life. As far as he was aware, it suited them both; it certainly suited Felix.

Now, however, that indifference had turned to what he could only describe as hatred. The precise moment when one transformed into the other, Felix could not say. It would be too easy to say that the change came with Adele Mills. The more he thought about it, the more Felix considered that Rowena's irrelevance to him had corrupted itself into dislike and, ultimately, hatred long before he had met Adele. If hatred had followed indifference, the hate itself was now usurped by a very definite desire to kill. The sudden awareness of the depth of his aversion to Rowena startled him. The whisky, more than ever, was needed, and he drank the second as swiftly as the first, promising himself that he would have no more.

"You don't need me to tell you it's far too early for that."

"I was thinking about Rowena."

Adele Mills laughed. "If we're doing that, I'll join you."

Felix, ignoring the promise he had made to himself, poured out two large measures of his father's best whisky. "I want to kill her, Adele."

Looking at him over the rim of her glass, with those sapphire eyes peering from under her long lashes, she displayed no emotion, as if the words did not convey a message of disaster or danger, only one of casual interest. Slowly, she sipped the whisky, and he watched the muscles in her throat deal with it, then watched as her tongue ran across her lips, seeking any stray drops.

"When did you have that bright idea?" she asked.

Felix shrugged. "I must have thought about it before without really taking notice of myself."

Adele smiled, but her expression was devoid of any genuine humour. "Then you're way behind me, my darling."

He knew that he should have been alarmed by the remark, not only by its stark confession, which was surely appalling enough, but also by the cold malice with which it had been spoken. But Felix, far from being shocked, felt as if a suspicion which he had long held had been confirmed. If anything about Adele's words came as a disconcerting surprise to him, it was that she appeared to have been nursing the idea of murder for far longer than him. Suddenly, it seemed desperately important to him that he shouldn't have any idea just how long Adele had been thinking about killing Rowena.

"I wish I could say I find it comforting," he said. "As it is, I'm terrified by the idea."

She sat down on the arm of his chair, the movement fluid and seductive, as if she had been poured from a bottle of sin. She crossed one leg over the other and began to play with the soft curls of his brown, boyish hair. He seemed, at first, not to notice her touch, although only seconds passed before he had leaned his head into her breast.

"You mustn't worry, darling," she said. "Everything will be all right."

This universally bland, almost meaningless platitude of assurance did not irritate him, but nor did he take any comfort from it. It was not her voice which soothed him, but the gentle twisting of his hair between her fingers, and the softness of her lips on the crown of his head. It was curiously maternal, this effect she had on him, and he was seldom able to resist it, no matter how much he might want to on those occasions, like now, when it seemed inappropriate. He knew that he should not feel this degree of security in the wake of a discussion, however brief, of murder, but it was impossible to deny how Adele affected him.

"Neither of us mean what we say, do we?" he asked.

"You know," she whispered, "I think that we probably do."

He looked up at her, as if to convince himself that she was joking. The smile on her lips still lacked any humour and appeared more than ever like a snarl of cruelty. "We never used to be like this, Adele."

She shook her head. "No."

"What happened to us?"

Her smile now softened, as if to acknowledge the naivety of his question and the childish innocence which his voice and expression conveyed to her. "Rowena happened to us, Felix. And she'll keep happening to us until we do something about it."

The logic seemed to Felix to be as infallible as it was terrible. He sank back in the chair and sipped the whisky. "I wish things would go back to how they were."

"They can," Adele said. "We can make it be exactly how it was."

How it was, he thought, when he and Adele were happy: before Rowena, before her threats, and before thoughts of murder. It was difficult to imagine that there had been a period of their life together that had not been blighted by Rowena Kettering, but Felix now forced himself to remember those early days of his relationship with Adele, when their existence had seemed to consist solely of music, dancing, and the continuous pop of champagne corks. There had hardly seemed to be a world beyond those evenings of careless, drunken abandon.

Felix had been the stranger, permitted entry into the group of already close friends. It had not been a cold greeting that he had received, but still, he had been conscious of an underlying doubt that he belonged. He would laugh when appropriate, be solemn when the conversation demanded it, and contribute to any discussions when invited to do so. His associates accepted him as part of their circle, but he remained unsure of the legitimacy of his presence. He had been introduced to them, after all, by a young man with whom Felix had only a passing acquaintance, so he could hardly call himself a friend of anyone in the bunch of people with whom he now seemed to spend most of his evenings. The uncertainty was entirely on Felix's part, and he knew it. The crowd had never indicated or suggested that he was unwelcome. If anything, Felix had wondered whether any of them really took any notice of him at all. For that matter, he thought, had any of them truly noticed themselves? Not for the first time, he wondered whether the cocktails, the dancing, the music, and the increasingly frequent lines of white powder had allowed any of those young people whom he had called friends to see or hear anything with any degree of clarity.

It had all changed when he had met Adele Mills. The party in question, held at a stockbroker's apartment overlooking the park, had been the usual bout of aimless frivolity. Looking back, Felix had come to realise that he had grown rather bored of the whole business. How many dry Martinis and erratic tangoes could a man tolerate before the shiny brilliance of the enjoyment of life began to smear? He had been thinking of throwing it all away and returning home when he saw her. The throng of people, dancing to a rhythm scarcely evident in the music being played, had parted suddenly before him, like the Red Sea before Moses, and she had been standing opposite him on the opposite side of the room. For Felix Kettering, the dancing paused, the music stopped, and the champagne evaporated to nothing.

He had walked across the room, pushing his way through the jostling of the dancers, always keeping his eyes fixed on her. She had held his gaze momentarily, before looking away with an apathetic roll of her eyes, as if desperate to give the impression of uninterested detachment. This aloof display had not deterred him, however; if anything, it had encouraged him. Her raised eyebrow, as seductive as it was contemptuous, fascinated him, and the pout of her lips as she raised her cigarette to them exhilarated him. Her hair was blonde, somehow naturally platinum, and the face which was framed by it was similarly pale, so that the sudden streak of scarlet on her lips and the cold blue of her eyes seemed all the more striking. Her gown was the same red as her mouth, and the long satin gloves, stretching to her elbows, were the same intense black of the heavy make-up around her eyes. The small, perfectly formed beauty spot at the corner of her mouth might well have been genuine.

"Good evening," Felix had said. "Would you care for a drink?"

She had looked across at him with a curious expression, a mixture of disdain and intrigue, as though something about him had been at odds with her expectations of him. "That's very kind."

Felix had smiled and stepped over to a tray of cocktails. He had handed her a Martini. She had taken the olive, skewered on its slim sliver of sharpened wood, and she had held it out to him.

"I despise olives," she had said.

Felix had taken the fruit between his thumb and forefinger and dropped it into his mouth. "I'm rather partial to them, myself." Then, when she had squinted at him, he had added: "I hope it doesn't count against me."

"No, why should it?"

And to that question, he had been able to find no answer. "I always feel a little out of place at these sorts of knees-up."

She had turned to face him, the red lips stretched into a smile. "I imagine you only feel at home in posh hotel bars. Tell me, is the Savoy as marvellous as I've heard?"

"It has its moments. Perhaps one day, you'll allow me to take you." He had drained his glass. "Would you like another?"

"I'd rather know your name," she had said.

"Forgive me, how rude," he had replied, holding out his hand. "Kettering, Felix Kettering."

She had taken his hand and inclined her head towards him. "Well, Felix Kettering, I'll do you a deal. Take me to some other place we can get a drink, somewhere which isn't here, and I'll think about telling you my name."

They had gone to a hotel not far from the stockbroker's apartment, and they had sat at a corner table, sipping Martinis. Felix had specifically asked the barman to put an olive in only one glass.

Slowly, they had come to know each other. They would meet regularly, always in public places and always, at her request, in corner tables. He would try to convince himself that her preference for tables in the shadows of the venues they chose was some sort of manifestation of her desire to keep him to herself, as if sitting at a bar or in the open space of a restaurant would mean having to share him with the other patrons. He was not unaware of the foolish self-indulgence of the idea, and he knew that if he voiced it, she would consider it to be little more than an adolescent ideal. In the end, he would come to learn and accept that it could never have been anything more in any case, and the truth was altogether more disturbing.

It had been one night only a few months before Felix's return to London that he had been woken from a disturbed sleep to hear knocking on the door of his apartment. Adele had been standing there, dressed in black, a hat and veil pulled low over her eyes. At her feet, Felix had seen the small suitcase which had made his stomach twist and a few pearls of sweat form on his temples. Adele had seemed entirely composed, her raised eyebrow and pursed lips seeming to display surprise that he had not invited her inside. He had done so, closing the door behind him, his mind suddenly alive with confusion. The suitcase now lay on the bed where she had placed it, like some personification of the pact they were about to make.

"We have to go," Adele had said. "Now."

"What has happened?" he had asked, his voice little more than a gasp of fear.

"It's over, Felix," she had replied. "We can't stay here."

"But where can we go? They'll find us."

Adele Mills had moved closer to him and, through the lace veil across her face, she had kissed him, a lingering display not only of affection, but of assurance and solidarity. Perhaps even of love. "Take me home, Felix. To your proper home. They won't find us there."

He could remember still that kiss on his lips and the resolve in her clear, sapphire eyes. Even if he had managed to forget them, her expression now would have reminded him of them, since they were now replicated in the kiss she placed on the crown of his head and the expression of determination in those same eyes. And he felt sure that Adele would be seeing in his own eyes, the same frightened glare of the frightened man he had been all those months ago in that rented apartment of which he now so seldom thought.

"I thought it was all behind us," Felix said. "I'd started to believe that you were right, that it was over, and nobody knew about any of it."

Adele, as serene in the face of disaster as she had always been, nodded. "And we were, Felix. For all these months, we've been happy, and what happened back then has meant nothing to us. But things change, my darling, and we have to deal with those changes."

He knew what she meant. How could he not? How Rowena had discovered the truth about Adele, he could not know. It would be foolish to think that he could ask Rowena about it, of course. To do so would have been both ridiculous and fatal. Adele had been quick to point out to him that how Rowena had discovered the truth was irrelevant. What mattered was that she knew about it. Thinking about her words now, Felix Kettering knew that Adele was right.

He rose from the chair and drained his final glass of whisky. "We both know she won't keep quiet, and there's no possibility of paying for her silence."

Adele, playing vaguely with her hair, smiled. "I'll say there isn't."

Felix was nodding, as if to convince himself of his conclusion rather than her. "There's nothing else for it then. We know what we have to do."

Adele rose from the arm of the chair and walked over to him. She kissed him, deeply, passionately, the touch of their lips almost fizzing with the unnatural glee of their wickedness.

"We know exactly what we must do," she whispered, and Felix, breathless, had never felt closer to Adele Mills than he did in that moment of sadistic sin.

Chapter Four

Matilda Royce had never liked the habit people had of calling her Tilly, but she had long since given up trying to put a stop to it, so that now it had become like an albatross around her neck, a curse which she could never escape because it was largely one of her own making.

It had started with her father, of course, but her hatred of him was not the only reason she despised the shortening of her name. She detested it for its foolishness, its suggestion of condescension, and its patronising odour. The fact that her father had been the first to use it simply added to her loathing of the name. He had not been an easy man to love, either for Tilly or her mother. She could still remember the smell of his breath, with its sickly-sweet tang of alcohol, as he screamed in her face, just as she could still recall the burning of her cheek or the salted taste of blood in her mouth after one of the frequent blows from his palm or, more often, his fist. She could still hear the sobs of her mother from somewhere in the distance, suffering her own physical and psychological wounds, powerless or, just possibly, too frightened to stop the assaults on her child. Perhaps, Tilly had thought more than once, her mother had been grateful that the object of his aggression was someone other than herself, no matter who that someone else might be.

When her father died, she had felt nothing except a sense of release. Here, at last, was an end to the bullying, the manipulation, the drinking, and the violence. And here, too, was an end to his intolerance of what his daughter was. Her mother had never addressed the issue, but her father had fluctuated between a cruel persecution of Tilly's nature and a macabre enjoyment in mocking it. With his death, it had all been forced to stop. He could not mock or denigrate her anymore. He had been reduced to nothing more than a collection of bones and rotting flesh, hidden forever under the soil. Her mother, too, had passed, and Tilly had felt some sadness, but nothing approaching what she considered to be genuine grief. If she ever felt fondly about her mother, Tilly would only think that her mother could no longer hide away while her daughter buckled under her father's anger, nor would she need to cover bruises with long-sleeved dresses or heavy make-up. No more excuses about clumsiness on the stairs or altercations with doors, and no longer any need to make false excuses to decline invitations to tea in case it invoked those alcoholic demons within him. He had no power over either of them, not when death had come to take them both.

The passing of her parents, one welcomed and the other only half-mourned, had demonstrated to Tilly Royce that death was somehow a unifier. It came to every living thing, regardless of nature, creed, or background, and it made everything neutral. It levelled out the strong with the meek, the rich with the poor, and the rulers with the oppressed. To death, saint and sinner were equals. It solved all problems and erased all prejudices and discrimination. Unlike her father, death registered nothing criminal about her, nothing unnatural about her, and nothing obscene about her. It made it all the sadder to her that the opposite was true in life.

From the moment Tilly had been able to understand the words, people had been coercing her, whether they realised it or not, into marriage, motherhood, and that particular brand of slavery that comes with both. Almost as soon as this conditioning to an accepted normality had begun, Tilly had known that it was impossible for her. Quite aside from not finding men attractive, she doubted that a normal family life could ever have been hers for the taking. Her father had robbed her of any belief that a man and woman could live in marital harmony, so she doubted that marriage to any man would have seemed to her to be possible. But even if her father had been a paragon of paternal virtue, Tilly Royce knew that her feelings would never succumb to male advances. She had been able to imagine herself only in the arms of a woman, just as she could only envisage herself living into old age with someone of her own sex, sitting comfortably by the fire in companionable silence with another woman, their lives uninterrupted by the presence of any men of significance. She had no reason to doubt the veracity or possibility of such a relationship. Her father had not been able to sully or corrupt that ideal. He had viewed her in much the same way as society itself did, as an unnatural entity, a birth defect, a natural mutation. She dared not think what lengths he might have gone to in order to attempt to cure her of what he would have seen as her mental affliction. He must have thought about it, even if he never threatened Tilly with any of it. There was no way of knowing how long it would be before he announced that something must be done about her, or how close it had come to happening before death had intervened. And Tilly suspected that whatever she imagined her father might have done would never be as terrible as anything he might have conjured up in his own mind. The irony of it was that her father would have tried to cure something that not only could not, and need not, be cured, but also something that he couldn't possibly have ever understood. And, she suspected, her mother had been no better. She had viewed Tilly's sexuality as another reason to anger her father, another motive for a punch to the face or a kick to the stomach, another cause for him to punish and degrade.

Even outside the scope of her own family, society ensured that Tilly remained an emotional prisoner. For her, true love would always be something to be kept secret, hidden away behind closed doors, boxed up like an unwanted memory in a photograph album in a dusty, cobwebbed corner of an attic. Love, it seemed, was only for those who decreed themselves capable of feeling it, a privilege for people of opposite genders, who were incapable of accepting that such feelings could apply to those who were different from them. To Tilly, it was not the imbalance or the prejudice that hurt and angered her, nor was it the blinkered view of the varied caprices of the world. Those things rankled, certainly, but they didn't offend her half as much as the unfairness of it all. Who decided that there should be this monopoly on love, that it could only be felt and enjoyed by those people who judged themselves what they considered normal? By their logic, Tilly was entitled to love too, because she considered herself entirely normal. She wasn't a maniac, or a psychotic, or a killer. She didn't harm babies, nor interfere with children. She didn't torture animals for pleasure. She didn't do anything which might be deemed to be abnormal. She was just attracted to women. So why was she not entitled to love except in secret, behind closed curtains or locked doors, and always in fear of a jail cell? There had never been any satisfactory answer, of course, certainly none which ever came within her grasp.

Tilly Royce had known love, even before she had met Rowena Kettering, but her affairs had been transient. The exception had been Anna, of course, with whom Tilly had fallen profoundly in love. Anna had taught her more than she had ever learned in school, about the world, about the arts, about what it is to be a human being driven by determination rather than by doubts. And Anna had taught her about love, in both a spiritual and physical sense. With Anna, there had been the exploration of body and soul, and each lesson had been a joy. Anna had been a few years older than Tilly, but the years had never seemed to matter to either of them. Her beauty was almost exotic, the skin a subtle shade of olive, the hair as black as a moonless night, and the eyes a vibrant, exciting shade of emerald. She had seemed thrilling to Tilly, unafraid of convention and respectability. She lived, like the spirit of humanity, free from any shackles of decorum. It wasn't that she was reckless or iconoclastic, simply that she believed in herself and her right to happiness.

But then Anna was gone. She had ended the affair, she said, for both their sakes. It was too precious to be permitted to turn stale. It was too pure to spoil with routine and habit. Its vitality should be preserved before tedium set in, and the best way to achieve that was to end it. That way, said Anna, they could both remember it as that period of endless summer and profound love. If the logic had seemed twisted, Tilly had not said so. Afterwards, she had not shunned love, but nor had she actively sought it out. And for the most part, her life had not seemed incomplete for its absence.

It was only when Tilly had seen Rowena Kettering for the first time that anything approaching the feelings that she had invested in Anna came back to her.

And yet, if Tilly had contemplated any suggestion of a serious love affair with Rowena Kettering, even based on that initial meeting, her hopes for it were instantly dismissed. It was sadly only too obvious, even from casual conversation, that Rowena and Tilly could never be linked romantically. Such was fate, such was the caprice of nature. But love, even when it is unrequited, is a powerful force, and, for reasons she only barely understood herself, Tilly felt that being close to Rowena in a platonic sense was better than not being with her at all.

"I'm not going to Ivor's party."

Rowena's voice, defiantly authoritative, broke in on Tilly's emotional recollections of her past. They were having tea in the drawing room at Campden Hill Square. The rain from earlier had stopped now, leaving behind it only the familiar, glistening sheen on the pavements and roads, and the soft sounds of traffic through puddles, which sounded like a collective demand for silence. What had prompted Tilly's journey into her memories she could not say, but the sudden intrusion of Rowena's voice was strangely welcome, although the topic of conversation with which she had chosen to break their companionable silence was not.

Tilly replaced her cup on its saucer. "Why not?"

"You must be able to guess."

Rowena did not look at Tilly when she replied, but instead kept her gaze on the world which existed beyond the window. Tilly found herself looking at the proud profile, with the strong cheekbones and elegantly pointed nose. The failing eyes, coloured like drops of chocolate, were heavy with emotion, and there were traces of tears, now a faded red, around them. And yet, they maintained something of Rowena's customary defiant dignity, which was mirrored and slightly emphasised by the raised chin. The hair, once the colour of hazelnuts, was now a darker brown, almost black, but streaked with the grey of age, and yet no less immaculate for it. In her youth, Rowena Steele had been praised for possessing the beauty of a princess. Time had matured that beauty, but it had not erased it, and Rowena Kettering, as she now was, possessed instead the majesty of a duchess. The transition from youth to maturity had not been unkind to her. On the contrary, if anything, it had enhanced her beauty, whilst simultaneously refining it. Tilly had seen photographs of Rowena Steele and had felt a passionate lust within herself for the girl she had seen. But Rowena Kettering, older and wiser than her former incarnation, inspired in Tilly nothing but the deepest love, something beyond carnal desire, but also something which made the impossibility of it all the more difficult to bear.

"I thought Ivor had agreed not to invite her," Tilly said now.

"He had, but Ivor obviously thinks that because this is a party for his sake, he has a monopoly on who attends it. The fact that I'm his wife and have feelings mustn't be allowed to interfere with that decree."

Tilly placed her cup and saucer, now empty, on the tray between them. "I can't say that I've ever noticed any empathy in Ivor. I suppose there's no reason why we should start seeing it in him now."

Despite herself, Rowena found the remark both offensive and unwarranted. "That's unfair, Tilly."

"Is it?"

"You don't know him like I do."

If Tilly thought the reply was obvious, she did not say so. "Well, let's take the girl instead. I'd have thought Daphne herself would have some shame and refuse the invitation."

"Not under Ivor's influence, I shouldn't think," said Rowena with a smile. "Ivor asked me for a divorce again earlier, and I refused him."

"He can't have been surprised."

"No, but perhaps he's thinking that divorce isn't the only way to be rid of a wife."

Tilly, shocked, glared at Rowena. "You're not serious."

But Rowena seemed not to have heard. "And we don't know what Daphne Clements thinks about my refusal to grant a divorce, do we?"

"She was perfectly amiable with you when you and Ivor went to tea the other day," argued Tilly.

"Affected politeness, nothing more," said Rowena, with scorn. "Biding her time, if you ask me, being nice to me in the hope I might see how much in love they are, take pity on them, and do what they would call the decent thing."

Tilly raised her eyebrows in defeat. "Nevertheless, I doubt that Daphne Clements has the stomach for…. Whatever you're suggesting."

Rowena shrugged. "She's a nurse, remember. Aren't so many of the murderers one reads about members of the medical profession?"

Tilly sighed, suddenly annoyed by the melodrama of the whole idea. "I'm sure you know best."

There was no attempt to disguise the brusque tone of voice and her obvious irritation with how the conversation was playing out. Rowena watched as Tilly began to tidy the tea tray, making rather more noise than was necessary, so that the clatter of china against silver seemed to be a manifestation of Tilly's suppressed exasperation.

"I'm sorry," Rowena said. "It's just that I can't bear how things are between Ivor and me."

"Perhaps you should let him go, then."

"Over my dead body." Rowena caught her breath at the tactless choice of phrase in the circumstances. "You think I should agree to Daphne coming to Longhampton?"

Tilly looked into Rowena's dark eyes. "I think you should be at a party which is to be held in your own house. What does it matter who else is there? What you need to realise is that if you are absent, people will think you're too frightened to attend."

Rowena held her gaze and slowly began to nod her head. "The show must go on, isn't that what we've always said?"

Tilly offered no response, but she knew she was right, and by her expression, so did Rowena. If Rowena were absent from the weekend in Longhampton, people would think she was afraid to show her face. Ivor, certainly, would see it as some sort of petty victory. Under no circumstances could Rowena allow him to think he had an open weekend. Her eyes hardened as a silent and defiant curse came to her mind, and she saw matters more clearly than ever before. If she was going to be forced to be uncomfortable this weekend, then Ivor could feel the same and be damned with him. Suddenly, Rowena felt as if she would rather be dead after all than allow Ivor's life to run smoothly.

The thought startled her, and sudden, unexpected tears began to roll down her cheeks. They were silent, but the pathetic sounds of the stifled sobs in her throat betrayed her. Kneeling at her feet, Tilly took Rowena's hands in hers, offering soothing sounds and sympathetic eyes.

"You mustn't let either of them dominate you like this," she said.

"It isn't only Ivor and Daphne," said Rowena. "It's all of them, Tilly. I don't trust any of them."

"But why?" asked Tilly. "What's the matter?"

Rowena took out a large, silk handkerchief, monogrammed with her initials. She dabbed at the corners of her eyes. Her sight might be failing, she thought, but she could not lose the capacity for self-pitying tears. "They all want me gone, Tilly, I know they do. They all want me in my grave. Edwin Jarratt, Felix, and Adele, all of them."

"You're being paranoid," said Tilly.

"Perhaps I should save them all the trouble."

"You must never say that."

"Why not? I'm getting old, Tilly. I'm losing my eyesight, I'm losing my husband, I've already lost my career. Worst of all, I've lost my son, and one day, I'll lose my daughter. What's left?"

Tilly felt the trembling of Rowena's hands in hers, gentle at first, but rising in intensity as each second passed, and it was this silent quiver of vulnerability which finally broke her resolve.

"You've got me," she whispered.

Rowena looked into her eyes, smiling despite the tears, and gently stroked her friend's cheek. "Dear old, faithful Tilly."

Tilly's throat suddenly seemed parched, her tongue so dry that it was like a leather strap between her teeth, but she ignored both sensations, concentrating instead on the moment that was passing between them and on pressing her own newly parted lips gently against those of Rowena

Kettering. The kiss, so long desired, was over before it began. Their lips had barely touched before Rowena had held up a defensive hand, whispering a hoarse "No," before rising to her feet.

From a velvet-lined case, she took a pair of dark glasses and placed them on her face, as much to hide the evidence of the tears as to protect those failing eyes from the daylight glare seeping through the window. "Please, don't do that."

Tilly, enraged with embarrassment, had risen too, but she remained where she stood, her fists clenched in outraged indignity. She was furious not only with the situation but with her awkward and misplaced confidence within it. She knew Rowena did not feel as she did, but she had succumbed to that temptation which had so long dangled itself before her, like the apple hanging from the branches of the tree of knowledge, or those bottles of whisky before her father on the kitchen shelf.

"I'm sorry," Tilly found herself saying.

Rowena did not look at her. "I told you after the last time, Tilly, it can never happen. If it happens again, we'll have to go our separate ways."

Tilly felt the fire rise in her cheeks. The flames were not simply those of shame or humiliation, but of a sudden anger and spontaneous hatred. Suddenly, at that moment, Tilly Royce imagined herself striding across the room and launching herself at Rowena, hands around her neck, the shame and regret transforming instantly into loathing and a determination to kill. But it was a fantasy only, and Rowena remained unharmed at the window, whilst Tilly tried to fight against the tears which had begun to roll down her cheeks.

Nothing more was said. The only sound to interrupt the silence was the low tapping of the low heels on Tilly's shoes as she crossed the room and walked out, leaving Rowena alone with her thoughts, her anxieties, and the stinging of her tears in those dying, chocolate brown eyes.

Chapter Five

For Dr Edwin Jarratt, the invitation to attend Ivor Kettering's weekend party at Longhampton provoked a conflict of emotions. His instinct was to decline it, and he had gone so far as to half complete a draft note to Kettering to say as much, but something stopped him before he could finish the message and seal it in an envelope. Instead, he had rolled it up into a small ball of discarded emotion and slammed it angrily into the waste bin under the desk in his consulting room. He sat back in his chair with a snort of frustrated anger, his fingers drumming hard against the desk blotter in front of him. Even there, there was no escape from his internal struggles, as his eyes fell almost immediately on the name of the girl he loved, which he had scrawled there in an adolescent gesture of desire and fidelity, but which he had crossed through immediately with another, more defiant stroke of his pen. Jarratt couldn't remember precisely when he had written and attempted to erase Josephine's name on the blotter, but he assumed it must have been some time ago since the ink now had faded. If only, he thought, he could say the same about his feelings towards her, but he supposed that love, or any profound human emotion for that matter, could not be expunged by a simple line of ink, even if it might be better for all concerned if they could.

Jarratt had never given serious consideration to love until he met Josephine Kettering. There had been women in his life, but the relationships that had followed, such as they were, had been little more than basic satisfaction of a mutual need. They had been pleasurable experiences for both parties, but they had been undertaken and concluded on an agreed understanding that they were no more than disposable pleasures. For Jarratt, it had been a sensible arrangement and one which he had not envisaged ever requiring the slightest modification. If he were to be honest with himself, he had not viewed Josephine Kettering in any other terms when he had first met her, but somehow the inclination for a casual affair seemed quickly to evaporate after that initial introduction. There had been an innocence about Josephine, which made any consideration of a meaningless flirtation seem like nothing more than a tawdry corruption of her naturally delicate naivety. It was not that the women who preceded her had all been sexually manipulative, but they had shared his preference for physical gratification without any emotional attachment being necessary. For some, he knew, it might have been possible that such an attachment might be coveted, but his aversion to a formal relationship, and certainly marriage, had been well known and none of those who might have secretly hoped for more had ever questioned it, and aside from those few, the remainder had viewed their contact with Edwin Jarratt on the same terms as him.

But, for some reason, it had been different with Josephine Kettering. It was not simply a matter of their difference in age. He was older, certainly, but not by sufficient years for it to be the sole cause of his reticence with her. He had tried to consider it in purely scientific terms, to find an explanation for it that was based on some logical foundation, but his endeavours had never resulted in any conclusion with which he could be satisfied. At last, at the climax of an evening of solitary indulgence in alcohol, he had come to realise that this reversal of attitude towards his interaction with women was the result of nothing rational or analytic, but purely a matter of love. For that reason alone, the notion of a casual affair with her seemed not only worthlessly impossible but disgustingly sordid, and he understood for the first time how his previous conduct, contrary to his beliefs, had been far less satisfying than he had imagined, for him and the women concerned. They had been nothing more than wasted opportunities to find what he now knew he could experience. To Jarratt, it had seemed not only to be a revelation but also a source of panic. He had never consciously felt love before, nor had he been aware of any reason previously to believe that love had struck him, but he knew in that moment of drunken clarity that it had done so now. And it had come in the form of Josephine Kettering.

Jarratt rose from his desk, the memories swirling in his head like leaves on the strongest of breezes. He felt the familiar waves of hatred breaking on the shores of his mind, as they so often did when he thought about his situation with Josephine. It hardly seemed fair to him that he could come to understand the nature of love so completely, only to have it rejected entirely. Even now, staring out of his consulting room window over Harley Street, Jarratt could not be sure whether Josephine's rejection of him would have been her personal decision, even if there had not been the external influence of her mother. He did not think he was deluding himself when he thought that Josephine had not been horrified by his expressions of love, which could only mean that it had been Rowena who had poisoned her daughter against him. Without this maternal interference, Jarratt suspected that he and Josephine could at least have given their feelings time to develop. As it was, she had rejected him completely.

"Are you saying you have no feelings for me at all?" he had asked.

Josephine had not looked into his eyes. "I've given you my answer, Dr Jarratt."

Not Edwin, but his professional title, which had seemed to slice through his heart like one of his own scalpels. "I don't believe you, Josephine. I can't accept that you don't have feelings for me."

"I can't say what you want me to say, I'm sorry." But she had still not dared to look him in his eyes.

He had taken a moment to consider his next words. "You can't expect me not to fight for you, Josephine."

She had shaken her head. "I think I can be expected to do just that, Dr Jarratt. You can't force me to love you. Or do you think that you have the right to do so?"

"Of course not."

"Are you sure?" She had looked into his eyes at that moment, and instead of the vulnerability which he loved so much, he had seen her absolute insubordination. "It sounds as if you consider yourself so entitled to me that you have the arrogance to assume that you have some sort of claim over my feelings."

"It isn't like that, I assure you. I just need you to understand that I love you."

"If you loved me," she had said, "you would allow me not to feel the same way."

If he had understood or appreciated the truth of her words, he was not in a position to admit it to himself. "I suppose I have your mother to thank for this."

She had said nothing in response, but no words had been necessary. The eyes had said all that was needed, with their glare of shocked anger in one moment and sickened disgust in the next. Later, Jarratt would despise himself for his petulance and the emotional immaturity that had prompted it, but in the moment, his rage had dominated his senses. When Josephine had turned on her heel to walk away from him, he had made no effort to stop her, and only afterwards had he been consumed completely by that uncontrollable fury, which manifested itself with the shattered glass and the smears on the wall of his consulting room, as the whisky slowly trickled to the floor.

"Damn you, Rowena," he said now, almost involuntarily but with no less spite for it. "Damn you to Hell."

He wondered whether telling Josephine the truth about himself would make any difference, or whether Rowena's poison had caused irreparable damage. What stopped him from putting his faith in her was as much a matter of cowardice as it was of stubbornness. On the one hand, he was afraid of Josephine's reaction, and he was not so delusional that he could not admit it to himself. On the other hand, however, Jarratt did not consider there to be anything about his past that required explanation. Was not everybody entitled to some corner of their soul that could remain private? Did love mean exposing every regret, every secret, and every skeleton in one's closet? If so, Rowena Kettering must surely be the worst type of hypocrite. Jarratt didn't know much about the world of the theatre, but he knew enough to recognise that nobody who lived within it was free from scandal and regret.

Not that Jarratt did regret what he had done, at least not absolutely, although nor was his reaction to it one of nonchalance. There were times when it haunted him, when he wished he could erase it from his memory, just as there were occasions when he would tell himself with fierce assurances that if he were in the position again, he would still act as he had done. Rowena had said there was blood on his hands, and it was undoubtedly true. But for Jarratt, it had not needed Neptune's ocean to wash it away, and a little water, a frighteningly small amount as he now remembered, had been enough to clear him of the deed. And yet, there had not been sufficient water to clean it from his memory. On occasions, the screams of agony and the scarlet horror of it all would invade Jarratt's dreams, where he would perform his crime over and over again, sometimes with a twisted expression of sickening glee and sometimes with a desolate glare of disgust.

Jarratt thought back now to when he had asked Ivor and Rowena Kettering for Josephine's hand in marriage, and he was struck, more vividly than ever, by how like an animal walking into a hunter's trap he must have seemed. Ivor himself had offered no objection to the match, but he had not seemed altogether interested in the whole question of the marriage of his daughter. No doubt, Jarratt thought both then and now, Ivor considered it a matter more within Rowena's purview than his. As with so many other things, as long as the marriage did not interfere or in any way damage Ivor's political career, there was very little for him to contribute to any discussion. If only the same could have been said for both of Josephine's parents.

Rowena had received him in the living room. She had been seated in a large armchair, her arms draped elegantly over those of the chair, and her legs crossed in a display of demure but professional defiance. Her eyes were covered by a pair of dark sunglasses, which he knew were a necessity for a medical condition, but they gave her a demeanour of glamourous pomposity, as if she were engaged in some theatrical or cinematic publicity. The impression was emphasised by the way in which she held her head, poised at an angle, the chin pointed upwards, so that she had given off the definite impression of royalty, or at least the desire to project it. She had not invited Jarratt to sit, and the wonton pettiness of the refusal amused rather than disturbed him. If Rowena had hoped that this minor display of power on her part was likely to intimidate him, she would be disappointed when, after he had left, she would realise it had not done so.

"You wish to marry my daughter, Dr Jarratt," she had said, making it seem more of a question than a statement of intent.

"I should very much like to do so, Mrs Kettering."

"You love her?"

"I do."

"Does she love you?" The question, as loaded and as deadly as a revolver pointed straight to his heart, was asked with a faint smile across her lips.

Jarratt had considered his response only briefly. "I would like to think so."

Rowena had smiled, although she did not address the slight evasion in his reply directly with him. "Tell me, Dr Jarratt, you have a practice in Harley Street, is that correct?"

"Yes."

"May I ask if it is profitable?"

Jarratt, incensed by the question, had felt the back of his neck flush with anger, but he had remained motionless and reserved. "I suppose you are within your rights to ask such a question."

"Let's agree to suppose so."

The response might have been rehearsed. She took such an obvious pleasure in it that Jarratt had been unable to accept that it had been a result of the natural improvisation of conversation. If it were, it displayed a quick and cunning mind behind the dark eyes and the sophisticated appearance of this former actress. Nevertheless, he had found the reply both conceited and confrontational.

"I make a very good living." He had stated it as a matter of business fact, careful not to inject into it any suggestion of boastful pride.

Rowena had smiled glibly. "I suppose one doesn't have a Harley Street gynaecological practice without achieving some degree of success."

Jarratt had returned the smile. "Again, we will agree to suppose so."

If Rowena had found the use of her own words against her amusing, she did not give any sign of it. In retrospect, it had been a mistake, both arrogant and mocking, and Jarratt had come to regret it. At the time, however, he had been pleased with himself, even if it had resulted in a shift in the atmosphere.

"Doctor, I shall be frank with you," Rowena had said. "I know about Florence Kendall."

The name had been like a second verbal gunshot in a matter of minutes, but this one seemed to hit him in the chest. He could believe, looking back, that he might almost have stumbled under the pressure of it, as if the words had been able to exert some sort of physical force over him. He had been shocked not only by the name, its memory flooding back to him like the waves of a violent storm over a helpless fishing boat, but also by the sudden sense of danger which had seemed to threaten to overwhelm him at that moment. Questions had poured into his head, mismatched and half-formed denials and explanations, none of which had seemed sensible or appropriate. Rowena had watched him, the red lips delicately smiling in pleasure at his obvious discomfort, but the dark eyes heavy with accusation and disgust.

"I see," he had stammered. "May I ask how?"

Rowena had given a vague shrug of her shoulders. "I hardly think that matters, do you, doctor? In a case of murder, there is only one point of any real importance, wouldn't you say?"

"Murder?" It was as if he had never heard the word before, let alone understood it.

Rowena had ignored him. "And that point is how to ensure that justice is done."

Jarratt had held up a hand. "Now, wait a moment, Mrs Kettering…"

Her eyes had burned with offended astonishment. "You're surely not going to deny the charge."

Jarratt had shaken his head. "You don't know the circumstances."

"I know enough about them, I can assure you."

"But you don't know everything," he had argued. "You can't possibly know."

Rowena had been unaffected by his protestation, and the aloof expression of superiority remained in place, along with the disdainful and dismissive smile. "I know enough to see you struck off and quite possibly enough to have you hanged."

The words terrified him—how could they not?—but he had managed to retain something of his composure. "Is that what you intend to achieve?"

Rowena had shrugged. "It is the usual penalty for murder, Dr Jarratt. And I trust what I have said," she had added, her teeth clamped together with a cruel determination, "is sufficiently clear as an answer to the ridiculous idea that I might allow you to marry my daughter."

It had been a dismissal, and Jarratt had recognised it as such. Any further discussion would have been pointless and, perhaps worse, could have made the situation deteriorate even further than was already the case. And so, Jarratt had left the room and the Campden Hill Square house, but not without a parting comment. It had been futile, he knew, and he doubted Rowena was troubled by it, but it would have been unthinkable to have walked out without leaving her with a final word of retaliation.

"Do your worst, Mrs Kettering," he had said, "but be prepared to pay the consequences."

At the time, he had thought it was a curt rebuke, a display of strength against her accusations, but looking back now, it seemed to be nothing more than a threat. As such, it had probably served no purpose other than to strengthen Rowena Kettering's suspicions that he was a killer. For the sake of his vanity, he thought now, he may have seriously compromised his position. If so, perhaps it would be as well to stay away from Longhampton that weekend. His presence would hardly be a soothing one, either for Rowena or Josephine. And if the rumours he had heard were true, he might well be intruding on Josephine's blossoming feelings for her father's private secretary, Lewis Davenport. Jarratt didn't know the man, but he would scarcely want to make Davenport's acquaintance if he were planning to walk down the aisle at the very ceremony that Jarratt had envisaged would be for him and Josephine.

And yet, Jarratt thought, with a flicker of mischief in his eyes, the invitation had come neither from Josephine nor Rowena, but from Ivor, with whom Jarratt had no particular quarrel. For that matter, he had no argument with Josephine who, he felt certain, would change her mind about him, if he could only force some distance from the woman he loved and the woman who controlled her emotions with venom and lies. It was Rowena who was the obstacle, Rowena who stood in the way of his happiness, his reputation, and possibly his life. It was Rowena who, more now than ever, he wished no longer existed, and it was Rowena with whom he had to have one final conflict if he was to do anything about this situation, both personal and professional, in which he found himself. And he would not be able to achieve any sense of peace or vindication if he did not engineer that confrontation. Ivor Kettering's invitation offered a prime opportunity for action, the chance to put an end to everything that plagued him once and for all.

With a malicious flourish of his pen, therefore, Dr Edwin Jarratt responded positively to Ivor's request to go to Longhampton and, in doing so, he cursed Rowena Kettering to damnation. The response was placed in an envelope, which was duly sealed and dispatched. He could have no way of knowing it, but Jarratt had contracted himself to a weekend in the presence of violent death.

Chapter Six

As the week that would see a series of events culminating in murder drew to a close, Lewis Davenport felt as if he had worked hard enough over the last few days and that a break from the responsibilities of Westminster and the smog of London generally might be welcome after all. A refusal of Ivor Kettering's invitation to Longhampton could scarcely be considered, of course, and it had been offered with a tone of voice and a choice of words which together had demanded acceptance. Initially, Davenport thought that he would have much preferred not to spend his weekend with his superior and whichever members of his family and friends he had deigned to invite. But, after the heavy toils of the past week, he began to suspect that the weekend would not be as awkward or as tiresome as he had feared. The presence of Josephine Kettering was always likely to be a persuasive factor, and it was useless to pretend otherwise, but Davenport had thought several times over the past few days whether her company alone would be sufficient excuse to endure the type of weekend that he loathed. And yet now, with the pressures of various ministerial matters that demanded close attention adding to the intensity of their professional environment, the prospect of a lonely weekend in London seemed infinitely more dismal than time in the cleaner, more vibrant air of the Norfolk coast, even if the company might largely leave something to be desired.

And yet, there was Josephine. If Davenport was to indulge himself in idealism regarding Ivor Kettering, he felt he could excuse himself for doing so in respect of his daughter, too. Davenport's mind went back to his first meeting with Josephine, at the dinner party in Campden Hill Square, not long after he had joined Ivor Kettering's government department. He had found himself feeling awkward, standing on the periphery of conversation, the Martini, though excellent, less dry than his own tongue. He knew nobody save for Ivor himself, who had been in conversation with other guests, and Davenport knew that he could not expect to monopolise his superior's attention, but his politeness on that aspect of etiquette left him feeling isolated in this assembly of strangers.

And then, he had been approached by the girl with the platinum hair and the oyster-coloured evening gown, whose shimmer seemed to be reflected too in the darker, more fascinating grey of her eyes. Davenport had known that Kettering had a daughter, and the eyes were sufficient to identify her, but her name suddenly eluded him, despite the fact that he knew without doubt that Kettering had mentioned it many times. Now, however, it was as if Davenport's memory had been erased of any droplet of information that it had ever been given.

"You look terribly bored," the girl had said. "And you haven't touched your Martini. I'm surprised. Daddy takes a special pride in his ability to make them."

"I'm afraid I'm not very good with people I don't know," he had said.

"Shy?" The girl had smiled, but there hadn't seemed to be anything mocking about it.

"A hideous trait on my mother's side," he had said. The smile on his lips, both coy and clumsy, seemed to suggest it was to be taken as a joke, but she had noticed that his eyes had not been let in on the prank. Behind the rims of his round spectacles, they had seemed to her to be pleading for reassurance, possibly even help.

She had held out her hand. "My name is…"

"Josephine," he had said, taking her hand, as if to keep himself upright. The surprise at recalling her name, so unexpectedly and so inexplicably, had threatened to buckle him. "Your father has often spoken of you," he added, by way of explanation. "I'm Lewis Davenport."

Josephine had raised her eyebrows in recognition. "And he has often spoken of you too, Mr Davenport."

"Nothing too awful, I hope."

"Of course not," she had laughed, "what a curious thing to say. I doubt he'll ever tell you this, but I rather think he likes you."

His cheeks had flushed, and he had pushed the spectacles up his long nose. "Thank you, that is very kind."

They had sat together at dinner, and he had found himself surprisingly at ease in her company. The food had been excellent, and he would have enjoyed it on any occasion, but her company seemed to elevate the tenderness of the meat, the richness of the sauce, and the bouquet of the wine. Afterwards, over brandy and cigars in the study, Davenport had found himself missing her and wondering what she was discussing with the other ladies in the sitting room. Briefly, he had dared to believe that she might even be thinking of him and wondering what thoughts were running through his head. If he had been able to read those thoughts, however, he might have suffered something of a disappointment.

Since then, he had met her several times, both by invitation, to tea or to lunch, and by accident at some formal event at which both he and Kettering had been present. Each time, he had succumbed further to his feelings for her, but never once had he been certain whether his affections for her were reciprocated. He had believed them to be so, and the stolen smiles across crowded rooms, the whispers in his ears about other people present, the shrill laughs at his mediocre but earnest attempts at humour, and the gentle kisses of farewell to his cheeks all conspired to give him hope. And yet, Josephine had never said anything definite that might inspire emotional confidence within him, nor had she provided any similar certainty that his feelings would not be returned. On the contrary, there had been suggestions that she did feel as he felt, and the few coy and hesitant kisses they had shared could only serve to boost his confidence. However, as the months passed by, Lewis Davenport became increasingly certain that he loved Josephine Kettering and that if anything was to be done about it, he would be the one to take decisive action.

In a sentimental display of what he assumed to be traditional chivalry,

Lewis Davenport had not asked Josephine herself to accept his proposal of marriage. Instead, he had approached Ivor Kettering in the first instance to request his permission to ask the question which had begun to gnaw away at his soul. The question had been difficult to ask, but the response he received had been worse.

It had been less than a week ago, and the raw pain of Ivor's reply still seemed to linger around Lewis' heart. He had been called into Ivor Kettering's office to deal with some minor departmental matters, for which he had assumed responsibility with his usual efficiency and diplomacy. The tasks assigned, Ivor had expected Lewis to leave the office immediately and set about completing them, but the younger man had hesitated.

"Is there anything else, Lewis?" Ivor had asked.

He had adjusted his spectacles and gently cleared his throat. "Sir, if I may, there's something I should like to discuss briefly with you."

Ivor had indicated the papers Lewis now held under his arm. "Our business is clear enough, surely."

"No, sir, it is not a question of the department's business. It's something rather more personal."

Ivor had screwed the lid back onto his fountain pen, placed it carefully before him on the desk, and leaned back in his chair. "I see."

Lewis Davenport had rehearsed the interview several times in silent moments of contemplative dread, but now the time had come to ask the question in reality, the words suddenly seemed impossible to say. He had caught his breath several times before he had found his voice. "It's about your daughter, sir."

"Josephine?"

"I have come to feel very strongly for her, sir. In a way which I could not have predicted."

Again, Ivor had said simply, but grimly, "I see."

It had been obvious to Lewis that the question was now redundant. It hardly needed saying, yet it seemed imperative to Lewis that he say it anyway. "I should very much like to marry her."

If Lewis had expected any sort of dramatic response, he was not to receive it. Ivor Kettering had sniffed, pulled at an ear lobe, and rose slowly from his desk. "Have you explained to my daughter how you feel about her?"

"I think Josephine knows how I feel, yes, sir."

"And does she feel the same?"

Lewis had looked down at his feet. "I haven't asked her, sir, but I think she cares for me."

"Then why haven't you spoken to her, man?" Kettering had seemed irritated by his subordinate's hesitancy.

"I wanted your blessing first, sir."

Ivor had considered the matter for a moment in silence. "Do you think it would be appropriate to marry my daughter and remain in your position under me in this government?"

The question had been unexpected, but Lewis had been able to parry it. "Sir, I would be sorry to leave your service, certainly, but if it were necessary, I would do so, if it meant being able to be with Josephine."

Ivor's face had remained dispassionate. "You had better speak to my wife. I suppose I can offer no direct objection, Lewis. I know you are honourable and faithful, and I cannot very well complain about your professional position. But Rowena is very protective of our daughter, and it would be as well for you to discuss the matter with her. At Longhampton, this weekend, perhaps. What better opportunity? You are still coming?"

"Yes, sir. I am looking forward to it." This last comment had not been altogether true.

"There you are then." Ivor had smiled briefly at him, a gesture of satisfaction that an unpleasant task had been successfully dealt with, if only by delegation.

Lewis had bowed. "Very well, sir, if you wish it."

"I should warn you, however," Ivor had added, walking towards him with a serious expression on his face and a crease of concern around his brows, "that you are not alone in your wish. There is Dr Edwin Jarratt to consider."

It had never occurred to Lewis Davenport that there might be someone else who shared his devotion to Josephine Kettering, and when he heard of it, Lewis had been consumed first by an overwhelming sense of defeat and then by a similarly devastating fire of jealousy. Lewis could not now recall the precise words he had spoken in reply, but he knew that they had been as ineffective as they had been incoherent. From that moment, however, the name Edwin Jarratt had seemed to plague him, and he seemed unable to escape from it. Even Josephine, unaware of the effect the name had on him, seemed to mention Jarratt with increasing frequency.

It was inevitable, of course, that Jarratt would be at Longhampton for the weekend and it was equally inescapable that Lewis could do nothing about it. Accordingly, there seemed little point in either fretting or protesting about the fact. It would be a waste of effort and emotion, and it was better simply to accept it. After all, Lewis thought to himself, as he turned off the office light and stepped out into the exterior corridor, there was nothing to be worried about. It was not as if Josephine had any feelings for Jarratt. From what she had said, the truth was quite the contrary.

As he turned into St James' Park, Lewis Davenport made a decision. The presence of Edwin Jarratt at Longhampton would mean nothing to him. His attention would be fixed solely on Josephine and Rowena, and his primary task for the weekend would be to obtain permission from one to marry the other. A smile drifted across his lips, and a sense of contentment swelled within him as he realised that once Rowena Kettering had given her consent, there could be no real obstacle to his happiness.

This optimism coursed so strongly through his veins that the possibility that Rowena would prohibit the marriage seemed barely credible, so he gave it very little thought. It was only later, sitting alone in the gloom of the late evening, a small glass of whisky at his side, that his thoughts turned against him. His mother had always said that pride came before a fall, and he knew that he was in danger of giving a truth to the proverb.

Obviously, it was possible that Rowena Kettering could refuse his request for Josephine's hand, and he knew that he had to plan against such a rejection. Suddenly, almost without being aware of his own thoughts, Lewis Davenport found himself wondering precisely what he was prepared to do if Rowena Kettering denied him permission to marry Josephine and how far he would be willing to go either to ensure Rowena's compliance or to terminate her influence over her daughter once and for all.

54

Chapter Seven

Daphne Clements had thought that a walk down by the river might clear her head, or at least distract her from the thoughts of dread and death which seemed to plague her so frequently of late. More than once over the last few weeks, she had tried to remember a time when she wasn't consumed by these dangerous and destructive ideas, which now seemed so common as to appear to her entirely normal, but she would find that if there had been such a period in her life then it was lost to her memory completely now. If she had expected, or even hoped, that she would feel some sadness at this realisation, she was to be disappointed. It wasn't sadness, regret, or distress that she felt about this perpetual misery that seemed to overwhelm her mind. Such feelings, although negative, were entirely normal emotions that one might face regularly, but with a determination to confront and deal with them. To that extent, Daphne supposed, they still possessed some degree of positivity in their assumption of a personal desire for redemption. What she now concluded she felt, what she now knew fuelled these dark and possibly fatal thoughts, was hatred, and from that she felt sure that there was no redemption or return.

The river offered no consolation. In the fading afternoon light it seemed to her to have taken on a more foreboding aspect than it could ever possess in the brighter skies of the day. Almost as if it could hear her thoughts, the water seemed to have blackened, and in its slow, ominous pulse through the city, it seemed to be making its own malignant plans. As the river passed by her, standing on the steps at Westminster Bridge, it seemed to Daphne that she was being called into the depths of the blackness of the water, to merge her thoughts with those of the river, to put an end to their curse once and for all. There was an almost hypnotic rhythm of the undulating ripples of water, as the invisible current below the surface worked its effects, and Daphne found herself almost succumbing to the desire to lift herself onto the parapet and launch herself first into the empty space between her and the river, and then into those icy depths below her.

She turned away and continued to climb the stairs, gazing down at the movement of her feet and concentrating on the grey of the pavement rather than the constant motion of the river. The immobility of the concrete beneath her feet was somehow reassuring, as if its motionlessness was the personification of cold and unswerving logic, far removed from the shifting surface of the water and the tumultuous ideas that had seemed to inspire within her. Away from its influence, Daphne's thoughts seemed themselves to be clearer, as if assuming the same granite personality of the paving stones. She knew that it was not her death that she desired, even if ending it would provide some kind of peace, and nor was it her death that would release Ivor from his personal prison. No, Daphne thought, if anybody should throw themselves into the Thames, it should be Rowena Kettering.

It was a thought that she had nursed many times before, but it never ceased to cause her shame. She would often feel gratitude for that personal sense of disgrace, because it seemed to Daphne to prove that there was still within her a human capacity for compassion, which in turn was sufficient to remind her that she had not degenerated into some sort of unknown form of existence which was fuelled entirely by hatred. Until recently, she had never consciously hated another person. There had been a few people during her childhood, the usual gang of schoolyard bullies, whom she had told herself at the time she hated, but which now she knew wasn't true. She felt anger towards them, certainly, for their ability to make her feel inferior, afraid, and ashamed of herself, but the way she felt now showed only too clearly that she had misconstrued those previous, less intense adolescent emotions. And, painful though it was to admit, she disliked her mother, whose opinions about women's work had always threatened to prevent Daphne's profound desire to be a nurse. She supposed that everybody had some people in their histories whom they had disliked, but she wondered how many people had felt sufficient cause to hate another human being as much as she abhorred Rowena. Feeling this profoundly negative reaction inside her for the last few weeks had made her realise that hate was a too frequently used word, one which might almost be said to have no meaning when used so casually, until such time as a person began to feel it consume them. Only then did the word reclaim its power and reassert its significance.

Although she had expressed her loathing of Rowena to Ivor, she had never said anything to him of those even more sinister thoughts, which came to her in deepest moments of despair, and which she had never envisaged might enter her mind. She had never wondered too deeply about why she had not said anything of them to Ivor, and she supposed now that it was easier to think about murder than to discuss it aloud. In her mind, it remained a fantasy, but speaking of it, putting words to the idea, was too harrowing to contemplate, as if expressing the desire to kill a person was as good as carrying out the deed. The idea was foolish, and she knew it, but it seemed to her to be no less valid for that, even if it were the product of a corrupting, guilty conscience.

The first glimmer of the idea of murder came to her when Rowena first denied Ivor a divorce. Daphne remembered now how eagerly she had waited for him to report back to her. They had decided to raise the issue with Rowena over an excellent lunch one afternoon in a Kensington restaurant. Daphne could remember the excellence of the food and wine just as vividly as she could recall the topic of conversation robbing her of the full enjoyment of them. It had been as if Rowena herself had been sitting at the table, a dominating spectre, which refused to allow the two lovers even a moment's peace to enjoy a fine meal. Not that Daphne could express any right, then or now, to expect the lunch to be uncontaminated by the seriousness of the issue which occupied both their minds.

Ivor had been adamant that the interview with Rowena would result in a successful outcome. Looking back, this optimism perhaps had allowed him to enjoy his chateaubriand and green salad with more gusto than Daphne, not sharing his confidence, had enjoyed hers.

"I don't see how she can possibly object," he had said. "After all, she can't be any less miserable in the marriage than I am. We've lived separate lives for longer than either of us would care to admit. What does she achieve by prolonging the misery?"

Daphne had considered it an unhelpful question, however rhetorical, and one which was posed by an idealistic point of view. "Perhaps she doesn't see it as misery."

"How can she not?" Ivor had taken a mouthful of wine. "The whole marriage was a mistake. Far too soon after my first marriage ended, I thought Josephine's birth would solve everything, but the marriage never really got over what happened to Peter."

"There must have been something between you once, Ivor," she had replied. "It's foolish to pretend otherwise, and I'm not too stupid to realise it, nor too delicate to cope with it."

Still, he had not conceded the point. "I shall simply say to her that the marriage is over, and prolonging it is going to suffocate us both slowly. Better to end it now, I shall say, than allow ourselves to grow to resent each other."

The next time she had seen him, he had been beyond deflated. His cheeks had been sallow, his eyes heavy with frustrated disappointment, and his lips taut with anger. Daphne had not needed to ask what the outcome of his discussion with Rowena had been. Somehow, it had seemed to her that asking for confirmation of her fears about it would have been rubbing salt water into open wounds.

"She refused to see sense," Ivor had said. "Just raved… Shouted like a mad woman. Said she wouldn't allow me to trample over her feelings just so I could have my way."

He had seemed bewildered by the response, but Daphne had been unable to expect any other reaction. "I don't suppose we should be surprised."

"I could strangle the bloody woman."

The words had been said almost without thought, like some sort of vocal spasm that he had neither expected nor been able to control. He almost seemed not to have heard it, since his eyes remained fixed on the floor between his feet, and his body motionless, save his hands, which flexed and squeezed, as if in some unconscious enactment of the very deed he had threatened.

Daphne had come to sit next to him. "Perhaps it might help if I speak to her."

"It'll make things worse."

"Do you think it could be any worse, darling?"

To that, Ivor Kettering had been able only to smile, but it was the smile of a defeated man.

Now, Daphne was suddenly aware that she was cold. Perhaps it was the rising breeze, but it could just as well be the chill of her thoughts. She began to walk more quickly than before, vowing to herself that she would enter the first tea shop that looked both accommodating and suitable. She found one without too much trouble and took a table at the back of the cosy interior. Her order of some fish paste sandwiches and a pot of tea was taken swiftly and efficiently, and she waited with patience for it to arrive.

Tea…

It had been an invitation to tea, which had formed the sequel to Ivor's unsuccessful discussion with Rowena. A little over a week ago, but it seemed like decades had passed. The idea had been foolish, of course, and Ivor had told Daphne as much, but she had refused to listen. Looking back, perhaps it would have been more hopeful if she had not buckled under Ivor's pressure and refused to allow him to attend. It had been her original idea that the invitation would be for Rowena only, and Daphne had hoped that a mature conversation between two intelligent women might have been more productive than the one between husband and wife. Daphne knew that Ivor was a catalyst for argument where Rowena was concerned, and she had thought his absence might be beneficial. But he had insisted on being there, and Daphne had realised that dissuading him was out of the question. And so, with reluctance, she had agreed, and the meeting had been all the worse for it.

It had started pleasantly enough, as far as any meeting between an estranged husband and wife and the woman responsible for the marital hostility could be. Rowena had been suspiciously polite, although Daphne could not help but think that the eyes behind the dark lenses of Rowena's protective spectacles were alive with malice. Ivor had struggled to maintain a dispassionate detachment from the simmering volatility of the situation. They had drunk the tea peacefully enough, although Rowena had been unable to resist the occasional petty complaint.

"Thank you for tea, Miss Clements," she had said, having finished her first cup. "Of course, I am accustomed to Indian tea only as a rule."

Whether it was true or not hardly mattered, but Ivor had made no effort to contradict her, so Daphne had assumed it was a statement of fact. "Perhaps I'll remember for next time, although I can't promise."

Rowena had smiled. "You think there will be a next time, do you? I rather thought this was an isolated incident."

Daphne had wanted to say that she was being polite, that she hadn't meant it, but there had been something about Rowena's tone of voice that would have made any retort seem both childish and impotent. "Perhaps we should talk about why we're here."

Rowena had thrown back her head and laughed, the shrill and mocking wail of a condescending banshee. "How very business-like you are, my dear. Do you talk to your patients in this brisk fashion?"

"No," Daphne had said, "but then I like and respect my patients."

Rowena's lips had quivered into a vague smile. "So, there is some fight in you, after all, my dear. That's just as well, because you'll need it if you think you're going to take my husband away from me."

Daphne had placed her cup down on the tray in front of her. "Isn't that rather a matter for Ivor?"

"Not exclusively," had been Rowena's response.

"May I ask you a question, Mrs Kettering?" Daphne had stared into the blankness of the dark lenses over her adversary's eyes. "Do you love your husband?"

The reply came after a pause, and it was accompanied by a malignant glare from those dark eyes of Rowena's. When she spoke, the words and their connotations shocked Daphne, a reaction which was enhanced by Rowena's austere and emotionless tone of voice.

"Love has nothing to do with it, Miss Clements," she had said. "You're a fool if you think it has."

Daphne had swallowed hard. "I rather thought that was what we were talking about."

Ivor had felt the need to assert something of his own authority. "She's goading you, Daphne. Don't rise to the bait."

Rowena had ignored him, as if unaware of his presence. "Let me put it another way, Miss Clements. What I feel for my husband and what he feels for me are none of your business."

It had been intended to sting, and Daphne had felt it. She had looked at him, and although he had offered no verbal defence, his expression had been alive with hatred and fury, all of which had been concentrated on Rowena. For her part, Rowena had seemed immune to everything.

"Tell me, Miss Clements," she had said, "what did you think this little gathering was going to achieve? Did you hope that offering me tea and sandwiches would persuade me to let you run away with my husband?"

Daphne had smiled. "I had hoped it would be possible for us to talk sensibly. You'll forgive me if I say that I was obviously mistaken."

Rowena had laughed again. "I do admire that spirit of yours. I can almost understand how Ivor feels about you."

"I doubt that."

Ivor had cursed. "Can't we talk like rational human beings?"

Rowena had scoffed. "You'd enjoy that, wouldn't you, Ivor? Two women fighting over you must be filling you with pride, but you can't stand the embarrassment of the sight of it. You'd prefer it if you could enjoy the masculine triumph of two women scratching their eyes out over you, without having to see the blood on their claws."

"I wouldn't put it quite like that," Ivor had grumbled.

"Wouldn't you?" Rowena had hissed. "I would."

And, surprisingly, Daphne had supported her. "If that's how you feel, Ivor, you should have stayed away, like I told you to."

Rowena had stared at the younger woman, her disbelief fighting for supremacy over her sudden but reluctant admiration. "You didn't want him here?"

Daphne had shaken her head. "I thought we stood a chance of having a more sensible discussion if he weren't here. He is, after all, rather the point of the issue."

Rowena had bowed her head. "Brains and beauty. Be careful, my dear, I might almost grow to like you."

The remark had been so unexpected that Daphne had almost fooled herself into believing it, but Rowena could hardly have expected the comment to be taken seriously. "Since he is here, Mrs Kettering, I suppose we must make the best of it. You asked me what the point of this meeting was, and I don't think I gave you a proper answer. I simply wanted to hear from your own lips whether you would even consider granting Ivor a divorce, and I wanted to be able to look into your eyes when you gave the reply."

Rowena's previous hostility, whilst not thawed, had seemed slightly less intense. She had crossed one leg over the other and offered Daphne a smile, but not one of mockery, or triumph, or spite, but curiously one of what Daphne could only call honour.

"A fair question, my dear," she had said, "and I do appreciate the candour of it. It deserves respect, and the best way to offer that respect is to be equally frank. I do not intend to allow my husband to divorce me so that he can marry you. The pair of you should be under no illusion about my position on this."

A brief silence had elapsed before Daphne rose to her feet. "Then there is nothing more to be said. Thank you, Mrs Kettering, for your honesty and your time. Perhaps now you will be good enough to leave my house."

And that had been the end of it. Ivor had tried to kiss Daphne on the way out, but she had turned her head away. It would have been as inappropriate as it was unwelcome at that moment. Daphne, suddenly, wanted nothing more to do with either of them, and she wanted the smell of them, and the memory of their presence, gone. In the silence that had followed their departure, and now as she sat in the tea shop, the cup of tea going slowly cold in front of her, it struck Daphne just how cruel it was for one person to have such power over another, to be able to exert such an influence over another person's life that they could dictate the happiness or sadness of that existence. Rowena had been given this power only by chance, by the cruel caprice of nature which had made Ivor Kettering fall in love with Daphne Clements. If she had never met Ivor, the situation would never have come alive, and Rowena would have had no hold over Daphne's emotions or her right to love. The cruelty of circumstance, the almost depraved entitlement of the woman to be in this position of dominance over another person's emotions, was impossible to accept. Even the contemplation of it enraged Daphne, and she found herself wishing devoutly that things were different. So many regrets: if only she had met and fallen in love with someone else, not Ivor, she might have been permitted happiness; if only Ivor had not been married in the first place; if only her life had been someone else's. But these were self-indulgencies, brought on by her pity for herself, and they were neither of consequence nor use. Her life was hers; it was Ivor she loved, and it was for their future that Daphne would have to fight. There was no reason why she should simply accept matters as they stood.

She paid for her tea and sandwiches and left the tea shop without anybody noticing her. In only a few moments, her place at the table was occupied by a pair of gossiping ladies, and it was as if she had never been there at all. It was as she marched back along the Embankment, inhaling the slightly stale tang of the river's odour as it was carried along on the early evening breeze, that Daphne Clements came to realise with a sudden and terrifying clarity what she supposed she had known for quite some time, that something would have to be done about Rowena Kettering and this malignant power which she seemed to possess over other people's lives.

Chapter Eight

Everett Carr sat in his Albany residence, cradling a glass of excellent whisky, and barely taking notice of Mahler's Symphony No.2, which was playing at a subtle volume from the gramophone on the small table in the corner of the room. The record had perhaps been ill-chosen. Carr hardly felt in the mood for a piece that had as its climax such an ecstatic message of resurrection, and which brought with it those defining reassurances of spiritual glory, but he had not listened to the piece for some time, and he had found himself longing to hear it once again. He wondered now whether this desire had been driven by the symphony's overall contemplation of life and death rather than its final declaration of redemption, but if so, his own thoughts of life and death, perhaps inevitably, had overtaken the music in any event.

It had been only a couple of days since he had met Josephine Kettering among the graves of the cemetery, but what she had said to him had lingered in his mind over the intervening period. Even now, the words seemed clearer in his recollection than much of the activity with which he had filled the past two days. And it was perhaps not only the words which the young girl had said about possible murder, but also her haunted expression and the certainty with which she had made the extraordinary statement, which convinced him that her fears were not without foundation.

As a former criminal barrister and judge, Carr had known unlawful death in its many forms. He had thought at one time that he had understood it, but he had come to realise that he did so only through the prism of the law, of legal argument and Courtroom theatrics. He had never belittled those crimes which he had prosecuted and, later, those on which he had adjudicated. He had never felt himself distanced, in empathy or sympathy, from the feelings and emotions that the bereaved families, desperate for justice and explanation, had experienced. He had always been, he hoped, a compassionate man. But dealing with murder and violence from an elevated bench, in an atmosphere of judicial prominence, draped in the traditional robes of his profession, now seemed to him to be far removed from the reality of those crimes. Professionally, he had viewed murder as a bundle of papers, bound together by red ribbons, of statements, exhibits, and testimony. For him, murder had been almost an academic exercise, a question of professional debate and evidential discussion. Only after he had retired did Everett Carr see murder in its brutal reality, committed in its gory immediacy, and only after stepping away from his profession did he witness personally the wreckage of life that murder left in its bloody wake. If anything, his retirement to date had become a more profound experience of learning and personal comprehension than those years of study, academia, and legal pomp and circumstance. And it was with this newly discovered understanding of violent crime that Everett Carr had listened to Josephine Kettering's fears, and it was that same comprehension of the harsh reality of murder which, he felt sure now, had convinced him that there were reasons to share those fears.

Carr sipped a little of the whisky and closed his eyes, plunging himself into thoughtful darkness. He wondered further about his newly refined attitude to murder, and it struck him that his personal experiences of it had always been beyond his control. He had been a witness to it only after the event. As ever, he thought about his wife and her vicious death, which perversely seemed to him to be almost meaningless. Not in the sense that it had carried no meaning, but that it had been without proper purpose: Miranda had not been the intended victim, since the bullets that had killed her had been meant for Carr himself. That was the cause of this incessant pain, in turn bearable and agonising, which infested the shattered knee, which still carried a sliver of shrapnel inside it. But it was not only Miranda's murder that occupied his mind and, as he thought further, another comment made by Josephine Kettering stirred in his memory.

She had asked him if he was a detective. He had denied it since he was not by profession an investigator of crime, so he considered that he had no entitlement to claim the title as his own. And yet, he had been involved in detective work, and he had insinuated himself into those investigations that had been undertaken by the official police. People might ask by what right he involved himself in such matters if he was not an official detective, and he had never quite given an answer that had seemed to him either wholly satisfactory or entirely honest.

"Every person has a moral and legal obligation to see justice done, have they not?" he would ask. "If I am able to assist the police in finding a guilty person, why should I not do so?"

But was there not something more to it than that? Was it not, if he were brave enough to admit it, that he somehow felt that he owed a debt to Miranda? She had died in his place, of that he had no doubt, and his knee and its associated pain were a sufficient reminder of it, even if he were tempted to try to forget it. Beyond those physical considerations, however, Carr wondered whether his past involvement in detecting murderers had been inspired by some kind of desire for atonement, as if bringing murderers to light, and helping in whatever way he could to bring justice to those whose lives were ripped apart by murder, might somehow make amends for Miranda's death. She would never have expected him to seek such redemption, and she would have hated to think of him torturing himself with thoughts such as these, but he found them increasingly difficult to dismiss from his mind. If they were a plague to him in that sense, they were also a comfort, since they offered some explanation and justification for his intrusion into matters which were none of his concern.

It was not that he actively sought out these situations. In many ways, it was misfortune rather than personal endeavour which meant he had been present when these terrible things had happened. Nor was it the case that he had enjoyed the process. On the contrary, exposing family secrets and hidden guilt could hardly be said to be a pleasurable exercise, but he believed that people were entitled to the truth, however unpalatable, and

Carr had a profound belief in the human spirit's ability to heal and mend.

But it was also true to say that any contribution on his part to the pursuit of the truth of murder had affected him as much as anybody else. He had been forced to expose, as murderers, people whom he had considered friends and people for whom he had a keen fondness, but these reservations had never prevented him from revealing their guilt. Did that fact alone not suggest some sort of compulsion on his part to pursue these killers, despite his personal feelings about them? He could certainly believe it, and he could only conclude that it was a result of this personal penitence about which he had speculated. Miranda had died, and he had not: that was the overwhelming tragedy and injustice in his life. If he could make some sort of retribution for it, he felt obliged to do so. He had known a man who had been unable to live with the fact that he had survived the Great War, but his brother had not. The man, Carr had learned with sadness, had been unable to live with the guilt and had ended his life in tragic isolation in his bath, with only a razor and whisky for company. Carr had not been able to comprehend it at the time, but now, sitting alone with the Mahler and the whisky, his thoughts darker than usual, he felt that perhaps he could fully understand the man's death after all.

Slowly, he opened his eyes and looked out across the courtyard towards Piccadilly. He rose from his chair, heaving a sigh from his lungs, and sipping once more at the whisky. He limped over to the window and looked out into the night, but he saw precious little of the Albany or the streets beyond it. Instead, he saw only his own features, reflected and blurred in the pane, staring back at him. The moustache, undeniably elegant, was white, as was the Imperial beard and his hair, but their colour was not what seemed to Carr to suggest age. Instead, he saw it in the eyes that looked back at him, and with the age, there was also a trace of sadness. Perhaps, he thought, a second whisky would not be sensible, however much he might crave its indulgence.

These thoughts of his relationship with murder were not necessarily the product of this uncharacteristic depression alone, however, and he reminded himself that there had been an original idea behind this grim reconnaissance of his past exploits and his darkest fears. His mind went back to the fact that his involvement in violent death had been after the event. In every case, the damage had been done, as it were, the life taken and the crime committed. His meeting with Josephine Kettering, and his subsequent agreement with her that there was some suggestion of danger manifesting itself in her family's relationships, had offered a possible change of circumstance.

This time, he thought, was it not possible that his presence at the centre of that family and its complexities might allow him to *prevent* a murder rather than investigate it? If Rowena Kettering was in danger, and if one of those people invited to the country house in Longhampton was planning murder, was it not morally incumbent upon Carr to use whatever understanding of the business of violent crime, and whatever skills he might possess concerning its detection, to stop that plan from being carried out?

Slowly, Carr began to wonder whether or not that chance meeting in a cemetery might have provided him with the opportunity to find at last this redemption that he feared he had been seeking so badly. His attention remained fixed on his reflection, but his thoughts remained far away.

Several minutes later, the Mahler had finished, but it wasn't until long afterwards that Everett Carr became aware of the sudden silence in the room, broken only by the distant crackle of the needle against the vinyl.

II

PART TWO: POISON HATH RESIDENCE

Chapter Nine

Rowena sat in the library of Marsden Grange, smoking a cigarette with a ponderous affectation and sipping at a gin and tonic which, even for her, was a little premature. It was almost but not quite eleven o'clock in the morning, and ordinarily, she would not have entertained the idea of alcohol at this time of the day, but somehow the occasion seemed both to justify and endorse it. And she would not gratify herself with any more than this one drink. It would be a solitary indulgence, a splash of strength with a twist of courage, and one which she felt was necessary and forgivable in the circumstances.

Her attention had been fixed on the curved gravel driveway, which arched its way from the main gates to the property, around the fountain in the centre of the garden, and back again to that same, wrought-iron entrance. From here, she had watched idly as the gardeners first industriously raked the lawns and then fastidiously clipped the hedges, and almost lovingly sprayed the roses. In the past, the beauty of the gardens at the grange had been something she had both admired and enjoyed, but on that morning, something about her mood and the anticipation of the weekend seemed to corrupt the idyll of the place. Or perhaps, thought Rowena with a bitter smile, it was just the gin.

But she knew that it wasn't simply the gin. The memory of the car in Campden Hill Square was still fresh in her mind, the sound of its engine and screeching still so loud in her mind that they might have been as real as they were on the day before she came to Marsden Grange. She had been crossing the road from the park to the house, her mind so distracted that she had not noticed the car coming from around the corner. If she had not been so preoccupied, she would have surely known that the car was travelling at such speed that its intentions could not possibly have been innocent. She could remember now looking over her shoulder, her senses suddenly awoken by that roaring engine and the banshee wail of the tyres against the tarmac, as the car veered around the corner. In an instant, the round headlamps had been upon her, glaring at her as if they were the widened eyes of some maniac intent on murder. Rowena's vision, so long distorted by illness, had seemed now clearer than ever, and in the looming monster of metal and glass, she saw her own death. The whole incident could only have lasted seconds, but it had seemed to last forever. She was conscious now of her body being thrown to the floor by some invisible hand of salvation, as the car had growled past her, furious at its failed mission. She had lain on the pavement, her mind and sight delirious with fear and panic, wondering whether she was in the last moments of life. Slowly, the realisation that the car had missed her, that whatever instinct had thrown her to the floor had saved her life, had seemed to overwhelm her, and her tears had stung in her closed, failing eyes. It had been an intentional attack, Rowena had been sure of it, and she remained convinced of it now, as her mind recalled the terror of those leering headlamps, the horror of the screaming engine, and the cold harshness of the pavement underneath her.

She closed her eyes, forcing the memory of this attack on her life from her mind. She took solace in the befitting stillness and silence of the library. There was a measure of peace that seemed to emanate from the leather-bound volumes in the fitted shelves that lined the two side walls, although she could not recall reading any of them. On the far wall, opposite the door, was a set of French windows, looking out onto the front lawns and the curved driveway, with a pair of heavy emerald curtains set on either side. On one side of the windows was a small writing desk and chair, and on the other was a side table used primarily as a drinks' cabinet, from which Rowena had helped herself to the gin. In front of the French windows, there was a small settee, with two matching armchairs set on either side of it. The small table, on which were fanned the Victorian periodicals, completed this central area of communal domesticity. On the fourth wall, next to the door, there was a large, marble fireplace, above which was a portrait of Rowena herself, in the part of Lady Macbeth.

It was a striking work, commissioned many years ago by Ivor, and which he had presented to her as a gift for a wedding anniversary. Their tenth, recalled Rowena, although she doubted Ivor would remember. She looked up at it now and saw the artificial version of herself glaring back down at her, the features still retaining some of the regal authority she had always felt the role demanded beneath the character's mounting insanity. Rowena was proud of the portrait: of the intensity of performance captured by the brush strokes, of the power suggested by the confident but manic glare, and of the artistic respect which she felt the entire portrait commanded. Felix once said that it was nothing more than a testament to Rowena's ego, a self-reverential round of applause framed for her own glory. If so, Rowena offered no apology for it.

She looked into the eyes of the portrait, and a sudden sadness overwhelmed her. The proud authority and demure assurance of the painted glare would never diminish, unlike the more fragile reality upon which it was based. The doctors had given her perhaps two years before total blindness overcame her, the news given in voices pregnant with grave condolence. What had caused the decline in her vision, she had never properly understood. They had explained it in technical terms, which had passed her by, her attention having been seized only by the implications of this terrible diagnosis, but she had been sure that the inference was that it was a natural deficiency, a personal tragedy which was inevitable. She had endured three years of increasing darkness in her world, the colours dimming, the clarity of her vision slowly blurring, and the previous joys of summer now becoming unforgiving flames of agony. Work had become intolerable, the spotlights and the greasepaint bringing pain where once they had brought pleasure, and retirement had been inevitable if not voluntary. Now, the portrait's perfection seemed to her to be in danger of mocking her instead of applauding her. It was difficult not to believe that it was some sort of punishment for her sins.

She drained the remainder of the gin, the ice tinkling against the glass, and she thought that perhaps one more would do no harm after all. Rising to her feet, she walked slowly to the small table in the corner of the room and went about the necessary business. No more after this, she told herself, until the usual hour for cocktails, before dinner.

Rowena looked back over the lawns and the driveway. For a moment, she hardly registered in her mind the vision of the man standing there, so that there was the impression in her mind that he had not been there initially and had now appeared as if from nowhere, like a small, black spectre from a world beyond her own. He was standing to the side of the fountain, looking up at the house, one hand clasped into a gloved fist over his heart and the other holding the silver handle of an elegant, black cane. He was dressed in black, a long overcoat reaching just below his knees and a sombre Homburg hat set perfectly on his head. From this distance, Rowena could see no splash of colour about him, but she was aware of the white of what looked like an improbable but luxuriant moustache and the suggestion, she thought, of a small beard below it. The overall impression was one of dapper sophistication, and even the suitcase, which stood by the feet, neatly placed together, seemed to suggest stylish formality. Rowena stared at him through the window, trying desperately to recall his identity to mind, but nothing came to her. Curious, and putting on a pair of dark sunglasses, she walked out of the library, pulled open the front door, and stepped onto the front steps of the house.

"Excuse me, can I help you?" she called.

The little man stooped to pick up the case and walked towards her. Rowena was surprised to see that he walked with a definite and obviously painful limp.

"My apologies, dear lady," he said, stopping in front of her and tipping his hat in greeting. "You must think me a careless and unwanted trespasser."

"Are you lost? I can easily give you directions to the town if you require them."

"No, no, I am not lost," he said with a smile.

"I see," said Rowena, although she felt she saw nothing at all. "Forgive me, but who are you?"

The little man bowed. "My name is Everett Carr." He reached into an inside pocket and produced a small card, which he handed to her. "I am a friend of your daughter's, if I may say so."

"Of Josephine?"

Carr bowed once more. "You are Mrs Rowena Kettering, yes?"

"Yes. But I'm afraid…"

"May I say," Carr said, gesturing with his hand across the front of the house and back over the lawns, "what a beautiful property this is."

Rowena, despite herself, smiled at the overt politeness, which was not only charming but somehow faintly ridiculous. "Thank you. We are rather proud of it."

"I had not expected the house to be so beautiful."

"I'm afraid one rather gets used to it."

"How very sad. One must never take beauty in the world for granted, dear lady, whatever form it takes. The roses in your garden, for example, the sea on the coastline, the sonnets in the poetry books, or indeed this house in its grounds. If one loses sight of those, one is left only with ugliness, and there is already far too much of that in the world."

Somehow, this dapper and eccentric little man had charmed Rowena out onto the driveway, so that now she stood next to him, looking up at Marsden Grange as if seeing it for the first time. The red of the bricks were of such a vibrant crimson that they almost seemed to shimmer in the morning light, an effect intensified by the glinting sun against the panes of the latticed windows. She saw a majesty she had never before recognised in the two turrets which flanked the house, each one capped with a sloping, conical roof of the same slate as the main house. The stone balustrades of the balconies on the uppermost of the three floors now seemed to her to possess their own sense of opulence, which promoted them above their rather more mundane, protective purpose. The flagged terrace which ran along the perimeter of the house was both inviting and somehow picturesque, so that she felt a sudden desire to be on the veranda at the back of the house, at which the terrace culminated, sipping that cocktail she had thought of earlier, in a gown of silk, as the sun slowly dipped down beneath the horizon, with the sound of voices and laughter ringing in her ears. Rowena supposed that she must have had these feelings when she first saw the place, but they had become buried under the soil of familiarity until they had been excavated by this stranger in black, to whom she suddenly felt a curious but profound gratitude.

"What an extraordinary man you are, Mr Carr," she said, "although I'm afraid I am still a little confused about why you're here."

Carr placed his hand on his chest. "Again, you must forgive me. I am here at the invitation of your daughter. As I said, we are friends."

"She has never mentioned you."

"It is only a recent friendship, I admit. She told me about this little gathering this weekend and asked if I would like to come. I have never been to the Norfolk coast, and I am afraid I have very little in my life which might be called social interaction." The lie, though shameful, was told with a pretence of gallant regret. "I fear Miss Kettering took pity on an old man."

Rowena smiled. "She really should have asked if my husband and I were agreeable."

Carr nodded adamantly. "Of course, of course, and I am sure she realises it. But, please, dear lady, do not be too hard on her. If I am intruding, I shall leave you in peace, just as you wish. But if I may make a small confession: it was not only Miss Josephine whom I wished to oblige this weekend."

"Oh?"

Carr smiled, the luxurious moustache stretching in genial amusement. "I have long been an admirer of your work, dear lady. Your Lady Macbeth, if I may say so, has yet to be surpassed."

"How very kind." Rowena was charmed and exhilarated by the praise. "You saw me perhaps at Stratford? Longer ago than I care to remember."

"There, and in London." Carr's smile remained in place. "Each time as impressive as the other, if you will accept an amateur's appraisal."

Rowena, suddenly embarrassed by the spectacles, removed them. She squinted at him through the pain of the sunlight. "Forgive these stupid things, Mr Carr."

He smiled, but there was a sadness in his eyes. "I'm sorry they are necessary, dear lady."

"They mean no more appearances at Stratford, London, or anywhere else."

"Then we must be grateful for the magic you have given us already, dear lady."

Gently, almost ashamedly, she replaced the dark glasses. "You're very sweet, Mr Carr. Do, now, come into the house."

He followed her into the main hallway, which struck him as being as impressive in its own right as the exterior of the house. The oak-panelled walls suggested antiquity without leaning towards ostentation, and the curved staircase, which seemed to erupt from the chessboard flooring of the hallway, emanated a luxurious dignity of its own, even without the ermine runner which cascaded down the stairs. As a space designed for welcome, perhaps it failed, but as an area which demanded respect and admiration, there could be no doubt as to its success.

Rowena showed Carr into the library, and only as she opened the door to admit him did she realise that she was still holding the glass of gin, and she wondered what he must think of her. Did he view her as a hopeless drunk, a woman capable only of surviving the morning with a chilled glass of one stimulant or another? Somehow, looking at him, she doubted it.

He had removed his long overcoat and Homburg hat, having left them with his case in the hallway, and he stood to her side now in a plain suit of black which, although clearly both well-tailored and expensive, somehow did not seem willing or required to boast of its own excellence. The skull with ruby eyes, which he wore as a lapel pin, was a little surprising, but it did not seem to Rowena to be as startling as the garish necktie and handkerchief, both of which were of such a livid lilac that they appeared outlandishly garish against the sombre simplicity of the black suit. Together with the white hair and elaborate moustache, the overall impression was one of perpetual mourning blessed with the bright colour of optimism and the stark white of wisdom.

Everett Carr was looking up at the portrait above the mantel. "A remarkable piece of work."

"It was a gift from my husband. He had it commissioned."

"It captures you in the role perfectly." Carr's dark eyes were alive with admiration. "It brings back to me not only the intensity of your performance but also the pathos of it."

"You are far too charming, Mr Carr," said Rowena, her laugh a show of modesty, but the glimmer in her eyes betraying her pride in his remark. "If only some critics were as kind as you."

Carr did not reply, but he gave a courteous bow and turned away from the portrait. Rowena gazed up at her image for a few moments longer, her thoughts largely abstract and meaningless, with only a few daring to linger on how happy she had been in years gone by, in those lost days when Ivor would commission portraits of her, present her with a reservation at a restaurant she had expressed a desire to visit months previously, or simply put his arms around her and tell her that if the sun burned out there would still be daylight in his life through her. Those little gestures which she now sorely missed, and which she knew were signs of a depth of love which might never be rekindled.

At last, she looked away and turned to face her guest. "I'm afraid you've taken us somewhat by surprise, Mr Carr, because we have no room ready for you. I shall have one prepared and see to it that your luggage is dealt with."

"How very kind of you," he replied. "I am sorry to have intruded on you like this. I had assumed Josephine would have told you that I was due to arrive."

Rowena raised her eyebrows. "Yes, it would have been helpful if she had done so, but it cannot be helped, and you are most welcome to stay, as I've said. I only hope the weekend isn't too fraught for you."

"Fraught?"

She looked into his eyes and saw that the questioning tone of his voice was not reciprocated in them, as if somehow, he knew what she meant but perhaps needed her to express it. "With you not knowing anybody, I mean."

His lips stretched into a smile, but the eyes remained fixed on her, and something about their intensity told her that he had not been fooled by her evasion or convinced by her lie.

"I'm sure everybody will be most accommodating, dear lady," Carr said.

He seemed to be on the verge of saying something more, and Rowena seemed to catch in those dark eyes a glimpse of a more austere aspect of his personality, both penetrating and calculating, but hidden beneath the casual amiability. What he might have said was to remain unknown, because the library door opened and Josephine Kettering walked into the room. Looking back to Carr, Rowena saw that the flicker of grim warning which had been in his eyes had vanished once more, and the affable smile was back in place. For the first time, Rowena became aware that there was perhaps something altogether deeper and more fascinating about this stranger in the house, and she began to wonder how much more lay hidden behind his outward gentility and politeness.

Josephine was breathless. "I am so sorry for not being here to meet you, Mr Carr. Unforgivably rude of me, but I'm afraid I had gone for a walk around the grounds."

"No need to apologise, my dear, I have been made most welcome."

Rowena took Josephine's hands. "It was really rather foolish to invite Mr Carr here without telling your father or me, darling. You should have asked us if it was convenient first, instead of embarrassing us all."

"I didn't think you'd mind," said the girl, her brows creasing and the bottom lip pouting. It gave her the sudden appearance of a spoiled adolescent, and the impression was magnified when her mother kissed her forehead and held her close.

"It doesn't matter, darling," Rowena said. "Mr Carr is perfectly welcome."

"I suppose Daddy will be angry."

"You leave him to me," came the reply, preceded by a short, scornful laugh. Rowena looked across at Carr and offered her hand. He took it, giving it a gentle kiss. "I must go and see about getting a room sorted for you, Mr Carr. I shall send in some coffee, or tea if you prefer."

He held up a dissenting hand. "Neither for the moment, thank you."

Rowena smiled. "Then I shall leave you with Josephine. The two of you must have much to discuss."

After she had gone, Josephine looked back to Everett Carr. "Have you spoken to her about what I said to you?"

Carr smiled. "Not yet. I thought it better to observe matters for a while first, to see things for myself, as it were."

"Then what did she mean when she said we must have much to discuss?"

Carr's eyes had grown serious. "Calm yourself, my child. She thinks that we are friends, but I am a stranger to her. She is naturally cautious about me. Her words are nothing more than that."

"Has she said anything to you?"

He placed a finger to his lips. "She did say one thing of interest. She said she hoped that the weekend was not too fraught for me, on account of me knowing nobody else here."

"That's rather typical of mother," said Josephine. "She likes her audience to be relaxed."

But Carr seemed not to be listening, and his voice, lowered and thoughtful, was filled with curiosity. "The suggestion that your mother thinks that I might find my time here tense surely indicates that she fears some sort of conflict or confrontation. If not, why would she not say that she was sure I would find the people here welcoming and amusing? Why use the word fraught?"

Josephine's impatience had dissolved into a sudden panic. "You think she anticipates something terrible, like I do?"

"I think many things, my child. What is important is that we remain vigilant. We must keep our eyes and ears open. Tell me," he added, his voice now as effusive and avuncular as ever, "am I the first to arrive?"

"No, no. My step-brother, Felix, and his fiancée, Adele, are here. I mentioned them, I think, and Lewis Davenport came down with Daddy last night. Poor Lewis, he thinks he is in love with me."

Carr smiled. "Does he not know it?"

But Josephine had no reply, other than to look down at her feet as the fire rose in her cheeks. "And Tilly Royce came with Mummy, so she's already here. A strange woman, but I'll let you make up your own mind about her.

So, only the damned Clements woman and Dr Jarratt are to come."

"There are no more guests expected?"

"No. You'll get to meet them all later, of course. Daddy insists on cocktails before dinner, usually at around six o'clock."

"I shall look forward to it." Carr smiled warmly at her. "Now, perhaps I might be permitted to find my bearings in this beautiful, but rather large house."

"Of course," said Josephine, laughing. "Do let me show you around."

But Carr held up a finger. "I should prefer to be alone, my child. And I think you may have one of your outstanding guests arriving."

She followed his gaze out of the library window, and only then did she hear the crunch of gravel under the tyres of a car, and feel the sudden slump of her heart in her breast.

Chapter Ten

The car belonged to Dr Edwin Jarratt, and Josephine had recognised it immediately. She had thought, for the briefest of moments, of making her way down the hallway to the kitchen and leaving through the back door of the grange, so that she wouldn't have to see or speak to him, but it would have been cowardice of the worst kind. Worse, she thought, it would only delay the inevitable. She could hardly avoid Jarratt all weekend and, in any case, she suspected that he would find some way of manufacturing a meeting between them or of tracking her down. And so, with a nauseating sense of distaste in her stomach and with her face exhibiting that same childish petulance that it had displayed earlier, she walked with Everett Carr to the front door.

Jarratt was standing on the doorstep, his suitcase in one hand and the fist of the other half raised to knock on the door. "What fortuitous timing, Josephine. Almost as if you were watching for me to arrive."

The arrogance of the man sickened her, but she refused to succumb to it. "I wonder if you would mind stepping aside, Dr Jarratt, to allow Mr Carr to pass."

"Certainly." The doctor, whose amiability and genial candour seemed to Josephine to border on the unctuous, stepped aside but held out his open hand. "I don't believe we've met, sir."

Everett Carr accepted the offered hand gently and gave a small bow of the head. "We have not, doctor. My name is Carr, Everett Carr."

Jarratt smiled. "A friend of the family?"

"Rather more a friend of Miss Kettering's, doctor. Now, if you will excuse me, I would like to take a walk around the grounds, and it does look rather as if rain has scheduled an appearance." And with another bow, he took his leave.

Jarratt watched him disappear around the side of the house, taking in with interest the limp and the difficulty with which Carr moved. "Funny little man. Where did you find him?"

Josephine, not about to reply, pulled open the door and stepped aside. "You'd better come in, Dr Jarratt."

He obliged, stepping over the threshold, placing his case on the floor of the hallway, and removing his hat. "I do wish you would call me Edwin."

"That would imply a degree of friendship."

"What a callous girl you can be, Josephine." The words were meant seriously, but he spoke them with a smile on his face, as if to admit the gravity of them would be to prohibit any hope that her feelings towards him might soften. "Is your Mr Carr staying for the weekend?"

"Yes."

"Then I shall look forward to getting to know him."

"I'm sure you will find him fascinating. I do."

But Jarratt appeared already to have lost interest. He had taken off his overcoat and tossed it casually on a nearby stand. "I suppose Lewis Davenport is here."

Josephine, ignoring the surge of nervous energy which passed through her at the mention of the man's name, made an effort to appear nonchalant. "Of course. He works for Daddy, and they have lots of things to discuss. They always seem to have matters to discuss."

Jarratt, a man for whom domestic politics had seldom held any allure, smiled simply. "Yes, I suppose that makes sense."

For a moment, the two of them stared at each other in silence. To Josephine, it seemed an age since she had last seen him, but it couldn't have been more than a couple of weeks. Still, it was as if she had forgotten not only how darkly sleek his hair was, brushed back from the low, almost atavistic brow, but also how cold and intimidating his eyes were. They were the clearest of blue, she knew that, but they reminded her not of oceans but of glaciers of ice, and their expression never seemed to lose some suggestion of suspicion or conflict, no matter how affable his manner might be. He was tall, which only increased the sense of imposing superiority. The shoulders were broad and the hands large, so that the possibility that he had been a proficient rugby player in his youth could not easily be dismissed, but his gynaecological profession meant surely that those same hands must be capable of delicate and sensitive work. She could easily imagine those hands on her, exploring her, and she was momentarily surprised to find that the thought stimulated her as much as it disgusted her. She supposed that a certain group of women would find him attractive without much difficulty, and she would be lying to herself if she did not count herself amongst them. A sole encounter of passion with him might be exciting, but Josephine could hardly bring herself to imagine a life with him. After all, he was not the sort of man who inspired any assurance of fidelity, and his allure could surely only be said to be of the moment. After that moment had passed, Josephine could envisage only mortification on her part and arrogant gratification on his. These prejudices had not been entirely of Josephine's own making. Her mother's dislike of the doctor, her unexplained reference to him being a monster, and Jarratt's vile words towards Rowena had been sufficient to crystallise Josephine's antipathy towards him. There could be no doubt that those factors soured any attraction which she might have felt for him.

"I thought it would matter to me that Davenport was here, Josephine," Jarratt was saying, "but it doesn't. I wouldn't have come if I thought he meant anything."

"Meant anything to whom?"

The eyes now seemed to be burning into her. "To you, to me, to us."

"Don't say anything else. Please, don't. You'll embarrass us both."

"I won't embarrass myself by speaking the truth."

Her arms folded, as if by their own volition, as some sort of physical barricade against him. "I wish you wouldn't do this."

"I can't help my feelings for you."

Her eyes now blazed with indignation. "Yes, you can. If I don't share them, which I certainly do not, then you can help your feelings. You can suppress them, you can bury them, you can forget them. These are the 1930s, Dr Jarratt, or hadn't you noticed? You've no right over my feelings."

His eyes, whilst not losing their cold intensity, now seemed to reflect a degree of genuine hurt. "I have no intention of behaving in the way you seem to imagine, Josephine. I can assure you of that. But I cannot dismiss my love for you with the casual ease which you suggest. If I could, I wouldn't feel the way I do for you. Surely, you can see that?"

Could she? In that moment, looking into those eyes and seeing the concern on his face, perhaps she could believe that he was not forcing himself on her, physically or emotionally. And yet, nor was it something which she felt able to disregard entirely. If he expected her to take his emotions and feelings seriously, she wished he would give her the same courtesy. She was on the point of saying so, her lips trembling with the effort and her eyes flickering between Jarratt and anywhere else but in his direction, when she heard her name being called.

"Is everything all right?" Lewis Davenport was walking towards them, his attention fixed not on Josephine but on Jarratt. Lewis walked slowly, his hands behind his back, and his eyes staring maliciously from behind the lenses of his spectacles.

"Everything is fine, Lewis, thank you," said Josephine. "Dr Jarratt was just going to his room."

Lewis, not to be deterred so easily, stood by her side. "Is there anything I can do?"

Jarratt snorted a contemptuous laugh. "You heard the girl, Davenport. Everything is fine. So, you can stop twitching that long nose of yours and toddle off back to where you came from."

Lewis permitted himself a slight, humourless smile. Any reply from him would sound unbearably trite and would surely give the impression that they were two jealous schoolboys, circling each other in the schoolyard, an image which he found unbecoming and which Josephine would certainly consider to be degrading, both to the two men and, more importantly, to her. But his silence still seemed like a weakness, and he found the urge to resist any kind of retort difficult to suppress.

"Josephine, I wondered if you might care to take a walk before your father insists on cocktails," he said.

Jarratt, not fooled by Lewis' circumvention, gave a short laugh and a genial shrug of defeat. He picked up his hat, coat, and case, and gave a short and rather insolent bow to them both. "No need to pretend on my account, Davenport, I know when I'm not wanted. Although perhaps someone could talk to me long enough to direct me to my room, at least."

She did so, briefly and with a sullen efficiency, and they watched him walk up the stairs and along the landing above them until he disappeared from view. Left alone, Lewis turned to face her. "Are you all right?"

She suddenly wanted to be away from both of them. "I didn't need rescuing, Lewis."

"Of course not." He seemed genuinely offended by the idea. "I didn't mean to give that impression, and I'm sorry if I did."

Josephine shook her head. She was irritated by it all now, by the two of them and by what she saw as her peevishness and indecision. Why did she allow either of them to make her feel like a foolish girl, incapable of rational and independent thought? Even more frustratingly, she allowed both of them to make her feel that way. She had always dreamed of love and romance, of marriage, of children even, but she had never expected two suitors to come along almost simultaneously. She supposed that some girls would find it thrilling to have two men competing for her. She had certainly read enough cheap novels on the theme. But she found it suffocating, as if they were both pressing a pillow down on her face with equal force, demanding devotion and commitment from her, when all she could provide was uncertainty.

"I'm sorry, Lewis," she said. "It's been a trying day."

He smiled at her, adjusting his spectacles unnecessarily. "Perhaps a little walk would be welcome, then?"

She nodded, suddenly feeling exhausted by what seemed to her to be the stale air of the house and its company. "You're right, yes. But would you mind if I had a little time to myself? Just to clear my head."

Lewis did mind, very much so. He wanted the time with her, the quiet walk in her company, and he wanted to be alone with her for as long as possible. But he also wanted her love and her respect. As he looked into her eyes, he knew that there was only one answer he could give. With a small nod of the head, he said simply, "Of course, I don't mind at all."

Josephine smiled, and it seemed to Lewis that an immediate relief and sense of gratitude passed across her face. She leaned forward and kissed him gently on the cheek. "I knew you'd understand. Thank you, Lewis."

He watched her walk away, open the front door, and close it behind her. The kiss still seemed to linger on his cheek, and, almost without thought, he touched the place where her lips had been with the tips of his fingers. In that brief moment, with a kiss of affection, perhaps, rather than love, she had seemed closer to him than ever before. The memories of their previous encounters, those hesitant and indecisive romantic clinches, now came back to him with such force that they seemed almost to drive the air from his lungs and swipe his feet from under him. He knew that he should not wish for too much, but that sense of envy and hatred which had threatened to consume him, when he saw Edwin Jarratt with her, now seemed to have disappeared, leaving him only with optimism and expectation.

He remained there for several moments more, all the time unaware that he was being watched. From the uppermost landing, Rowena Kettering had watched the little drama unfold, her eyes narrowed with contempt, and her lips pursed with a particular breed of malevolence.

Chapter Eleven

Is walk around the ground of Marsden Grange did much to lift Everett Carr's mood, so that some of the anxieties and concerns which had plagued him since he first met Josephine Kettering had eased. They had not vanished completely, but the beauty of the lawns, shrubs, and woods surrounding the house was a vibrant and soothing tonic for him. Carr was not necessarily a man who was heavily influenced by his surroundings, but he appreciated as much as anyone the elegance of the natural world. The colours of the flowers, the majesty of the trees, and the lush greens of the elegantly cultivated lawns all combined to impress on him a sense that there was goodness and beauty in the world, even when one's thoughts were consumed by darkness.

He stood silently beside a small sundial, at the fringe of the woods which stretched beyond the east side of the gardens, and listened intently. So different to the noises of London, with its hiss of motorcar tyres along the rain-drenched streets and the hawking of newspaper vendors, mixing with the general buzzing of urban existence. Here, there was only the sound of a fresh breeze and, from somewhere in the distance, the faint chirping of birds. Somewhere beyond the house, there was the coast, where the sound of the sea against the shores and cliffs would dominate the headland, but even that sound of raging tides would seem beautiful when compared with the mechanical clamouring of city life. Carr had never thought about it in such terms before, but the sound of nature, however primal, from the delicate songs of the birds to the most violent of storms, was always more beautiful and alluring than any sound of industrial progression made by man. And here, in these gardens of a stranger's country house, they seemed more beautiful and peaceful than ever, and Carr was almost able to forget the dark business in which he had involved himself and those thoughts of murder which had dominated his attention over the past few days.

He realised now that he was grateful for his decision to explore the grounds, that he was thankful for the tranquillity of nature's surroundings, and that he was keenly appreciative of the beauty which he saw. Not because of their obvious attraction, but because they reminded him that these malignant and troubling considerations of impending death were not his natural psychology. He was, by nature, a man who thrived on finding the best in people, in wishing that their hopes and aspirations would come to pass, and that the human spirit, however tested by adversity, would prevail. Here, in the gardens of Marsden Grange, Everett Carr seemed to find himself once again, and somehow, he felt able to believe in himself once more. In a moment of forgivable self-indulgence, he permitted himself time to enjoy the sensation.

After a few moments of this solitary contemplation, Carr became aware that he was not entirely alone. From a distance away to his right, he saw a couple walking in his direction, although they were too engrossed in their conversation to be aware of his presence. From this distance, Carr could tell little about them other than very broad outlines of their characteristics: the man's height and slender frame, his dark hair, and obvious elegance of appearance, and the girl's platinum hair, pale skin, and equally elegant stature. As a couple, they appeared well matched, their contrasts complementing rather than jarring with their similarities. If a novelist had wished to create an image of a couple destined to be in love forever, he might have chosen these two figures as his models from life. Carr's sense of optimism, newly invigorated by the gardens, was given an additional galvanisation by this appearance of young love in full bloom.

Had he been able to overhear the discussion between them, however, his admiration and his joy in the tenderness of young love would have been cruelly shaken.

"We've got to be better prepared," said Adele Mills. "We didn't think it through before, but this time we will."

Felix Kettering shook his head and inhaled deeply on his cigarette. "I can't believe we're doing any of it. We must be mad."

"We promised each other," she replied, her voice perhaps louder than she might have wanted or expected. "You promised *me*."

"I know. But talking about it is one thing. Doing it is something else entirely."

Adele had been linking his arm, but she now unravelled herself from his grasp and moved away from him. It was a single step, almost imperceptible, but to Felix, it had seemed as if it had been acres that she had put between them.

"I never thought you'd fail me, Felix."

He took hold of her again. "I won't fail you."

She looked into his eyes, into their granite hardness, the colouring the only physical feature which he shared with his father and Josephine. "It's not as if Rowena's your mother. She doesn't mean anything to you."

Felix had tightened his grip on her. "I won't fail you, Adele. I didn't fail you before, did I? And I won't now."

She kissed him urgently. "Tonight, do it tonight."

Before he was able to give her any verbal guarantee of his pledge, he had seen Everett Carr. Felix gave a warning squeeze of her arm. "Be quiet, now. Who's that?"

Adele looked over at the dapper man who was walking towards them. She was conscious at once of a large white moustache, of its elegance and size, and perhaps more acutely, she was immediately aware that the man limped badly. She had a sudden vision of her grandfather, a man who had both loved and treasured her, one of the few who had shown her genuine affection, and she felt a sudden wave of nostalgic fondness wash over her. As the man approached, however, Adele saw that he was not as old as she had imagined. It had been the white hair which had deceived her, perhaps, but he could not have been many years over fifty. And yet, there was something about him which suggested an age beyond his year—the hair, the limp, the formality of dress, and the rounded shoulders.

"A beautiful afternoon, is it not?" this stranger said. Adele was struck at once by the darkness of his eyes, which seemed to contrast with the gentleness of his voice. The eyes suggested a profound intensity of thought, but the voice evoked nothing but kindness and gentility.

"Very beautiful," said Adele. She was smiling now, betraying none of the conspiratorial seriousness which had dominated her features until that moment. She looked up at Felix. "Isn't it, darling?"

"Very much so." Felix's voice was similarly ingratiating, but his eyes could not disguise their suspicion. "Forgive me, sir, but I don't believe I have had the pleasure."

Carr, smiling benignly, nodded. "You have not, my boy."

Felix, despite himself, laughed. "May I ask who you are?"

"My name is Carr," said the little man, holding out a hand. Felix took it. Then, taking Adele's hand, the man added, "Everett Carr, at your service, dear lady." And he kissed Adele's fingers gently. The hair of his moustache was soft above the lips, in contrast to the waxed tips, so carefully styled and which seemed to her so brittle that they might snap.

"It's a pleasure to meet you," she said. The voice seemed to him to be enchanting. There was something exotic about it, a faint accent perhaps, a quality which struck him as so alluring that he had a momentary vision of the mythology of sailors being lured to their deaths.

Felix was watching Carr with interest. "I'm Felix Kettering. This is my fiancée, Adele Mills."

"I am enchanted," said Carr, with an elaborate bow, "to meet you both."

"I suppose you're here by invitation of my father," said Felix. There was something about the sombre formality of Carr's suit which seemed to Felix representative of the corridors of power. "Do you work for the government?"

Carr was both amused and horrified by the suggestion. "I fear I am a man too bound by his own integrity to have such employment." Before Felix could protest at what he may have considered a monstrous implication, Carr continued. "It is your step-sister whom I am honoured to call a friend."

"Josephine?" Felix frowned. "She has never mentioned you."

Carr's smile broadened, and he gave a casual shrug of his shoulders, as if to suggest that he could offer no explanation for Josephine's reticence, nor would he attempt to do so. "These really are magnificent gardens. I was just thinking to myself how they make such a change from London."

"Yes, I always like to get away from the city and come here. We try to do it as often as possible, don't we, darling?"

Adele nodded. "Sometimes, it is safer to bury yourself away in these remote parts."

Carr inclined his head. "I quite agree."

"You're staying here for the weekend, I take it, Mr Carr?" asked Felix.

"I have that privilege, yes."

The young man smiled. "Well, you're very welcome."

He smiled now, and Carr was impressed by the change in his demeanour. Without the acute suspicion in the iron-grey eyes, there was a warm amiability about the handsome face. He shared his father's dignified but aloof expression, and the intelligence of the forehead was reflected in father and son. There was not yet the permanent crease above the nose which Ivor Kettering possessed, but the foundations for it had been laid. And yet, Felix's features were softer than his father's, so that what appeared to be simply ruthless intelligence in the father appeared in the son to be compassionate astuteness. There was perhaps the suggestion of ruddiness at the cheeks which might indicate a life of social engagements and artificial stimulants, but their effects were not yet so profound as to be permanent, and Felix Kettering gave the impression of being a gregarious man of the world, in whom one could expect a degree of empathy and a casual charm. In Adele Mills, Carr thought, Felix had found a companion who emphasised his own allure by possessing a similar attraction of her own, except where Felix offered amiable assurance, Adele promoted a sardonic seductiveness. They were so different in expression and appearance that it was impossible, paradoxically, for Carr to imagine a better pairing for either of them. If coupled with people of similar appearances or attitudes, they would have appeared bland and predictable. As it was, their combination appeared vibrant enough to illuminate a cinema screen.

"It promises to be an interesting weekend, if nothing else," Felix said. "I suppose you've heard about the dreaded Clements woman, Mr Carr?"

And there it was, thought Carr, the crack in the otherwise perfect veneer. The comment, the use of that particular word to describe the girl concerned, had been unnecessarily spiteful and vindictive, so that Felix's natural charm now seemed corrupted by cynicism. Carr might have been forgiven for hoping that Felix would have risen above such petty slanders, but it had been too much to expect.

"I have heard something about her, yes," said Carr gently.

"I only hope Rowena can keep her emotions under control. Otherwise, there could be hell to pay." Felix inhaled on his cigarette and flicked the end across the lawn.

Adele smiled briefly. "I don't think you should stir things up in front of Mr Carr, Felix."

Felix bowed in apology. "She's quite right, sir. Take no notice of me. I can't pretend to like either of them, but it doesn't do to set fires where there are already flames."

"A very wise precaution, dear boy," said Carr, his voice polite but laden with caution. "You will, I am sure, forgive me, if I return to the house. I must unpack, acquaint myself with my room, and dress for dinner. It has been a pleasure," he added, not altogether dishonestly, and gave a small, courteous bow.

As he walked away, Adele said softly, "You scared him away."

Felix smiled. "Perhaps that's no bad thing."

"What do you mean?"

"I don't trust any stranger in the house, not right now. What's he doing here?"

Adele kissed his cheek. "You're paranoid, my beautiful boy. Nobody suspects a thing, least of all that silly little man."

For Felix, it was sufficient consolation, if only for the moment. "Shall we take one more turn around the grounds, darling? Or do you want to go back inside?"

"One more turn," she replied. "But this time, we don't talk about killing anyone."

By the time Carr reached the house, he felt in need of little more than his own company, a cup of coffee, and some time either with his thoughts or a book. Before dressing for dinner, he thought he would bathe. He often found a hot bath to be not only relaxing but also conducive to serious thought, as if the steam from the water acted as a relaxing balm to his mind as well as his body. For such a simple necessity of human existence, Carr found soaking in a hot bath to be a special luxury.

These thoughts of relaxing comfort were interrupted by the sound of commotion from the library. Carr realised now that he had been conscious of some voices as he entered the house, but they had barely registered in his mind. Now, they intruded into it without invitation or apology. It was Rowena's voice which he recognised first, raised and outraged, carrying in it a disturbing tone of defiance.

"Don't you dare lecture me. Who do you think you are? You may act as if you're somebody of importance, but believe me, you're nothing but a secretary, one step up from a servant. If you were halfway competent to be in a position of power, you'd hold it by now. You'd be giving orders instead of receiving them."

The vitriol in her voice was obvious, and Carr could not help but wince at it. He felt suddenly as if his presence in the hallway was an embarrassing one, as if he had been cast in the role of eavesdropper against his will. He began to make his way up the stairs, but some instinct paralysed his legs and left him motionless on the first step.

Another voice, unmistakably a man's, came to his ears from the library. "I'll ignore your insults, Mrs Kettering, and remind you again that it is in your interests to listen to what I have to say."

"Anything you have to say can mean nothing to me," said Rowena.

"I know things, Mrs Kettering," said the other, "and you would do well to listen to what I know. It can only be to your benefit."

A shrill laugh. "So, as well as being a civil servant of no importance, now you show yourself up as being a nasty little blackmailer."

"It isn't blackmail."

"Threatening to expose some sordid little secret you think you've uncovered unless you get your own way? It sounds very much like blackmail to me."

"Very well, call it what you like. It doesn't alter anything. Can I take it that you agree to my proposal?"

"Agree to it?" Rowena's laugh this time was dangerous. "I'd rather be dead than let you near her."

"That is unfortunate. You leave me with no choice, Mrs Kettering. I can only suggest you reconsider, or you'll be sorry."

The silence that followed was somehow indicative of movement. Carr walked as briskly as he was able up the stairs, looking back only once as he heard the library door open. A man emerged and crossed the hall. Carr did not recognise him, but in only a short space of time, as cocktails were prepared and sipped, he would be introduced to Carr as Lewis Davenport, a proposed suitor of Josephine Kettering, the professional assistant to Ivor Kettering, and, to use Rowena's own words, a nasty little blackmailer.

Chapter Twelve

Daphne Clements had arrived at Marsden Grange as late as she dared, despite Ivor Kettering's insistence that she should not have any anxieties or fears about being present. It was not a question of anxiety, she had told him, nor was it one of fear. It was simply a matter of convenience. She knew that if she arrived too early, she would be condemned to time in isolation in whichever bedroom they had prepared for her or to walk around the grounds in the outside air. She could hardly expect to be able to have the freedom to wander around the house and into any room she chose, nor could Ivor expect as much. Similarly, she had said, she did not want to spend her time sitting in the company of comparative strangers or those members of a family who might despise her. Ivor, with some misguided sense of chivalry, had said that he would sit with her, or walk with her, or that they could have some time in Longhampton itself, but Daphne had resisted all his suggestions with vigour.

"Honestly, Ivor, I would much rather make my own way there and in my own time," she had said. "You will have work to do with Lewis Davenport, and I would hate to interfere with it. In any case, I wouldn't want anybody to have the impression that you were some sort of bodyguard for me. It would be much better if I arrive at such a time as will allow me to unpack and prepare myself for your usual cocktails and dinner. That way, it is all done on my own terms."

"Very well, Daphne, as you wish," he had replied, but his tone of voice had indicated that he was not altogether content with the arrangement.

Her journey had been pleasant enough, but not without some element of trepidation, caused not only by that ever-lingering unease at seeing Rowena but also by the prospect of seeing Felix and Josephine. It was a natural feeling of dread. If she did not feel it, Daphne told herself, she would hardly be experiencing normal, human emotions. All the same, she wished that they were less savage than they felt as the train rattled through the countryside, and the town of Longhampton drew ever closer to her.

She had taken a local bus service from the station to the town and walked the final mile and a half down the narrow country lanes that led to Marsden Grange so that when she arrived, she was breathing heavily and was warmer than she had anticipated. She had taken a moment at the iron gates to compose herself, before walking along the gravel driveway to the house itself. She had been prepared to meet Rowena almost immediately, or either Felix or Josephine, and she had silently rehearsed her greeting and responses to any comments in her mind as she undertook the lonely walk to the house. These private preparations had been part of the reason for her choice not to be collected from the station or to take a taxi, but, as it transpired, she had needed none of them. The door, almost uncannily, had been opened by Ivor. For a moment, she had stood before him in silence, not sure whether she was happy or enraged to see him, but he had spoken before she could draw any definite conclusion.

"I was watching out for you," he had said. "You told me which train you were getting, and I knew you'd either get a taxi or a bus and walk."

"I told you I didn't want you to act as a bodyguard," she had protested.

But his smile had been close to endearing. "I'm not. I'm acting as a genial and welcoming host."

And despite herself, she had returned that smile. "You're also acting like a fool."

Now, although the smile had faded slightly, the eyes hardened. "Can't you let me act like the man who loves you, even for one moment?"

And she had relented. Perhaps, she thought now, sitting on the bed in her room, she had been rather too eager to distance herself from him. He was in as difficult a position as her, she supposed, and it seemed both curiously selfish and unfair not to recognise the fact. They ought to be presenting a united front against Rowena, instead of fighting each other, even if it was Daphne who was doing most of the fighting. She had come here to confront Rowena for the sake not only of her own happiness, she reminded herself, but that of Ivor as well.

He had shown her to the room which had been set for her. Standing there, foolishly awkward for a few moments, they had kissed passionately at last and declared their love. It had strengthened Daphne's resolve, just this brief reassurance of their relationship, so much so that she regretted her earlier reticence. She said as much, and received another kiss from him, equally passionate and as if by way of absolution.

He had left her alone, and Daphne had gone about the business of unpacking the small suitcase which she had brought with her. It took her no more than a quarter of an hour, after which she bathed quickly and began to prepare herself for the evening. Now, dressed in a gown of black, with a simple necklace that had belonged to her grandmother hanging around her slim throat, she sat in the first shadows of the early evening, slowly brushing her hair in front of the dressing table mirror. A few days ago, she would have dreaded the prospect of an hour of cocktails and conversation, just as she would have loathed the idea of trying to engage in polite discussions over a dinner table at which she was not welcome and barely acknowledged. But now, as she styled her hair, the eyes that stared back at her from the glass seemed to convey a silent, internal calm that seemed almost alien to her, as if the impassive expression that looked back at her was of someone else, a person about whom Daphne knew nothing at all, someone who felt only an entitlement to happiness, and a sudden desire to pursue it at any cost. If only her and Ivor's happiness could be secure, she thought, it would hardly matter what people said, because she and Ivor would have won and Rowena would be out of their lives forever.

An involuntary laugh escaped from Daphne's mouth at the prospect of such an idyll. If she could have detected how malicious the sound had been, she would have been shocked, perhaps even a little disgusted, with herself. As it was, she simply repeated the sound and put the finishing touches to her hair and appearance.

Chapter Thirteen

Ivor Kettering's fondness for a pre-dinner cocktail was evident in his skill at preparing them. He combined the gin, vermouth, and ice with the ease and dexterity of a chemist preparing toxic solutions for various experiments, and he did so with a flair that was hardly suggested by his sombre demeanour. What had created and instilled in him this affection for what was nothing more than a common tradition, nobody, including Ivor himself, could say. He showed no signs of wishing to apologise for any childish pleasure he took from it, and, for their part, his guests, who had assembled in the library for the pleasure, never sought any such apology.

Everett Carr was standing alone by the French windows of the library, looking back out over the lawns that he had so enjoyed earlier that afternoon. His solitude was not by choice, but nor was it by any particular design. He was a stranger in the midst of the social assembly around him, which was engaged in its various conversations, and Carr's natural politeness prohibited him from intruding into those discussions. Instead, he sipped gently at his martini, dabbing his lips and moustache with a precisely folded handkerchief. Cocktails had never featured prominently in his habits and tastes, but he was by no means averse to them, and when he chose to have one, or one was offered to him, it always seemed to him to be a rare and exotic indulgence. The present example of its kind was undeniably excellent.

He turned away from the window and allowed his eyes to wander slowly over the assembled throng. There was as yet no sign of Rowena Kettering, and Carr assumed that she would still be preparing herself for her guests. He supposed that a woman of her temperament and nature would be unable to resist the making of an entrance, even if it meant not being there, as a simple hostess, to greet her guests. This task had been left to her husband who, Carr noted, had performed the social duty with ease. Perhaps he preferred to undertake the task alone, without the threat of any overshadowing from Rowena's tendency to melodramatic excess.

"You look as if you're in a world of your own, Mr Carr."

He must have been, he thought, since he had not been conscious of Josephine Kettering approaching him. Carr bowed gently in greeting. She was dressed in a red evening gown, whose colour was so deep that it made her pale skin seem so delicate that it might shatter at the slightest touch, and the platinum hair was made all the more exclusive by its contrast with the stark crimson of the gown. A string of pearls hung around her slender neck, providing an elegant accessory to the overall impression of beauty and grace, an impression damaged only slightly by the ostentatious use of a cigarette holder.

"I am a solitary man, my child," Carr said with a smile, "and such men are often alone with their thoughts."

"Mother's waiting to make one of her entrances, of course. How very tiresome it all is."

Carr thought a change of topic might be appropriate. "You stayed behind to greet Dr Jarratt earlier?"

She tossed her head towards the man concerned, who was watching her and Carr with close attention. "I was rescued by Lewis Davenport, I am happy to say, so I didn't have to suffer Dr Jarratt for longer than was necessary to say hello."

"Tell me," said Carr, softly, "do you still believe that one of the people in this room is likely to do something terrible?"

She looked at him, her eyes like flint. "You don't have to be delicate about it, Mr Carr. Do I think one of these people is planning to kill my mother? Yes, I do."

Carr sipped the martini. "Which one, would you say?"

"I don't know, that's partly what scares me."

"If you were to guess…" prompted Carr.

Josephine smoked intently for a moment. "It could be any one of them, Mr Carr. Daphne Clements could easily do it. She certainly has a motive in my father, and she's a nurse. Easy for her to slip poison into a cocktail or a bedside glass of water."

"Tell me, which of them here is Miss Clements?" Carr made a show of looking around the room.

"The one making eyes at Daddy, of course," said Josephine, with perhaps more venom in her voice than she might have intended.

Carr followed her gaze and found himself looking at a woman whom he might describe as handsome rather than beautiful. There was something feline about the features, suggested perhaps by the high cheekbones and the almond-shaped eyes, in which Carr could detect the clear impression of practical intelligence so necessary in her profession. The hair was sleek and dark, styled back from a broad and intellectual forehead, under which the eyebrows arched in a curve of interested inquisition. The dress was black, exuding a simple if funereal elegance, although it might have been more fashionable a few years earlier. Nevertheless, she wore it with dignity, although Carr had the idea that she would have been more at ease in sensible tweeds or her professional uniform than in socially sophisticated silk.

"She's not beautiful," said Josephine, "not like Mummy. I don't know what Daddy sees in her at all."

Perhaps not, but Everett Carr could see it plainly. Rowena's beauty was obvious, the beauty of a successful stage actress. Daphne Clements did not and could never possess it, but she had an attraction of her own in her earthly, more practical fashion. It was like being asked to admire two pieces of art, one which was so obviously a masterpiece that it required no comment or thought to appreciate it, and the other less obvious in its genius, requiring longer to gaze at it and to appreciate it. The genius was there, but it required effort to discern it.

"Everything has beauty, but not everyone sees it," murmured Carr.

If Josephine recognised the quotation, she did not say so. "I suppose you're right. But I wouldn't be surprised to learn that Daphne has her fair share of wickedness, too."

Carr looked at her. "Indeed?"

"Something I heard her saying earlier. I presume she was talking to Daddy since nobody else will speak to her here, but what she said gave me the real chills." Josephine lowered her voice so that Carr had to bend towards her to hear. "She was talking about morphine, Mr Carr, and just how much of it she has in her possession."

Carr's dark eyes had narrowed, and the brows were creased in concentration. "As a nurse, she might be expected to have such a drug, of course."

Josephine rolled her eyes dismissively. "Yes, obviously, but in view of everything else, doesn't it make you wonder? You said yourself that you thought my fears were well-founded."

Carr was nodding slowly. "I cannot deny it, my child."

"And on top of that, Daphne was talking about how much morphine she can get her hands on. You don't have to be a chemist, or even read too many detective stories, to know that morphine is deadly. And why would she need to be talking about how much she has of the stuff if she wasn't intending to use it?"

Carr held up a warning finger. "Do not leap to conclusions, my dear girl."

"But why else would she feel the need to discuss her supply of the drug? It's hardly an everyday type of conversation, is it?"

With that, at least, Carr was in agreement. "It is an interesting fact, my child. All we can do with it for now is remember it, docket it, and look out for something else which may bear upon it."

She looked at him, her grey eyes wide with horror, and her naturally pale skin now whitened further by something altogether less natural. "I'm so frightened, Mr Carr. Hearing Daphne talking like that has made everything seem so real."

Carr placed his hand on her arm. "We must be vigilant. Anything you hear or see which troubles you, tell me."

Gently, she placed her fingers on his. "I can't tell you how pleased I am that you're here."

Whatever he might have said in reply was to be left unspoken, as Carr saw Felix Kettering walking towards them.

"How's the martini, Mr Carr?" he asked.

"Excellent," replied Carr, smiling, "although I am no expert, I'm afraid."

Felix winked. "You can trust the old man to know his way around a cocktail shaker. Hello, Josie. Everything all right? Can we expect pistols at dawn between Davenport and Jarratt?"

It was said in such a sneering and condescending way, in a tone of voice that recalled schoolyard bullies, that Josephine wanted to feel angry about it and retort accordingly, but she found that the only feeling she could muster was a self-pitying mortification. She looked over to Carr, as if to offer some silent apology for her own embarrassment, and then she spat out a futile wish that Felix would mind his own business and leave her alone, before walking away to find an alternative conversation.

"A very emotional girl, my step-sister," said Felix with a smile. Carr, who had not approved of the remark, offered no direct reply. Felix took a mouthful of his cocktail with the lascivious glee of the glutton. "I hope Adele and I didn't frighten you away when we met earlier, Mr Carr. She was rather afraid we had done."

"Not at all, Mr Kettering."

"Felix, please." The smile broadened. "No need to stand on ceremony here. The house is an Eden far too filled with serpents for any such formal civility."

Carr smiled darkly but said no more. His eyes remained fixed on the portrait of Rowena as Lady Macbeth, which glared down at him from above the flames in the hearth. Within moments, however, his attention was broken, first by the sound of the library door opening, and then by the appearance of Rowena Kettering as she entered the room. She wore a resplendent and expensive dress of the deepest claret, and although the eyes were shaded by the dark spectacles, Carr was certain that they glittered with mischievous conceit.

"Am I the last to arrive?" she said. "How frustrating of me."

The words were flippant and perhaps should have been spoken with a theatrical arrogance that would have illustrated their frivolity. But, despite the smile on her lips, Rowena's eyes were heavy and Carr thought he could detect not only the redness of past tears but also a current glimmer of bitterness and spite in her expression. Whether anyone else had noticed it, he could not say, but the intended humour suggested by her greeting was not matched by the sudden shift in mood which had occurred when she entered the room. Given that Felix was standing so close to him, Carr first noticed this souring of the atmosphere in the young man's face. The eyes had hardened and the jaw had clenched, as if a sudden primeval fear had manifested itself before him. Carr looked swiftly across to Adele Mills and in her eyes, he saw reflected the same sudden anxiety but it was accompanied by a definite twist of pure hatred. Carr's instincts rose on their hackles, like a cat suddenly aware of some impending disturbance or danger.

Looking around the room, he saw similar expressions of dark emotions. He looked across to Josephine, who was standing now with Lewis Davenport, and he saw in the young man's eyes the unmistakable fire of loathing. Interestingly, Carr thought, Dr Edwin Jarratt had not glared at Rowena's entrance with any degree of repugnance or malice. Instead, and in some ways more devastatingly, he had turned away from her, as if she were some sort of Gorgon, whose presence was so horrific to him that he could not bring himself to look in her direction, not through any fear that she could turn Jarratt into stone, but rather that she could turn him into a killer.

It was a natural instinct to look across at Daphne Clements, not least because of Josephine's talk of morphine possession and intended murder. In the eyes of the others, Carr had detected hatred and loathing for the woman in the doorway, but in Daphne's eyes, he detected not only those adverse emotions but also a quality that was lacking in them. It was a sense of defiance. Something about the narrowed eyes beneath those arched eyebrows suggested some sort of resolve or purpose, and it was this glimmer of determination that, coupled with the obvious and common hatred of Rowena, caused Carr such disquiet.

Rowena had accepted a cocktail from a distant but dutiful Ivor, although no obvious hostility passed between them. He had glared at her, challenging her to speak to him, and she had responded in kind, as if looking at him or acknowledging him at all would be to infect herself with some disease. There had been words, Carr felt sure of that, and something in their relationship had shifted. And yet, Rowena was an actress, and no product of any marital disharmony would interfere with her public appearances, even if those were taking place in her own home. She was now making her way through the assembly of guests.

Tilly Royce followed in her wake, keeping a polite distance, and sipping disinterestedly at the cocktail which Ivor had passed to her. Her eyes were fixed on the back of Rowena's head, but her expression lacked the twist of contempt and malice that was so evident elsewhere. If anything, Tilly's face was entirely neutral, and Carr found himself wondering whether or not that canvas awaiting its paint was not the most disconcerting face of all.

He remained silent and watchful, his senses alert to any indication of which of the minds in the room, if any, was planning to kill.

Chapter Fourteen

Carr could hardly have hoped that the atmosphere of dread and malice that had been so evident in the library would have dissipated entirely by the time they reached the dining room, but he was pleased to find that it had abated slightly once the party had been seated. He supposed it must be the gradual splitting of the group into smaller sections, as the gentlemen escorted the women to the meal, and dinner conversation companions were selected and agreed upon. It did not relieve the impression of some malignant presence in the room, but it proved a distraction from it, and Carr was grateful even for this small mercy, not least because a bad atmosphere at dinner always affected his enjoyment of the food, which in this instance was excellent.

The conversation was polite but not stilted, although it was dominated, perhaps predictably, by Rowena. More than once during one of her tales of theatre life, Carr found himself straining to hear the more muted, but less conceited, discussion at the other end of the table between Ivor, Davenport, and Jarratt. He could not make out the topic properly, but it seemed to be a political discussion rather than one of any personal animosity between the three men. And animosity, thought Carr, could so easily be expected to permeate any of the discussions around the table. Beneath the apparently calm surface of the polite chatter, Carr was conscious of an undercurrent of tense unease, and he might have been forgiven for thinking that this barely concealed hostility could make itself known at any moment and with potentially disastrous consequences. And it came, with all its dreaded inevitability, towards the end of the meal.

It was Ivor Kettering who made the comment which began the episode. "But surely, there are matters about which there can be no debate about what is right and what is wrong. Murder, for example. We must surely all know that there cannot be a conflict of opinion there."

"Can we be that certain, sir?" asked Lewis Davenport.

Ivor was amused. "In what circumstances might murder be justified?"

"Suppose a man discovered the identity of the person who violated his wife or his child. If he murdered that individual, would you condemn him to the hangman's rope?"

Ivor's answer was immediate. "Of course. His tragedy doesn't justify his crime."

"Are you saying you wouldn't understand the man's actions?" asked Dr Jarratt, slowly drawing a circle on the tablecloth with his forefinger.

Again, Ivor's response was immediate. "It isn't a question of understanding his motives. Of course, I could understand it, and I might even empathise with him, but my point is that no amount of social empathy or moral justification gives you the right to take another person's life. If it did, we'd all be free to murder with impunity, not least because we'd all be able to justify that killing to ourselves."

Lewis held up a finger. "Ah, there your argument must fail, surely, sir. It isn't for my hypothetical man to say whether the murder he commits is justified or not."

"How can it not be?" asked Ivor. "Who decides what is justified or not, or when an abhorrent act is justified or not? How does one define it? Surely it is a subjective matter. We cannot expect a jury to decide whether a killer acted reasonably or not. What one juror considers reasonable, another may not. It would surely be impossible to resolve."

"But isn't that what juries do all the time?" replied Lewis. "Don't we ask any jury to determine whether someone intended to kill, or whether the killing occurred out of a particular set of circumstances? So, does it not follow that we must, by definition, be asking juries to determine whether a killing was justified or not?"

"Precisely," said Jarratt. "After all, there is such a thing as manslaughter.

Isn't that what we're talking about, the difference between manslaughter and murder?"

"I don't think it is," said Ivor. "Manslaughter is when someone kills without malice aforethought. Am I right on that, Mr Carr?"

Carr, somewhat embarrassed by this unavoidable inclusion into a debate he did not care for, nodded slowly. "That is correct."

Ivor seemed to think his point was proven. "There we are, then. This man Davenport has dreamt up would be acting with malice aforethought, no doubt about it. He is actively going to seek revenge for what his proposed victim did to the wife or child. If that isn't malice aforethought, what is?"

"And what about the public hangman?" It was Felix who asked the question. "He is sanctioned to kill, after all. Does it make any more sense for a killer to be killed himself? Isn't it all rather Biblical? An eye for an eye and so forth."

"You would prefer to turn the other cheek, would you, Felix?" asked his father. "Allow a murderer to continue to have the right to life which he took from another?"

Felix, as if unable or unwilling to answer the question, looked instead to Carr. "You must have a view on this, Mr Carr, being a former exponent of His Majesty's law once upon a time."

It was not designed to be a malicious goading, or even a mischievous one, but Carr still had no inclination to engage too far with it. "I swore to uphold the law, Mr Kettering, not to make it."

Ivor gave a growl of agreement. "Besides, the law is what it is, and until it is changed, if at all, it is what we must accept. Besides, Felix, your argument is too facile. When a man kills his wife, he has committed a crime. When a hangman pulls that lever, he is performing a duty. The two deaths are not synonymous, nor are the two motives behind them, so a comparison is worthless."

Carr looked around the table, wondering whether anyone else besides himself had noticed the ease with which Ivor had selected the hypothetical murderer and victim to make his point. Had it been purely accidental, or had the choice been one which occurred to him because the scenario had been so closely on his mind?

Lewis Davenport was speaking. "I tend to agree with your father on that particular point, Felix, but that isn't to say that the original point of discussion has any merit."

Josephine looked across at him but addressed her comment to the table as a whole. "Whatever merit it may or may not have, might we change the subject, please? It's horrible."

Jarratt sipped some wine. "Yes, perhaps we should move on."

Despite herself, Josephine smiled across at him, albeit with a hesitant reluctance. But his support of her wishes could hardly have gone unnoticed. When she happened to catch Lewis Davenport's gaze, she saw the fierce envy and the flush of outraged contempt in his expression. She looked away, unsure what to say or how to respond. Everett Carr, sitting silently, apparently noticing nothing, noticed everything.

And then, without warning, there came Rowena's voice, a sultry but now seemingly less than sober drawl of amused spite. "Really, Dr Jarratt, I would have thought that you would have particularly strong views on the matter."

The comment, so overt that it was both shocking and unexpected, produced a sudden and bleak silence in the room. Eyes flickered between Rowena and Jarratt, the former smiling and the latter glaring at the empty plate before him, the tendons in his neck like cords of rope and the skin around the back of his ears and on his cheeks aflame with indignation.

"I don't know what you mean, Mrs Kettering," he said, seemingly without caring whether anyone detected the lie.

"Well, you're a doctor," said Rowena. "You must surely see your fair share of life and death. I just assumed that you would have a clear idea of when it might be acceptable to commit murder."

Jarratt's hands had clenched into fists. "I thought we were changing the subject."

Felix raised his glass in a toast. "Quite so. Let's forget the whole thing and talk about something else."

Rowena shrugged. "I thought Dr Jarratt's views on the subject would be quite straightforward, in the circumstances."

Ivor cleared his throat. "I think that's enough, Rowena. Whatever it is you're implying no doubt has little merit and, in any event, this would hardly be the place to discuss it."

Rowena scoffed. "I was only following your own topic of conversation, Ivor, so I shouldn't think you can afford to be so meritorious."

Ivor had got to his feet. "Rowena, I am serious. This stops now. I won't have my guests embarrassed in this fashion. If you can't act sensibly and with decency, perhaps you ought to leave us."

Far from being dissuaded by the command, Rowena laughed at it. "Why don't you be honest, Ivor? It isn't simply that you want me out of the room, is it? You want me gone altogether."

"What do you mean by that?"

"Isn't it obvious?" Rowena looked across to Carr. "Do you suppose it was a sheer coincidence, Mr Carr, that my husband's hypothetical murderer was a man who had killed his wife? Don't you bet on it. A little glimpse into Ivor's private world, that's what it was."

Carr was intrigued by this common train of thought between Rowena's interpretation of Ivor's comments and his own. If Ivor's example of a husband killing his wife had struck the two of them, how many more people had picked up on the point? Slowly, and not a little uneasy in his position, Carr looked across at Ivor. The man's face, usually gaunt and pale, was flushed with mortification, and his eyes were like bullets behind the lenses of his spectacles. Some people, like Carr, were staring at him, waiting for a response; others, too embarrassed to look into his face, concentrated on their plates, glasses, or laps.

Ivor spoke, his voice retrained. "You're being ridiculous, Rowena, as usual."

"Not to say melodramatic," said Felix. "Again, as usual."

Rowena glared at him. "Keep out of it, Felix. You have enough troubles of your own, wouldn't you say?"

Flames of malice exploded across Felix's cheeks. Carr watched as Adele laid a hand on his leg, a silent effort to calm him, to convince him that rising to Rowena's bait would be a mistake. A sensible gesture, Carr thought, but he could not mistake the obvious malevolence in Adele's own eyes, which were fixed on Rowena now with what seemed like murderous intent.

Ivor was still on his feet. "I don't know what's got into you, Rowena, but you're embarrassing yourself and our guests. Now, either this stops, or you can go. The choice is yours."

"Why do you suppose you can order me out of my own dining room, Ivor? This is my house as much as yours, darling. I have no intention of leaving." Rowena held his gaze with defiance, before breaking it and looking across the table to Daphne Clements. "I'm not going to allow you to spend any time alone with that bloody woman, Ivor, not as long as I am around to stop you."

Daphne, who had been one of the guests who had striven to keep her eyes averted from the unpleasant confrontation, felt a sudden wave of nausea wash over her as she became aware that people were staring at her. They seemed to expect some sort of response, as if silence would condemn her. She did not look at Rowena, but her voice, when it came, betrayed no indication of fear or intimidation.

"How can you be so spiteful, so damned selfish?" she asked.

Rowena cackled with mocking delight. "Well, found a voice, have you? How very entertaining. Let me tell you something, Daphne. My looks may be failing me, and I may lack your youthful allure, but one thing I will always have over you is experience. I've seen things, done things, and learned from them, my girl, and I've done it more times than you. So, you'll never get one over on me."

"I don't want to get one over on you, Rowena," replied Daphne, as calmly as she could manage. "I just want to be happy, with the man I love."

Another cackle, which might have shattered the wine glasses. "That's rather hard luck, isn't it, dear? Because the man in question just happens to be mine and I won't give him up."

"He doesn't want you," said Daphne, her voice breaking.

Rowena looked at Ivor. "Yes, he does. Deep down, he does. I know it, and sooner or later, he'll remember it."

Daphne looked at Ivor. "He despises you, Rowena. He loves me."

There was no cackle this time, only a contemptuous snigger. "You're an infatuation, Daphne. You aren't the first, and you certainly won't be the last. You're a minor distraction from his life with me, nothing more."

Daphne's control was dwindling. She looked again at Ivor, tears brimming in her eyes, begging for him to retaliate, to defend their love against Rowena's accusations of transient romance, and to give some sign of reassurance that he did not feel the way this dreadful woman was claiming. But Ivor's eyes were fixed on Rowena, as if she were all that existed in the world. Daphne saw no love in his glare, only hatred, and she was curiously grateful for it, but it offered no comfort to her. Suddenly, it wasn't enough that he despised his wife. What Daphne needed from him, more than anything, was solidarity with her, and Ivor's inability or, worse, his refusal to look at her was too intolerable to forgive.

Rowena, as if aware of Daphne's private emotional instabilities, smiled cruelly. "You're a passing phase, Daphne, and you may as well learn it now as later."

Daphne's restraint collapsed. With an outburst of anger so unexpected that it seemed more intense than she might have imagined, she slammed both hands down on the table and got to her feet. She stared across at Rowena, her face illuminated from below by the candles which ran down the centre of the table, which gave her expression an ethereal, almost supernatural quality, which, in turn, heightened the look of uncontrolled venom on her face.

"You're wrong, Rowena," she shouted, her voice quivering with a blend of emotions, in which fury and loathing fought for supremacy. "Ivor loves me, and I love him. And that's what you can't stand, isn't it? That's why you're acting like this."

"Like what, dear?" The tone was insulting.

"A jealous, nasty, wicked old bitch." The tears had started to fall now, but there was no sadness in Daphne's eyes, only raw, unfiltered hatred.

The words must have stung Rowena more than she either expected or realised, for her features hardened into a cold mask of spite. "Be careful, Daphne, your true colours are beginning to show."

"You've never tried to hide yours, have you?"

"You stupid fool," spat Rowena. "Do you think your histrionics are going to do you any good at all?"

Daphne seemed not to have heard. "Ivor loves me, and I love him. That's just something you will have to get used to."

"Repeating it over and over doesn't make it true, dear," goaded Rowena.

Daphne shook her head, as if refusing to hear the torments. "Ivor and I will be together, Rowena, and we will be happy. And you can do nothing about it. We will be married, and you'll be the one left with nothing."

Rowena shook her head slowly. "Over my dead body, dear."

"If need be," said Daphne, the tears still falling, but the voice suddenly, dangerously calm. She glanced over to Ivor, who remained standing, motionless, but with the eyes, fixed on Rowena, burning with loathing. If Daphne expected him to react to her, she was to be disappointed. At last, feeling as ridiculous as she was enraged, Daphne walked out of the room, slamming the door violently behind her.

The silence that followed was brief and uncomfortable. It was Ivor who broke it. "Congratulations, Rowena. If you intended to ruin the evening and embarrass everybody here, you've done a remarkable job."

In a sudden movement, followed by a violent shattering noise, Rowena threw her glass onto the floor. "You sanctimonious hypocrite, Ivor. The whole scene only occurred because of your feelings for the girl and your insistence on inviting her here."

Felix laughed. "I hardly think you can blame Father for what we've all just witnessed."

"Why don't you stay out of it, Felix?" hissed Rowena

Ivor slammed his fist down hard against the table. "For God's sake, Rowena! Haven't you done enough? Won't you be satisfied until everyone around this table despises you?"

"They do already," muttered Adele Mills.

Josephine glared at her. "How dare you say such a thing?"

Felix was looking at Rowena. "Why shouldn't she? It's true, and we all know it."

Jarratt leaned forward. "It doesn't need saying, then, does it?"

Before there could be any further remonstration or argument, Rowena screamed violently and rose to her feet. Her face was pale, ashen with humiliation and outrage, and her eyes were wild with fury. Staring up at her, his lips parted in a bewildering mixture of fascination and fear, Everett Carr felt as if he were looking at the face of terrified madness. Rowena seemed about to speak, her features contorted in a malignant fury and her concentration reserved solely for Ivor, but no words came. Instead, in the flickering of a second after getting to her feet, Rowena fell to the ground. Her knees buckled and her arms flailed to find some support, but all she found was the tablecloth, bringing down with her a clattering of crockery and cutlery as she dropped to the floor, limbs splayed, as if she had been a puppet whose strings had been cut.

Carr got to his feet, but he was too slow. Tilly Royce had acted with more speed than he could manage. She was on her feet at once, allowing her chair to tumble to the floor, and she knelt by Rowena's body, cradling her head in those practical and dextrous hands, and calling for a glass of water. It was Carr who obliged.

Ivor had moved away from the table. "For God's sake, look at yourself. You're drunk. Tilly, get her out of here and into her bed. Let her sleep it off."

Tilly, with some assistance from Carr, hauled Rowena to her feet. She placed an arm around the actress' waist and held her tightly to her side. Together, they moved ungainly to the door, as if trapped in some terrible parody of a dance, whose only accompanying music was the incoherent moans from Rowena's mouth. Ivor moved to the door and pulled it open, but Tilly offered no word of thanks, nor did he expect or demand one. Instead, she looked back over her shoulder at the ruins of the dinner party.

"You should all be ashamed of yourselves," she said.

Carr found it impossible to disagree with the condemnation. If any of the others shared his dismay, they did not express it. There were some muted words of polite excuses for Rowena's behaviour from Ivor Kettering, and similarly subdued comments of regret about the unpleasantness of the evening, but nothing approaching an apology came from anybody's lips. Slowly, the assembled throng began to dissipate, leaving the room without words. In the silence that followed, only Everett Carr remained, standing where Rowena had fallen, his eyes seemingly unable to avert themselves from the shards of broken glass lying at his feet, and the memory of his hostess lying supine on the floor still lingering in the back of his mind.

Chapter Fifteen

leep was impossible, despite his best efforts, so Carr now sat in silence, looking out of the bedroom window across the back lawns of Marsden Grange. Even in the darkest hours of the night, illuminated by nothing but the moon, the majesty of the trees and the fields beyond the boundaries of the property was unmistakable. Although shrouded in the blues and blacks of the night, the impression of extensive natural beauty was so profound as to be almost tangible. In other circumstances, Carr might have ruminated happily on the wonders of the natural world, of their splendour both in daylight and under cover of darkness, but his mind was too distracted to permit any such philosophical contemplation.

The unpleasantness at dinner had been good neither for digestion nor for rest, and Carr was feeling the unhappy effects of the lack of the proper function of both. The bed had promised to be both inviting and comfortable, but when he had climbed into it, his mind had refused to settle and, no matter how hard he tried, comfort persisted in eluding him. And so, after consulting his watch for the fifth time in less than half an hour, its chain and fob scraping across the wood of the small bedside cabinet and producing a sound that seemed in the stillness of the night to be louder than thunder, he had given up the attempt and all hope of sleep. There was a small wooden chair set against a writing table in one corner of the room, and he had taken it and placed it at the window of the room, easing himself down onto it, and he had remained there since a little after midnight. He did not check his watch for a sixth time, but he estimated that he had been sitting there for a little over an hour.

He had not stayed long in the dining room after everyone else had departed. It might only have been a few moments, but when he had limped slowly away from the scene of the bitter altercations, there had been no sign of any of the other guests. It was of no importance to Carr, and he had no particular wish to see any of them at that moment, but he wondered how many of them had gone to bed and how many were still up, dissecting the evening and picking over the bones of Rowena's outburst.

Once upstairs, he had seen Tilly Royce coming out of a bedroom at the far end of the corridor. He had called gently to her and walked towards her. If she had hoped she might avoid an audience with him, Tilly was to be disappointed.

"Forgive me, Miss Royce," Carr had said, "but have you just come from the room of Mrs Kettering?"

"Yes."

"I wondered if I might have a very brief word with her."

Tilly had shaken her head. "She's very tired."

"I will only be a moment," he had insisted.

"She doesn't want any visitors."

Carr had smiled. "Perhaps if you came with me and we left the door ajar?"

"I must insist, Mr Carr, I'm sorry."

And he had relented. After all, he knew when a battle was lost, and he doubted anything would have been achieved by pressing the point. Tilly Royce was hardly a woman who would succumb easily to any insistence or charm from him.

Now, he rose to his feet and limped slowly across the room to the bed. Despite his earlier reluctance, he did check his watch once again and saw that his previous estimate had been accurate. The time was now a little after one in the morning, but sleep seemed further away than ever. Experience had taught him that reading often helped during these bouts of insomnia, and he decided that a book from Ivor Kettering's library might be of some benefit, and he set off to obtain one.

He was halfway down the stairs when he heard the scream.

For a moment, he failed to register the noise as what it was. It seemed alien to him, a sound that had no context or meaning for him, like the plaintive call of some unknown species of bird drifting across the night breeze over moorland fields. But almost immediately, this lack of understanding gave way to very real comprehension, and with it came the natural consequence of fear and alarm.

He could see the light emanating through the open door of the library. It was only one of the table lamps, judging by the relatively meagre beam which sliced its way through the gloom of the hallway, but it was sufficient to show Carr where to go. He looked back over his shoulder but saw nobody following him, and he heard no noises which would suggest any waking from slumber upstairs. There was only him, Everett Carr, alone to face whatever was lurking in the library. At that moment, as if the sudden realisation of his own solitude had been a silent call for assistance, he became aware of another sound. Somehow, it did not belong, an incongruous noise, a dull but persistent and rhythmic banging. The front door, thought Carr, his brows furrowing in confusion. Someone was hammering at the front door.

As he reached the bottom of the stairs, he became aware of a shaft of light piercing the gloom of the hallway, coming from a room to the left, and Carr turned to face it. Ivor Kettering stepped out of his study into the hall. Behind him, the door to his study was open, and the dim glare of a desk lamp glowed from within.

"What's this damned racket?" he barked.

"Did you hear a scream just now?" asked Carr.

Ivor seemed uncertain. "I thought I heard something, but it seemed so unlikely that I assumed I had imagined it."

The banging on the door persisted. Carr pointed to it. "You must have a key."

"All the main keys are locked away at midnight by the butler, Bates, except for a spare set I keep in my study desk." He marched to the front door and banged against it with his fist. The external hammering ceased. "Who is out there?"

"Jarratt," came the muffled reply.

Carr frowned, but he did not ask the obvious question. "Fetch your keys, Mr Kettering."

Ivor obeyed, reappearing within seconds and fumbling with his personal set of keys. "What the devil is Jarratt doing out at this time of night anyway, the damned fool?"

He thrust the key into the lock and pulled open the heavy oak door. Edwin Jarratt entered, dressed still in his dinner suit, save that he had discarded the jacket and bow tie, and removed his collar. The evening rain had begun to soak his shirt to his chest, and his hair was flecked with droplets of the inclement weather.

"Hello," he said cheerily, "a welcome party."

"What in blazes have you been up to?" roared Ivor.

Carr did not wait to hear the reply. Instead, he moved back to the doorway of the library and looked inside. At once, he saw the horror of it all, and in that moment, he seemed unable to see anything else. Similarly, the extraneous noises of the movements and voices behind him seemed to vanish, as if all his senses were entranced by the sudden presence of death.

And death it was.

It was sitting in one of the armchairs in the library, the one set to the left of the room. From around the wing of the chair, he saw the familiar blank stare of the dead, the eyes rolled back towards the corner of the lids. They were no longer human eyes. Now, they looked as if they were made from glass and painted that deep chocolate brown colour, like those of a doll. The mouth was open, and the tongue protruded slightly from behind the two rows of teeth from which the once proud lips were drawn back. One arm hung loosely over the arm of the chair in which the body was slumped, the exposed flesh seeming inhumanly pale even in the dim light afforded by the desk lamp on the table by the side of the chair. The other arm lay uselessly across the stomach, the fingers curled slightly into a half-formed fist. The legs were stretched out, the feet splayed at an ungainly angle, a posture that might have looked comical if the circumstances were not so horrific. A silk nightgown was visible under a matching housecoat, and Carr had the foolish idea that such garments could hardly offer any practical protection against the cold night air. Similarly, the low-heeled satin slippers hardly seemed sensible or appropriate, and they looked hopelessly ridiculous, hanging off the cold, motionless feet. Carr felt an inappropriate but genuine sadness that in death, Rowena Kettering lacked the confident elegance that she had demonstrated and carried so easily in life.

Standing opposite the chair in which the body was sprawled was Daphne Clements. She seemed unaware of Carr's presence, just as she seemed to be oblivious to her surroundings. Her eyes were fixed on Rowena's lifeless figure, and her expression suggested that this mass of silk and flesh was all Daphne could see, as if her entire world now consisted only of that dead thing and its staring eyes of glass. In one hand, she held a small bottle, which seemed to be empty, but which Carr could identify easily as a phial of some poison or other. In the other hand, he saw a hypodermic needle, her fingers still inserted through the metal rings on the barrel and her thumb still resting on the piston. Carr stared for a long moment at the tip of the needle and then, almost involuntarily, his eyes drifted to the exposed flesh of the arm which hung loosely over the chair. He must have seen it immediately, but only now was Carr aware of the little bubble of red that protruded from the joint of the arm, so tiny and insignificant that it was almost invisible, the only physical evidence of the use of the needle in Daphne's hand. What had been injected into Rowena Kettering was impossible to know for the moment, and it hardly seemed to matter. What was of consequence was the fact of unnatural death and the very real possibility of murder.

Carr said her name softly, but Daphne seemed not to have heard him. He took a cautious step forward, but the movement failed to distract her, and she remained frozen, staring at the body, her eyes lingering over it, as if in admiration of it. But it was not admiration that Carr saw in Daphne's eyes. No more was it fear, shock, horror, or any other similar emotion that he might have expected to see. And, perhaps more surprisingly, he could not say that he saw any clear evidence of malicious triumph or satisfaction in those eyes either. If anything, Daphne's glare struck him as being as lifeless as Rowena's, as if in the end, the two women who had hated each other so much in life were oddly reconciled in death.

Such fanciful ideas were of little value to him and, in any case, they were driven from his mind by the more practical and grounded clamour of voices in the hallway. Carr glanced at Daphne, paralysed for a moment by sudden indecision and confusion, until, with a snarl of frustration, he forced himself to move.

He stepped back into the hallway and became aware of movement on the stairs and the flicker of candlelight. He saw Lewis Davenport and Felix Kettering, their faces illuminated by the flames of the candles. Behind these two commanders of this nocturnal investigative group, Carr could see Josephine Kettering, peering between the shoulders of Lewis and Felix, her face alive with fearful curiosity. Behind her stood Adele Mills and Tilly Royce, each staring down into the confusion of the hallway with similar expressions of alarmed fascination, which was exaggerated by the flickering flames of the candles.

Carr gave them no more than a passing glance. His attention was fixed on Ivor. "How long have you been in your study?"

"Half an hour or so. I went up to bed after our disastrous dinner but could not sleep, so I came down here to do some work."

"Did you see anyone in the hallway during that time?"

A shake of the head. "No."

Carr simply nodded. "Mr Kettering, might I ask you to be so kind as to have your cook and parlour maid roused from their sleep?"

Ivor glared at him. "What on earth for?"

Felix had now stepped off the stairs and approached his father and Carr. When he spoke, his voice was as serious as it was curious. "What's happened, Mr Carr?"

Lewis was by Felix's side. "Yes, what's going on?"

And then, before anyone could speak further, there was a scream from the stairs. Carr turned round swiftly, in time to see Josephine Kettering collapse against the banister. Swiftly, Adele bent forward to catch her, and she eased both of them down to sit on the stairs. Josephine fell back against Adele, as if unable to sit upright, and her eyes flickered wildly, fighting the impulse to faint completely. Jarratt made a move to run towards her, but Ivor held out an instinctive hand and pointed towards the library door. Simultaneously, as if they were some sort of macabre choir, there was a collective intake of breath, a hiss of shock and horror.

Daphne Clements stood in the doorway to the library, the hypodermic needle still in her hand, and the blank, impassive expression still etched onto her features. Slowly, as if she had only now learned the power of speech, she spoke. The words came thickly, as if her tongue were too large for her mouth.

"She's dead, Ivor." The dull, emotionless tone of her voice matched the lack of empathy or sentiment in her eyes. "She's dead, and we're free of her at last."

Chapter Sixteen

The collective reaction of the guests at Marsden Grange was one of dreadful silence. For a long moment, they all remained quiet and still, looking ridiculously like actors in a melodrama, waiting expectantly for the curtain to fall. But this was not the end of an act, only a terrible moment in time that would change each of their lives forever.

Daphne was staring ahead, but her eyes remained glazed. It appeared that she was looking at Ivor, who stared back at her as if she were some foul demon rising from an abyss.

"My God," he whispered. "My God…"

Felix spoke in a violent growl of malice. "She's killed her. She's murdered Rowena."

Then, a scream, from Tilly Royce, her hands clasped now to her cheeks, and her eyes widened with horror. "It isn't true!"

"Of course it's true," said Felix. "She's as good as admitted it. We must telephone for the police."

This onslaught of voices and opinions was both unhelpful and dangerous. Carr took a step forward and turned his back on Daphne, as if presenting himself as a barrier of protection from their accusations, and he banged his cane against the hallway floor. The noise, unexpected and jarring, was a shrill but authoritative demand for silence.

"Perhaps I might have your attention," he said into the resulting quiet. "Yes, we must call the police. For now, it is as well to be as far from this room as possible. Might I suggest people move to the drawing room?" He looked at Ivor. "If you would summon your cook and parlour maid, as I asked earlier, we can leave Miss Clements in their care for now. She must not be in contact with any of us until the police have interviewed her."

Lewis stepped towards him. "Under what authority do you issue these orders, Mr Carr?"

Carr bowed and smiled. "Under no authority, Mr Davenport, other than common sense and decency. I am asking nothing which the police themselves will not ask or accept."

Ivor gave a word of approval. "I agree with Mr Carr. Everyone, please, move to the drawing room and I shall arrange for some coffee."

"You don't expect us to stay in there for the rest of the night, surely," protested Jarratt.

It was Carr who replied. "For the moment only, doctor, if you would be so kind."

There was a general reluctance, but it was expressed only in apathetic murmurs. Ivor watched them move into the drawing room, asking Adele and Felix to care for Josephine until he could join them. Once the drawing room door had closed, he turned back to Carr. "Is it really necessary to isolate Daphne, as you suggest?"

"I am afraid so, sir."

Ivor seemed desperate to argue the point, but something about the sudden seriousness in Carr's dark eyes demanded compliance rather than debate. For the first time, Ivor became aware of the imposing command that could be summoned from beneath Carr's usually gentle and polite exterior. "Very well. I shall summon the staff at once."

Carr bowed in gratitude and watched him leave. Left alone with Daphne Clements, he took a moment to stare into her eyes. He saw now that the emotionless trance that had seemed to grip her was either passing off or had been an illusion all along. Looking back at him, he could see in the girl's eyes a mixture of emotions. Shock was evident, and to be expected, but behind it, lurking like a deadly fish under the surface of the ocean, he saw fear. It was a fear he had seen before, and he recognised it only too well, like the face of an old adversary coming back out of the past. He had seen it in the eyes of those people to whom he had handed the death sentence. It was the wide glare of panic, entreaty, and disbelief at the realisation that their life could only come to an end now with a hangman's noose. Carr had done his duty in the past, and execution was the most serious effect of that duty, but his acceptance of the fact was not evidence of his immunity to it. Putting on the notorious black cap before sentencing a prisoner to death was never something he had done lightly, and nor had it ever been merely a perfunctory task, as he knew it had for some of his contemporaries. To Carr, the symbolism of that small square of black fabric had never diminished. Instead, it had retained its power and significance with fierce tenacity, and it continued to do so, even when he was no longer required to wear it. It would be an overstatement to say that he remembered the face of every person he had condemned to death, but it was no such exaggeration to say that he recalled the collective impact of those faces in the wake of their own mortality. And now, in that darkened hallway of a Norfolk country house, he thought he saw it reflected in the eyes of Daphne Clements.

From the pocket of his dressing gown, Carr took a handkerchief. Slowly, as if he were dealing with a frightened child, he took first the needle and then the small medical bottle from Daphne's hands. She offered no resistance, although he whispered gentle words of encouragement to assist in any event, and within seconds the two objects were in his care, wrapped in the protective shroud of his handkerchief. Gently, he placed the package of evidence into the pocket of his dressing gown. Any fingerprints would be preserved as well as could be expected. Throughout the procedure, Daphne's eyes remained fixed on him.

"She's dead," she repeated. "It's all over now."

Carr smiled gently, the extravagant moustache prickling with kindly assurance. "Be brave, my child. Everything will be all right."

She looked into his eyes but gave no response to his pledge. He wondered whether she believed it. Perhaps he wondered whether she had even heard it. No more was said until Ivor Kettering arrived with the female members of staff. On Carr's orders, they took Daphne upstairs to her room, both promising not to leave her alone. Ivor made a small effort, almost involuntarily, to follow, but Carr blocked the way with his cane.

"The police, Mr Kettering," he encouraged.

Ivor looked over Carr's shoulder to the open door of the library. In the gloom of the hallway and the dim lighting in the library, he had the overwhelming and nauseating impression that the sickeningly pale arm was suspended in the air as if supported by some macabre and spectral force. Suddenly, Ivor had an unprecedented need to see Rowena, no matter that she was dead and no matter how terrible the sight might be.

"I have to see her," he said, the voice thick with dread.

Carr shook his head. "I would strongly caution against it."

Ivor's eyes raged, but his voice came out in a hoarse but furious whisper. "Damn it, Carr, she's my wife."

The hypocrisy of the statement seemed not to have occurred to him, and Carr saw no reason to emphasise it. "Nevertheless, I advise you to join the others. The room must be left as undisturbed as possible. The police will not only expect it, but they will demand it."

Ivor removed his spectacles and rubbed the palm of one hand vigorously over his face. "This is madness. No, it is beyond madness. I can't believe any of it is happening."

"Can you not, Mr Kettering?"

There was something in the cadence of Carr's voice that unsettled Ivor. "Are you suggesting I know something about this?"

Carr shook his head and made a calming gesture with his hand. "I am suggesting nothing, Mr Kettering, other than that the police are called without any further delay."

Ivor held his gaze defiantly. "I don't know anything about what has happened, I assure you." He waited for some response from Carr, his eyes no longer confrontational but expectant, almost as if he needed some reply or assurance from the little man beside him, but none came. Ivor, defeated, merely sighed. "Given my position in the government, Mr Carr, I wonder if it would be as well to telephone Scotland Yard."

Carr inclined his head. "By all means, sir, but notify the local station as well. We need a police presence here as soon as possible, and Scotland Yard will not be able to get here until morning. Tomorrow, if you insist on involving them, be sure to ask for Inspector John Mason. It might be of some assistance if you tell him I am here."

"Indeed?"

Again, Ivor seemed hopeful of some further reply, by way of explanation, but Carr did not oblige. Instead, his attention remained fixed on the doorway to the library, and his mind returned to the horror of what lay beyond it.

Chapter Seventeen

There was nothing about the body which struck Carr on his second examination of it that had not occurred to him at first sight. He looked again at the slumped figure, the splayed legs, and the glazed eyes curled back in their sockets, staring intently but sightlessly at the corner of the room. He saw again the tiny red circle against the pale flesh of the arm, the exposed tongue, and the lips pulled back from the teeth. He took in again the delicate silk of the nightgown, housecoat, and heeled slippers, whose combined elegance in life now seemed only to glorify the fact of death. None of it was new to him, and nothing about it stirred any instincts that had not been awoken on his first discovery of the tragedy. Gently, he rested the back of his hand on one of the cheeks, closing his eyes against the proximity of the face of death, and he was not surprised to find it was still warm to the touch. It was an incongruous sensation, feeling the warmth so obviously associated with life on the skin of something so obviously dead, as if the body were trying to convince him that it was still alive, that the appearance of death was nothing but an illusion. The corpse seemed to Carr to be striving to be thought of as a human being and not a collection of dead tissue, muscle, and bone. But the face, with the bared teeth and the staring eyes, was too cruel a reminder of the reality. The body might be warm, but the face spoke only of the coldness of death, and it was not the bracing cold of the sea, nor the refreshing cold of a cooling drink on a humid day, but the unforgiving chill of the grave.

"I'm sorry," he heard himself say, in a voice as gentle and morose as the touch of his skin against hers.

And sorry for what, he thought. For her death or his failure to prevent it? For a moment, he stood in respectful deference, one hand behind his back, the other curled around the handle of his cane, and his head slumped onto his breast. It was the accepted stance of dignified reverence, except that the dark, intense eyes were not lowered in mournful veneration. Instead, from under the heavy brows, they stared with a definite purpose into that face of death.

Turning away, he seemed to be aware for the first time of cold and the swirling hisses of a night wind. With it came a tapping noise, incessant and irritating, a sound which seemed paradoxically to be both familiar and alien to him, one which he knew he recognised but which he was momentarily unable to identify. This audible riddle was solved by the swelling of the emerald curtains that covered the French windows of the room. Frowning, Carr limped across the room and pulled wide the curtains with his cane. One of the windows was open, the key still in the lock, and the tapping noise being caused by the wind catching the door and knocking it against the frame. A mystery solved, perhaps, but one which gave rise to a second, perhaps more dangerous one, whose answer might be obvious but whose implications were no less sinister for it. Carr thought about closing the door of the windows. The temperature of the room might be critical, but it was not for him to make any such decision. It would be a matter for the local police once they had arrived. They could not, he thought, be very far away.

It was when he turned away from the windows, pulling his dressing gown around himself as protection from the intruding wind, that he saw it. The portrait of Rowena as Lady Macbeth, whose majesty and prominence had so impressed him earlier, was now in ruins. Carr walked slowly across the room, taking in as much detail of the vandalism as he could in the dim light. Someone had used a sharp blade, a knife, or a razor to slice at the canvas, creating a central and prominent saltire of wickedness that lacerated the image of the dead woman from corner to corner. It seemed to Carr that these two slashes would have been more than sufficient to make the point, but the culprit had seemed to disagree, and smaller, but no less violent, cuts had been made across the painting. There did not seem to be any pattern to these lesser acts of sabotage, and they gave the altogether more disturbing impression that they had been inflicted not with precision but with uncontrolled rage.

He was standing at the mantelpiece now, the damaged portrait looming above him in its newly tattered, ruined shame. He realised at once that the perpetrator must have climbed onto the mantelpiece or, perhaps more likely, used one of the chairs to provide additional height. The deduction was facile but important, since it demonstrated that almost any of the guests at the Grange could have been responsible. With the aid of a chair, any one of them could have been able to reach up to slash the painting, even if they had been compelled to stand on the tips of their toes on a chair. If the mantelpiece had been scaled, the person responsible must have been athletic. Carr leaned forward and examined the mantelpiece. It would have been possible, if precarious, for an acrobat or a sailor to have mounted it, but Carr doubted the likelihood of it, and there were no visible marks on the marble to suggest any such climb had been attempted. No, he thought, a chair was more likely to have been used, and that meant that everybody must be under suspicion of vandalising the painting. Just as they must all be under suspicion of murder.

Carr walked back to the body, giving it one final look, his eyes lingering over the small puncture mark in the middle of the arm. An image of Daphne holding the hypodermic needle and medical phial came into his mind once more, swiftly followed by another recollection, of Josephine's conversation with him over cocktails before dinner. He remembered the essence of her talk rather than the actual words, but he knew without doubt that she had said she had overheard Daphne talking about possessing morphine and how much of it she could lay her hands on. Josephine had assumed, perhaps not unreasonably, that Daphne had been talking to Ivor Kettering, but in the moment, it hardly seemed to matter. What seemed to Carr to be of more immediate importance was the fact that Daphne had been discussing morphine at all. Taken in conjunction with the needle mark in Rowena's arm, the hypodermic needle, and the phial, it now seemed to Carr to be an inescapable conclusion that Rowena Kettering had been killed by morphine poisoning. It would need a medical examination to confirm it, but Carr felt sure that he was right, and if a post-mortem proved him wrong, he would be suitably astonished.

He walked out of the library slowly, crossed the hall, and opened the door of the drawing room. At the sound of his entrance, the conversation, already muted and hesitant, stopped completely, and a series of wide and inquisitive eyes, set in suitably expectant faces, turned towards him. Carr looked at nobody in particular, fearing that doing so would make him feel compelled to say more than he intended. Instead, he simply asked for Dr Edwin Jarratt.

"Would you come with me for a moment, please?" he asked.

Jarratt politely edged his way through the others and followed Carr out of the room, closing the drawing room door behind him. The two men went back to the library, Carr stepping aside to allow Jarratt to enter. The doctor paused.

"I thought we were trying to keep out of there," he said.

"It is best to avoid as much unnecessary traffic as possible, certainly." Carr smiled. "You, at the moment, doctor, are not unnecessary."

"How kind of you to say so," Jarratt replied, without humour. "May I ask why?"

"I would welcome your thoughts on the time and cause of death."

"I'm a gynaecologist, Mr Carr, not a pathologist."

"But you are an intelligent man of medicine, nevertheless."

Jarratt was not swayed by the flattery. "Isn't what you're asking a matter for the police?"

Carr nodded. "And is it not our duty to do what we can to help the police?"

Jarratt smiled, not without appreciation. "What a mysterious man you are, Mr Carr. Very well, I suppose you know what you're doing."

Jarratt walked slowly into the room. As he did so, his eyes were caught by the disfigured painting above the fireplace. "Good Lord."

Carr nodded. "One of several mysteries, doctor, but not the most pressing just now."

Jarratt accepted the point without further argument. He turned his attention away from the slashed canvas and looked down at Rowena's body. He was not intimidated by death, and nor did Carr expect him to be, but he approached the body with caution, as if murder demanded a heightened degree of trepidation not required for any natural fatality. He looked at the face with uncertainty, as if he expected those staring eyes to follow him as he moved around the chair, and he kept his distance so that he did not have to engage with the indignity of stepping over the outstretched legs. There was something almost theatrical about the care with which Jarratt moved, a sense of unreality that troubled Carr, if only because he could discern no probable cause for it. Jarratt, now to the side of Rowena's body, leaned into it. He touched the skin briefly and with the professional care one might have expected, and he peered with intent into the rolled-back eyes.

"I'm not an expert in such matters, Mr Carr," he said at last, "but I would say she's been dead for no more than an hour or so. Two, at the absolute outside mark, but I'd be surprised if it is that long. I'd say around one o'clock."

"The French windows are open, doctor," said Carr. "Does that affect your judgement?"

Jarratt shook his head. "I wouldn't say so. I mean, it might affect the time estimate to a degree, but not by very much, I wouldn't think. The windows can't have been open long, surely. On a night like this, the body would be colder than it is if they had been open for any significant period."

"I'm inclined to agree with you," Carr said. "And the means of death?"

Jarratt pointed to the prick on the arm. "We know what caused that, of course. We saw the Clements girl holding it. It is surely obvious that she was injected with some poison or other. The pupils are heavily contracted, almost to pinpoints, which would suggest an opiate of some sort."

"Morphine, for example?" suggested Carr, keeping his voice as bland as he was able.

"Possibly, yes. If so, she will have fallen into a coma very quickly, and respiratory failure would have followed."

"How quickly?"

Jarratt looked up at him. "Frighteningly so. Death would have occurred within five or ten minutes from the injection."

Carr nodded. He had suspected as much, but the doctor's confirmation was helpful. "*There is poison in the fang of the serpent, in the mouth of the fly, and in the sting of the scorpion.*'"

Jarratt rose to his feet. "*But the wicked man is saturated with it.*'"

If Carr was impressed that Jarratt knew the quotation from an ancient Indian philosopher, he did not show it. "Thank you, doctor, that is all."

III

PART THREE: QUESTIONS AND LIES

Chapter Eighteen

Everett Carr sat alone in the drawing room.

He had slept little, and what sleep he had managed had been disturbed. And yet, despite his lack of rest, he felt strangely alert, as if the drama of the preceding evening had served as its own form of revitalising restoration. As was his custom, he had wanted little more than strong coffee for his breakfast, and he had helped himself to a cup from one of the several pots which had been prepared and which stood now in the dining room, for the guests' convenience. Nobody had been in the dining room when Carr entered it, and he had not been altogether sorry or dismayed by the solitude, which persisted now in the drawing room.

The local police had arrived soon after Carr and Jarratt had walked out of the library. Carr had spoken to them at some length, explaining the position with candid but economical clarity. There had been some preliminary questions for all those present, but Ivor Kettering had made it known early and with certainty that he wanted Scotland Yard to be summoned at the earliest possible moment. The local inspector, although quick to assure them all of the capability of his force, had seemed neither worried nor surprised by the demand. There had been a brief examination of the corpse, and Jarratt's conclusions had been vindicated by the police surgeon, although the inspector was in no doubt that the men from the Yard would wish to have their own expert evidence on the point. The body had been removed to the mortuary, however, and the library had been locked. Carr had indicated to the inspector that the French windows were open, and the decision was taken to close them. It could hardly matter, thought Carr, given that he, Jarratt, and the inspector were witnesses to the fact of them being open, and the official detective had commanded that they be closed and locked.

Daphne Clements had been interviewed briefly and in private, and the inspector had placed her under arrest on suspicion of murder. She had been driven away to the station in the requisite sombre, black Wolseley. Ivor Kettering had insisted on accompanying her, but the inspector had refused. For her part, Daphne had raised neither objection nor any protestation of innocence, but it had been clear to Carr, and presumably to anyone who had cared to notice, that the young nurse was still in a state of shock, so that the grim reality of her situation and its wider repercussions were still unclear to her. Details of the guests and their addresses had been taken, assurances provided that nobody would leave Marsden Grange until the Yard had approved as much, and a police guard had been placed on the house to ensure those assurances were honoured. Some people had voiced what Carr had taken as being obligatory and perfunctory words of protest, but in time, they had retired to their beds and succumbed with various degrees of success to sleep.

On the morning after the tragedy, it seemed to Carr that the house was unnaturally still. The air seemed almost toxic with suspicion, which seemed to hang heavily on the atmosphere of the house generally. It was not reserved for the library, where it might be thought to be safely contained within the locked room. It was as if the repugnant stench of malice had somehow infected the whole of Marsden Grange like an invisible plague. Despite his encounters with violent death in the past, Carr was not immune to the sensation that murder caused an almost physical change to the place where it was committed, and his previous experiences had in no way anaesthetised him to it.

He sipped the coffee, grateful for its rich and bitter stimulation of his senses. There were points about the murder of Rowena Kettering that intrigued him, others that puzzled him, and some that seemed entirely obvious to him, but he tried to give none of them any particularly profound thought. There would be time enough for that, especially if calling in

Scotland Yard meant the case being handed to Inspector Mason. Carr hoped his request that Mason be notified would be heeded by both Ivor Kettering and the local inspector, to whom Carr had repeated it. Time would tell, of course, but it was a factor outside of Carr's control, and so it could only ever remain a matter of optimistic anticipation.

The door opened, breaking into his thoughts, and Josephine stepped into the room. Carr rose immediately, placing his cup of coffee on a small table beside his chair, and walked over to her. She had evidently not expected him to be in the drawing room, and he had the immediate impression that she would have preferred to be alone and that any company, perhaps his in particular, was unwelcome. Her eyes were enflamed with raw emotion, their lids so livid in colour that it made the paleness of her skin seem almost ethereal. She had about her an aura of exhaustion, which perhaps had less to do with lack of sleep than it was to do with the relentless sobbing that she so obviously had endured.

Carr was conscious that words in such circumstances were almost always inadequate. Nothing that could be said could possibly hope to alleviate the pain or make amends for the tragedy that had taken place. Nevertheless, silence would have been both insensitive and intolerable, and some words of condolence, however futile, were better than none. But he knew the wisdom of keeping those words simple and brief. "I am so very sorry, my child."

Her head nodded vaguely in recognition of the words, but her gaze remained fixed on the floor, as if looking at him might compel more tears to fall. "I was right, Mr Carr. All those fears, everything I told you about, I was right about it all."

"Indeed." His voice was barely audible.

"We did nothing to stop it, did we?" With an effort, she raised her gaze to meet him. There was no retribution in the words. She spoke them only as a matter of fact. "Even so, I can't believe any of it is real. I know it is, but it seems impossible to believe."

Carr had no reply for her, certainly not one which he felt was either appropriate or beneficial. Josephine's reaction to her mother's death was not unique, and Carr had witnessed it in others, this immediate but incredulous grief at a loved one's death. When that death was unnatural, it seemed impossible to rationalise, so that there was a delayed shock at the reality of it. Grief was instantaneous and within one's comprehension, but murder was not, and the mind needed time and distance to confront it.

"It all seems so unfair," Josephine was saying. "Mummy has lost her life, Daphne will lose hers, and Daddy will end up with neither of them. It isn't unfair, it's just a complete waste. What has any of it been for, what did any of it matter in the end?"

Tears had now returned to the eyes, but those exhausting sobs which Carr expected did not come. He placed his arm gently around her shoulders, and she fell against him, her face nestling between his shoulder and neck. The sounds of grief which roared from her were muffled by the lapel of his jacket. They could have stayed in that awkward but oddly comforting embrace only for a few seconds, but it had seemed like hours.

When she pulled away from him, Josephine was filled with apology. "I am so sorry, Mr Carr. I'm afraid that I'm finding all this rather difficult to deal with."

"There is no need to apologise, my child."

"You're so kind. Even if we didn't stop this terrible thing from happening, I'm so very glad you're here."

He smiled, pleased by the words, but his eyes remained darkly serious. "You ask me what any of it mattered in the end. Let me answer you: all of it mattered. It was all significant and it was all necessary, because she was your mother, and because she loved you. And you were her daughter, and you loved her. That is why it matters, Miss Kettering, and nothing which happened in this house last night, and nothing which occurs here in the days and weeks to come, can change what she meant to you or prevent it from being significant. You see, Miss Kettering," he added, "there must be some things that even murder cannot be permitted to destroy."

She had listened to the words carefully, not only because she had a sense that they were meant sincerely but also because there was a gravity about his expression that seemed to demand attention. What he had said seemed to require her to find some inner courage, a moral strength to face up to what had happened and not allow her life, her beliefs, and her memories to collapse under the catastrophic force of murder. Looking into his eyes, Josephine had the sudden knowledge, the absolute certainty, that Carr believed what he had said, and she felt an irresistible obligation to do him the courtesy of reflecting and honouring that belief.

"Thank you, Mr Carr," she said. "Thank you so very much."

If either of them felt there was anything more to say, they would not be granted the opportunity, since the sound of approaching cars and the sudden visibility of the official-looking vehicles announced the arrival of both the local police and Scotland Yard.

Chapter Nineteen

Inspector John Mason had received the call during the night. Initially, he had expressed both a concern and a reluctance to take on this particular case, partly because he was well aware that the Norfolk police were perfectly able to handle a murder investigation without the need for Scotland Yard, but also because the case, as it had been swiftly and concisely explained to him, appeared to be so straightforward that it required almost no investigation at all. Surely, he had argued to his senior officers, it was merely a matter of taking statements and obtaining a confession from the woman already arrested. The response, delivered to Mason with customary intransigence of official orders, had been that the scene of the crime was a house owned by a government minister, who had specifically requested the presence of Scotland Yard. And here was the truth of it, thought Mason: a straightforward case treated with an importance beyond its merits, an enquiry (however routine) taken out of a local force's hands, and Mason's personal circumstances wholly inconvenienced simply because a member of the establishment demanded it, and those wishes, like the expectations of a rampaging toddler, were to be granted without question. How Mason despised the politics of it all.

"Besides, Mason," his superior had said, "you're looking tired. A bracing trip to the coast might be just what the doctor ordered."

"Surely, sir, you mean just what the senior minister demanded?"

The retort, bitter but satisfying, could not have been ignored, but the chief superintendent had seen no reason to acknowledge it. "You might take a less cynical approach to the assignment, inspector, if you knew that you were specifically requested to undertake it."

Mason had frowned. "By whom, sir?"

"One of the guests." The chief superintendent had checked his notes, the relevant name escaping his memory for the moment, and Mason had heard the impatient sound of flicking pages. "Do you know a man called—let me see—Everett Carr?"

Despite himself, Mason had smiled. "I shall take the first available train to Norwich, sir. Perhaps somebody could telephone ahead and request the local force send a car to meet me. It would be as well if I went straight to Marsden Grange."

The chief superintendent, curious as to the sudden change in attitude of his junior officer, did not question it, and Mason's requested arrangements were swiftly made.

Mason could not recall precisely how long had passed since he had last seen Everett Carr, but he could recollect only too well that it had been during their combined investigation of the murders connected with the Icarus Club. He wondered idly, as the train rattled its way out of London, whether Carr was still a member of the club and, if so, whether he visited it regularly still. Or was it that the killings, which had led to the uncovering of a terrible tragedy, had poisoned Carr's mind against the cosy opulence of the place? Mason knew that Carr was a man of sensitivity and compassion, and he would not be surprised to learn that Carr's sensibilities towards the Icarus Club had been corrupted by the murders connected with it. It was a matter of no consequence, but Mason knew, if he could only dare to admit it to himself, that his mind was toying with these ideas largely because of the mention of Carr's name, and the knowledge that he had requested Mason's presence at Marsden Grange in particular, had prompted in the practical and experienced police officer a degree of sentimental nostalgia. And perhaps there was an element of guilt, a self-condemnation that Mason had not contacted Carr since the Icarus Club investigation. Would a telephone call, or a telegram, or even a knock on the Albany flat's door have been so difficult? But perhaps Mason's sudden disgust at himself was unfair. After all, there had been no communication from Everett Carr either, had there?

The journey had been so peaceful and relaxing that Mason was sorry when it came to an end. With the exception of these initial lapses into recent memory, and a nap of indeterminate length somewhere between Brentford and Colchester, Mason spent the journey considering the scant details he had received of the death of Rowena Kettering and enjoying the greens and browns of the countryside, as it rolled pleasantly past the window of his carriage. He told himself that he didn't leave London for the country half as much as he should do or would like to do, and he made a mental note to rectify the error. The truth, however, as he well knew, was that within a matter of weeks, he would have forgotten his pledge.

He knew less about Rowena Kettering than he did about her husband. The theatre, particularly Shakespeare, was a forum that had never appealed to Mason, beyond the occasional music hall show. Like the cinema, he found these artificial representations of life too broadly presented to be truly reflective of human existence. He saw enough of the wickedness of the human soul, that to see it idealised or otherwise depicted in anything other than its harsh reality made it too banal for Mason's appetite.

He had a similar dislike for politics but for entirely different reasons. Ivor Kettering's name was known to Mason, both as a minister in the Treasury and as a politician of impressive credentials in his own right. To Mason, these plaudits meant very little. He distrusted politicians intensely and had seldom met one who did not give him the impression that they were in some way interested only in themselves. And yet, he knew that Ivor Kettering was lauded throughout Westminster and the press, both for his values and for his policies. Now, Mason thought, Kettering's name would be mentioned in the parliamentary corridors and the offices of Fleet Street as much for his connection to a violent murder in his own country retreat as for his political ambitions.

At the station, he was met by a uniformed officer and a local detective sergeant, both of whom welcomed him with professional courtesy if not personal warmth. Mason got to business at once, asking for the name of the local inspector and ordering that a message be conveyed to him that Mason would like a conference with him, and the chance to interview the prisoner later that day, possibly after lunch. The detective sergeant had assured Mason of co-operation and, when prompted, provided the names of several local hotels and inns which might be suitable for Mason's stay. He handed him a folder filled with papers, containing the local inspector's reports and comments, and a key.

"To the library, sir," the sergeant had explained. "It was locked after the crime was discovered and Miss Clements was arrested."

"Excellent work, sergeant," Mason had said. It had not been meant to be either condescending or offensive, but only a statement of fact, and it had been acknowledged as such without any fuss. Mason had been grateful for it.

The drive from the main station at Norwich to Longhampton seemed longer than its twenty minutes only because it was conducted in silence. Mason had not found it uncomfortable or awkward, only marginally petulant, but he was still rather relieved when it came to an end. Mason climbed out of the Wolseley and took stock of his surroundings. Although they would never have said it to him, the two local officers thought that the Scotland Yard man seemed to suit the lawns and woods of Marsden Grange. Mason was large, his bulk due not to lack of exercise and poor food, but to the effects of middle age on a naturally muscular bulk. The cheeks, flushed pink, and the clear blue of his eyes suggested a cheerful honesty, a combination which suggested something of the appearance of a country farmer to the man. The impression of agricultural heritage, which had occurred immediately to the local officers, was intensified by the tweed suit that Mason chose to wear as a matter of course. Whatever his external appearance suggested, however, Inspector Mason was nothing less than an experienced and dedicated police detective.

Having been admitted into the house, he found himself standing in the majestic hallway of Marsden Grange. It was suitably impressive, although Mason had seen his fair share of domestic opulence, just as he had witnessed what passed for living at the other end of the social spectrum. He had ceased to be awed by wealth, because he was only too aware of the existence of areas which displayed the opposite, and he certainly felt nothing approaching envy for those people who could afford such luxury. To Mason, his professional presence at any location, whether it was the largest mansion or the dirtiest slum, was because it was the scene of a crime. As such, it deserved his objectivity rather than either his admiration or condemnation. Beyond its relevance to the enquiries he was obliged to make, a house had no significance to him, nor could he allow it to have.

"Good morning, inspector. I see that you have made good time."

The voice, as familiar as it was unmistakable, brought a gentle smile to Mason's lips. He turned to face those intense black eyes, the contrasting white hair of the extravagant moustache and neatly trimmed Imperial beard, and the dapper yet mournful elegance of Everett Carr. Mason walked towards him and shook his hand, courteously but warmly. "Mr Carr, how good it is to see you again."

"I'm only sorry about the circumstances," said Carr. "It seems we are destined to meet only when a life has been taken."

It was a reference to the Icarus Club murders, and Mason knew it, but he saw no reason to resurrect the past. "I have had brief details of the events of last night, of course. Perhaps I should speak to Mr Kettering, but then I would welcome a conference with you, Mr Carr, if I may. Although it all seems rather straightforward, I must confess."

"So straightforward as to be inexplicable."

Mason smiled. "I suspect I'm not supposed to understand what you mean by that just yet."

Carr shrugged, but his voice remained serious. "I have no wish to speak in riddles, inspector, but I have my doubts that matters are as simple as they appear."

Nothing more was said, but an arrangement was made to meet outside the library door once a quarter of an hour had passed. Mason sent word to Ivor that he had arrived and desired to speak to him on a preliminary basis, and Carr took advantage of a breath of fresh air. His short walk around the grounds was a solitary one. He neither met nor saw anybody and as the moments passed, he found himself enjoying the quiet of the surrounding fields and woodlands so that when the first spots of rain began to fall, he was sorry to have to return to the house.

He did not ask Mason for any details of his discussions with Ivor Kettering. It was not a formal interview, and it was a conference arising purely out of professional politeness rather than from any official interrogation. As such, Carr doubted it would have elicited anything either of importance or interest, and he trusted that if it had, then Mason would inform him. As it was, the inspector arrived at the library door with commendable promptness. He took the key that the detective sergeant had given him on arrival from his jacket pocket and opened the door. He and Carr stepped inside, and Mason silently shut the door once more, leaving them alone in the room.

It did not smell of death, nor did it seem as if the memory of murder lingered in the air. Such notions were for detective novelists, but it was still difficult for Carr to erase the corpse from his recollections. The chair in which Rowena had died was empty now, but it seemed unnaturally vacant without her body sprawled in it, as if the chair had somehow been designed for the sole purpose of having Rowena die on its seat. There was no physical trace of her death in the room, but it was impossible not to feel that the library had somehow changed. It now no longer appeared as a room of solitary reflection and literature, but rather as one in which no pleasure could ever again be derived. It was now less a library and more of a mausoleum. Fanciful ideas perhaps, but Carr could not resist having them.

"Perhaps you could tell me briefly what happened last night Mr Carr," said Mason, walking slowly around the room.

Carr knew that he did not simply mean the finding of the body. Such information would be in the file that Mason had been carrying with him since his arrival, set out in the mundane and oppressively factual language of official police reports. What Mason wanted now was a personal perspective, an idea of the human emotions and conflicts which led up to those cold, inflexible words in his reports. Carr was happy to oblige, giving his account concisely but without missing any vital detail. When he had finished, Mason remained silent for a few moments.

"Dr Jarratt's estimate of the time of death seems to have been fairly accurate," he said at last, checking the details in the folder. "The local doctor reached the same conclusion of around one o'clock in the morning."

"In which case, and as I suspected at once, the murder must only have been committed moments before we all arrived in the hall," said Carr. "There will still be a formal post-mortem, of course."

Mason nodded. "We should have a preliminary report by tomorrow. Not that it will tell us anything that we don't already know. Morphine poisoning is bound to be the cause, just as one o'clock is certain to be the time. Beyond that, we don't need to know very much more."

If Carr found this dismissal of a vital scientific procedure as flippant, he did not say so. Instead, he remained silent, his brows furrowed and his lips pursed in concentration beneath the heavy moustache. One finger tapped against the silver handle of his cane.

Mason closed the folder of official reports once again. "From what you've told me, Mr Carr, it seems obvious that more people than just the Clements woman might have wanted Rowena Kettering dead?"

Carr nodded. "But only Daphne Clements appears to have gone through with it."

Mason looked across at Carr. "What troubles you about the matter as it stands, Mr Carr?"

"Only a few points," came the reply. "The French windows, for instance."

Mason looked over his shoulder at them. "What about them?"

"They were open. Did the local police not tell you?" Carr tutted. "How remiss. Yes, inspector, one door was wide open, but with the key still in the lock."

"Meaning someone could have got in through them."

"Possibly." It was evident from Carr's tone of voice that he disagreed. "That would assume, would it not, that the doors had been opened from the inside in order to allow someone to enter from the outside."

"A pre-arranged meeting, perhaps, and presumably with Rowena Kettering."

"For what purpose? If Daphne Clements is the killer, she wouldn't need to creep in through the windows, since she was already in the house."

Mason was growing a little impatient. "Mrs Kettering might have been too warm, felt the need for some fresh air."

The idea was beneath him, and both he and Carr knew it, even with the latter's frown of disappointment. "It was a chilly night, inspector, and nobody would have opened those windows because it was too hot in the room." He shook his head and tapped on the floor with the ferrule of his cane. "No, no. The facts suggest only one explanation. Someone was in this room, for reasons which may or may not be obvious, and they wanted to escape from it but felt unable to do so through the door. The French windows offered the only other alternative."

Mason nodded slowly. "Taking that as true, this person of yours must have been in this room with the body."

"And so, two things must follow. One, that this person is the true killer of Rowena Kettering, and Miss Clements is innocent; and two, that the true killer was then outside the house when we all descended into the hall."

"Dr Jarratt, you mean?"

Carr smiled. "The only person who was not inside when the murder was discovered."

"But there's no proof that he opened the windows." Mason had begun to walk around the library, his hands behind his back and the folder tapping against his legs. "There is another possibility. That Miss Clements is the killer, and she opened the French windows in order to confuse the issue."

"If she wished to do that," said Carr, "why would she allow herself to be found with the body and the murder weapon? No, inspector," he added, banging his cane more vehemently on the floor, "Daphne Clements did not open those windows. But somebody did, and that is of the utmost importance."

"A defence barrister would make much of it, that's true," said Mason, "but how much importance can it have when set against the fact that Clements was holding the murder weapon, that she was found with the body, had a motive, and all but confessed to the crime in front of witnesses?"

Carr conceded the point with a small shrug of his shoulders. "Why Miss

Clements was in the library at that precise moment is certainly a point of interest."

"Perhaps Mrs Kettering caught her in the act of doing that." Mason pointed to the portrait above the mantelpiece. He crossed the room and stared up at the slashed depiction of Rowena in her professional prime. He was no art aficionado, but even Mason could see that the brushwork was both experienced and accomplished.

"I had the privilege of seeing it before it was destroyed," said Carr, coming to stand by the inspector's side. "It was a remarkable piece, and it captured Mrs Kettering with impressive accuracy. She is shown as Lady Macbeth, a role I was fortunate enough to see her play. Many years ago," he added softly, as if the period of time was of importance.

Mason gave a suitably appreciative murmur, but nothing more. "The knife work is of more interest to me than the brushwork. It suggests a particular type of malevolence."

"Unquestionably it does," replied Carr, with genuine sadness in his voice. "Our murderer wanted to add malicious insult to fatal injury."

Carr held up a cautionary finger. "Can we be sure that the killer did this?"

Mason looked down at him. "Who else could it have been?"

"What does the killer achieve by it? He wants to end Rowena Kettering's life and he has done so. Why would he proceed to slash the portrait? It adds nothing to the principal crime."

Mason found it hard to disagree, although he was not yet able to relinquish his argument. "But we don't know that it was done after the murder. As I said, perhaps Mrs Kettering disturbed the vandal in the act."

"And he killed her? Inspector, the idea is beneath you. Is it credible that our murderer would violently slash this canvas with a knife and then, when he is discovered, would calmly sit Mrs Kettering in a chair, fill a hypodermic with morphine, and inject a fatal dose? Is it not more likely that in the frenzy of destroying the portrait, and fuelled with such obvious hate, he would stab her with the very same knife he has used on the painting?"

Mason was frowning. "For that matter, how would anybody get Rowena to sit in the chair while they inflicted a fatal dose?"

Carr smiled. "It would be simple enough if Rowena were already sitting in the chair. The murderer comes in behind her, grabs her arm, and thrusts the needle into it."

Mason was frowning. "The more I hear, the more I am convinced that the simplest solution to this case is the correct one."

"Occam's razor," murmured Carr.

"Clements is a nurse. She'd have access to morphine. Medical professionals have access to a lot of suitable methods of murder, and it is entirely logical for a nurse to use those methods."

Carr did not argue. "And she was overheard talking about morphine."

Mason was immediately intrigued. "By whom?"

"Josephine Kettering."

"Talking to whom?"

Carr was less inclined to reveal the name but saw that he had little choice in the matter. "To Ivor Kettering."

Mason's eyes burned with satisfaction. "There we are, then! Clements is in love with Kettering, and Rowena is in the way. So, Clements tells her lover of her plans to solve that problem, using a poison she has in her possession. She takes a hypodermic needle, fills it with the poison, and finds Rowena in here. As you say, she grabs her arm, and the deed is done. She waits for the dose to take effect, but you find her in the aftermath of her crime."

"And the painting?"

Mason smiled. "It is as you say. Someone else did that for their own reasons. But insofar as the murder goes, it all fits."

"Except for the French windows," said Carr, pointing with his cane.

"There will be an explanation of that," said Mason. "Perhaps Ivor Kettering can tell us. If he can't, I'm sure Daphne Clements can. I don't think there can be any doubt about it, Mr Carr. She did it, and she'll hang for it."

Chapter Twenty

Inspector Mason had permitted Carr to come to Rowena's room alone, a gesture of friendly confidence which had touched Carr, but Mason had professional duties to perform, none of which had been of particular interest to Carr. They were largely administrative: giving orders to subordinates, advising the people of the house that interviews would commence shortly, and making arrangements for him and Carr to interview Daphne Clements in her police cell. This last was of definite interest to Carr, but the practical organisation of it had not. And so it was that he was alone in the same bedroom in which, only hours before, his pleas for Rowena to be wary of the dangers hanging over her had gone unheeded.

The room seemed to feel her permanent absence from it, as if it knew that she would no longer brush her hair in front of its mirrors, no longer sit at its windows and look out over the lawns, and no longer sleep in the comfort of its bed. The room, quiet and still, seemed to be in a peculiar state of bereavement of its own, with Carr, standing alone in the centre of it, acting as some solitary but intrusive mourner. It was large and expensively furnished, but it was too extravagant to be considered entirely elegant. There was evidence of Rowena's tendency for dramatic opulence, most noticeable in the lace trims of the bedsheets and the exotic but unnecessary decadence of a four-poster bed, whose ornate silk curtains were tied at the middle with pink ribbon and secured to the centre of the carved wooden posts. The cushions appeared almost too large for genuine comfort, and the blankets were heavy and embroidered, giving the impression of the bed of a princess in a romantic fairy tale. This was a place to be admired, rather than one in which the body's necessary restoration could be achieved.

The furniture, too, suffered from the same uneasy blend of practicality and decadence. The chairs were there to serve their purpose, but they were covered in silk upholstery, patterned with roses and doves, and the idea of sitting on one seemed barely capable of proper consideration. The theme of roses and doves was continued in the decorations on the dressing table and a small strongbox at the foot of the bed. There was an odour of rose water in the room, too, faint but unmistakable, and with it came an irresistible impression of nocturnal pampering, of cosmetic luxury after a hot bath. It was a little excessive, Carr thought, and he had the sudden idea that the design of the room was intended to remind Rowena of her childhood nursery, or the bedroom she had enjoyed as a little girl. There was something nostalgic about it, something which seemed desperate to reflect its obviously Victorian heritage. The realisation made his initial impression of the loneliness of the room all the more tragic, because this recent death served only to make the room appear to be not a room of peaceful rest but a hopeless museum to an irretrievable past.

The impression was heightened by the chaos in the room. Carr could hardly believe that Rowena had caused the mess, particularly given the obvious care with which the room had been maintained. It would be an insult to this shrine to her past to have tarnished it with such angry disarray. The two wardrobes on either side of the bed had been ransacked, the clothes from inside now lying in untidy clusters around the floor. The drawers of the dressing table and those of the writing desk, which stood next to it, had been pulled out, and the gaps which they left in the tables now seemed to gape at him in ridiculous parodies of surprise. The contents of the drawers were tossed onto the ground, a curious mixture of personal and private possessions: papers, pens, envelopes in a peculiar duck egg blue colour, a bottle of ink, and old theatre programmes now lying next to hairbrushes, hand mirrors, vanity cases, stockings, and underclothes, with the odd box of cigarettes and matches adding to the confusion. As evidence of a search being undertaken for something, it was obvious, but it struck Carr as an unforgivable invasion of the privacy of a dead woman.

The object of the search was impossible to know unless Carr could find some clue to it amid this confusion of belongings, but if the person responsible had found whatever it was, then it was surely reasonable to assume that it had been removed or destroyed. Nevertheless, Carr moved slowly around the room, his eyes ignoring the obvious details and concentrating on those points about the room which did not suggest themselves immediately upon entry. With the ferrule of his cane, he sifted through the scattered clothes but found nothing amongst them that seemed to be of significance. Indeed, there seemed to him to be no reason for these clothes to have been tossed around the room in such a manner. It seemed suddenly to Carr as if it had been a waste of effort on the culprit's part. What could he or she possibly have thought was hiding amongst these gowns, dresses, and skirts? What might Rowena have concealed in her blouses, jumpers, and nightgowns? A coat might be a suitable hiding place for something, but the rest suddenly seemed to Carr to be thrown around purely for the sake of it.

And then it struck him. It was not aimless vandalism at all, but a carefully orchestrated diversion. Carr almost smiled in admiration. The best place to hide a needle, he thought, was not in the proverbial haystack, but among hundreds of other needles. Similarly, the ransacked wardrobes, the discarded clothes, and the general disorder were all designed to mask one particular but smaller instance of burglary.

If the clothes were a diversion, it seemed to Carr equally certain that the discarded drawers of the dressing table were a similar blind. It was hardly likely, he thought, that anybody could have wanted to steal or discover anything of importance among the personal items of female grooming which so obviously belonged in these particular upturned drawers. It was not impossible, but Carr thought it improbable. It was surely more reasonable to suppose that the intruder's goal had been the writing desk. He might have suspected the bedside cabinets, but those drawers were still firmly in place, which Carr took as evidence that the culprit had found whatever he was searching for, meaning that no search of those cabinets was required.

He knelt carefully, his knee protesting with a bolt of pain along his leg, and he began to look gently through those items which had obviously been in the desk drawers. There was little of interest, and he wondered for a moment what he had expected to find. As he had thought earlier, if the search had been successful, then the person responsible would have taken away whatever they were looking for, or else they would have destroyed it. And if they had not found it, there was no possibility of Carr doing so. The thought intrigued him: whoever it was must have thought they would find what they were searching for in the desk drawers, so why would they not have been successful? Carr's eyes widened, and a smile flickered under his moustache and beard. The answer to his question was obvious: the intruder had not found anything, because Rowena had already destroyed it.

He looked towards the small fireplace set in the far wall and limped over to it. Again, the shattered knee growled at him as he knelt in front of the cold iron of the grate. He stuck the ferrule of his cane into the ashes, hardly daring to hope that he might find something. Then, with a surge of excitement, he saw a scrap of white paper, peering out from the grey ashes like the peak of a mountain through low clouds. Gently, using only the fingernails of his thumb and forefinger, Carr pulled at the tip of the paper. It was small, delicate, the merest sliver which had survived the flames. And yet, even from this fragment, Carr could tell that it was expensive, peculiarly strong and stiff, and of the highest quality. It was hardly the sort of paper one would use to write a note or even any type of casual correspondence. It was more akin to the type of paper used to write wills, perhaps, or commercial and business letters.

Carr rose to his feet and took one of the envelopes that had been scattered around the room. He placed the sliver of paper from the fire into it and dropped it into his jacket pocket. It might mean nothing, and it might not be of any use, but Carr had an intuition that Mason should be made aware of it. He walked to the bedside cabinets. The intruder had not opened them, but Carr wondered what he might have found if he had. There were two of them, one on either side of the bed. On the one closest now to Carr, there was a small reading lamp, some paperback editions of various Shakespeare plays, a collection of Auden's poetry, and, perhaps incongruously, the latest Dorothy L Sayers detective novel. On the one near the writing desk, Carr could see only a carafe of water and a glass, half-filled. He sat on the bed and pulled open first the drawer and then the doors of the cabinet nearest to him. The drawer was empty, but the main storage area of the cabinet contained a shoe box, which Carr now pulled out and placed in his lap.

Removing the lid, the contents suggested at once a box of memories. There was a selection of theatre programmes, some dating back to the early 1920s, and each one from a play in which Rowena had performed, so that they formed an informal record of her professional career. In addition, there were napkins from restaurants around the world, neatly folded so that the name of each restaurant was clearly visible, and menus from the same and other restaurants. There was a black silk purse, in which Carr found a selection of coins from various countries, kept as mementoes, Carr assumed, of touring productions on the continent and further afield. There was a bundle of newspaper pages, taken from various editions of the *New York Times*, the headlines declaring a number of diverse stories: the President's plan to cut farm debts; the disappearance of a crucial witness to the Mafia assassination of Salvatore Ferrara in Manhattan; the Federal Bureau of Investigation assuming conduct of the Lindbergh kidnapping case; the granting of power to Hitler's cabinet to act as a dictatorship. The editions spanned a period from March to October 1933, presumably a period in which Rowena appeared in theatrical productions in New York City, prior to her retirement later that year. Some of the newspapers were not kept so neatly folded, however, and, wrapped in crumpled pages of some editions, Carr found a rather ugly and less than impressive model of the Sphynx, fashioned out of pot and painted with only obviously mediocre sculpting skill. Carr thought it distasteful, and he was not surprised that Rowena kept it shut away in a cabinet by her bed. It was not fit to be on display, certainly, but Carr supposed that it was the sentimental meaning that had mattered rather than the workmanship of the souvenir. He wrapped it back in its newspaper shroud and replaced it in the box. The contents were fascinating as relics of Rowena's travels abroad, but beyond that, Carr saw no importance in them, and he replaced the box in the cabinet.

He rose from the bed and walked around it to the other cabinet. There was nothing in the drawers or the storage area, and Carr gave a small sigh of disappointment. It was only when his eyes drifted to the glass of water and the carafe, which he had noticed earlier, that his attention was seized once more, as if it had been grasped by the ice-cold, skeletal fingers of fear. It was not the sight of the glass and the carafe that troubled him, but the specks of crystalline powder that were scattered close to the base of both. A passing glance might have suggested a slight spilling of sugar, but to Carr's mind, there was a much more sinister possibility. He looked at the glass, wondering whether Rowena had sipped from it and how much of the white powder had been tipped into it. And by whom, he wondered, and when.

Until now, he had taken it for granted that Rowena had been killed by a lethal injection of morphine. It had been an obvious conclusion. But Carr knew arsenic when he saw it, and the light dusting of white on the bedside cabinet was almost certainly traces of it. It was inconceivable that any killer, whether it was Daphne Clements or not, would try to murder Rowena twice and with two different lethal substances. Carr shook his head against the suggestion. It could not possibly be a conclusion which he could take seriously. But there was another explanation which was not only much more likely but also infinitely more terrifying.

As he stepped out of the room, gently pulling the door closed behind him, Everett Carr felt certain that there were two unidentified poisoners at large in Marsden Grange.

Chapter Twenty-One

The cell was at the end of a grim, damp corridor, whose stone floor and white walls of faded and soiled paint only increased the melancholy of the place. The ceiling was low, making the space seem cramped and suffocating, and intensifying the overall impression of oppressive gloom. The windows were filthy, and the sunlight which was able to penetrate through the grime was muted and dimmed, so that the bars across them cast only faint shadows across the floor, as if even they had been corroded away by the misery of this long, narrow passageway. Throughout it, clinging to the senses like leeches to the skin of the sick, there was the distinct odour of dirty water, which only partially masked the more repellent stench of human waste and stale vomit. It was the sort of place where hope came to die.

Daphne Clements sat on a small wooden chair beneath a large, rectangular window high above her head. The walls surrounding her were brick, painted a colour which had once been white but which now had faded almost to grey. There was a bed on one wall, but it looked as if it was incapable of offering any comfort or meaningful rest, so that it seemed to her as welcoming as the heavy metal door which had been closed on her, with the tiny square of its peephole offering a tantalising but cruel glimpse of the freedom available beyond it. At least with the door closed, she could not smell the corridor outside, whose stink had caused her to retch violently when they had dragged her down it. Had they chosen the end cell on purpose, to force her to endure the reeking smell for as long as possible? It seemed unnecessarily cruel, and she couldn't quite believe it was true, but it was by no means certain.

She was cold now, and she pulled her knees up to her chin, clasping her hands around her shins. Suddenly, she craved a hot cup of tea, even of the foul stuff they had given her when she had arrived, piping hot but with the consistency and appearance of pond water. She had drunk it, but it had made her choke, although now she would do almost anything for another cup of it.

She thought about Ivor. She wondered whether he would come to see her or whether the sight of her standing over the corpse of his wife would have corrupted his mind entirely against her. The words which had come out of her mouth, but which had seemed to be spoken in a voice which was not hers, came back to her: *She's dead, and we're free of her at last.* Why had she said it? She knew now that it sounded like a confession, but she hadn't meant it to be one, and she cursed those damning words with such passion that she could almost taste the rage in her mouth. But the words were not the only factor that would tell against her. There was her love for Ivor, the hypodermic needle, the bottle of morphine. They would all conspire together to see her hang. If she closed her eyes tightly, she could almost feel the length of rope coil like a vengeful serpent around her neck.

She did not notice that she was crying for several minutes.

It was only when she heard the rattle of keys on a chain and the subsequent clicking of the key in the lock of the cell door that she wiped away the tears. She stood up as the door clanked open, as if she were welcoming guests into her parlour instead of watching her accusers march into her cell. She saw at once that it was not the local inspector who had arrested her who now walked into the cell. It was a large bear of a man, who carried an air of authority which marked him as a police detective. Scotland Yard, Daphne presumed, which surprised her a little, until she realised that Ivor must have made some insistent calls. Whether it was good news or bad, Daphne could not say, but she supposed she had as much chance against Scotland Yard as against the local force.

She was not shocked by the appearance of Inspector Mason, therefore, but the sight of the man who accompanied him bewildered her entirely.

It was the same little man with the enormous moustache who had been at Marsden Grange. She could see no reason for him to be there, but he was. Against the background of that fetid corridor and this dreary cell, he looked strangely flamboyant. The elaborate moustache, the lurid violet necktie and handkerchief, contrasting with the sombre black of the suit, and the twinkling ruby eyes of the silver skull lapel pin he wore, all seemed excessively decadent in comparison to these morbid and miserable surroundings. And yet, as he looked at her, she saw in his face a kind empathy, which emanated from his unusually dark eyes and extended to the gentle and compassionate smile beneath the hair on his face. In him, in this man whose name she could not recall, Daphne felt a sudden but curious sense of comradeship, as if he had both the means and the intention to help her. If he had been there alone, Daphne felt sure she would have burst into thankful tears.

It was the other man who spoke. "Miss Clements, I am Inspector Mason, from Scotland Yard, and this gentleman is Mr Everett Carr."

The name now was instantly recognisable. The little man bowed courteously and removed his hat and gloves. He indicated the bed. "May I sit?"

She had recalled seeing that he was lame, so many details now coming back to her, and she nodded her agreement. "Please do. Would you prefer the chair?"

"You sit on the chair, dear lady. I shall be quite comfortable here, thank you."

Mason, having no desire to sit, remained standing in the centre of the cell. "We have some questions we must ask, Miss Clements."

The words were spoken with seriousness but without hostility, but Daphne was not sure what answer to give or whether any was strictly necessary. She surely had no choice in the matter and would be required to answer any questions which were put to her. There was, however, one query of her own which she wanted to raise, and she asked it with an obvious fear but also with as much courage as she could muster. "How long do I have to stay in here?"

The question did not surprise Mason. He had expected some sort of query from her regarding her situation, her release from it, or possibly about her rights to legal representation. None of them would have seemed unnatural or unexpected. What had surprised him, however, was the hauntingly innocent voice with which the question had been asked. It was like the voice of a frightened child, who had recognised that some unknown danger had passed at last, and who now only wanted to know if it was time to go home. Despite the hardening of his senses which the nature of his official business inevitably caused, Mason found himself feeling touched by the girl's naïve gentleness, even if he were not so assured of her legal innocence.

"That will rather depend on what you tell us now," he said. "You have not been charged with any crime as yet. I think it is best if we hear about this whole business from your point of view."

Daphne lowered her gaze. "I wasn't aware that my point of view mattered. Don't the facts speak for themselves?"

It was Everett Carr who spoke. "As yet, dear lady, we don't know all the facts."

"Aren't they obvious?"

"Very little about what happened last night seems obvious to me. Why you were in the library at all, for example."

Daphne looked at him. "To murder Rowena. Isn't that what people say?"

Carr smiled gently, but his eyes glared at her with a hypnotic allure. "For the moment, we are only interested in what *you* say." He pointed an encouraging finger towards her.

Mason stepped forward. "So, you see, Miss Clements, it is in your interests to speak to us."

Daphne shifted her weight on the chair and clamped her hands under her thighs. Again, Mason had the impression of a child, this time awaiting some sort of retribution for a minor transgression. The girl now looked up at them both and gave a short nod of her head.

"Very well," she said. "You've asked why I was in the library, so I'll tell you. I had a note, pushed under my door, asking me to meet someone there at one o'clock."

"Do you still have this note?" asked Mason. His tone suggested disbelief in her story.

"No, I burned it."

"Why?"

Daphne shrugged. "I didn't think it was worth keeping. I could hardly be expected to think it might help to prove me innocent of murder. Besides, the note demanded it."

"Didn't that strike you as odd?"

Had it? She tried to remember. Whether it had seemed strange or not wasn't something she felt able to say. The question relied entirely on hindsight, and it required an assumption of knowledge after the fact, which could not possibly have been in her mind in the moment. The question seemed, on those terms, grossly unfair, but she did not say so. Instead, she replied with as much honesty as she felt she could give. "I don't think I gave it much thought."

Carr nodded his understanding. "That seems natural enough to me. And this note, it was from Rowena Kettering?"

"No."

He had clearly expected the answer to be so obviously the opposite that her single syllable of denial seemed like the blade of a guillotine coming down with savage finality. His eyes widened, but their darkness seemed to shimmer with excitement, and the moustache and Imperial seemed to bristle with fascination. "I beg your pardon, Miss Clements. Then, please, do say who sent it."

"It was Lewis Davenport."

The response was so unexpected that, for a moment only, it seemed to both Carr and Mason that the name was unfamiliar to them. Mason walked slowly to the wall of the cell and leaned against it. For the first time, he wished there was a spare chair for him to use. If what Daphne said was true, there was, of course, sufficient doubt, at least in the hands of a defence barrister, that she was in the library with the express intention of committing murder.

"You recognised his handwriting?" he asked.

CHAPTER TWENTY-ONE

"No. I've never seen the handwriting on the note before."

"Then the note was signed in Lewis Davenport's name?" asked Carr.

Daphne looked at him. "Yes, and it was about Ivor's work. Lewis is his private secretary and confidant, so it seemed natural that he would have written the note."

"And what did this note say about Mr Kettering's work?"

"Just that Ivor was in some sort of trouble. It made it clear that there was some sort of political scandal brewing and that Ivor was going to find himself in the centre of it."

"Did it give any details of this possible scandal?" asked Mason

Daphne shuffled on the chair to face him. "No. I assumed Lewis would tell me those when we met."

Carr smiled. "And you thought that Lewis Davenport assumed that a secret shared was a secret halved?"

"I suppose I did."

Mason pushed himself away from the wall and walked into the centre of the cell. "When did you receive the note?"

"I noticed it pushed under my door as I was leaving my room for dinner."

"You didn't ask Mr Davenport about it? There was ample opportunity during the cocktail hour, for instance."

"No, inspector."

Carr began to turn his cane between his fingers. "You sat next to Mr Davenport at dinner, I seem to recall. What about then?"

"No. For one thing, Ivor was next to Lewis, as you will also remember, and I was afraid he might hear. But the note asked me to say nothing to anyone."

"You read it before going down to dinner, then?"

"Naturally."

Mason was pacing now. "And what did you do after dinner?"

"I went straight to my room. Rowena had made a spectacle of herself, as Mr Carr can tell you, and I just wanted some peace. I'm sorry to say that there was something of a scene between us."

"You were heard to say that you and Mr Kettering would be together, even if it meant over Rowena Kettering's dead body."

Daphne's hands clasped tightly together, the knuckles whitening. "Yes, I did say something like that, but I swear I didn't mean it. Not really."

Mason smiled, but his words offered no comfort. "You'll appreciate, Miss Clements, how hard that might be for someone to believe, especially given your later statement, in front of witnesses, that you and Mr Kettering were now free to be together."

Despite herself, and her voice strangled with guilt and regret, Daphne recited those terrible, damning words: *"She's dead, and we're free of her at last."*

Mason turned on her. "What exactly did you mean by that?"

"Just what I said."

"It sounds like a confession, Miss Clements," insisted Mason, "a confession and a justification for what you'd done."

Daphne was shaking her head violently. "It wasn't that. It was nothing of that kind at all."

"But you can't deny you said it," demanded Mason.

"No, and I don't deny it. I did say it, but I don't know why. I wish I hadn't. Please, you must believe me. I didn't kill Rowena."

"It doesn't look that way, Miss Clements," said Mason. Even if the note had been delivered by Lewis Davenport, all it could suggest was an alternative reason for Daphne to be in the library. There was nothing to suggest that she did not plan to use that note as a possible alibi, just as she was doing now. Assuming, of course, that the note had ever existed at all. Lewis Davenport would need to be asked about it, but assuming his reply was what Mason anticipated, the only evidence of the note would come from Daphne herself, and she could not produce it in support of her claim.

A silence had descended over the cell, although only Everett Carr seemed aware of it. Mason was glaring at the accused woman, who in turn refused to look up into those fierce and demanding eyes. It seemed to Carr as if Mason had reached a decision and that his version of events was entirely concluded in his own mind. For his part, however, the more Carr heard, the less he understood. And the more childlike Daphne Clements seemed, the more Carr came to suspect that not only was she innocent but that a peculiar and sinister trick was being played on them all.

Into the silence, there came the gentle clearing of his throat. "Excuse me, Miss Clements, but I wonder if we might go back a little. What did you do between getting back to your room and one o'clock?"

"Nothing. I read a little, but I couldn't concentrate. I didn't want to go to sleep in case I missed the appointment." Her voice lowered. "If Ivor was in trouble, I would naturally want to help if I could."

Carr inclined his head. "Of course. Now, at the appointed time, you went downstairs, yes?"

"Yes."

"Did you see a light in the library?"

"No, the door was closed when I got to it."

Carr seemed pleased with the answer. "Now, this is very important, dear lady. Did you see anyone else in the hallway or on the stairs?"

"No." The tone of her voice was hesitant.

"You're certain?"

"Yes." The hesitancy intensified.

Carr waited for the truth to be told, but nothing came. He smiled gently. "What about the person you saw on the stairs?"

A sudden fear flashed across her expression. Carr looked at her kindly, his mouth smiling warmly beneath the magnificence of the moustache, and the dark eyes now softening with encouragement. Mason was alert with interest, his own eyes narrowed, and his brows creased with fascination.

"I saw nobody on the stairs," said Daphne, but the tremble in her voice betrayed the agitation she felt. She desperately wanted to look away from Carr's stare, but she found that she could not do so, as if he had some emotional hold of her which he would only relinquish when the full truth had been told. "It's true, I saw nobody on the stairs," she added, almost pitifully. "It was on the landing."

Mason was irritated by the pedantry of the reply, but Carr merely nodded humbly, as if the error had been entirely his and without excuse. He said with a calmly apologetic tone, "And who did you see on the landing?"

"Josephine Kettering," said Daphne, after a long moment of hesitation.

Carr, slightly taken aback, stared impassively at her, his eyes probing for any suggestion that the answer was a lie. "Where exactly did you see her?"

"She was about halfway down the corridor, just standing there, as if she might be trying to decide something."

"Did she see you?" asked Mason.

Daphne, who seemed to have forgotten Mason's presence, was startled by the sudden intrusion of his voice. "No. She had her back to me."

"But she might have seen you going down the stairs, if you made a noise, perhaps?" asked Carr.

"No, because I waited until she had gone before I made any move."

"Did you see where she went?" said Mason.

Daphne nodded. "Back into her room."

"But you have no idea where she might have been going, or coming back from?"

"No, inspector. I only know that I saw her there."

Carr placed a finger to his lips and thought for a moment in silence. "Tell me now, dear lady, about the hypodermic needle and the bottle of morphine."

Daphne closed her eyes against the memories, as if the very act of recalling them would prove her guilty of using them. She knew what he wanted to know, and she wished she could give him a sensible explanation. Somehow, she doubted that either man would believe the truth because she could scarcely do so herself. Even to her mind, the idea that she had somehow felt compelled to pick up both the hypodermic and the empty phial seemed too fanciful to be accepted as any version of the truth, distorted or otherwise. It was too melodramatic to be credible, and yet that was the only answer she was able to give. She looked at Mason and saw at once the inevitable disbelief in his eyes, swiftly replaced by the sardonic and contemptible expression of condemnation. She could not blame the inspector for his reaction to her testimony. If anything, she doubted it herself.

And yet, in the eyes of Everett Carr, she saw neither mockery nor disdain. Instead, she saw a deep fascination, as if she had said something that might be of immense importance if only he could fully understand it. "What was it about them that compelled you to touch either of them?"

Daphne shrugged. "I thought they were in the way. Someone might have stood on them when they came into the library."

"It was instinctive?" asked Carr.

Daphne nodded. "It didn't register with me, not at first. As soon as I picked them up, I saw Rowena in the chair. I must have gone into immediate shock. I don't remember walking over to the chair. All I can really remember is the look on her face, and then walking out of the library and…" But no more words came.

Mason glared at her. "Did you touch the body at all? To verify death, perhaps?"

She shook her head. "It was obvious that she was dead."

A smile, or perhaps it was a lascivious sneer, crept over Mason's face. "Of course, it would be obvious to you. Being a nurse, I mean."

"It would have been obvious to anybody," argued Daphne.

"As a nurse, you'd have access to morphine and needles?"

Daphne looked down at the floor of the cell. "Yes, of course."

"Had you seen either of them before?"

"They were fairly conventional. I've seen hundreds like them."

Mason allowed the response to hang in the air between them, as if somehow it served not only as a piece of damning evidence against her but also as some sort of corroboration of his own thoughts and ideas.

Carr rose from the bed with difficulty. He began to exercise his leg by walking up and down the meagre length of the crude prison cell. "As part of your professional life, Miss Clements, do you have access to morphine?"

"Yes."

"As part of a hospital supply only, or in your own possession?"

"In my possession, for house calls and so on, where required." And suddenly, as soon as the words were out, she felt that she knew the reason for his question. "How did you find out?"

"Find out what?" snapped Mason.

She looked from one to the other of them. "Isn't that why you're asking about having the stuff in my possession?"

Mason now loomed over her, like some demon from the pit. "How did we find out about what, Miss Clements?"

"About the missing morphine…"

Chapter Twenty-Two

It was apparent that the dark business at Marsden Grange had already begun to take its toll on Ivor Kettering. Looking into the man's eyes, Carr saw that particular mixture of emotions that he knew were the customary aftermath of such a tragedy: horror, shock, and undeniable grief. But it was not just the eyes that struck Carr. The colour of Ivor's skin seemed to have paled, so that the cheeks now seemed thinner than before, the forehead now appeared to be permanently creased, and the features, previously noticeable for their quiet and dignified authority, appeared anxious and on the perpetual verge of collapse. He had invited Carr to his study, but once seated, he had not looked directly at his guest. Instead, those grey eyes had danced around the top of the desk, seeing but not focusing on the piles of paper, the collection of pens and pencils, the paperweight, and the telephone, as if what Ivor was seeing was a confused muddle of objects as indeterminate as the doodles, blotches, and scribblings on the desk's blotter. His fingers, too, were equally active, clasping and unclasping, and the hands rubbing themselves together at irregular intervals.

Carr was pleased that Mason had stayed at the local police station. His official presence might have been too much for Ivor to handle in the immediate aftermath of violent death. There would have to be a formal interview, of course, but Mason had felt that he required more time with Daphne Clements and that there was work to be done with the local police. There was also the inquest and post-mortem to be arranged and attended. Carr had felt no such inclination to speak with Daphne further at this stage, and the official business of unlawful death was not a matter that he felt should necessarily concern him, so he had returned to Marsden Grange.

"You have seen Daphne, Mr Carr?" Ivor said now. "How was she?"

There was no easy way to answer the question. A lie would be easily detected, and the truth seemed the only option, however difficult it might be to tell and to hear. "It is useless to deny that Miss Clements is in considerable danger."

Ivor nodded. "She must be so terribly frightened, poor girl. I wish there was something I could do."

"Before the events of last night, Mr Kettering, would you have said that she was capable of murder?"

Ivor considered Carr's question. Could he believe Daphne capable of murder? It was impossible to deny that they had seen her with the body, holding the needle and phial, and that she had seemed to confess to the crime in front of the whole assembly of guests. But this was not what Carr was asking, and Ivor dismissed those facts from his mind. Carr's question demanded an emotional response, not an intellectual one.

"No," said Ivor. "To be quite frank, I can't imagine her doing anything of the sort."

Carr nodded. He could hardly have expected a man in love with the accused woman to say anything else, but he doubted whether the reply had been the result either of purposeful dishonesty or of blind devotion. "If Miss Clements did not do it, of course, then a more sinister explanation for the events of last night must be considered."

Ivor's eyes finally came to rest on Carr's face, and the fingers brought their nervous dances to an end. "Yes, I quite realise that."

"Nevertheless, Miss Clements has the means, the opportunity, and the motive."

Ivor's eyes rested briefly on Carr. "Insofar as Daphne's motive goes, I presume the police will take it for granted that I share it."

Carr smiled, not entirely without humour. "For that matter, you might also have had the opportunity."

Ivor seemed genuinely surprised by the comment. "I was in here, you know that. We met in the hallway."

"Indeed, but there is nothing to say that you did not come out of this room, cross the hallway, kill your wife, and then return. You could do that in silence and unobserved, very easily. You need only then wait for the alarm to be raised, and reappear in the hallway, just as you did."

"Where would I get morphine from?"

It was a poor response, and Carr's expression showed that he thought as much. "Miss Clements is a nurse, Mr Kettering. You could easily have used her supply of morphine and hypodermic needles. She may even have given them to you."

Ivor was silent for a moment, before rising to his feet and walking slowly around the desk. "You must have a very poor opinion of me, Mr Carr, if you think that I would commit such an act, with Daphne's knowledge or not, and then let her take the blame for it."

As a response, it was certainly a better one, and Carr acknowledged it with a smile. "What if I were to tell you, Mr Kettering, that you and Miss Clements were overheard discussing how much morphine she was able to lay her hands on?"

"Who says so?"

"Do you deny it?"

"I could argue that I don't have to deny it to you." He waited for Carr to respond, but nothing came to fill the silence. Ivor paced the room for a moment and then sat back at the desk. Carr had remained motionless throughout the performance. Ivor smiled darkly. "Has anyone ever told you that you have a talent for making people confide in you, Mr Carr? As a matter of fact, we did discuss Daphne's morphine, but it wasn't about how much she could get. On the contrary, it was about how much she had lost."

This, at least, corresponded with Daphne Clements' confession that some of her personal supply of morphine had gone missing. It had been a deliberate manipulation, but Carr was not about to confess it. "I see," he said, blandly.

"Daphne had found a phial of the stuff missing from her bag. She has been attending to a patient recently who has to have double injections of the stuff, one in the morning and one at night. She had replenished her supply a week or so ago, and when she came to check, she found one missing."

"Did she offer any explanation?"

"She assumed she had miscounted. Or the hospital dispenser had."

Carr spoke softly. "That is still her explanation of the matter."

"Perhaps because it is true. After all, Daphne is not the only medical professional with access to morphine."

"You mean Dr Jarratt?"

Ivor nodded. "He and Rowena were hardly the best of friends."

"Do you know the cause of their animosity?"

"Rowena never went into details, other than to say that she knew that Jarratt had committed murder."

"That is a very serious charge," said Carr, sombrely. "Did she have proof?"

"Rowena wasn't the sort of woman to allow a meaningless thing such as proof to detract from her beliefs," said Ivor.

Carr was saddened by the unnecessarily hostile comment, although not so naïve that he could not recognise the possibility that the spite was masking a deeper grief than Ivor would care to admit, either to Carr or to himself.

"Did you love your wife, Mr Kettering?" he asked, gently.

Ivor was taken aback by the question. As if to delay having to respond, he removed his spectacles and cleaned them vigorously with his handkerchief. When he replaced them, the eyes themselves seemed to have been cleansed, and he looked up at Carr with a more assured expression of clarity.

"Once, very much so. One doesn't abandon all feelings for a woman, simply because one has fallen for another. Wouldn't you agree, Mr Carr?"

Carr nodded slowly. "I don't think human emotions are so straightforward as that, certainly."

"Rowena wasn't an easy woman to love. She was capable of deep selfishness, for one thing, quite apart from her jealousy. And her nature was almost uncontrollably melodramatic and it came with a malicious acidity, too. You may have witnessed something of it in your short time here."

Carr, never one to speak ill of the dead, merely smiled, but there was no humour in it. "She was a woman whom life had treated cruelly, I think."

Ivor frowned. "What do you mean by that?"

CHAPTER TWENTY-TWO

"Her failing eyesight, for example."

"Oh, yes, of course." It was evident that Ivor had thought Carr's comment was a reference to something else.

"How bad was her condition?"

"The doctors thought she would lose her sight completely within two years." He lowered his gaze, and the tone of voice became tinged with regret. "She took it very badly. Perhaps one can sympathise."

Carr was in no doubt of it. "Did the doctors give any cause for it?"

Ivor nodded. "They gave a long and detailed explanation, of course, but it was all bewilderingly technical, but the gist was that it was hereditary. Somehow," he added, "the idea that it was inevitable depressed Rowena even more. She likened it to fate in Greek tragedy. All very melodramatic, of course."

"But perhaps understandable," said Carr. After a moment, he said, "Your daughter loved her mother very much, I think."

Ivor nodded. "Yes, Josephine is very loyal to Rowena. She was, I should say."

"They were close?"

"Perhaps too close, Mr Carr. I never said this to Rowena, and I certainly wouldn't to Josephine, but it always struck me that we spoilt the girl. Rowena did certainly, although I allowed her to. I couldn't do otherwise, not really."

"Why was that?"

Ivor removed the spectacles once more, this time not to clean them but to rub at something in his eye. If it was a tear, it was a lonely and unwelcome one. "I've mentioned Rowena's jealousy. It was the reason she never really accepted Felix as a stepson. She couldn't bear the thought of my first wife being alive in him and still being part of me through him. An example of her melodramatic point of view, you understand."

"So, she wanted a child of her own with you?"

"Precisely."

"So, when Miss Josephine came along, she spoilt her?"

Ivor shook his head. "Not quite, Mr Carr. You see, before Josephine, there was another child. A son, Peter. He…drowned." The words came now with difficulty, as Ivor strove to suppress the memory. "A little before his second birthday."

Carr felt the obvious sadness, and it struck him personally. He and Miranda had never had children, but parenthood had been something both of them had coveted, so he could well appreciate the depth of pain caused by the Ketterings' loss.

"You have my deepest sympathy," he said.

Ivor did not acknowledge the condolence. "You asked if I loved my wife, Mr Carr. In moments like this, and recalling the death of our son, I can feel as if I love her now more than ever. Does that make me a hypocrite?"

"No, Mr Kettering. It makes you a human being."

Ivor rose from his desk and walked to a small drinks tray, set on a low table by the window. It was early, but the measure of brandy that he poured for himself was less of an indulgence and more of a comforting restorative. The offer of a drink to Carr was little more than a polite gesture, and the refusal a similar display of manners.

"Well, there it is," said Ivor. "When Josephine was born, there was an element of being grateful for having her. I tried not to succumb to it, but Rowena couldn't help herself. To her, Josephine was a second chance, a gift from a God I doubt Rowena believed in. There is a Shakespearean quotation about it, I believe. Rowena mentioned it once, but I can't recall it now."

Carr thought he knew the one. "*I am one who loved not wisely, but too well.*' Othello, although said in quite different circumstances."

Ivor smiled. "I suspect Rowena knew what she meant by it. In my darker moments, Mr Carr, I realise that there is a more cynical way of looking at the situation, that Josephine was nothing more than a substitute for Peter."

"I am truly sorry." Carr's face was dark with sadness. "May I ask exactly what happened?"

Ivor drained the brandy and walked slowly back to his desk. He sat down once more, his nerves now steadied, and he clasped his hands together on the blotter. "It was on a short holiday in Scotland. Rowena found him, face down in a small river near the cottage we had rented. She had taken him for a picnic, got distracted, and then the next thing she knew, he was in the river. Naturally, there was a period of blame, which I regret now, but it was surely inevitable. We tried hard to fight against the culpability, but it was only with the birth of Josephine that Peter's ghost seemed finally to be laid to rest. If, indeed, something like that can ever be laid to rest."

Carr said nothing for a long moment. No words seemed either relevant or appropriate, and he allowed the fragile silence to endure. At last, with a polite clearing of his throat, he offered another word of mournful apology.

"I wonder if we might return to the point about Miss Clement's missing morphine," he said at last. "Assuming that Miss Clements did simply misplace it, or that there was a dispensing error, then we must account for the morphine that was used to kill Mrs Kettering."

"Naturally."

"Morphine is not easy to obtain, as you will be aware. It requires an official prescription and must be obtained from a registered pharmacist. The question, then, becomes one of opportunity. Only a doctor, a nurse, or a chemist would be able to get hold of the drug with ease."

"I would tend to agree."

Carr smiled. "So, we have three possibilities, have we not? Either Miss Clements killed Mrs Kettering and used the morphine from her bag, or someone else stole that morphine and used it to commit the murder."

"And the third?"

"Someone else with access to a supply of morphine is the murderer."

Ivor gave the matter some thought and, satisfied, nodded. "I can't see how anyone could have stolen Daphne's morphine. Nobody would have the opportunity. And I cannot believe Daphne is a killer."

Carr's smile broadened. "Therefore, we must fall back on other people with easy access to morphine. Does that not bring us back to Dr Jarratt?"

Ivor was contemplating the point, and a sudden flame of inspiration flickered in his eyes. "It does, but there is someone else to be considered. Tilly Royce was a nurse during the war. You remember, Miss Royce?"

"I remember," murmured Carr. "Does she still practice as a nurse?"

"I don't know, not for certain. Tilly and I don't have much to do with each other."

"So, either Miss Royce or Dr Jarratt would have been able to obtain morphine with ease."

"Meaning that if Daphne is innocent, as I am sure she is, either one of those two must be guilty."

Carr held up a cautionary hand. "We must not run before we can walk, Mr Kettering. Obtaining the poison is not the same thing as administering it. Dr Jarratt or Miss Royce might have secured the poison only to pass it to someone else."

"An accomplice?"

"Possibly."

"But who?"

Carr shrugged. "I cannot say. It is an idea only, and we can be sure of nothing. It is possible to make a case against anybody in this house."

"Including me?" Ivor hissed, recalling now Carr's previous speculations.

Carr merely shrugged. "Arsenic, of course, is altogether easier to acquire. You will have some in the house, no doubt?"

Ivor, alarmed by this sudden change of topic, nodded vaguely. "I expect so, yes."

"Yes, most houses will have some around, no doubt. Tell me, is there a pharmacy or chemist in Longhampton?"

"Several, but we always use Danforth & Brierly, in the high street. Is that important?"

Carr merely smiled. "May I ask a rather delicate question, Mr Kettering?"

"If you must."

"Was it really necessary to bring Daphne Clements to Marsden Grange this weekend?"

The question startled Ivor, but whether it was the implication or the arrogance of it which shocked him, he could not say. "Is that not a grossly impertinent question?"

Carr's eyes remained darkly intense, but his lips creased into a wicked smile. "Perhaps, but also unquestionably pertinent."

Ivor was not amused by these linguistic games. "I don't see it is any of your business, Mr Carr, but I suppose the police will ask the same thing. They may even think that I did it so that we could murder my wife together, a suggestion you have put to me already."

"That was not the reason?"

"No." Ivor leaned forward for emphasis, but he resisted slamming his fist against the desk. "As a matter of fact, Mr Carr, Rowena and I quarrelled about that very subject. I will tell you what I told her. This weekend's party was my idea, to celebrate my appointment to government. Who attended, who I invited, was a matter entirely for me."

Carr's smile remained in place, but he felt no amusement. The reply given to his question was one whose honesty he did not doubt but whose arrogance he despised. It was in cruel contrast, he thought, to the deep emotion Ivor had displayed a few moments ago, as if the remembered and mutual pain Ivor and Rowena had shared over the death of their first child was now no longer an important factor to him. It prompted a series of questions in Everett Carr's mind, not least amongst them the one about how deeply Ivor still felt for his dead wife. Had his earlier display of sadness been a diversionary tactic, an act designed to suggest deeper emotions than he felt? As a deception, if that is what it had been, it was skilfully done. If genuine, this present callousness and arrogance seemed difficult to reconcile with it.

For the moment, Carr could think of no further questions for the man, and he seemed suddenly desperate to leave the study behind. He rose from his chair and nodded his head in gratitude. The expression on his face betrayed no similar sense of amiable thanks.

"You have been most amenable, Mr Kettering, and I thank you for it," he said. "If I am able to throw any light on your wife's death, I shall be glad to do so."

"Are you a detective, Mr Carr?"

"No."

"Then what business is it of yours to throw light on anything?" Ivor, too, had risen to his feet. "Shouldn't you leave the question of solving this crime to the police?"

"Undeniably so," smiled Carr, "but I am a curious man by nature."

"I am not sure I like the idea of you walking around my house playing amateur sleuth," said Ivor, "and I have no doubt the police won't approve either. Perhaps it is a question of respect."

"And what of the truth, Mr Kettering?" asked Carr. "It is down to all of us to seek and wish for the truth, is it not? You talk of respect, Mr Kettering, but we owe respect only to the living. To the dead, we owe only the truth."

Ivor could find no meaningful argument to the contrary. "That is what you believe, is it, Mr Carr?"

"Not me, sir," replied Carr. "Voltaire."

With a small but courteous bow, Carr stepped out of the room and closed the door behind him.

Chapter Twenty-Three

"Have they charged her yet?"

The voice, as unexpected as it was belligerent, took Carr by surprise. He turned around and found Felix Kettering standing in the hallway behind him, his hands clenched into fists and the cheeks flushed not only with the customary excess of alcohol but also, Carr thought, by an obvious and perhaps understandable outrage. How long Felix had been there, Carr could not say, but the idea that he had been listening to Carr's conversation with Ivor seemed impossible to deny. There was nothing to suggest it, but the suspicion of it seemed to Carr to be both natural and forgivable. He took a moment to digest Felix's attitude of fury. The arms were by his sides, and the feet were perfectly balanced on the toes, the shoulders hunched forward in confrontation, like a boxer primed for a fight. Only the unhealthy crimson of the cheeks, both from the excesses of alcohol and his obvious anger at the present situation, spoke against him. Carr noticed now, for the first time, the specks of spittle that foamed in tiny clouds at the corner of Felix's mouth, and the sight struck him as, perhaps unfairly, as wholly repugnant.

Carr walked slowly towards him. "There is still much to establish before any charges can be brought."

Felix took a step back, as if the reply, as unexpected as it was unwelcome, had been capable of physically wounding him. The fingers spread themselves out of the fists, flexed, and then curled back in on themselves. "What's the difficulty? We all saw the Clements woman. We all know what she did and why she did it."

"Certainly, it would seem so."

Felix laughed, and one of the clouds of spittle exploded. "I don't see how anyone can doubt it."

Carr gave a polite, almost apologetic shrug of his shoulders. "I wouldn't doubt it at all if it were not for the fact that so many people seemed to despise Mrs Kettering."

Felix stared at him for a moment, the eyes blinking quickly, as if the fundamental idea of Carr's words had not occurred to him, let alone their significance. Slowly, the tension in his limbs seemed to ebb away, as swiftly as a tyre with an unexpected nail in it lost its pressure. The shoulders suddenly slumped, the fists unfurled, and the legs loosened. The eyes flickered with confusion, and the lips stammered silently in unspoken reply. Only the fierce red of the cheeks remained constant. At last, Felix looked into Carr's eyes, and the lips broke into a humbled smile.

"I suppose it's no secret," he said. "Rowena was difficult to like."

Carr smiled. "I have heard as much."

"Father told you, did he?" Felix nodded, as if a formal response was not required, an affirmative taken for granted. "I think he suffered it most, poor chap," Felix added. "But he wasn't alone."

Carr nodded his understanding. "You had an altercation with Mrs Kettering yourself, I believe. A week or so ago, perhaps?"

Felix glared at him. "How could you know about that?"

The answer, if Felix had thought about it carefully enough, was obvious. It was not difficult to imagine, Carr thought, that it had been Josephine Kettering who had told him about the argument, but Carr had no intention of revealing the details of his discussions on that first day with Josephine. Even if Felix were to draw his own conclusions on the matter, Carr would neither have confirmed nor denied them. As it was, Felix did not press the point.

"There's no use denying it, I suppose," he said. "All right, yes, I didn't get on with Rowena. But disliking her, however intensely, is no motive to kill her."

Carr seemed to acknowledge the point with a nod of his head. "Why did you dislike her?"

Felix shrugged. "Can any chap like a woman who has taken the place of his mother?"

It seemed a strangely childish and petulant response, but Felix delivered it with such animosity that for a moment, Carr felt able to believe it. And in that moment, Felix's features seemed to dissolve into those of a disgruntled schoolboy. For the first time, Carr became aware of the abstract pattern of freckles that mottled those ruddy cheeks, whose colour now seemed to hark back to childhood exertions on the playing fields as indulgence in alcohol, and the malice in the eyes, momentarily, became the product of that peculiar adolescent sadism which would pull legs off spiders rather than poison stepmothers.

"Surely," said Carr, "there was something more than that. Does such resentment, however understandable, still rankle after all these years?"

"Perhaps not," said Felix, "but perhaps it never entirely disappears either."

Carr, not one who had suffered the loss of a parent and its replacement by a stranger, did not feel he could argue further with conviction, but he remained dissatisfied with Felix's explanation. "You're suggesting that the argument last week was fuelled by this parental resentment?"

"In part, perhaps."

"But there was something else?"

Felix's eyes shimmered with suppressed outrage. "If there were, Mr Carr, I don't see that it is any business of yours."

If it was designed to intimidate, Carr did not oblige. Instead, he smiled gently and nodded his head in agreement. "True indeed, dear boy, but it will certainly be the business of the police."

Felix smiled, but it was a twist of the lips that was confrontational rather than amused. "Then I'll tell you what I shall tell them. An argument between Rowena and me was no unusual thing. This one was about Adele if you want to know."

"About your fiancée?"

"Rowena had made a snide comment about Adele being of low character. Rowena was a terrible snob, if you want to know the truth, Mr Carr. Well, a chap can't have his lady talked about like that, can he?"

Carr smiled. "Not at all."

Felix grinned and lit a cigarette. "Besides, if having a bust-up with Rowena was likely to lead to murder, I'd have killed her years ago, believe me. But I couldn't possibly have done it. I was in plain sight of everyone after dinner until I returned to bed. I went to Adele's room, and I was with her until we heard the commotion down here. You can ask her."

Carr did not reply. As an alibi, Miss Mills' testimony would be less of an exoneration of guilt as Felix seemed to suppose. As lovers, not to say betrothed to each other, they could perhaps be assured of providing mutually supportive alibis for murder. And if Felix hoped that his dismissive attitude to his argument with Rowena, or his explanation of it as a regular and almost meaningless occurrence, could be taken as the truth, then he was surely either naïve or desperate.

"Look here, Carr," Felix said, "is there any suggestion that the Clements woman didn't kill Rowena? After all, it seems rather obvious that she did, don't you think?"

"It never hurts to be thorough where murder is concerned," said Carr, somewhat sententiously.

"I suppose not, but one can't help thinking that it is all rather a waste of effort looking for a solution elsewhere when it is so clear what happened."

"But you know yourself, Mr Kettering, how many other people in this house last night had reason to cause harm to your stepmother."

Felix nodded. To have denied any such knowledge would have been unnecessarily foolish. "But, damn it, she was found bending over the corpse with a hypodermic needle full of bloody morphine."

Carr ignored the inaccuracies of the statement. "Did you know that a phial of morphine had been taken from Miss Clements' supply?"

"No."

"The hypodermic needle and the phial, she says, were on the floor, and she merely picked them up. Does that seem likely to you?"

"No." Felix spoke with more emphasis.

"There is nothing to disprove her statement," said Carr, carefully. "And if she is telling the truth, is it not possible that someone else murdered Rowena and did all they could to fix the blame on Miss Clements?"

"Make her a patsy, you mean?" The idea seemed to amuse rather than fascinate Felix. "Very possibly, I suppose. But she as near as damn it confessed to the crime. You can't get away from that. I mean, she said what she did. We all heard her. It's a fact."

"Perhaps," murmured Carr. His eyes had narrowed, and the heavy brows were drawn over them so that the bridge of his nose creased in thought.

Felix glared. "Perhaps? You don't mean to say you think we all misheard what she said, that we suffered from some sort of collective deafness at that one moment?"

The guttural laugh that concluded the statement broke Carr free of his reverie. He smiled at Felix. "Not at all, dear boy. The idea is laughable, is it not? No, no, not deafness. It wasn't that at all."

If Felix had hoped for some further explanation, he was to be disappointed. Carr's attention had been distracted by a movement on the stairs. Adele Mills was walking down towards them, one hand stroking the banister with an almost seductive caress, whilst the other was plunged deep into the pockets of a pair of ocean blue, high-waisted, wide-leg trousers. She wore a white collared blouse which complemented rather than exaggerated her porcelain skin. The platinum hair bobbed as she came down the stairs, and the lips were parted in an ingratiating but alluring smile. She seemed to exude a casual finesse, but Carr had the impression that beneath her style, there remained something of a dangerous seductive prowess.

"What are you two gossiping about?" she asked, coming to rest by Felix and kissing him briefly on the cheek.

"Mr Carr is just wondering whether I murdered Rowena," said Felix.

"My, what a strange idea," Adele purred. Her voice was so mocking and assured that Carr could almost believe that she had imagined the fear. Almost, he thought, but not quite.

Carr shook his head. "I have many strange thoughts, dear lady. You must pay very little attention to me. I am a fanciful old man."

Adele was smiling, but her eyes might have frozen the Thames. "I very much doubt that, Mr Carr."

Felix blew smoke towards the ceiling. "Besides, darling, I've told Mr Carr that we were together after dinner until we heard all the banging and shouting from down here. So, I don't think he believes me guilty any longer."

Carr did not reply, but his smile remained in place and his eyes stayed fixed on Adele. She said: "Which is true, we were together. Felix came to my room a little after half past eleven, and we stayed together until we heard all the commotion from downstairs."

"Neither of you left the other alone during that time?"

"Not for a moment," said Adele, linking her arm through Felix's and pressing her body against his. "Only the hullaballoo from down here interrupted us, right, darling?"

A raise of Felix's eyebrows and a roll of his eyes seemed to be sufficient response. Carr smiled. "Neither of you was on the landing, for example?"

Felix shook his head. "Not us."

Carr smiled. "And neither of you saw anyone go into the library?"

"Again, no," said Felix, this time with a more dangerous edge to his voice.

Adele, however, was smiling at Carr. "Unless you mean Daphne Clements, but we only saw her after she'd killed Rowena, as you know."

Carr's eyes drifted from one to the other of them, and he wondered for a moment what trick, if any, was being played on him. At last, however, he smiled cordially, shook the hand that Felix Kettering had offered to him, and bowed to Adele Mills. "Please accept my apologies, if I seem to be intrusive. On my word, I meant no offence. Murder breeds suspicion, I'm afraid."

Adele nodded slowly. "I know what you mean, Mr Carr. It's fair to say that neither Felix nor I cared much for Rowena, but neither of us would have wished this on her. I must say," she added, after a moment's thought, "I would hardly have believed Daphne Clements capable of doing such a thing. When one thinks about how doctors and nurses are supposed to save lives, not take them. It gives me the shivers."

Carr asked, softly: "You are sure of her guilt?"

Adele looked strangely at him. "Of course. Who else could it have been?"

"More than one person might be said to have had cause to do it, dear lady," said Carr, his eyes filled with a seriousness matched only in his voice.

Felix stepped forward. "Neither of us, as I've said. Come on, darling, let's get some air. This house is becoming almost too suffocating for words."

But Adele's eyes remained fixed on Everett Carr. "Could you get my hat and coat, Felix? I'll wait here."

Obligingly, almost like a puppy obeying its master, Felix jogged up the stairs and vanished from view. Carr had followed him with his eyes, which now slowly returned their attention to Adele. He was aware suddenly of an undercurrent of unease simmering beneath the surface of her expression, and he was surprised to find it not only deeply fascinating but somehow strangely alluring, as if this suppressed emotion, so at odds with the coolness of her external demeanour, made her seem so overwhelmingly vulnerable that it was impossible to resist the urge to help her. He understood now that asking Felix to fetch her outdoor garments had been not a request for assistance but a dismissal.

"Could we go into the drawing room, Mr Carr?" she asked in a whisper.

He would have agreed, but she gave him no choice. She marched across the hallway and pulled open the drawing room door, stepping inside swiftly but strangely surreptitiously. Carr followed behind her, as quickly as he could manage. She had given no thought to his leg and she offered no apology for it.

"I'm sorry if I seem melodramatic," she said, closing the door, "but I didn't want Felix to hear what I'm about to say."

"I am at your service, dear lady."

"What you said just now about more than one person having a reason to kill Rowena," Adele said, her sapphire eyes wide with anxiety. "I didn't think anything of it, until just now. I took it for granted that Daphne was the killer. I mean, we all did. So, what I overheard that day didn't seem relevant."

Carr's fingers curled around her forearm. "What did you overhear?"

"It was just before we had cocktails. I was walking along the landing and

I passed Rowena's room. I could hear voices. They were muffled, but it was obvious that whoever was in there, they were having a serious argument."

"Did you recognise these voices?"

Adele gave a hesitant nod of her head. "It was Rowena and Josephine."

Carr felt a cold fist tighten around his heart. "Miss Kettering?"

"They were arguing like old enemies, Mr Carr." Adele rolled her eyes. "I feel as if I'm telling tales out of school."

"We must have the truth, Miss Mills," urged Carr, his expression and the cadence of his voice both serious and authoritative, like those he would adopt when addressing a witness, a jury, or the condemned.

Adele sighed deeply. "The worst of it is that I can't be sure what I heard, not exactly. I'm fairly sure, but I could have been mistaken. It all seems so unlikely."

"You must tell me, dear lady."

She looked into those dark eyes, which both encouraged and demanded honesty and co-operation. "It was mostly Rowena talking, as usual. She said something about Josephine knowing nothing about someone. A man, I presumed. Rowena called Josephine a naïve little fool, and she said that if Josephine could condone either murder or blackmail, then she was no daughter of hers."

Carr frowned. "She said that? Condoning murder and blackmail?"

"Yes. And there was something else. Something which made no sense to me." She fought for the words, as if saying them herself would make them seem even less intelligible than they had been at the time. "It still doesn't make any sense."

Carr tightened his grip on her forearm. "Please, dear lady, tell me all."

"I don't know why Rowena would say this," Adele said, "but I am sure I heard her tell Josephine that she was changing her will."

"Her will?" A dozen thoughts and ideas raced through Carr's mind.

Adele nodded. "She said that if Josephine continued the way she was acting, she was leaving Rowena with no choice. Rowena said something like, 'Of all the tragedies I've had in my life, this feels like the cruellest of all.'"

CHAPTER TWENTY-THREE

"And did Miss Josephine respond?"

Adele nodded. "She said something, but I couldn't make it out. But then," she added with emphasis, "Rowena said something else."

"What?" Somehow, Carr seemed to know what the reply to the question would be before it was given to him.

Adele stared into his eyes. "Rowena said, in no uncertain terms, that she was left with no choice other than to speak to her solicitors. Mr Carr, Rowena was going to disinherit Josephine Kettering altogether."

Chapter Twenty-Four

As the morning began to drift into the afternoon, Josephine found herself increasingly desperate for fresh air and solitude. The house had become almost insufferably claustrophobic. It seemed to her that whichever room she entered, somebody she had no desire to speak to was already in there. It might be a couple of policemen, either detectives or uniformed officers, or just possibly a combination of both, or it was a member of the household, all of whom now seemed to her to have morphed into figures of suspicion. Before the events of the previous night, she would never have taken any of them as being capable of murder, but it was as if the fact of that terrible and uniquely wicked crime had been able somehow to contort their expressions into masks of malevolence, or at least had managed to twist her interpretations of those same expressions into portraits of malice.

Before now, when her fears of murder had only been vague glimpses of her paranoia, she would have put such thoughts down to her imagination. But now, it all seemed frighteningly real. For the first time, Josephine could imagine the bite of the rope around Daphne Clements' neck, the gasps of breath shortened by fear, the sudden darkness of the hood over her eyes, and those final moments of uncertainty before the trap door was released. She could bring to mind the swinging of the legs, the kicking of the feet, as futile as it was degrading, and the sudden, terrifying stillness that would follow it, whose silence would only be broken by that horrifyingly slow rhythm of the creaking of the rope.

Josephine felt a sudden urge to vomit. She looked over the fields, across the vast expanse of green which stretched ahead of her to the Fens and the coast. She looked, too, at the collection of trees that formed the woods that bordered the grounds of Marsden Grange. She tried to remember the times when she must have played in those woods and fields, of how she would have marvelled at the scope and size of them, and how endless the summers here must have seemed. Now, she doubted she would ever want to return to the place. The fields and the Fens seemed desolate, unwelcoming, and wild. The trees showed only their naked branches, like the gnarled fingers of old women pointing at her with cold, unfeeling accusation, and the house itself, which had once seemed so proud and magnificent to her, seemed to have buckled under its own sense of guilt and morbid depression. Nothing was the same, not in the wake of murder. One act of violence and nothing would ever be the same again.

Josephine was conscious of a sudden chill, and she thought it would be as well to return to the house. She had a novel she could try to finish, but she remembered at once that it was a detective story, whose lurid contrivances and deductive extravagances were so far removed from the reality of murder that they could hardly be considered credible or even entertaining. Not for the first time that morning, she felt the curiously infuriating sensation of inactivity of the reality of a murder investigation. She had expected the police to interview the members of the house immediately, and she had waited her turn, but it had not yet arrived. She felt unable to settle, as if giving her statement and answering the official questions put to her would be some sort of exorcism of at least part of the horror of the previous night. But the opportunity had not come, and the delay had only served to intensify her feelings of claustrophobia and suffocation. Josephine thought back to the detective novel on her bedside table, and she doubted that she would ever pick it up again at all.

It was as she turned away from the fields at the back of the grounds that she saw Everett Carr walking towards her. Her instinct was to flee, but she realised that it would be both childish and pointless even to make the attempt. He had not only seen her, but he had waved at her. If she made any attempt to ignore him, it would serve no benefit. She raised her hand in greeting but allowed herself a gentle sigh of apprehension to escape from her lips. It hissed between her teeth like the whistle of a newly boiling kettle.

"I wondered whether you might have come outside for some fresh air, my child," said Carr. He was slightly out of breath, the thin cheeks delicately flushed, and his eyes were narrowed by what Josephine understood as pain. Presumably, she thought, the walk over the lawns had strained his shattered knee, so that his breathlessness was as much in response to that pain as to the natural exertion.

"Yes, indeed," she said, "the house was getting rather stuffy."

Carr was now beside her. "I only wish to help you. You know that, do you not?"

"Of course. And I am so grateful."

But Carr's eyes showed that he was not seeking gratitude. "If I am to help you, I must know the truth."

"The truth about what?" Her confusion seemed genuine. "We know the truth. Daphne killed Mummy because she wanted her gone so that she could marry Daddy. I don't suppose that will happen now. It can't if they hang her."

Carr seemed not to have been listening. "I must know the truth about you, my child."

"About me?"

Carr nodded slowly. "About the argument you had with your mother before dinner last night."

Josephine stared at him, her cheeks flushing slightly, before she looked away swiftly, giving a small snigger of deceit. "Argument? I don't know what you're talking about."

"The truth, dear lady," urged Carr.

"Don't talk to me about truth. Whoever told you I was arguing with Mother is the person who's lying."

Carr paused for a moment. "So, there was no threat to disinherit you, possibly because of your involvement with a man?"

Now, the snigger became a shrill laugh of contempt. "What an outrageous accusation! Whoever told you such a thing?"

"Is it true?" Carr's voice was gentle.

Josephine glared at him, her eyes brimming with tears, but behind the sadness, there was the unmistakable stain of fear. "I thought you were my friend. You pretend to be so nice, so kind, but all you want to do is pry into private matters and intrude into other people's grief. I think it's horrible. Worse, I think it is wicked."

Carr could not claim to be unaffected by the accusation and, not for the first time, he wondered why he felt this compulsion to interfere in police business. Was it nothing more than an intrusion, as Josephine Kettering said, or was it that long-suspected psychological quest for atonement for surviving the attempt on his life that had killed his beloved Miranda? If so, did his selfish desire for retribution entitle him to interfere in other people's lives? Was his guilt at his survival of death any justification for these investigations into the deaths of others? He wondered whether he would ever know the answer and, suddenly, he was aware of a profound sadness swelling up inside him.

"I have no wish to cause you pain," he said, "but the truth must be told."

Josephine's eyes retained their terrified sadness. "So you keep saying."

"You have not yet denied it, my child." He waited for some response, but it was not to come. "May I tell you something, Miss Kettering? Your mother's room had been ransacked. Now, I learn that you may have been told that your mother was changing her will against your favour. You will forgive me if I treat those two matters as being cause and effect."

"It's a lie."

"You were seen on the landing outside your mother's room."

"By whom?"

Carr doubted that telling her it had been Daphne Clements would have garnered any favour or produced any result. "Are both these pieces of information—seeing you on the landing and the argument about your mother's will—false?"

Josephine shook her head in confusion. "What is all this supposed to achieve, Mr Carr?"

"I simply seek the truth."

"Who told you I was on the landing?"

Now, unless Carr wished to engage in circular arguments, there seemed no way of avoiding the answer. "Miss Clements."

"Daphne! A suspected murderess? If you think you can take her word for anything, Mr Carr, perhaps you're not the judge of character I took you to be."

This time, the words did not sting. Instead, the shrill but evasive reaction convinced him that Miss Clements had been telling the truth. "And is Miss Mills also a suspected murderess, my child, or can I take her word as the truth?"

"What's Adele got to do with it?"

"Miss Clements saw you on the landing, but it was Miss Mills who overheard your argument with your mother. Should I not believe either of them?"

"Adele is nothing but a common tart," snapped Josephine. "She used to be a dancer in a nightclub, did you know that? And I don't mean she was foxtrotting in a ball gown like Ginger Rogers."

The implication did not shock Carr, but it saddened him, as did the petulant malice with which the words had been spoken. "Does that make her a liar, Miss Kettering?"

"I would have thought it made her less than reliable."

Carr inhaled the cool afternoon air with some relish. It had a strangely cleansing effect. "Why would both these women tell lies about you?"

"I don't know. For that matter," Josephine added, looking into his eyes, "why would you believe such women so easily over me? A murderess and a burlesque dancer?"

It was clear to Carr that this crude but condescending unpleasantness was a continued attempt to evade the purpose of his questions and to deflect his suspicions away from her, and he could perhaps understand her reasons for doing so, but he found her attitude disappointingly and sadly distasteful. He had begun to wish that he had never started the discussion at all, although he knew that it would have been not only inevitable but necessary to be undertaken at some point. And his feelings could hardly have been expected to change on account of any delay. Whenever the conversation was had, she would have said the words, used the tone of voice, and burdened his conscience with this same sense of sadness and disgust.

"It may not be certain that Miss Clements is a killer," he said. "There are other possibilities, as you have always suspected."

"But we saw her, holding the needle, and we heard what she said."

Carr nodded slowly. "What we see and hear are not always the truth, my child. Your father's relationship with Miss Clements and your mother's hostility towards it were common knowledge. Someone with reasons of their own to harm your mother might have used them as camouflage."

"It seems rather theatrical."

Carr smiled softly. "Perhaps it does."

"Well, if it's Adele putting these ideas about me into your head, perhaps she also used Daphne and my father as camouflage, as you put it." Josephine seemed pleased with the idea. "Yes, suppose she did want to kill my mother and blame Daphne for it, then throwing suspicion on me might be a sort of safety net, in case her original plan went wrong."

"But it didn't go wrong," argued Carr. "Miss Clements was arrested, after all, and Miss Mills only told me about hearing your argument with your mother after that arrest."

Josephine bit her lower lip. "Oh yes, I see."

Carr noted with some satisfaction that she raised no further objection to the references to her being seen on the landing or the argument with Rowena. His casual deflection of her attention had served its purpose, and he took her omission as evidence that what Adele Mills and Daphne Clements had told him was true. Josephine had argued about her disinheritance with her mother, and she had been outside her mother's room on the landing. He felt reasonably confident, therefore, that it had been she who had searched Rowena's room, looking for evidence of any change of Rowena's will or any intention of it. Had she found any, he wondered. Before he could debate with himself whether asking the question would be beneficial, she was speaking again.

"There's someone who nobody would suspect of killing Mummy, but I wonder whether she did." Josephine was staring at him, her eyes filled with some sort of sudden realisation. "I didn't give it any thought before, because I'd taken it for granted that Daphne killed Mummy, but then you started throwing accusations around and put the idea that Daphne might have been framed in my head."

"Who do you mean, my child?" asked Carr.

"Tilly Royce."

Of all the names she might have said, this was not one Carr had anticipated. He was visibly taken aback, and he was unable to disguise the fact. "What makes you say so, dear lady?"

"Yesterday, before everyone arrived, I saw Tilly in the library, staring up at the portrait of Mummy as Lady Macbeth." Josephine caught her breath and put a hand to her mouth. "It must have been Tilly who slashed it."

Carr was growing unusually impatient. "Why? Because you saw her staring at it?"

"No, no," said Josephine, looking at him as if he were some sort of idiot, "because of what she said when I passed the open door. She was staring up at the portrait, and I heard her very clearly, utter the word *bitch*."

Carr did not reply, and for a moment Josephine wondered if the use of the word had offended him. He stared ahead of himself for a long moment, the eyes flickering with fascination and the luxurious moustache twitching in deep concentration. "Did she shout the word, or whisper it under her breath?"

Josephine needed no time to think. "She hissed it, through gritted teeth. It was spoken with hatred, Mr Carr."

"But I understood Miss Royce to be a very close friend of your mother's."

Josephine shrugged. "I can only tell you what I heard, Mr Carr. Or are you going to disbelieve me again?"

Carr bowed, but the remark had irritated him. "You think that Miss Royce killed your mother and violated the painting?"

"I don't know, but it seems possible. Wouldn't it make sense? For whatever reason, she and Mummy have a disagreement over something,

Tilly is in a rage, she kills Mummy, slashes the portrait, and makes it look as if Daphne was responsible."

"Do you have any idea what this possible disagreement between your mother and Miss Royce might be?"

"No."

"Did you know that Miss Royce was a nurse during the war?"

"No. Who told you that?"

"Your father."

"Mummy never mentioned it. But it would mean she'd be able to get her hands on morphine, wouldn't it?"

And Carr, with the briefest of smiles forming on his lips, had no option other than to concede that it would.

Chapter Twenty-Five

I t was by pure coincidence that Carr met Tilly Royce on the driveway. He supposed that, like Josephine Kettering, she had begun to feel stifled by the atmosphere of the house and now craved fresh air and a change of scenery. Police orders would have prevented any lengthy journey, leaving the extensive grounds of the estate as the only viable option for escape. Carr blamed neither woman for their sense of entrapment, which seemed to him to be both natural and understandable. When ordinary lives were disrupted by extraordinary circumstances, it was forgivable that some of the people affected might come to experience a desire to flee.

He approached her as quickly as he was able and called her name. She turned to face him, startled by the voice, and he was struck at once by the proud nobility of her features. It was only when he was standing in front of her that he realised that previously he had taken very little notice of her. He had glanced at her briefly during cocktails and across the dinner table, but he had taken no particular notice of her. Now, he found himself confronted with an almost patrician face, emphasised by the arched and aristocratic eyebrows which led to the long, sloping nose. The eyes, almost as dark as Carr's, were shaped like almonds, but the lids seemed to hang heavily over them so that they appeared permanently half-closed in casual but seductive arrogance. The lips were full but parted slightly, and a glimpse of regular, pearl-coloured teeth could be caught. The hair was as dark as the eyes, cut short and curled, and the black, wide-legged trousers and jacket, worn over a white silk blouse with a brooch at the neck, gave her a touch of professional elegance.

Carr bowed with similar grace. "You are taking a tour of the grounds, perhaps?"

"Yes," said Tilly. "Just to get away from this place, if nothing else."

"I wonder if I might join you."

She eyed him cautiously. "You've been out already, surely."

He smiled warmly. "Quite so, but my walk was a solitary one."

If she detected the lie, she did not say so. "Then, please, do come along. I should like the company." And if he detected that lie, he was likewise too polite to express it.

They walked slowly, partly on account of Carr's leg, and partly to enjoy the freshness of the air. Tilly was gracious enough not to enquire about the cause of his lameness, and Carr was anxious not to thank her for accommodating his speed, lest it encourage such an enquiry. There were occasions when he felt able to talk about the incident and the tragedy surrounding it, but this was not one of them. His moods on the subject were changeable: sometimes philosophical and accepting of it, sometimes saddened and outraged by it. Recently, the latter had dominated.

"I'm very sorry about Mrs Kettering," Carr said. "I know you and she were close friends."

Tilly felt a sudden sadness slam into her chest. It was as if the fact of Rowena's death hit her, with the force of a speeding train, only when it was spoken aloud to her. Until then, she could have almost convinced herself that it was unreal, that it hadn't happened at all, that it was part of a story she never wanted to finish reading. Carr's words somehow seemed to strip her of that comforting distance from reality. She had the immediate urge to weep and, strangely, to vomit, but she managed to retain control of herself.

"We were close," she admitted. "I was perhaps closer to her than she was to me."

"You have been friends for a number of years, I think."

"Several, yes. She asked me to be her companion as if she were one of those old dowagers in romantic novels."

"But you were not a companion of that type?"

Tilly scoffed. "Lord, no. I've never been a servant to anybody, Mr Carr, but I have no family and very few friends. Rowena and I were good company for each other, so I agreed. It was only ever going to be temporary, but we never really found a natural point to end it. Now, of course, it has been ended for us."

"And, again, I offer my condolences." Carr bowed. "Forgive me for saying so, but she seemed to me to be a lady who upset people very easily."

Tilly laughed, a coarse and curt bark of grim humour. "She made enemies more easily than she made friends, that's true, God knows. She wasn't an easy woman to like. Does saying so make me a bad person, now that she is dead?"

Carr needed no time to consider the question. "Not in the least. It makes you honest. Liking someone, caring for someone, being close to someone means all the more if we can accept their vices as well as their virtues."

"I've never thought of it like that," said Tilly with a doubtful shrug. Almost immediately, she thought about her drunken sadist of a father. She supposed that nobody, however wicked, was entirely without redemption, but Tilly had never been conscious of any virtue in him, and the notion of accepting or forgiving his many vices for the sake of his considerably fewer virtues made her feel physically sick.

"Did you and Mrs Kettering ever have disagreements?" asked Carr.

Tilly laughed again, the same curt bark. "As I say, she was a very difficult woman in many ways. You had to know how to handle her. The theatrical ego, for example. One had to know when to massage it, when to ignore it, and when to put it back into its kennel. Too many people failed to learn the lesson."

"But you did, dear lady?"

"Passed the test with flying colours," said Tilly, smiling. "Our arguments never lasted for very long."

"You never bore any sort of grudge?"

The question grated on her nerves, like a fork across a china plate. "What are you trying to suggest, Mr Carr? That I killed Rowena?"

He gazed into her eyes. "Did you have reason to, dear lady?"

"No." The answer was definite, but it sounded no less hollow for that certainty.

"When was the last time you did have one of these arguments?"

"Is that any of your business?"

He shook his head. "No, but I see no harm in talking about it. We can change the subject, of course, if you prefer."

Tilly smiled. "Doing that would breed suspicion, I suppose, so best to get everything out in the open and be thought of as honest. What a manipulative little devil you are, Mr Carr."

He was not offended by the remark, but did not smile back at her. "I do not wish to make an enemy of you, Miss Royce."

The smile grew warmer. "You haven't, don't worry. One doesn't like to be cross-examined, although I suppose one will have to get used to it. The police won't politely suggest changing the subject, I expect."

Now, Carr did smile. "Of that, I think you can be assured, dear lady."

"I'll tell you what I shall tell them. Rowena and I had a little disagreement only a couple of days ago. About Daphne Clements, as a matter of fact. Rowena got it into her head that she wasn't going to come to Longhampton at all this weekend because Ivor had gone back on his word and invited Daphne, even though he'd given a solemn oath to Rowena that he wouldn't. Not that a solemn oath would mean anything to Ivor. Then, he changed his mind completely and told Rowena so, in such a manner that he gave her no choice other than to accept it."

"How was it that you came to quarrel about it?" asked Carr. "Was the dispute not a matter for Mr and Mrs Kettering?"

"Yes, but how Rowena dealt with it was what angered me. She was furious, as you might expect. Her revenge was to refuse outright to come. She thought it would make Ivor look foolish." Tilly snorted. "I told her that all it would do would be to make her look afraid."

"And so, you changed her mind?"

She nodded her head, but the sadness had already risen in her eyes. "I wish I hadn't now."

Carr looked across to her. "As far as you and Mrs Kettering were concerned, that was an end of the matter?"

Tilly frowned. "What is it you're driving at, Mr Carr?"

He was careful not to exaggerate his embarrassment. "You have caught me red-handed, dear lady. It seems rather foolish to say it not, but you have been so candid with me that I am obliged to return the kindness. I was thinking of the damaged portrait of Mrs Kettering. You have heard about it?"

"A nasty bit of spite, and quite unnecessary. The painting may not have been by one of the Masters, but it was efficiently done, and Rowena was proud of it."

"You did not deface it yourself, then?"

Tilly stopped walking and glared at him. "Absolutely not. Do you have reason to think so? The idea is as ludicrous as it is offensive."

Carr gave only a small shrug of his shoulders. "Dear lady, I am only trying to make sense of so many small details that puzzle me. One of which is the fact that you were seen staring up at the portrait only yesterday, and you were heard to refer to Mrs Kettering in rather an unpleasant fashion."

Tilly laughed, but her cheeks flushed slightly. "Whoever told you that?"

"Is it true?"

"No. Even if Rowena and I did fall out sometimes, it was never enough to make me want to slice paintings or poison her. If anyone is saying otherwise, or trying to imply it, they'd better make sure I don't hear them. There are more people in this house with better reasons to hate Rowena and slash a painting of her than me."

"Do you have any specific candidate, dear lady?"

"A few."

"Daphne Clements, for example?" Carr's eyes were darkly provocative.

Tilly picked a small branch from one of the trees and began playing with the leaves. "You know, it would be funny if it wasn't so tragic. Everybody is saying how much Rowena and Daphne hated each other, but it isn't true. Not entirely."

"Indeed?" Carr's voice was bland, devoid of the sudden confusion and fascination which swept across his mind.

"Rowena fluctuated. Sometimes, she hated Daphne for ruining her marriage, sometimes it was Ivor she hated, not Daphne. She wasn't entirely consistent."

"But how did she really feel, would you say?"

"If Ivor had chucked Daphne for good and gone back to Rowena, she'd have welcomed him with open arms and the affair would never have been spoken of again."

Carr nodded. He had not known Rowena Kettering at all but what little he had seen of her would have convinced him that she would have acted in such a fashion, so that he had no hesitation in accepting Tilly's answer as the truth.

"A week or so ago, Ivor and Rowena had tea with Daphne, at her invitation," Tilly was saying, "and I am sure Rowena only accepted to see if she could like the woman."

"But why should she do so, when Miss Clements was threatening to ruin Mrs Kettering's marriage?"

Tilly shrugged. "I think she felt that if she was going to lose Ivor, then it would soften the blow if it was for someone she could respect. She might even have thought that if Daphne could like her, it might dissuade her from pursuing Ivor."

Carr thought for a moment. "Was Mrs Kettering capable of such a manipulation?"

"I should say so, and the same idea works in reverse."

"I do not follow."

"It's equally possible that Daphne was biding her time, being nice to Rowena in the hope that she would have seen how happy and in love Daphne and Ivor were, so grant them a divorce."

"Of the two scenarios, Miss Royce, which do you say has the more psychological accuracy?"

Tilly smiled. "I'm sure Rowena would have manipulated Daphne far more easily than the other way around."

Again, Carr nodded his agreement. "Quite so."

They walked in silence for a few moments, each alone with their thoughts, and the gentle breeze bringing with it the smell of fauna and foliage. Carr began to wonder about the peacefulness of the countryside, its stillness and its soothing calm, so absolute that it could almost seduce even a man of his urban proclivities. But no amount of rural tranquillity could erase the darkness of the violence that had taken place at the heart of this façade of pastoral peace.

"Miss Clements denies committing murder," said Carr.

"She would, of course."

"Nevertheless, there are other people who might have benefitted from Mrs Kettering's death."

"Who?"

Carr, whose mind had returned to the arsenic in Rowena's bedside glass of water, merely shrugged. "It is a sad fact of life, dear lady, that death benefits more than one person."

Tilly shook her head. "But surely in this case, it is obvious what happened last night."

"There are other matters to consider."

"I can't see what. I would have thought that there were enough witnesses to put the matter beyond all doubt, yourself included. What else can the police be considering? If the police can't see what is perfectly clear to everyone else, perhaps they should be told that this wasn't the first time Daphne tried to kill Rowena."

For a moment, it seemed to Carr as if time itself had stopped. It was as if there was nothing in the world for him now except Tilly Royce and the words she had spoken, which echoed in his mind like church bells over the silence of a sleeping valley. He was conscious now of a dull ache in his fingers, and he realised that his grip had tightened around the handle of his cane, but he had not been aware of the impulsive reaction to her words, any more than he had known that the breath was held in his lungs until they, too, began to burn in protest. "You will have to explain, dear lady."

"What's to explain? Daphne has attempted to murder Rowena before, but she failed."

"But when was this, dear lady?"

"A few days ago."

"Where?"

"In London. Rowena was walking through Holland Park back to the house in Campden Hill Square, when a car came out of nowhere, driving all over the road, according to Rowena, but heading for her. She had to throw herself to the ground to avoid it."

"Was she badly hurt?"

Tilly shook her head. "She was shaken, of course, and nobody could blame her for that. Apart from some cuts and grazes, caused when she threw herself to safety, and tears to her coat and stockings, she was uninjured, I'm happy to say. It was her pride which suffered the most."

"And she was convinced that the car was heading for her?"

Tilly nodded. "Absolutely certain. She was disorientated, I think, because she said it came in the wrong direction. She was shaken by the whole incident, as you can imagine, so her immediate recollection was a little garbled, but she was adamant that the car drove at her deliberately and at great speed."

"Most interesting," murmured Carr. "Did she see the driver?"

"No, although now it seems obvious that it was Daphne."

Carr did not seem inclined to argue the point. "Did Mrs Kettering confront Miss Clements about the incident?"

"Not that I know of."

"But she told her husband."

Tilly shrugged. "Presumably so, yes."

"Did Mrs Kettering report it to the police?"

Now, the shake of the head was vehement. "She had a couple of stiff drinks, smoked like a chimney for half an hour, and had a bath. After that, she said she felt like a new woman and didn't want to relive the incident, especially not multiple times to multiple police officers. Her words, Mr Carr, not mine," Tilly added with a smile.

"And after this incident," said Carr delicately, "there was nothing else?"

"Not until last night." Tilly looked into his eyes, and he saw a fit of profound anger as well as an acute sadness, and it seemed to him that when she spoke, those confused and suppressed emotions were equally evident in her voice as in her stare. "Except this time, Mr Carr, Daphne Clements was a damned sight more successful than she had been in Holland Park."

Chapter Twenty-Six

Lewis Davenport checked through the bundle of documents that Ivor Kettering had passed to him, his long fingers flicking over the pages, and his keen, eager eyes ensuring that each memorandum and letter had the minister's signature in the appropriate place. From across the study desk, Ivor watched the younger man as he worked, the lips moving almost imperceptibly in concentration as if he were compelled to mouth the words contained in each document. It was a curious habit, one which Ivor had often noticed, but it had never struck him before how irritating he found it. It was a foolishly childish habit, as if his pubescent self had been unable to read any text without forming the words silently with his lips, and the custom had continued into adulthood. Now, as if only seeing it clearly for the first time, Ivor found it infuriating. He rose from the desk and turned to the window.

"Is everything in order?"

Lewis did not reply immediately, preferring to complete his task before giving any definite report. At last, he shuffled the papers back into the neat pile they had been when Ivor passed them to him, and he nodded. "Yes, sir. I shall arrange to have them sent to the House first thing on Monday."

"Good. And thank you." The expression of gratitude was as perfunctory as it was official. It was not genuine appreciation, but an obligatory conclusion to the morning's business.

Lewis placed the papers into his briefcase and rose from his chair. "Is there anything else, sir?"

Ivor turned to him. "Do I sense a rebuke, Lewis?"

"Sir?"

"Perhaps you think doing parliamentary work in the wake of the disaster which has taken place in this house is distasteful."

Even if he had, Lewis would not have said so. "Not at all, sir."

"I know what you're thinking, Lewis." Ivor looked back out of the study window. "You're thinking that everything we've done this morning could have waited until next week. I'm well aware of it. The truth is, Lewis, I wanted a distraction from everything that is happening."

This sudden desire to confide, the need to explain, disconcerted Lewis. "I can understand that, sir."

"Have the police questioned you yet?"

"Not yet."

"Will you have anything to tell them when they do?" Ivor looked over his shoulder.

Was it Lewis' imagination, a product of his guilty conscience, which saw the glimmer of accusation in Ivor's eyes? Lewis became aware suddenly of a dryness in his throat. "Not very much at all, I don't imagine, sir."

"Do you think Daphne killed my wife, Lewis?"

In other circumstances, the question would not have derailed Lewis Davenport, for all its sudden directness, but he was already so disorientated by this spring of guilt which had welled up inside him that he struggled initially to provide any answer. "I find it difficult to reach any other conclusion, sir."

It seemed for a moment as though Ivor would retaliate with some sort of outburst of protest. The eyes behind the spectacle lenses glared and the lips pursed tightly, as if fighting to contain that same burst of retaliation which, as it turned out, never came. Instead, Ivor looked back out of the window and shook his head.

"I cannot believe it," he said. "There must be something else behind all this. There simply must be."

"Someone else with a reason to kill Mrs Kettering, you mean?"

"That would be logical, wouldn't it, assuming Daphne is innocent?"

"Yes, no doubt. But who?" Lewis leaned over the desk. "What you're suggesting, sir, is that someone in this house is a killer, and, forgive me, that would have to include members of your own family."

Ivor could hardly be unaware of the fact, and Lewis did not expect him to be ignorant of it. The minister turned away from the window and sat back down at his desk. He latticed his fingers across his stomach and looked up into his secretary's slim, eager face.

"I'm aware of that, Lewis," he said. "But it must also, by necessity, include others who are not members of my family."

Suddenly, Lewis felt the prickle of guilty paranoia menace the back of his neck. "Do you have any suspicions, sir?"

Ivor held his gaze. "Do you?"

"I haven't given it any thought," lied Lewis. "The matter seemed so obvious."

"And is that what you'll tell the police?"

"Of course, unless you wish me to say something else."

There was a long, silent intake of breath, betrayed only by the rising of Ivor's stomach and shoulders. They fell silently again as the breath was exhaled. "You must tell the truth, as you see it, Lewis. As we all must."

"I agree, and I intend to do so," Lewis lied again. "Will that be all, sir?"

Ivor nodded, giving a word of thanks and a wave of dismissal. Not ungratefully, Lewis took the briefcase and walked out of the room. He was barely halfway across the hall when he saw Everett Carr.

"Good afternoon, Mr Davenport," said Carr, "I wonder if I might have a word."

"I was just doing some parliamentary work with Mr Kettering," Lewis said, not quite understanding why he felt the need to explain himself.

Carr nodded gently and looked over to the study door with definite empathy in those dark eyes.

"Mr Kettering does well to keep his mind occupied," he said. "The situation cannot be easy for him and it will help if he is able to use his work as a distraction."

Lewis nodded. "I rather fancy that was his idea."

Carr smiled. "He must have much to consider, and he must be grateful for your assistance as his secretary."

"I do as much as I can to help him."

"A loyal employee, yes?"

"I like to think so," replied Lewis, suddenly wondering what Carr's motivations were. The smile was in place amid the luxurious moustache and Imperial beard, but there was something about the dark eyes which perturbed Lewis, as if they were probing him for some hidden secret or watching out for the one detail in his expression which would give some clue to it.

"Yes, that would explain it," said Carr, almost to himself.

"Explain what?"

Carr stared at Lewis as if surprised that the question was necessary. Almost immediately, he stammered a word of apology and shook his head as if in frustration at himself, and he tutted loudly in self-reproach. Lewis waited for a reply, largely fooled by Carr's frivolous performance and only slightly suspicious of it. When he spoke, Carr's voice was casual, almost indifferently genial.

"Well, the note, of course."

"Note?"

"The one you sent to Daphne Clements." Carr nodded, as if this all now explained the matter. "Such loyalty, my boy, that Mr Kettering is lucky to have you."

But Lewis only stared at him. "I'm sorry, Mr Carr, but I don't know what you're talking about. What note?"

Carr's eyes were now widened with theatrical alarm. "Miss Clements swears that you sent her a note, explaining that Mr Kettering was in danger of some scandal or other and that you needed to speak to her about it. That is why she was in the library, she says, because your note asked her to go there to meet you."

Lewis stared, in confusion as much as in disbelief. "But it isn't true. It's a complete fantasy."

"There is no possibility of any scandal surrounding Mr Kettering's political career?"

"None."

"You deny writing any such note?"

"Absolutely, although I would very much like to know who did write it. Has Miss Clements shown you this note?"

"No, she destroyed it."

"Very convenient," said Lewis, raising an eyebrow. "Do the police believe her story?"

"I rather suspect not." Carr smiled gently. "It is clever, though, is it not?"

"Clever?"

"If the note is a forgery," said Carr, "using your name was ingenious. As you said, you are a loyal employee, and whoever wrote that note knew it. It explains why your name was used. It would be perfectly natural for you to wish to protect Mr Kettering from any scandal, and equally natural for Miss Clements to believe what the note told her. Using your name added a truth to what you now suggest is a lie."

"Yes, I see that," said Lewis.

"Assuming, of course," said Carr judiciously, "that it was written at all."

Lewis nodded, allowing himself a small smile. "Yes, there's no guarantee it exists, and we only have a suspected murderess' word for it."

Carr offered no reply. "Let us assume for the moment that it did exist, and that its reference to a scandal concerning Mr Kettering was true, who would know about such a scandal apart from yourself?"

"Nobody," said Lewis. "Mr Kettering was very careful with whom he spoke about government matters."

"Would he have told his wife about any possible scandal, for example?"

"I very much doubt it."

"His children?"

"Even less likely." Lewis gave a small, almost sneering grin.

"But if this note is genuine, and Miss Clements is not lying, then someone must have written it. If not you, then who could it be?"

Lewis' eyes narrowed momentarily, as if in concentration. "Nobody, which perhaps is all the more reason to assume it never existed."

Carr nodded slowly. "Forgive me, but purely for the sake of argument, if the note was genuine, what might this scandal be to which it referred?"

"I cannot imagine." Lewis said the words with conviction.

"Mr Kettering is in no danger politically?"

"None at all."

Carr held his gaze, but Lewis offered no further response. "He is not, for example, being blackmailed?"

Lewis laughed, but it was a spontaneous and involuntary rasp of surprised humour. "Blackmailed? About what?"

Carr's mind had turned back to the recent past, to the argument he had overheard between Rowena and Lewis, and to her final words, which had concluded it: *a nasty little blackmailer.* "Perhaps by whom would be a better question, Mr Davenport. That might tell us about what."

"I'm afraid I don't understand. Ivor isn't being blackmailed about anything. If he were, I'd know about it."

"And Mrs Kettering? Have you ever heard anything which might suggest to you that she was being blackmailed?"

"No, never."

Carr watched Lewis carefully for a long moment, but no more was volunteered and no more was sought. At last, Carr raised his eyebrows and smiled warmly. "You must forgive me, Mr Davenport. I am a man with a tendency to enquire, I mean no harm by it."

"Think nothing of it, but I can assure you that Ivor wasn't being blackmailed about any scandal, and this note, if it exists, didn't come from me."

"If there is no possibility of any political danger to Mr Kettering, the note makes no sense, would you not agree?"

Lewis smiled. "I think I would have to, Mr Carr."

Carr bowed politely. "Then that is the fact we must face. There is no proof of any scandal and there is no proof of the existence of this note. Only the word, as you say, my boy," he added deliberately, "of a suspected murderess."

Carr's smile remained in place, and the farewell bow which he gave was fastidiously courteous. As Lewis watched him walk away, noticing almost for the first time the painful limp, he felt there was something that had been left unsaid, and he called back to Carr with a hesitant but polite urgency. The little man stopped and turned around, the brows raised in expectation and the moustache and Imperial beard bristling with civil enquiry.

"Is there any doubt about Miss Clements' guilt?" asked Lewis.

If Carr thought it was a curious question, he did not express it. "What makes you ask such a question?"

Lewis looked back to the study door. "I was in no doubt at all until Mr Kettering said something just now."

"And what was that?"

"He asked whether I thought Miss Clements killed his wife. I answered as tactfully as I could, saying that the facts seemed to speak for themselves, but he said that there might be other people who wished to see his wife dead."

Carr's brow creased with fascination. "Did he say whom he might suspect?"

Lewis shook his head. "I told him that what he was saying would have to include his own family, and he accepted as much, but he said that there were others who would have to be considered." He smiled, a nervous laugh escaping from behind the stretched lips. "He seemed to be accusing me."

Carr shared the smile, but his eyes remained gently hostile. "Would it be offensive to ask what you were doing in the moments before the murder was discovered?"

"I was in my room. I had gone over some official papers, and I had just got into bed when I heard all the noise. I rushed downstairs with everybody else."

Carr pointed a mocking finger at him. "That is no alibi, my boy."

Lewis laughed, with more assurance this time. "No, I suppose it isn't! But I'm afraid it is a case of no alibi and no motive."

Carr's smile widened, still benign, but his eyes were dark, and his mind was thinking only of blackmail. "Did you have the impression that Mr Kettering might know who the killer was?"

Lewis shook his head. "Not so much that, but he is certainly thinking that the police have it wrong. I can't see it myself, but I'm well aware of Mr Kettering's intelligence and instincts. He isn't often wrong about important matters. It has set me thinking, that's all."

"Tell me, Mr Davenport," said Carr, carefully, "has Mr Kettering ever mentioned to you another attempt on his wife's life?"

Lewis glared in amazement. "Never."

"Has Miss Josephine ever suggested as much?"

"No." Lewis' amazement had turned to confrontation.

Carr smiled warmly. "It is nothing more than a rumour perhaps. If the family has not mentioned it or discussed it with you, it cannot be of any importance."

The flattery, so blatant that it was almost unctuous, nevertheless achieved its aim of deflection. "I do rather think I would have been notified of such an event."

Carr's smile widened. "I am sure of it. But, Mr Davenport, he added conspiratorially, "let us suppose that Miss Clements has been wrongly accused, who would you say the real killer is?"

"If anyone in this house could be taken as a killer, I would have to say my money would be on Edwin Jarratt."

Carr was not surprised by the answer. "A doctor is trained to save life, Mr Davenport, not to take it."

Lewis scoffed. "Plenty of doctors turn into killers, Mr Carr, you know that."

Carr nodded, his gaze drifting to the floor. "And what would make you suspect Dr Jarratt?"

"Something Rowena once said. It was Mr Kettering who told me, and I must confess to breaking a confidence in telling you, Mr Carr. Rowena was convinced that Jarratt was a murderer."

So, Carr noted with interest, Lewis Davenport knew about Rowena's suspicions of Jarratt being a killer. "Did she have any proof of it?"

"I doubt it. Otherwise, she would have done something about it, I'm sure." Lewis looked around himself, making sure they were alone. "That's why Rowena refused to let Josephine marry him and, in part at least, it is why

CHAPTER TWENTY-SIX

Josephine despises him, too."

In the moment, however, Carr was less interested in such romantic matters than he was in murder. "Did Mr Kettering tell you who Dr Jarratt was supposed to have killed?"

Lewis shook his head. "No, and I doubt he knows. But you see what I mean, don't you, Mr Carr? If Daphne Clements is innocent, the only other person in this house who could reasonably be considered a suspect is the man who seemingly has been involved in murder already. And that man is Dr Edwin Jarratt."

Chapter Twenty-Seven

Dr Jarratt, sitting alone in the drawing room, knew nothing of this conversation taking place in the hallway, and perhaps it was for the best.

Jarratt had spoken briefly with Josephine, but her attitude towards him had been hostile, and it was clear that she did not want either to speak to him or to hear his words of condolence. He had spoken harshly in return, which he now regretted, but her incivility in the wake of his genuine concern and sympathy had been particularly frustrating. "If you're not able to put aside this unfounded personal animosity towards me, Josephine," he had said, "and recognise a display of simple decency and compassion, then there's more of your mother in you than I realised."

It had been said in anger, but he wondered whether it was entirely unjustified. Perhaps Josephine would never love him as he loved her, and it was becoming increasingly clear that she would only ever despise him, but surely, she could recognise that his sympathy had been genuine and not a cynical ploy to sway her affections in his favour. And if she couldn't, perhaps he didn't want anything to do with her after all.

Apart from this brief and unsatisfactory exchange, Jarratt had spoken to nobody. He had seen Josephine and Carr in the garden, but he had wondered only idly what their discussions might be about. He had heard doors open and close in the hallway, but he had made no enquiry as to who was moving around. He wanted to see and speak to no one. The only company he desired was his own. He needed the silence and the personal seclusion to give himself time to think about the events of the previous night and what his next move should be.

But clarity of thought would not come. Whatever strategy he concocted became lost amid the recollections of Rowena's corpse, the blank stare of the sightless eyes, which had seemed to him to be fixed solely in his direction, a dead glare of accusation and condemnation. His thoughts were clouded by images of Rowena's unnaturally white flesh, the pale patina of death, and the memory of those parted, hanging lips that seemed to scream silently that he was a killer.

He extinguished one cigarette and lit another. The action was mechanical, the movement of an automaton rather than a human being. What he really needed, he told himself, was a drink, but he knew that it was both unwise and reckless, not to say too early. The very act of having a steadying drink would be noticeable, and it could, he reasoned, arouse the very suspicions which he was trying to avoid. The need for a drink would have to wait until it could be satisfied at a more reasonable hour. For now, he would have to content himself with tobacco, resilience, and patience.

He thought about the police investigation. It had been slow so far, almost as if there were no sense of urgency about it. He supposed the arrest of Daphne Clements might have slowed things down. If the police thought they had discovered the killer so quickly and so easily, perhaps the type of murder investigation one might have expected from one's knowledge of detective stories became redundant. Perhaps, after all, he would not be questioned and his resolve would not be tested in the manner he feared. It would be a relief, certainly, if that were the case, but Jarratt was neither so optimistic nor so naïve as to take the matter for granted. And there was the inquest to consider. He would be called as a witness, of that he had no doubt, not only because of his presence at Marsden Grange but also on account of his preliminary examination of the body at the request of Everett Carr. It would not be the first time he had given evidence at an inquest, and there could surely be no doubt about the verdict. It seemed inevitable that the coroner would find that Rowena was the victim of murder at the hands of Daphne Clements.

These thoughts must have consumed him more deeply than he had imagined, since the approach of Everett Carr startled him. He had not heard the door open and close, nor had he heard the uneven rhythm of Carr's limping approach. Instead, he had become aware suddenly of a presence over his shoulder, like an omen announcing its intentions, and the dark shape of Carr had appeared suddenly by his side. Jarratt gasped instinctively, and a mild curse escaped from his lips. He clasped his hand over his heart and stuttered out Carr's name, whilst Carr, with his usual and inherent politeness, stammered out a simultaneous apology.

"I didn't hear you come in," said Jarratt. "I was lost in thought, I'm so sorry."

"No apologies from you, doctor, please," said Carr, resting his hand on Jarratt's shoulder. "The fault is entirely mine, and you must forgive me for intruding into your peace."

"I'm afraid there's precious little chance of peace now," said Jarratt. This, at least, was something honest he could say.

Carr sat down beside him. "I wanted to thank you for your assistance last night, doctor. I hope you didn't mind my calling on you like that."

"Not at all, glad to help."

"Have the police spoken to you?" Carr watched Jarratt shake his head. "I wondered if they had asked you about your movements last night."

Jarratt smoked heavily. "Not yet. I suppose it is only a matter of time. As a matter of fact, there isn't very much to tell. I couldn't sleep. The conversation at dinner had hardly been amicable, after all, and it certainly wasn't conducive to good digestion. I've never been very good at lying awake in bed, so I got up and went downstairs. I thought some fresh air and exercise might help me to sleep, so I nipped out of the front door and wandered up and down the terrace."

"What time was that?"

"Around half past midnight."

"Did you hear or see anything while you were walking on the terrace?"

"Only a fox in the fields beyond the house. I appreciate that isn't what you mean, though, Mr Carr. No, I didn't see anything out of the ordinary."

For a reason which he could not define, Carr expected more to be said, and when Jarratt did not comply, Carr became suddenly acutely aware of the silence of the room. With the single exception of the delicate ticking of a clock in the distance, there was no noise, but the stillness seemed oddly unnatural, and the quiet was more oppressive than soothing.

It was Jarratt who broke the silence. "Have you seen Josephine today?"

Carr nodded slowly. "You care for her deeply."

"I'm in love with her." The confession was too obvious to be startling, but its frankness was still capable of having an effect. "Rowena never approved of me, of course. I doubt she would have considered anybody good enough for Josephine."

And here, Carr thought, was the opening for which he had been searching. He smiled warmly. "I would have thought a successful doctor was a more than suitable match for any woman's daughter."

Jarratt gave a short, vaguely cruel laugh. "So would anybody, I should say. As a suitor, I don't think I'm too shabby, to be brutally honest about it. I have a successful gynaecological practice in Harley Street, I'm not badly off financially, and anybody can see how I feel about Josephine. But Rowena was set against me from the start."

Knowing the answer, in part at least, Carr was obliged to feign confusion. "Why was that, do you suppose?"

But Jarratt was not so easily fooled. "Don't tell me people haven't been gossiping about me, Mr Carr. Haven't you heard that Rowena Kettering thought I was a murderer?"

Carr bowed slightly. "Perhaps some people have hinted at it, yes."

"Lewis Davenport, no doubt." Jarratt's voice was acidic, and he lit a cigarette as if to banish the taste of bitterness from his mouth. "You'll have gathered that he and I aren't exactly the best of friends."

"He has similar feelings for Miss Josephine, I fancy."

Jarratt snorted. "He says so. I rather doubt it myself. Much more likely that he's looking after his own interests."

"I'm not sure I understand."

Jarratt inhaled deeply on the cigarette, but it did nothing to vanquish the taste of resentment. "He's Ivor's little lapdog, you see. Davenport is an ambitious little runt. Much easier, I'd say, to climb the political ladder if one's senior minister is also one's father-in-law. Or do you think I am just a jealous and paranoid rival in love?"

Carr doubted it was wise to offer any direct answer to the question. Instead, his mind had turned back to Lewis Davenport and the question of blackmail. "Perhaps he is not as favoured as you imagine."

Jarratt, it seemed, was too consumed by his dislike to notice the comment. "Davenport is a snake. He'd do anything to discredit me, even if it meant pandering to Rowena's insane delusions about me."

Carr gently stroked the silver handle of his cane. "What cause did she have to suspect you of such terrible things?"

Jarratt looked across at him. "That's just the point, Mr Carr. She had no reason to think it. And, for what it's worth, I'm not guilty of it, not that anyone seems to care about that."

"She must have felt she had some basis for saying it," insisted Carr gently.

Jarratt shook his head. "She was delusional. Rowena was a complicated woman, Mr Carr. It wasn't enough for her to say that she simply didn't like me. There would have to be some reason for it, even if it was a fabricated one. And, of course, it would have to be something dramatic. Nothing less would suit Rowena."

"So, she dreamed up this accusation of murder?" Carr shook his head. "It seems highly unlikely."

"Unlikely and irrational, but that was Rowena Kettering. In one of our many arguments, I asked her what right she had to be so pious. I asked if she'd never done anything she was ashamed of."

"And what was her reaction?"

"She looked at me as if I were the Devil incarnate. Of course, all this is a gift to someone like Lewis Davenport, who would inevitably use it for his own advantage." Jarratt rose to his feet. "I'm aware of how bitter I sound, Mr Carr, but at least I'm honest enough to admit it. As I said earlier, I didn't like Rowena, but one would never wish something like this to happen to anybody."

He had walked to the window and was staring now out over the lawns.

Carr remained seated, one hand resting on the silver handle of his cane, the other gently massaging the shattered knee. Without quite knowing why, he had the sensation that he was being deceived about something that he could not identify. It was as if something about Jarratt's demeanour, his words, his attitude, and his inferences sounded hollow, like a false panel in a wall or a flat key in a badly tuned piano. But the nature of the deception was evasive, and it remained beyond the reach of Carr's perception. He found it profoundly frustrating.

Jarratt was still talking. "I must confess, I would never have thought Daphne Clements was capable of doing such a thing."

"Do you know her well?"

Jarratt laughed softly. "Not all that well, no. I suppose I have no right to voice any opinion on what she may or may not be capable of."

Carr was not judicial on the point. "But she doesn't strike you as being a murderess?"

"No." Jarratt turned away from the window and looked back at Carr. "That's to say, she didn't strike me as such. Then again, what do they say about still waters?"

"*'Smooth runs the water where the brook is deep,'*" quoted Carr.

Jarratt completed the verse. "*And in his simple show he harbours treason.'*"

"You think Shakespeare's words could describe Daphne Clements?"

"Let me respond to your question with one of my own: do the facts not suggest it?"

Carr smiled. "Perhaps, Dr Jarratt."

Jarratt was surprised by the lack of certainty on Carr's part. He felt a tremor of what he could only imagine was fear pass through him, a sensation that was not entirely unexpected but no less unsettling for that. For a brief moment, he wondered just how much of the truth this dapper little man knew. It could not be much, surely, Jarratt thought, but nevertheless, his instinct told him to be cautious.

"Perhaps all it takes is a motive and the opportunity," he said, "and Daphne had both."

"In the right circumstances, I should think any one of us could be capable of murder," replied Carr solemnly.

Jarratt looked at him closely. "Do you include yourself in that assessment, Mr Carr?"

Carr thought back to that fateful day outside the Old Bailey when it had seemed to rain bullets for a few swift and terrible moments. He saw himself falling to the ground, and he heard Miranda screaming his name before she was sent sprawling across the pavement. He saw the speeding cars, heard the fatal chorus of successive guns, and saw the explosions of light and smoke that accompanied them. He could not see the faces of the men in the cars, but he never could. They were hidden by the shadows and the gunshots, but his imagination always conjured up impressions of snarling malice and violent hatred. It was of these faceless killers who had changed his life forever that Carr now thought.

"Oh yes, Dr Jarratt," he said, "I fear that I could easily commit murder in the correct circumstances."

There was something about the hardening of Carr's eyes which suggested to Jarratt that any enquiry into what those particular circumstances might be would be unwelcome, but the topic seemed not to have come to its natural conclusion. "It certainly looks as if Daphne Clements found her correct circumstances here last night."

"Were you aware of another attempt on Mrs Kettering's life?"

Jarratt frowned. "When?"

"A few days ago."

"Who told you about this?"

But Carr only smiled. "Were you aware of it?"

Jarratt, his eyes wide with what might have been amazement but might also have been confusion, shook his head. "I've never heard anything about it. Josephine certainly hasn't mentioned it to me. She may have told Davenport about it, I suppose." It was clear that the idea, though feasible, was abhorrent, just as the jealousy in his voice appeared to be both malicious and oddly petulant.

"I rather think she didn't," said Carr, casually. "I doubt she knows about it."

Jarratt nodded. "That would make sense. Rowena was so protective of Josephine, and something like that would terrify the girl."

Carr offered no definite agreement. "Can you imagine Miss Clements in a speeding motor car, driving straight for Mrs Kettering? Does that strike you as likely?"

"What are you saying exactly, Mr Carr?" asked Jarratt. "You can't think Daphne is innocent, surely. You were there. You saw what we saw."

Carr nodded slowly. "Oh yes, Dr Jarratt, we all saw the same thing, certainly. My concern is that we didn't see what we thought we did."

Jarratt glared at him. "You do think Daphne is innocent, don't you? But on what evidence exactly? And if she didn't do it, then who did?"

Carr rose slowly and painfully to his feet. "Someone else with motive and opportunity, Dr Jarratt. Someone who had a passing knowledge of morphine and needles. And someone who found themselves in the right set of circumstances at Marsden Grange."

Dr Edwin Jarratt did not reply. There was nothing he felt he could say. He could not deny an indictment which had not been made, and it occurred to him that to refute any allegation which had only been implied might in itself lead to some inference of guilt. And so, he remained silent, smiled only once, and turned his back on Carr to look out of the window once more. Nothing more was said, beyond the polite word of farewell from Carr as he took his leave, but the air remained heavy with the silent suspicion of guilt and the unspoken accusation of murder.

Chapter Twenty-Eight

Inspector Mason did not return to Marsden Grange until the following day. He had not been idle in the interval. There had been much to determine, to discuss, and to report. As it was, however, matters now seemed clear to him. The facts, as they appeared to the inspector, could permit only one interpretation of the case, and it seemed to Mason that the murder of Rowena Kettering was solved. That in itself did not mean that his job was over. There was still the inquest to be held, formal charges to be brought, and final reports to be submitted before the matter could come to trial. Unlike much of the detective fiction he had read, which was minimal, since the inspector found the genre to be both trite and of almost no merit, a case of murder did not end when the guilty party was identified. But that point had been reached, and the second phase of a murder enquiry could soon be set in motion.

Mason found Everett Carr walking in the gardens of Marsden Grange. It struck Mason that if his own demeanour was one of triumph, Carr's attitude seemed to depict directly opposing emotions. For a long moment, he watched Carr walk aimlessly in circles, his head sunk on his breast, and one hand clenched into a fist behind his back whilst the other gripped the familiar cane with an obvious intensity. Mason would have confessed to a curious surprise at Carr's apparent melancholy if he were not already closely acquainted with what he saw as Carr's tendency to seek complex solutions to such matters when more obvious answers were self-evident. When Mason walked across the lawns to greet Carr, therefore, it was without any indication of rebuke or conceit.

"I don't think there can be any doubt about the case now," declared Mason. "The lab has worked hard to get its results to me so quickly, but they are fairly conclusive."

Carr smiled, but his eyes remained fixed on the ground. "Everything is as it appeared, then?"

"Dr Jarratt was fairly accurate in his estimation of the time of death," replied Mason. "Our man puts it at around one o'clock in the morning. He also agrees with Jarratt's guess that death would have occurred within five or ten minutes of injection."

"There was never any doubt about that," said Carr. "I find those five or ten minutes very suggestive, don't you, inspector?"

If he did, Mason did not say so; he seemed not to have heard the question. "There was never any doubt, no, but it helps to have it confirmed. The pathologist also commented on the difficulty in obtaining morphine. It is either prescribed or obtained professionally for that purpose. One doesn't simply walk into a chemist's shop and ask for it."

"That is not proof that Daphne Clements obtained and used it," cautioned Carr. "Dr Jarratt and Tilly Royce both have the professional knowledge and ability to acquire and use morphine."

Mason smiled. "That may be so, but only Daphne Clements' fingerprints were found on the phial and the hypodermic needle."

Carr frowned. "There is no mistake about that?"

"None."

Carr pondered the matter for a long moment before turning the conversation in a different direction. "What about the white powder I found in Mrs Kettering's bedroom?"

"Arsenic, as we thought." Mason frowned. "Curious, I admit. Why would Daphne Clements try to kill Rowena twice?"

Carr smiled. "For that matter, why should anybody try to kill her twice? There seems to me to be a very simple explanation."

"Two poisoners," said Mason, nodding. "Yes, I'd thought of that. But surely the coincidence is too monstrous to accept."

Carr shook his head. "I think not, inspector. In a house where a woman makes many enemies, I think it is entirely within the realms of expectation to assume that more than one person might contemplate murder."

"The arsenic, you mean?"

Carr nodded. "And the attempt on Mrs Kettering's life in Holland Park."

Briefly, Carr explained what Tilly Royce had told him. Mason listened intently but shook his head decisively once Carr had finished. "There's nothing to say that Miss Royce isn't correct. Clements will deny it, of course, but it's as likely that she was behind the wheel as anyone else, more so when you consider everything else."

"And the arsenic?"

"That does suggest a second murderer, I admit, but I still don't see how it makes any difference." As he spoke, Mason counted off the points on his fingers. "Even if someone else did try to poison Rowena Kettering, it wasn't anybody but Daphne Clements who was found standing over the body, and it wasn't anybody else's fingerprints we found on the murder weapon. And Clements certainly had a motive. Not only that, she was witnessed having a quarrel with the dead woman at dinner. Did she not say that she'd have Ivor Kettering for herself over Rowena's dead body? And there are her words to Kettering himself, again witnessed by several people. Including you, Mr Carr," he added with a smile. "I don't see any way out of it."

Carr was frowning heavily. "You make a very good case, inspector."

Mason put away his notebook. "I think it is more a question of the facts speaking for themselves."

"Perhaps," mused Carr.

And here it was, thought Mason, this habit of looking for difficulties even in the most straightforward of cases. He permitted Carr a moment of quiet indulgence, a wry smile creeping across his lips.

"There seems no doubt that the inquest will return a verdict of murder against Daphne Clements," said Carr at last.

"I should think it likely, yes."

"And then the matter will proceed towards trial, imprisonment, and the hangman." Carr spoke frankly, but there was an element of dark regret in the cadence of his voice.

"That's the way of these things," said Mason, "as you know."

"Quite so." Carr looked at him, and Mason saw in the dark eyes a glimmer of despondency. Mason knew Carr was an optimistic man by nature, and it struck him forcibly that the usual good humour made this opposing mournful demeanour all the more disturbing.

Carr's prediction about the inquest proved to be correct. The proceedings, which took place in the centre of Norwich, in the shadow of the city's Norman cathedral, could hardly have been expected to reach any other conclusion. Certainly nothing Everett Carr could say would influence the coroner and the jury to such an extent that their findings and verdict could be any different than it was. Sitting at the back of the assembly, Carr watched in frustration as evidence was given, questions were posed and answered, and medical findings were presented. When he had been called to give his own version of the events of the night of the murder, Carr did so with a calm and polite honesty that betrayed none of his internal unease. Of all the people sitting in the coroner's court, Carr had the unwholesome sensation that he alone believed in the innocence of Daphne Clements and that only he had the almost tangible suspicion that what had been seen, heard, and given in testimony was not the truth but only a macabre manipulation of it.

More than once, Carr looked over to Daphne Clements, seated between two police officers, and he was struck on each occasion by her staring eyes and vacant expression. She seemed divorced from the events of the inquest, as if she were both uninterested and unaffected by them, as though they were happening to someone else entirely. When her name was mentioned, when it was connected to the terrible crime of which she was accused, it hardly seemed to register with her. Carr could not decide whether it was a symptom of disbelief or an acceptance of what now seemed to be the inevitable. Either way, he was frustrated by it, and his anger at both the situation and himself seemed to pierce his soul like a knife through flesh. Once the verdict was given, as swift as it was condemning, Carr had no wish to linger. The court and its processes had seemed to become suffocating to him. Briefly, he locked eyes with Mason, whose duty was now clear. He rose to his feet and walked swiftly towards Daphne Clements. Carr watched the formal words be spoken, but the prisoner barely seemed to hear them. Daphne's silence, her disassociation from the reality of her situation, stirred in Carr an immense whirlpool of pity and fury. Something, he thought, must be done. He paused only to watch Daphne Clements be escorted away, her expression still a pathetic mask of indifference, before he marched out of the court and into the disinterested bustle of the high street.

He was joined almost immediately by Ivor Kettering, whose arrival by his side almost indicated that he had followed Carr purposefully out of the court. His expression was livid, his cheeks and neck burning with a furious fire. His teeth were clenched and his brows creased, the eyes behind the lenses of his spectacles narrowing in baleful rage.

"The coroner is a bloody fool," he hissed, "and the men of the jury are no better. How can they possibly think that Daphne is capable of doing such a thing?"

"There is the evidence, Mr Kettering," said Carr softly.

"Evidence be damned," snarled Ivor. "It's nothing of the kind. It's all circumstantial."

"It is highly likely to persuade a jury at trial."

"If it is evidence, as you say, Mr Carr, then it must have been interpreted incorrectly. There has to be another explanation for what happened to Rowena. There simply must be."

"Wishing something is true does not mean it is so," cautioned Carr.

"Spare me the platitudes, Mr Carr," barked Ivor. "I've been wondering about you and I'd lay good odds that you're not convinced by this mindless verdict either." If he expected or demanded any reply, he was to be disappointed. "I'm right, aren't I? You think Daphne is innocent."

Carr spoke gently. "I think there may be alternative answers to the problem, certainly."

"Then, for God's sake, help me to prove Daphne didn't do it."

"I am not certain that she didn't." Now, Carr looked into Ivor's eyes. "Be under no illusion, Mr Kettering. You must not put words into my mouth. There are questions about this tragedy that have not been answered satisfactorily, and in those questions, I see the possibility of other solutions to this mystery. But until those questions and alternative theories are dispelled, I offer no guarantee of innocence or guilt. If my questions are answered but they do not exonerate Miss Clements, then so be it. I will be satisfied. My hesitation in accepting the coroner's verdict is not proof of my belief in her innocence."

"Argue semantics if you wish, Mr Carr, but the fact is that Daphne is innocent."

Carr reflected for a quiet moment. "Tell me, Mr Kettering, did you know that your wife was the victim of another attempt on her life?"

A moment of importance seemed to pass between the two men, but Carr was not for the moment entirely sure whether Ivor's startled reaction was born from incredulity or astonishment that Carr knew of the incident.

"When?" The word came out of Ivor's mouth as a gasp.

"A few days before she came to Longhampton, as I understand it."

"What happened?"

"A car was driven directly at her in Holland Park. She did not tell you about it?"

Ivor shook his head. "Why did she not say anything?"

There was, thought Carr, an obvious and understandable reason, possibly even two. Rowena might have thought that Ivor would not care enough about the incident on account of his love for Daphne Clements. A darker extension of the thought was that she might have thought he would wish the attack had succeeded. The second reason was not unrelated: had Rowena believed that Ivor himself had been driving the car?

"She told Miss Royce," said Carr.

Ivor was not surprised. "Yes, she would have done, of course. Thick as thieves, those two. Did Rowena say that it was Daphne driving?"

Carr simply shrugged. "She could not be sure who it was."

Ivor glared at him. "I'm afraid I can be in no doubt about it at all, Mr Carr. You see, Daphne cannot drive a car."

It would not have been unreasonable to assume that Carr would have displayed some degree of astonishment or surprise at the revelation, and Ivor himself had expected it. He was shocked, and perhaps a little disappointed, therefore, when Carr offered no dramatic response to his remark, other than to murmur, "I see." His eyes had hardened, however, and he began to preen the elaborate moustache with his finger and thumb, which suggested that the news of Daphne's automobile incompetence had interested him, even if it had not surprised him.

"But it is proof, isn't it?" Ivor said. "Of her innocence."

"It is proof she did not drive a car at Mrs Kettering," said Carr, nodding, "but it is not proof that she is innocent of her ultimate murder."

Despite his words, Carr was thinking of the arsenic found next to Rowena's bed. He had suspected when he found it that there might be two killers at Marsden Grange. The attack on her life in Holland Park and Daphne Clements' inability to drive now seemed to confirm those suspicions.

"Tell me, Mr Kettering," he said, his eyes narrowed in thought, "do you know of any communication your wife might have received on the night of her death?"

"Communication?"

"From anyone in the house?"

Ivor shook his head. "She said nothing to me. What sort of communication?"

Any reply Carr might have given was interrupted by the arrival of Felix Kettering. He marched towards them, his florid face alive with a fierce blend of satisfaction and outrage. Adele Mills, Carr noted, was talking to Josephine Kettering a little distance off, but her eyes were fixed on her fiancée. The man himself nodded a greeting to his father and Carr.

"Never any doubt about the outcome, I suppose," he declared. "I'm sorry, Father, I appreciate how difficult this is for you."

Ivor put his hand on his son's shoulder. "She didn't do it, Felix. I'm going to try to prove it."

"But the verdict?"

"I don't care about the verdict." Ivor's voice was harsh with pain. "Someone else killed Rowena."

Felix glared at his father. "Who?"

Ivor looked across to Carr. "Whoever tried to kill her in Holland Park."

"Holland Park?" Felix frowned, his eyes fluttering in startled confusion. "What happened in Holland Park?"

"Someone tried to run down Rowena in a motor car," replied Ivor. "She didn't tell you about it, I suppose."

"No." Felix lit a cigarette with a slight but noticeable clumsiness. "I'd have told you about it if I'd known, Father."

"She didn't tell anyone, it seems, unless she confided in Josephine."

Felix exhaled cigarette smoke. "Or Tilly bloody Royce. She knew, no doubt."

"But you see the significance?" Ivor said. "Daphne can't drive a car, so she couldn't have run down Rowena. And if she didn't do that, who's to say the person responsible didn't murder Rowena and frame Daphne."

"Isn't it all a little melodramatic?" Felix looked at Carr. "I seem to remember you saying something similar to me the other day, Mr Carr. I couldn't believe it then, and I can't believe it now."

Ivor's indignation was palpable. "Can't you see at all how matters look from my perspective?"

"I'm sorry, Father, but no. I understand why you're thinking this way, honestly, I do, but you must face facts. All you can prove is that Daphne didn't try to kill Rowena in Holland Park. Assuming it happened at all, of course. But the innocence of one crime isn't proof of the innocence of another. All we can say for certain is that there are two culprits—a definite killer and a would-be one."

Ivor, deflated, took off his spectacles and cleaned them with his handkerchief. It seemed almost to be a strategy to prevent himself from breaking down in tears. "So Mr Carr has been advising me."

"I'm pleased someone is remaining realistic," smiled Felix, oblivious to his insensitivity.

Ivor replaced his spectacles. "Nevertheless, I feel I should tell Inspector Mason about the Holland Park episode and Daphne's lack of driving ability. I shall get her exonerated. Mark my words."

Felix and Carr watched him walk away, but whilst their eyes stared in the same direction, their expressions could not have been more opposed. Carr's eyes were intense with concentration, his glare as hard and cold as diamonds, and his lips pursed with suppressed and confused frustration. By contrast, Felix was smiling widely, his cheeks puffed out like summer apples, and his eyes glowing with amusement and a little pity.

"He'll do his best, too, the old bugger," he said, to himself as much as to Carr. "But I fear he's sailing himself into tragedy."

Carr barely heard the words. "What did you mean just now, when you said the Holland Park attack might not have happened at all?"

Felix frowned. "Did I say that?"

"It was implied, certainly."

"Well, not speaking ill of the dead and all that, but Rowena was prone to a few tall tales."

"You mean lies?"

Felix seemed not to like the term. "Exaggerations of the truth. Can we agree to call it that? If she tripped in the street and grazed her ankle, she'd probably tell people she almost broke her leg. It was part of her profession as much as it was her psychology. She was melodramatic."

"And Holland Park?"

"If she were crossing the street and this car, which we've heard so much about, came a little fast around the corner, Rowena's mind might have interpreted the event as an attempted murder."

Carr's eyes now glittered with interest. "That is most interesting, not to say very insightful, if I may say so."

Felix inclined his head and flicked the end of his cigarette into the gutter. "Don't mention it."

"Tell me, Mr Kettering, have you ever been to America?"

The jovial expression became guarded as much as confused at this sudden and seemingly arbitrary change in the topic of discussion, and the smile faded slowly from his lips. "What a strange question. No, as a matter of fact. Why do you ask?"

If Carr had detected the lie, he did not show it. "Just a question which occurred to me, Mr Kettering. I have an active mind."

Felix could hardly be expected to believe the excuse and nor did he, but Carr was not about to allow him to question it further. With a short but graceful bow and a tip of his hat, Everett Carr turned on his heel and limped slowly away. Only when he was far enough away did Adele Mills, who had been watching from close by, approach Felix.

"Josephine's heading back to Marsden Grange," she said. "I said we'd stay here for a while longer. I thought we could do with a drink."

But Felix had only half paid attention. "A drink is a bloody good idea."

Adele took hold of his arm, her eyes now wide with apprehension. She looked at the retreating back of Everett Carr, now slowly disappearing into the crowds. "Why, what's the matter?"

Felix's reply came through gritted teeth, a hiss of suppressed but fearful hysteria. "Carr knows, Adele. For God's sake, I think Carr knows who you are."

Chapter Twenty-Nine

As it turned out, Josephine Kettering did not return to Marsden Grange straightaway. Once Adele Mills had mentioned staying in town, Josephine realised the idea was a good one. It was too soon to return to the house. The inquest had brought it all back to her, the memory of the night before last and all its dark and tragic events now as fresh in her mind as if they had happened only moments before. She had not been able to forget them, of course, but the reiteration of the events of that night, and the cross-examination of witnesses and experts, which had seemed to Josephine to continue for hours, had made the horror and the shock of it seem all the more vivid in the reliving of it than it had been in the reality. To go back to the place where it had all happened seemed, in the moment, therefore, to be almost impossible.

Instead, she decided that a walk through the crowded streets might be beneficial. It was curious, she thought, that she should consider it so. It would normally never occur to her to lose herself among the masses of people whose business, private and professional, compelled them to fill those streets with their presence. Ordinarily, in a mood such as this, she would want isolation and the privacy only of herself and her thoughts. But now, strangely, it was the company of these faceless, nameless strangers that she coveted. There seemed to be some sort of strange sense of safety amongst these unknown people. Why should that be, she wondered. Was it perhaps the very fact that they were strangers, people whose lives were untouched by murder, violence, and death? Were they a reminder that there was a life which could still be said to be ordinary, which was being lived by hundreds of other people untainted by the horror which had blighted her own existence and, she supposed, that of all those present in Marsden Grange that night? Whatever the reason, Josephine was glad to be amongst them, and she was grateful for their anonymity.

For around a quarter of an hour, Josephine walked slowly through the throngs of people, idly turning corners and only half-registering where she was going. Not that she had any definite destination in mind, of course, but the shop windows which she passed, with their various enticements to enter the shops concerned, only made the vaguest impression on her. There were china ornaments, leather-bound volumes, framed prints of famous art, cakes, bottles of various wines and spirits, and stationery, all neatly packaged in commercial displays. Josephine looked at them all but saw none of them. When, at last, she decided that she wanted a drink, and had persuaded herself that perhaps something stronger than tea might be permitted in the circumstances, she found that she could recall very little of her wanderings, save the overall and distinct impression that she had found them both soothing and liberating. Perhaps a celebration of the feeling, rather than an immunisation against the ordeal of the inquest, was the proper cause for a drink. Fortuitously, she found herself reaching the conclusion at the door of *The Black Boar*. As she entered, her only fear was that she would meet Felix and Adele, a proposition which she found strangely disconcerting, but one which fortunately did not come to pass.

She ordered herself a gin with tonic, feeling a sudden sense both of guilt and madness that she should be standing alone in a public house ordering afternoon spirits, and she felt a surge of mild paranoia that the other patrons were staring at her in judgemental disgust. She contemplated leaving, but the drink was already being prepared, and not only did she fear that her voice might fail her, but she also felt a defiant glow of obstinacy. It was nobody's business what she drank, where, or when, and if people thought badly of her then it was their luck out. Perhaps they hadn't suffered what she had over the last few days. Her first sip of the cocktail was like an insolent disregard and rebuttal of any disapproval or disdain, imagined or otherwise. She took her glass, sat down at a vacant table, and lit a cigarette. At least then, she thought, it would appear as if she were waiting for someone.

She looked around her. The pub was hardly glamourous. She had not even known it existed until she had stumbled across it now, and it hardly seemed to be the sort of place that she would have come to by design. Its decorations were obviously from the previous century, but the varnish had faded, so that it was no longer a vibrant and polished oak, but a dull veneer long since marooned by age. The upholstery of some of the stools poked through the torn leather, like unruly hair protruding from under the brim of an ill-fitting hat, and the tables were freckled with the charred holes of careless cigarette burns. The windows behind her were frosted but decorated with elaborate stencilled flowers, and the designs, one of the legacies of the pub's Victorian heritage, and she thought that they might have been beautiful were the panes not so grimy and the sills mottled with the occasional but overlooked body of a dead fly. And yet, she thought, despite its shortcomings, there was an honesty about the place. It pretended to be nothing more than it was. It demanded nothing more of itself. Anybody who entered it but was disturbed by the decorations or the disposition of the place did not have to stay, and it seemed to Josephine that the pub would have had no problem with such people leaving it in peace. How much more honest it was, she thought, than the splendour and hypocrisy of some hotel bars and pretentious restaurants which she had known. She smiled to herself. Heaven knows, she thought, what Lewis Davenport would say if he knew she was sitting there alone, drinking gin, and not caring about the torn seats and insect remains.

Almost wittingly, Lewis was now in her head. She had not meant to think about him, and she had not intended him to occupy her mind at all. But it had happened, and now that he had invaded her thoughts, he was impossible to dismiss. There had never been any genuine doubts about her feelings for him, and, despite her coy dismissal of them to Everett Carr, she knew that Lewis had no misgivings about his feelings towards her. So why, she thought now, had she experienced this foolish hesitancy which had so far prevented her from accepting what was so obviously a genuine proposal and acquiescing to her own no less genuine feelings? The answer was only too painfully obvious to her, but Rowena was now dead and could no longer dictate how Josephine ran her life.

There was her father, of course, who might not welcome this less romantic marriage of personal and professional life, but Josephine smiled at the thought of him having to accept it, whether he was happy about it or not. This, now, was surely the gin's influence. And yet, her father had no concerns about Lewis, as far as she was aware. He had often praised Lewis for his efficiency, his tact, and his loyalty. There seemed no reason why he would not likewise praise such values in a son-in-law. And so, amid the dingy charm of *The Black Boar*, Josephine Kettering reached her happy but still important decision that she would accept Lewis Davenport's proposal of marriage.

And Dr Edwin Jarratt? He would be disappointed, no doubt, but she doubted he would remain so for long. Her relationship with him, such as it was, had never seemed simple to her. Certainly, her feelings towards him were complex. She had always made a show of disliking the man, partly because of her mother's prejudices against him, but also on account of her dislike of his cool arrogance, his easy confidence, and his cynical sarcasm. She found his manner altogether too casual, which made his seriousness, when it came, seem somehow dangerous. The intensity of it when set against his otherwise flippant attitude unsettled her, and she wondered how often this darker shade of his personality might manifest itself and how predictable it might be. When she dared, she wondered what caused it, but her answers were always too vague and uncertain to offer any satisfactory explanation. Except, of course, when she took into account her mother's own beliefs about Jarratt being a killer. In her darker moments, Josephine could be startled to discover that she did not always find the idea too monstrous or outrageous to be inconceivable.

And it was this quality about him which, when she permitted herself to succumb to it, Josephine found irresistibly enticing. With Lewis, there was no doubt of security and safety: he would provide for her, care for her, dutifully make love to her, and treat her with respect and dignity. Jarratt might do likewise when it suited him, but she also had the impression that he would surprise her, even shock her, perhaps sometimes unnerve her. If Lewis were dutifully predictable, she suspected Jarratt would be dangerously passionate. Such thoughts thrilled and frightened her, but she wondered whether a time in her life would come when the security of Lewis Davenport would be preferable to the unpredictability of Edwin Jarratt. Hadn't someone said once that the flame which burned twice as bright only did so for half as long? She could not remember exactly, but she was sure it was true, and when she thought about Edwin Jarratt, it seemed to her to be undeniably so.

"May I join you, my child?"

The voice was at once familiar, but it was so unexpected in these surroundings that it seemed for a moment to be entirely unknown. She looked up and saw Everett Carr smiling down at her, his extravagant moustache curling with amusement, and the dark eyes glittering with amiability. He held his hat to his chest, in an affectation of humble servitude, but his other hand held the silver-handled cane at an angle of dapper elegance. His suit was, as ever, funereal, and the bright emerald of his necktie and handkerchief was almost garish in its contrast.

"Mr Carr, what a surprise!" She made an effort to stand, but he waved her down with a flourish of his hand. "What are you doing in such a place? Hardly your style, I'd have thought."

"Nor yours, if I may say so."

She felt herself flush. "I didn't even know it existed. I stumbled across it."

"And I saw you come in and thought you might not object to company."

"Of course not," she smiled. He had no reason to think it was a lie. "I don't make a habit of coming into public houses on my own. I didn't want to go back to the Grange."

Carr smiled and looked at her now-empty glass. "In the circumstances, perhaps another?"

"I shouldn't."

He gave a small bow. "Nor should you allow an old man to drink alone."

Within a few moments, he was back with her. She had offered to help with the drinks, on account of his leg, but he had refused. Instead, with gallantry or stubbornness, he had insisted on making the two trips required to bring her the second gin and tonic and then his own glass of red wine. She noticed he was breathing slightly harder than before, and he sipped the wine with gratitude, but it prompted from him only a nauseous grimace.

"Sometimes, one's need outweighs one's prejudices," he said, to himself rather than to her, smiling and dabbing at his lips with the gaudy handkerchief. "Now, my child. Tell me, how are you?"

She fidgeted. "First of all, I think I owe you an apology. Our last meeting was rather hostile. I'm sorry about that."

Carr smiled and lowered his eyes. "Think nothing of it."

"I do, nevertheless. I can only blame it on everything that has happened."

"Murder is disruptive, my child. In every way."

Josephine sipped at her gin. "I'm sorry for suggesting Tilly Royce might have killed Mummy, too. Today's events make it clear she didn't."

Carr's eyes were serious. "You did not come here, my child, to think about the day's events. I would say, rather, that you came to escape them."

Josephine laughed gently and sipped more gin. "You're right."

Carr gave another dismissive flourish of his hand. "Then we shall change the subject."

"I find it difficult to think about anything else. I keep thinking about Daddy, you see, and how awful he must be feeling. None of us particularly like Daphne, but that doesn't stop him from loving her. He must feel as if everything has turned into rather a horrid mess."

Carr did not feel the compulsion to repeat his view on the disruptive and destructive nature of murder. It did not need to be said again, and he had the impression that even if he had considered it necessary, it would have been unwelcome. And yet, the concern in her eyes and the nervous flexing and drumming of her fingers suggested that there was something deeper troubling her, something which perhaps was of more personal concern to her, and which vexed her more closely than any natural consideration which she might have for her father's troubles.

"Is there something else that worries you, my child?"

As she had in the cemetery on their first meeting, Josephine wondered what it was about this dandified little man that made it so easy to confide in him. Was it only his ingratiating manner, his gentle voice, and the polite kindness of his manner? It could not be so, she thought, but whatever else it might be, she could not define it.

"I was thinking about marriage when you came into the public house, Mr Carr," she confessed. "I was debating it with myself."

Carr's response was guarded. "Debating the sanctity of marriage or the choice of person with whom to enter into it?"

She smiled, but there was no humour in it. "Your tone of voice makes me think you know the answer."

"It is a choice between a certain doctor and a certain private secretary to your father?"

"There was a time when I thought I'd never get any proposals of marriage, Mr Carr. Now, I have more than I need or want."

"Might I ask whether you have made a decision?"

She nodded slowly. When she gave the name, Carr confessed a mild surprise to himself. He had never been a gambling man, but if he had been, it would have been Dr Edwin Jarratt on whom he placed his wager. As it was, he was saddened to discover that he was not only surprised by her choice but also a little dismayed by it, and when he offered his congratulations, the voice that spoke the words was laced with a cautious disappointment.

"You don't seem pleased for me," said Josephine. "Perhaps I've shocked you, and you don't know quite what to say. I can understand that. I'm shocked and stunned myself. And Mummy would be furious, although I don't suppose I can think about that. I don't think Daddy will mind, assuming he can spare a thought for it. He rather likes Lewis, you see, although he'll probably worry that Lewis' work will suffer."

The words tailed off, and she looked away from him, as if embarrassed by her rambling speech. For a moment, he thought tears had begun to fall, but he was mistaken. Slowly, softly, he cleared his throat.

"May I ask you a personal question?" he said.

She looked at him, confirming once and for all his error about her tears. "If you like."

"Do you love Mr Davenport?"

"He loves me."

Carr was not fooled by the evasion. "That is not what I asked."

"No, I know." She held his gaze for a long moment. "That's just the thing, Mr Carr. I think I do love him. I've pretended otherwise for so long that I'd almost convinced myself I didn't."

"And why was that?"

Now, a single tear did fall. "Because of Mummy. She didn't like Lewis or Edwin, as you probably know, and somehow, I didn't want to disappoint her. But now, and this is what worries me the most, I feel able to accept and decide what I want. I feel free. Does that make me sound wicked?"

Carr shook his head. "I can understand it perfectly. But will you allow me to give you a word of advice, my child? You must not enter into marriage without being certain of your feelings. If you do, your life may not be what you hoped it would be."

Strangely, she laughed. "That reminds me of something Mummy once said. She was giving me one of her usual warnings about Edwin Jarratt, in the early days when he had first shown an interest in me. I remember clearly what she said: *It will make you feel totally alone if you love someone who can't love you back.*' And now, you're saying the same thing."

"Because it is true, my child."

"Perhaps, but it doesn't apply. Lewis loves me, and I love him. And now, there won't be any obstacle for us, because we will still have my money."

She knew it had been a mistake as soon as the words were out. Looking back, she would be unable to explain to herself why she said them. Carr had not coaxed them out of her, and the discussion had not needed them. Speaking to them had been nothing more than an impulse, and she could blame nobody but herself for their consequences. Except, she thought, Everett Carr's gentle ability somehow to manipulate people into confiding in him.

His expression had been serious, and it remained so. He gave almost no indication that he had heard the words, let alone appreciated their importance, and it was only the faint smile across his lip and the slight raising of one eyebrow that showed Josephine that she had betrayed herself. And yet, he offered no gesture or comment of reproach or condemnation. On the contrary, he simply clasped the silver handle of his cane with one hand and raised the glass of wine to his lips with the other.

"I see, my child," he said, "and I understand."

She was staring at the table, and her hands were clasped in her lap so that she looked like a recalcitrant schoolgirl awaiting admonishment. "I lied to you, Mr Carr. I'm sorry. For someone who has been so kind to me, I've treated you very badly."

"It is of no matter, my child. What is important now is that we have the truth. No more secrets, no more lies." He allowed his words to take effect and waited for her to look into his dark, persuasive eyes and nod her agreement. "Miss Mills was telling me the truth, was she not? She did overhear you and your mother arguing."

A nod of her head. "I'm afraid so."

"And the disinheritance?"

Another nod. "Mummy said it in a rage. I don't know if she meant it or not. Sometimes, she would say things in anger that she didn't mean. I thought this was one of them."

Carr smiled. "But you couldn't be sure?"

"No."

"Which is why you searched her room on the night she was killed? You were looking for proof that she had changed her will."

The tears that rolled down Josephine's cheeks were fuelled by guilt and shame. She let them fall, as if wiping them away would be to erase those same emotions which, in turn, would be to deny them.

"I couldn't sleep," she said, "so I went to Mummy's room and knocked on the door. There was no answer, and I thought she might be asleep, so I gently pushed open the door, but she wasn't there."

"It was a terrible risk, my child. Your mother might have returned at any moment."

"I don't suppose I was thinking that clearly," she hissed, forcing back the sobbing. "And the worst of it is that I found nothing. And all the time I was rooting through my mother's private possessions, she was being murdered only a flight of stairs away."

Carr offered her a soothing word and, more practically, a clean handkerchief. She dabbed at her eyes, the silk softly cooling against her reddened cheeks.

"She did burn her copy of the will," he said slowly. "I found a scrap of burned paper in the grate of her fire. It was strong, stiff paper, the sort of legal paper on which wills are drafted. I am sorry, my child."

She shrugged. "I don't suppose it matters. The solicitors will still have a copy. Mummy couldn't have notified them in time, could she?"

Carr was unsure of the answer, but still could not share her optimism. "She may have decided on her course of action far earlier in the day."

"But the argument we had was…"

He held up a cautionary finger. "Your argument with her did not lead necessarily to the burning of the will, my child. She might have burned it before the argument. We cannot know for certain until we know Mrs Kettering's reason for burning the will. Just as we cannot know for certain whether she had spoken to her solicitors until we speak to them ourselves."

Josephine's brows were furrowed in confusion. "But why would she attempt to disinherit me before she and I argued?"

"Perhaps because she had been provoked into it by somebody else." He could see that she still did not understand. "Who else might be affected by your disinheritance?"

"You mean Lewis?" She waited for a response, some acknowledgement of assent, but he provided none. "What could he have done to make her react so violently against him?"

Carr offered no direct reply, but his mind was polluted by the memory of blackmail. "According to Miss Mills, during your argument with your mother, Mrs Kettering said something about the tragedies in her life, and this being the cruellest of all. Do you remember her saying such a thing?"

"Yes, I think she did."

"Do you know what she meant?"

Josephine shook her head. "No. She said so many hateful things that I can't remember them all. I don't even know if she meant them, and now, of course, I never will."

Sadly, and with a regret that he found almost too heavy to bear, Carr thought he knew only too well whether Rowena Kettering had meant what she had said, but he said nothing. He doubted he could have brought the necessary words to his lips.

Josephine had finished her gin. A third was out of the question. She looked into his eyes and attempted to smile. "It wouldn't mean anything, you know. Even if she has disinherited me, it won't mean anything. Lewis loves me for who I am, not for my money." With a word of farewell, she rose from her seat and walked slowly out of the pub.

To Everett Carr, it had seemed to be the saddest confession of all. Whether it was her naivety or his own concerns about Lewis Davenport's motives and nature, the faith that she placed in his feelings for her, and which was so evident in the voice that had made the claim, seemed to deflate Carr's natural optimism. In other circumstances, away from the crimes at Marsden Grange, he would have rejoiced in the devotion that she showed to a man she loved. Away from the shadows of death and deception through which they walked, he would have been overjoyed by their happiness, of the prospect of their love growing and maturing over time. But here, in this dingy public house, amid the conversation of disinheritance and murder, he could not summon those natural impulses. Instead, all he could do was remember Rowena Kettering's words to Lewis Davenport, which he had overheard and which came back to him now, from beyond the grave: *as well as being a civil servant of no importance, now you show yourself up as being a nasty little blackmailer.*

There was a sudden sour taste in his mouth, but it had nothing to do with the cheap red wine, the remnants of which he left untouched in the glass, as he sat alone in troubled silence.

Chapter Thirty

After the inquest, Lewis Davenport had hoped to travel back to Marsden Grange with Josephine, but Ivor had made a point of holding him back to discuss the verdict, and Lewis had seen Josephine first talking to Adele Mills and then walking away in the direction of the town. As Ivor spoke, Lewis had silently urged Josephine to look back in his direction, but she had not. Instead, she had walked away from the coroner's court with her head sunk on her breast, her hands clasped behind her back, and what seemed like a weight of conscience hanging heavily on her shoulders. Lewis had turned his attention back to Ivor Kettering and had made the desired and dutiful remarks and noises, but the truth was that he felt nothing but resentment at Ivor's monopoly of his company, especially when it was solely to complain about the outcome of the hearing and of voicing what seemed to Lewis to be strangely mewling protestations of Daphne Clements' innocence.

His return to Marsden Grange, therefore, was marked by frustration and bitterness. He was suddenly consumed by a desire to be back in London, although whether this was a genuine desire or simply one that had sprung from his current mood, he was unable to say. Certainly, it seemed to him now that the panelled walls and oak furnishings of the Grange were in danger of appearing to close in on him, and the chequered flooring of the hallway seemed now to blur his vision. The place had taken on an aspect of horror and menace that had never struck him before. Everywhere around him, behind the closed doors of each of the rooms leading off the hallway, and up the main staircase to those above his head, it seemed to Lewis that the stench of death, the taste of murder, and the sounds of deceit closed ranks and conspired against him. He longed now only to escape them.

It was in the fog of these fears that Everett Carr confronted him. Lewis had not heard him approaching, and when the little man appeared at his elbow, as if conjured from the air itself, Lewis gave an involuntary gasp of surprise. He gave a breathless laugh of relief. "My goodness, Mr Carr, how you startled me."

He looked into Carr's eyes, expecting to see the benevolent smile under the extravagant moustache, and the glitter of amiability in the curiously dark eyes. The expectation was banished from his mind by the reality, which struck him with all its ferocity when he took stock of it. The eyes were hard, oddly dangerous in their intensity, and the lips under the moustache were pursed with grim intent.

"I wonder if I might have a word, Mr Davenport."

The words, at least, remained polite, but the tone of voice in which they were spoken was vaguely hostile. Lewis, although he would have preferred to decline, felt unable to do so, and he had the notion that any refusal would have been ignored in any event. He nodded in agreement, and Carr motioned towards the drawing room.

"We shall need privacy," he said.

Lewis did not argue. It hardly seemed appropriate, and Carr's demeanour suggested that any objection would be neither welcome nor tolerated. He walked behind Carr, allowing for the older man's slowness of step, and closed the door behind them once they were both in the room. If it was privacy Carr desired, Lewis was happy to provide it.

"You seem very serious, Mr Carr," he said, placing his hands behind his back, as if an efficient attitude might both be necessary and provide some sort of protection from Carr's anger. Professionalism, he had found, suggested that impropriety was not only unlikely but impossible and, as such, was an effective line of defence.

Carr, however, kept his back turned away from the younger man. "You will know, I think, that I am fond of Miss Josephine."

"I had assumed as much, yes."

"I should be very sorry to learn that she has been harmed in any way, physically or emotionally."

Lewis frowned. "What, exactly, is it you're suggesting, Mr Carr?"

"I know about Rowena Kettering's threat of disinheritance." The reply came with a polite calmness that its effect was almost devastating. Lewis said nothing. "I know that Miss Josephine was searching her mother's room on the night of the murder, looking for evidence of it."

"I see."

"You see the contradiction, no doubt."

Lewis frowned. "I'm afraid not."

Now, Carr did turn to face him. The heavy brows were drawn tightly across his brow, and from under them, his intense eyes glared out with onyx menace. Now, Lewis saw nothing dapper, nothing foppish, and nothing ludicrous about this little stranger to whom previously he had attached no importance. It seemed to Lewis that everything which he had once found foolish now seemed darkly threatening.

"You surprise me," said Carr. The voice remained polite, but it had darkened in tone. "I should have thought that a man of your intelligence would have been quite capable of seeing my point. Mrs Kettering loved her daughter; she was fiercely protective of her. You must know as much, given your close relationship with Josephine's father. What could Josephine have done to bring her mother to cut her off without a shilling? What would be so unforgivable for a mother as possessive as Rowena Kettering to feel such a step was necessary?"

Lewis' throat was dry, and he feared that his voice might fail him. "I can't possibly say."

"I think you can, my boy." The salutation, which in ordinary circumstances would have been avuncular in its amiability, was now nothing less than dangerously condescending.

"You mean marriage to me?" Lewis saw little point in further pretence.

"Naturally."

"Well, you're quite wrong. If Josephine had said she was marrying Edwin Jarratt, perhaps Rowena would have disinherited her."

"No doubt, but that does not mean she would not have felt likewise about you." Carr's voice lowered. "*A nasty little blackmailer.*' That is what she called you, did she not?"

The words seemed to freeze the blood in Lewis' veins. "I don't know what you're talking about."

"I overheard your argument with Rowena Kettering on the day she was killed, Mr Davenport," Carr said.

"You're mistaken," insisted Lewis. "It wasn't me."

"I asked you once before if you had any idea why someone would blackmail Mrs Kettering, and you said you had not. That was a lie."

"I don't have any idea. There is no lie."

"Another lie!" The raising of the voice, so unexpected that it was terrifying, was followed by the angry stomp of his cane against the wooden floor. "Of all people, you know who would have such a reason, because you were the person blackmailing her."

"Now, that *is* a lie," hissed Lewis. "And I don't have to listen to any more of them."

He moved to leave, but Carr's voice stopped him as effectively as if a hand had gripped his collar. "*Agree, or you'll be sorry.*' Your final words to Rowena that afternoon. Agree to what, Mr Davenport?"

Lewis was silent for a long moment, his only movement the gentle, almost imperceptible clenching and unclenching of his fists. Slowly, he turned awkwardly, as if unsure of whether his legs would support him, like an infant finding its feet for the first time. Carr's eyes were fierce.

"Agree to marriage, perhaps?" he asked, his voice barely containing his rage. "That was it, wasn't it? You gave Rowena Kettering an ultimatum. Your blackmail didn't involve money or payment, however, only the hand of your victim's daughter."

Lewis shook his head. "You're wrong."

"Then explain the words I overheard. You will admit that your parting words sound like a threat, and Mrs Kettering used the word *blackmail* specifically."

Lewis stared blankly at him for a long moment, his lips slightly parted, and his eyes glaring wildly. At last, he gave a short laugh, as embarrassed as it was nervous, and he removed his spectacles and began to polish them vigorously with his handkerchief. Carr wondered briefly whether the gesture was to ensure that he could no longer see Carr clearly, as if by doing so he could banish Carr from the room.

"It will sound so foolish and petty now," he said.

"It won't," said Carr softly, "if it is the truth."

The spectacles were replaced, the handkerchief stuffed back into his pocket, and the hands thrust into his pockets. Lewis gave a nod of the head and a resigned raise of his eyebrows. "It was about money. Aren't all arguments worth having about money?"

"Or love," said Carr, but it might have been said only to himself.

Lewis, certainly, seemed not to have heard. "I've worked for Ivor Kettering for a long time now, Mr Carr. Some might say too long. I have been loyal, I have been dedicated, and I have undertaken every task he has delegated to me with, if I may say so, diligence and tact, even with discretion. But never once, I'm sorry to say, have I had an increase in salary. It seems filthy, doesn't it? We're so frightened of discussing the very thing which we need to live our daily lives."

If he had expected a reply, Carr was not about to oblige. Instead, he looked back at Lewis from under his heavy brows, his head slightly inclined in concentration, but his expression revealing nothing of the emotions that stirred inside him. Lewis began to walk slowly around the room.

"I tried to discuss it with Ivor, of course," he said, "but I was always dismissed, sometimes with a flea in my ear, more often with a gentle word of encouragement. Either that or the topic was passed over in favour of some aspect of our work. Anyway, in the end, it became clear that a direct request for more money was going to get me nowhere, so I decided on a different approach."

"You asked Mrs Kettering to exert some influence over her husband?"

"Not initially. First, I asked Ivor for more responsibility. I thought if he granted me that, I could use it as justification. More duties, more salary."

"Would Ivor Kettering have been able to grant you this wish?" asked Carr.

"Surely, it would have been a matter of the public purse."

Was it his imagination, or did he see a trace of crimson flush the young man's cheeks? If so, Lewis was quick to hide it, with a shrug of his shoulders and a turn on his heel.

"Perhaps," he said, "I don't think I gave the practicalities much thought. I just wanted more money. I felt I deserved it, for one thing, and I wanted to be in a better position to support Josephine, for another."

"I see." Carr's expression remained impassive.

"Ivor still didn't respond," continued Lewis, "so I asked Rowena. I suppose, as you said, I hoped she might exert some influence over him. Looking back," he added with a smile, "it was a pretty desperate plan. And you obviously overheard how successful it was."

Carr looked keenly at him. "She used the word *blackmail*, Mr Davenport."

"Yes, that was unfortunate. You see, I threatened to resign if I didn't get my way. Rowena saw straight through me. I had no intention of resigning, and she knew it. So, she called me a nasty little blackmailer, and threw me out."

"And your final words to her?"

"*'Agree, or you'll be sorry?'*" Lewis shrugged coyly. "I felt humiliated. I wanted to have the last word." Now, he looked into Carr's eyes with a defiant assurance. "But there was no blackmail, not in the real sense of the word. The only person to use it was Rowena."

"And you account for her use of it as an example of her dramatic tendencies?"

Lewis smiled without humour. "Well, she was always rather melodramatic. But I swear, Mr Carr, that is all there was to it. Now, does that answer your question?"

There was a long silence. Carr watched the younger man keenly, his fingers and thumbs idly stroking at the Imperial beard. Lewis stared back at him, but there was no pleading for innocence in his expression and no exaggerated display of candour. It was the gaze of a man who had told a tale and was willing either for it to be believed or not. Had there been some insistence of the truth of it, Carr might have suspected deceit, but he had to confess that he found this confident disinterest in the acceptance of the explanation dangerously convincing.

Slowly, Carr smiled. "Well, it is an answer, certainly."

Lewis nodded. "Then I shall leave you in peace."

He walked to the door, and suddenly Carr knew. The expression might have been nonchalant, but the stride to the door was too swift to be innocent. It struck Carr as being not so much an exit as an escape. Now, his smile broadened, and he saw the lie he had been told in all its improvised but shining brilliance. He waited until Lewis had opened the door before he called his name.

"You are a clever and resourceful man, Mr Davenport," he said, "but always be aware that there are those who are more intelligent and more cunning. I offer you that as a word of advice from an older man."

"Thank you," said Lewis. "Anything else?"

Carr gave a short, slow bow. "Alongside that word of advice, a word of warning. If you do anything to harm or upset Miss Josephine, I shall come for you. Be under no illusion about it, my boy. I have seen too many of your kind to be fooled. You are very plausible, Mr Davenport, but I have eyes that see everything and ears that hear everything. And I see and hear you."

He pointed deliberately at Lewis' heart, the finger seeming suddenly like the mark of divine condemnation. Lewis offered no further reply, other than to close the door slowly and silently, as if hearing it shut behind him might be to hear the sound of the hangman's trap door before the noose was pulled tightly around his neck.

Chapter Thirty-One

Tilly Royce had returned alone to Marsden Grange. For her, there had been no desire to discuss the verdict, nor had there been any desire or need for alcoholic stimulation in the wake of it. The proceedings had unfolded much as she had expected, and she doubted anyone could have held any genuine belief that matters could have progressed any differently. She had given her evidence, such as it was, in a calm, almost disassociated fashion. She had rehearsed it, of course, before the mirror and when staring out of her bedroom window, just so that she could be confident of what she would say and how she would say it. Such preparations might have been considered natural, she supposed, and when the time came, she had been grateful for them. Her evidence had been presented to the court, documented, and taken into account. There was nothing else to be done.

She had watched the others during the proceedings, and she had seen the varied masks of concern, fear, and agitation. Felix and Adele, sitting together with their arms interlinked, had seemed especially interested in the official process of the inquest, watching each witness closely, and looking at each other at certain moments, as if to satisfy themselves that things were going according to some plan which Tilly could not fathom. Josephine Kettering, too, had paid close attention to what was said, but her face had been half-hidden by her handkerchief, held up to her mouth as if in expectation of some imminent display of tearful emotion. For his part, Ivor had remained admirably collected, which had both surprised and impressed her. She could hardly have blamed him if he had broken down with emotion, given that one woman in his life was about to be found guilty of the murder of another, but such considerations seemed far from his mind. But Tilly was not so naïve that she could not recognise the taciturn control of male reserve, adopted by men like Ivor almost as a civic duty. It would be a betrayal if he displayed anything but respectable reticence, at least in his own eyes, and not for the first time, Tilly had found herself loathing the man for such foolish attitudes but also, perhaps more strongly, for his position in Rowena's life. The jealousy, spiteful and adolescent, irked her as much as its cause.

She had caught a bus back to Longhampton and walked from the village back to the grange. She had walked slowly, her hands behind her back and her gaze turned to the ground, so that it took her rather longer than it should have done to reach the gates of the property. It had been one of those walks that had been so consumed by her thoughts that she now could remember none of it. She must have passed people, perhaps even acknowledged them, but she could recall nobody. Likewise, she must have taken note of the usual landmarks—the village green, the bandstand, the wishing well, the row of shops, and the war memorial—but none of them seemed to have registered in her mind, and it seemed almost a surprise to find herself so suddenly at her destination.

She pulled open the gates and stepped onto the gravel driveway. She crunched her way towards the house, wondering now how long she would stay. She would be needed for the trial of Daphne Clements, but that was not a requirement to stay at Marsden Grange. There was no need for her to remain in the house after today, and she could return to the Campden Hill Square residence whenever she chose. She had given its details to Inspector Mason and he knew he could reach her there.

She had almost made up her mind to leave immediately, at first light tomorrow at the latest, when the thought struck her. Without Rowena, what right did she have to stay in the London residence? She had never paid rent or had any agreement from Ivor that she could live there. Rowena's word had been sufficient invitation and authority. But now, Rowena was gone, and what would Tilly do? She could hardly rely on the goodwill of Ivor, even if she wanted to, because there was no guarantee that he would continue to provide it. Suddenly, Tilly felt an uncharacteristic sense of hopelessness and, more worryingly, of loneliness. Her logic, fighting for supremacy over this emotional indulgence, tried to convince her that she would endure, just as she had done in the past, but this time it was different, and she knew it. It was not the first time she had been left alone and, unbidden, the memory of Anna came back to her mind. She had not thought about her first love for so long that the sudden intrusion of the memory into her thoughts alarmed her. It was as unexpected as it was irrelevant, however, and she quickly dismissed it. Anna had left, and Tilly had survived the pain, but the difference was that there was always the possibility of seeing Anna again. With Rowena, there was an unfillable void, no hope of any sort of reconciliation or reunion, and Tilly's capability to endure suddenly seemed drained of its power, and with the loss of it, there came a frightening doubt about the future, her security, and her happiness. She leaned against the fountain on the driveway, the stone so cold against her buttocks that it felt damp, and she wept.

Silently, softly, she sobbed.

From the window of the drawing room, Everett Carr saw her. He had been sitting alone in silent contemplation, following his confrontation with Lewis Davenport. He had been arranging his thoughts, testing and finalising those theories and ideas which he felt could transform into definite conclusions about some if not all the mysteries at Marsden Grange. The central mystery of who murdered Rowena Kettering remained, but those extraneous puzzles seemed to him to be largely settled. Beyond, of course, the always thorny issue of the question of proof. He had been considering the problem of evidence when his attention was distracted by the appearance of Tilly Royce, her disturbance of his peripheral vision breaking his chain of concentration and focusing his mind elsewhere. He could not, in all honesty, claim to be irritated by the interference. He rose to his feet and walked painfully out of the drawing room, into the hallway, and finally out onto the drive.

Tilly had brought her sobs under control by the time she knew he was approaching. The uneven rhythm of his limping gait across the gravel was her first indication: such a sound could have been made by nobody but him. But the flash of black and contrasting colour in the corner of her eye, caused by the dark suit and gaudy necktie and handkerchief, was the final confirmation. She might have thought she preferred peace and solitude, but Tilly found that she neither flinched nor was irritated by his presence. If anything, she found the white of his hair and moustache, also so stark against the black of his clothes, to be a strange comfort, like a kind grandfather or uncle checking on a favourite niece or grandchild, but who is conscious that his company might not be required or desired.

"You will allow me to join you, dear lady?" he said. "I thought you might wish some company, after the ordeals of the morning."

She dabbed at her eyes with the gloved fingers of one hand. "I'm terribly sorry, Mr Carr, you've caught me in a moment of weakness. I feel rather foolish."

"There is no need, dear lady." He was so polite that he did not look at her, fearing that to do so would be an intrusion too far. She found herself smiling, but feeling grateful for such a genteel and unnecessarily fussy consideration.

"I walked from the village," she said, suddenly needing to explain herself. "I wanted some time alone. You can understand that, I'm sure."

"Very much so. Sometimes, people mean well by talking in times of trouble. They think it is a comfort, but it can so often be an intrusion."

Despite herself, Tilly laughed. "I knew, somehow, that you'd understand only too well."

Carr smiled. "Tell me, Miss Royce, what do you know of Lewis Davenport?"

The statement took her by surprise, and she was unable to conceal it, even if she had felt it was necessary. Carr did not look at her. Instead, he massaged his moustache with one hand, whilst using the other to draw abstract patterns in the gravel with the ferrule of his cane. Despite his apparent abstraction of thought, she seemed to know that he was listening intently.

"I don't know much about him at all," she said. "I know he's in love with Josephine, and that he's loyal to Ivor, but beyond that, I've nothing very much to say about him. I don't have any personal feelings towards him."

"Did Mrs Kettering?" He still did not look at her, but he had registered the flicker of hesitation in her reply.

"She wasn't altogether keen, I don't think," said Tilly. "Certainly, she objected to his attentions towards Josephine."

"Did you know that she had threatened to disinherit Miss Kettering if she married Mr Davenport?"

Tilly seemed embarrassed by the question, but she knew that a lie would be unconvincing. "You've found out about that, have you?"

"I have," said Carr, needlessly.

"Yes, I did know about it. At least, I knew that Rowena was thinking about it."

"You were a true confidant, dear lady," smiled Carr.

Tilly seemed close to offended by the remark. "We were close friends, Mr Carr."

Now, he did look at her, the dark eyes brimming with compassion and understanding. "I think I knew that too, Miss Royce."

"Rowena didn't have too many friends," said Tilly. "She had people who said they were her friends, but they weren't. They were far too interested in what they could get out of her."

"On the night she died, did Mrs Kettering say that she had received any communication from someone?"

"From whom?"

Carr shrugged. "Anyone at all?"

"No." There was no suggestion or betrayal of a lie. "About what?"

"A meeting, perhaps?"

Tilly shook her head. "Nothing at all."

"May I ask you a delicate question, dear lady?" Carr's eyes remained fixed on her, and when the question came, he had the distinct impression that it was not the one she had expected. "Was Mrs Kettering being blackmailed?"

"Blackmailed? By Lewis Davenport, you mean?"

"By anybody," said Carr, dispassionately.

"Not that I'm aware of. And I can't imagine what anybody would have against Rowena, which could be used as a levy for blackmail."

"She had no secrets?"

Tilly smiled. "We all have secrets, Mr Carr. But they're not all worthy of extortion."

It was a point which he felt must be conceded, and he did so with a smile and a glance into her eyes. "*Touché*, my child."

"Even if she were being blackmailed, what does it matter now? The verdict has been given."

"There will still be a trial," Carr said.

"It's hardly likely to have a different result than the coroner's court, surely."

Carr shrugged his shoulders but offered no definitive reply. "Did you know that Mrs Kettering had a son before she gave birth to Miss Josephine?"

Tilly gazed into the distance. "Little Peter, yes. I didn't know her at that time, of course, but she told me about it."

"A tragedy."

"It explains why Rowena was so protective of Josephine." Tilly pushed herself off the water fountain and began to walk around in small circles in front of him. "She blamed herself for what happened. Peter drowned, you see, when Rowena had taken her eyes off him."

"In Scotland, I believe?"

"Yes, they were on holiday. Rowena had turned to pack up a small picnic, and when she looked back for Peter, he was lying face down in the river."

Carr now eased himself off the fountain, too. "Mr Kettering was not there?"

"No. Rowena had begged him to go with them, but he was busy. He said he had important matters to address. Obviously, they were more important than his wife and child."

Carr stopped walking. "Those sound like the words of Mrs Kettering, rather than your own."

Tilly nodded. "They are. There was mutual blame, Mr Carr. Ivor blamed Rowena for not keeping watch on Peter, and she blamed him for not going with them. Two pairs of eyes would always be better than one, she said, but as it was, she had to do everything and lost concentration."

Carr gave a sigh of regret. "So often in tragedy, people blame each other for what is, in reality, something out of their control. An accident, a force of nature, an act of God."

"In Peter's case, more an act of the Devil." Tilly turned to face him. "Rowena accepted it was all her fault. In the end, I mean. She stopped blaming Ivor, assuming she ever really had done."

"You doubt it?"

Tilly shook her head. "I don't know. Does it sound plausible that it could have been Ivor's fault?"

"No," conceded Carr with a smile.

"I don't like the man, but it never seemed fair of her to blame him." Tilly looked away now into the distance. "Or to blame herself. It was an accident, caused only by a child's eager fascination with the world and a parent's momentary lapse of concentration."

Carr gripped the handle of his cane as tightly as he could. "Only people without children could talk as we do."

"You have none of your own?"

"My wife and I were not blessed. We tried, but it never happened." And now, it never could. Tilly was not sure whether any reply was appropriate or, if it were, what it was she should or could say. She had no wish to enter into an emotional debate with this man, however kindly he was, and nor did she think he desired such a discussion. She felt instead that he had simply answered her question, but that his reply had in some way opened up an old wound, which neither required nor deserved any further examination.

"It is getting chilly," she said. "I should perhaps go inside. A cup of strong tea is in order, I think."

Carr, still enveloped in his thoughts, seemed momentarily not to have heard her. At last, however, it seemed as if the silence that had descended had affected even him, and he smiled at her, giving a small bow of apology. "Forgive me, my mind was elsewhere."

"I was just saying that I might go inside now."

"By all means. I might have a walk around the grounds. Exercise this confounded leg of mine." He gave another bow. "I trust I don't intrude into your privacy, dear lady, but may I ask what you will do with yourself after this is all over?"

She smiled at him. "Where will I live, do you mean? If you want the honest truth, I don't know. I was thinking about it just now. Perhaps I'll travel. Get away from here. Try to forget it all."

Carr listened with sympathy and understanding. He could appreciate the difficulty in which she would find herself, and it was a situation that required resolution sooner rather than later. He suspected Ivor Kettering would not be so ungenerous as to evict her instantly, but his kindness could not be expected to be indefinite. In any event, Carr doubted that Tilly Royce would want to live amongst the Kettering family without the bond and company that Rowena had provided. If she did decide to travel, she struck him as being intelligent enough to realise that it was a question not of broadening her horizons but of fleeing from a painful chapter in her life. Perhaps fleeing from pain and sorrow was not to be criticised but advocated. Certainly, it was not for him to pass any comment. There was no mandate or social obligation on how to deal with grief. If there were, perhaps it would make life all the easier to bear. As it was, however, there was only one's personal attitude to coping with loss and death, and Everett Carr was only too experienced in such matters.

He watched Tilly Royce walk back into Marsden Grange, before finally beginning to walk towards the woods and fields which surrounded the perimeter of the property. His leg ached with a dull and throbbing rhythm of agony, this permanent reminder of his tragedy, from which he had never fled but, equally, from which he had never entirely healed. It was always there, the memory and its associated guilt, both seemingly personified in the permanent limp and associated anguish. Again, perhaps more strongly than ever, the feelings of guilt at his survival of that tragedy, in the face of Miranda's death because of it, swelled up inside him and, as if in some mental and physical alliance against him, his shattered knee began to sear with unforgiving pain.

Chapter Thirty-Two

She remembered the inquest and its aftermath only in fragments: accusing stares, condemning phrases, official words. But even in their disjointed state, the memories told the same despairing story. She was guilty of the ultimate crime, and she would hang for it. Murder: the word seemed almost unreal to her now, for all its implications of violence and horror, as if it had lost all its connotations and was no longer anything but an indictment against her, nothing more than a legal term which she could no longer understand and which meant something tangible only to those men who uttered it with no emotion other than professional authority. Policemen, coroners, members of a jury, and later it would be barristers and judges. For her, though, the word meant almost nothing anymore, other than being a precursor to another, more vivid horror. Murder, she thought, had happened, but its terrifying sequel, her hanging, was yet to come, and she had always feared the future more than the past.

How much pain would she experience when the time came? Would she feel the pull of the rope as it tightened around her throat, or would it break her neck too quickly for her to register any sensation at all? Surely that was how she must hope it would be. The alternative was altogether too terrible to contemplate. She had visions of the past, which came to her in terrible clarity, of witches and traitors dangling from the end of the rope, their lower limbs jangling in a hideous parody of some sort of frenetic dance. Surely, it was no longer like that. Humanity must have progressed over the last few hundred years. She should be able, she thought, to have some expectation of advancement and progression in her own species, which would mean that her execution would be swift, efficient, and as humane as possible. Or was she hoping for too much? She should assume, perhaps, that the point of her death was that it would be horrific. It was, after all, a punishment. What right did she have to expect it to be so easily discharged?

It was strange, almost bizarre, even to be thinking of such things. How far she had come, she thought, since the days of her childhood. Her existence now was so far from where she had intended it to be that it seemed almost to be occurring to someone else. Her parents, both dead, would be bewildered by it. She wondered if there was a moment when she could say that her life had started to go wrong. Was it only when she had met Ivor Kettering? However logical it seemed, she felt it was too simplistic to equate her downfall to that one event. Perhaps falling in love with Ivor was only the catalyst, and things had already started to go wrong long before. Had it been when she stole a shilling from her mother's purse that time, but had felt so riddled with guilt that she had not dared to spend it? It was the first act of serious wrongdoing that she could remember, so it was reasonable to assume that was when her character had been corrupted. She could not recall now what had made her do it: the thrill of it, greed, or simple malice? Not only could she not recall it, she could not now understand it. Perhaps it had been wickedness for the sake of it, a petty act of rebellion, just to see if she could get away with it. And she had. Her mother had put down the loss of the shilling, so vital and so badly needed, to her miscalculation and forgetfulness, but never to stealing. Even if the idea of theft had occurred to her, she would never have suspected her daughter, whose innocence was taken so much for granted that it made any confession all the more impossible to make. Well, punishment had to come at some point and now it had arrived. Fate had come to take its pound of flesh, she thought, and just maybe it was not a day too soon.

She thought again of those executions of the past. It was not only witches and traitors who suffered, but thieves also. And she was a thief. Not just of that shilling from decades ago, but also of another woman's husband. Too late, she realised that she had no proper claim over Ivor Kettering. That, too, had been a dream. There had never been any possibility of Rowena giving him up, and she had begun to wonder whether he would have left her in any event. In her darker moments, this was undeniably the case; sometimes, she dared to believe the opposite. The truth was that she couldn't be sure one way or the other. Her circumstances, her plight, and her confined existence conspired against her, blurring her perception of reality, as if her dread of the future could manipulate her knowledge of the past and the present. She was on the course of being condemned and hanged as a murderess. Years ago, even weeks ago, such an idea would have been laughably impossible, but now it was not only possible but happening. So, what did reality matter? This was her reality, and it was nothing but madness.

Ivor had been to see her, of course. They had allowed her that kindness, at least, but she feared that the visit had been less than successful. If Ivor had hoped for some sort of revelation or reprieve from the impending disaster, he had been disappointed. He had insisted that the verdict was wrong, voicing the opinion with such emphasis that she felt as if he were trying to convince himself as much as her. Worse, he had spoken as if saying the words out loud was sufficient to make them true, and that his voice was enough to change the mind of those twelve men on the coroner's jury and to persuade another twelve different men at the trial of her innocence.

"We shall get you the very best defence," he had said. "Money doesn't matter. We can burn it as long as we see you free."

She had not replied. There was nothing she could say. The inevitability of it all seemed now to be so overwhelming that it was suffocating her, robbing her not only of hope but of her voice. Ivor had persisted.

"The jury were fools, and so was the coroner, but it doesn't mean that we need to assume the next jury will be fools also. If anything, we must expect them to be the opposite."

He had said as much several times over, the words always different but the meaning still the same. She had barely heard the exact words, but their effect had not been lost on her. In the end, she had told him to stop. She could not bear to hear his frustrated optimism anymore.

"I'm sorry," he had said. "It's just the injustice of it all. How can they think you did such a thing? I don't care what evidence they say they have, either.

It's not a question of evidence but of human nature. And you don't have murder in you."

It seemed as if the situation had been rehearsed. There was no better time to voice what had been in the back of her mind all along, but it still seemed alien to hear herself say the words aloud, as if her voice had been seized by thoughts and words which were not her own.

"Are you sure about that, Ivor?" she had said.

He had been visibly confused. "Of course."

"Because I wonder. Maybe I did do it, after all. I certainly wanted to kill her. Perhaps you didn't, but I did. I wanted Rowena dead, and now she is. So, maybe I did kill her."

"Wanting her dead and killing her aren't the same thing."

"Not remembering killing somebody and being innocent of murder aren't the same thing either." If it was a confession, Ivor either couldn't recognise it as such or refused to do so.

"This place, everything which has happened, has warped your sense of reality," Ivor had said. "You don't know what you're saying. And for God's sake, don't repeat it to anybody."

"What if it's true?"

"It isn't. It can't be." Again, he had spoken as if his words alone were enough to make the statement true. "We will get you out of here, my love, and we will survive this."

Now, she wondered whether his use of the word had been tactless or accidental. Had he meant to say that they would survive? It was difficult not to see it, yet again, as a reference to her death. She would cheat death, that was his assurance, his spoken guarantee of something that he could not possibly know for sure. Her life was not in the hands of Ivor Kettering, and he had no authority over it. All he could do was offer optimistic platitudes and words of banal comfort. But her fate rested with the twelve men of a jury, a judge, and an executioner. They were her puppeteers, and it was to their morbid tune of condemnation that she must dance.

And here now was a new sensation: the realisation that she was no longer in control of her own life. She no longer belonged to herself but to those figures of authority who would convict and condemn her. She had no say over her life any longer. Somehow, it seemed to her that this was the cruellest of all the injustices. Accusations of murder, the defilement of her name, and the robbing of her reputation all seemed strangely bearable when set against this seizing her own will and her ability to control her destiny. If she had to give them everything else, she would not provide them with the satisfaction of that final indignity. She would retain control of that one piece of her humanity that had not been surrendered to them. If her life were to reach its climax at the end of a rope, she would ensure that the rope was one of her own making and that the culmination of her existence was on her own terms.

As she tore her sheets into strips for the purpose, Daphne Clements looked up at the little tent of blue which she now called the sky, and wept.

IV

PART FOUR: THE TRUTH WILL OUT

Chapter Thirty-Three

The news reached Marsden Grange on the following morning. Inspector Mason had arrived at the house early, already bearing the weight of responsibility that the events of the previous night had brought upon him. He had asked Carr and Ivor Kettering for a private meeting in the latter's study, and it was there that he broke the news. He was too seasoned an officer to handle the situation badly, and experience had told him that the most efficient and, perversely, the kindest way in which to deliver unpleasant news was to be simply factual, professional, and to offer few, if any, platitudes of sympathy.

"I'm sorry to have to tell you, sir," he said, "that last night, Miss Clements attempted to take her own life. She did not succeed, but it was a close thing. She's now in the prison hospital."

Everett Carr, he noticed, mouthed a silent word of sadness and regret, but said nothing aloud. It was either tact or shock, possibly a blend of the two. Ivor Kettering, for his part, offered no immediate response, other than to draw his brows into a crease of confusion, as if the words had been spoken in a language with which he was not familiar. His lips moved, seemingly of their own accord, but no words managed to escape from them, the only sound being a small, humourless, and deeply incongruous laugh.

"Kill herself?" Ivor said at last. Slowly, he sat down in his chair behind the desk, his hands gripping the arms tightly, as if he were afraid that his knees might buckle underneath him. "How?"

Mason knew it would be impossible to avoid the details, but he wished that it could have been otherwise. "She tried to hang herself, using the bedsheets."

"Hang herself?" Ivor searched for some meaning in the words. The cruelty of the irony was lost on nobody, but none of the men in the room deemed it appropriate to comment on it.

"She was found by the duty sergeant, who had gone to check on her," Mason explained. "He raised the alarm immediately. His speed of action probably saved her life."

The details, delivered flatly and without emotion, were no doubt unwelcome, but Mason felt obliged to provide them. Ivor heard them but seemed incapable of understanding them. The inspector allowed only a brief moment to pass before speaking again.

"Does she have any family, sir, anyone who needs to be notified?"

Ivor shook his head. "No. There's nobody, only me. Can I see her?" This last question was asked almost as if it were an afterthought, and it was delivered in a tone of voice which suggested that Ivor was furious with himself for not thinking to ask it sooner.

Mason shook his head. "I'm afraid not, sir. Not for the moment, at least. I'll let you know when it's possible."

Ivor shook his head in bewilderment. "She must be so desperate to do something like this. I went to see her after the inquest, and I wondered then about her state of mind."

Everett Carr looked sharply at him. "In what sense?"

"She seemed distant, divorced from reality, as if her mind was unable to engage with her situation." Ivor struggled to find the words. "I can't explain it. She asked me if she'd killed Rowena after all, but just couldn't remember it."

Mason's eyebrows raised. "Did she, indeed?"

"It means nothing, of course. Her mind has been twisted by circumstances." Suddenly, Ivor seemed to grasp Mason's implication. "For God's sake, don't take it as a literal confession. She's not thinking straight. And who can blame her for that? I'm sure she isn't the first innocent person to lose their grip on reality. I don't suppose you can fathom it, can you, inspector? You probably see what Daphne has done as an act of justified penance by the guilty rather than a cry of desperation from the innocent. No doubt you think she should have succeeded and saved the hangman a job and the courts the time and trouble of a trial."

The outburst was unfair and regrettable, but somehow understandable. Certainly, Mason offered no defence to the allegations, nor did he feel any animosity on account of them. Instead, he simply clasped his hands behind his back and lowered his gaze to the floor. If it was designed to humble Ivor into an apology, it was successful.

"That was unwarranted, inspector," said the minister, "I'm sorry. Blame the shock, blame my feelings of inadequacy about everything that's happened, blame my feelings for Daphne. Hell, blame anything you like. I didn't mean what I said."

Mason cleared his throat gently. "I think perhaps you did, sir. At least, I think you meant the part about not taking what Miss Clements said as a literal confession."

"And nor do you, I think, inspector," said Carr. "You know full well what a defence barrister would make of it, I'm sure, and it wouldn't be too far from what Mr Kettering has said. It seems to me that this tragedy cuts both ways. It could easily be read as a sign of guilt or, equally, of innocence."

Mason nodded. "For the avoidance of doubt, I read nothing into it one way or the other. That said, I deal in evidence, and, taking what I have into account, I am bound to infer that Miss Clements' motives for what she has done were driven by guilt rather than innocence."

"Be that as it may," said Carr, "it alters nothing. The attempt is what must take priority. The lady has survived it, but is seriously ill. For the moment, her health must matter more than any questions of guilt or innocence."

Ivor sat back in his chair and looked over to Carr. "Quite so. Thank you for telling me, inspector, and thank you also for doing so before anybody else. That courtesy is appreciated. Now, I wonder if you would allow me some time alone."

It was not an unreasonable request, and there was nothing more to be said. Mason gave a curt nod of the head and turned on his heel. Carr gave a gentle bow and walked slowly out of the room. The present interview was concluded.

"Do you still suggest the Clements' girl is innocent?" asked Mason once the study door was closed.

"I have not reached any definite conclusions," replied Carr.

"But you have your own ideas, I'm sure."

Carr inclined his head. "Certain things do occur to me, but nothing I can prove."

"Well, I can prove that Daphne Clements handled that needle and phial," said Mason. "I can prove a motive and an opportunity. You can't deny any of that, can you?"

"No." Carr spoke frankly but without concern. "But you must guard yourself against running in the wrong direction, my friend."

Mason winked. "That's just it, Mr Carr. I don't think I am running in the wrong direction."

"Then you must finish your race, inspector. First, I wonder if I might ask a favour of you."

"Of course."

Carr gave a smile of gratitude. "Have your researches into Mrs Kettering's affairs provided you with the name of her solicitors?"

"Yes, a firm in Norwich and one in London. Apparently, Ivor Kettering insisted on having city solicitors and a local representative." The inspector reached into his pocket and brought out his official notebook. "The London firm is Galbraith, Simmonds & Ford. The firm in Norwich is Temple, Marsh & Kemp."

"I wish to pay a visit to them, and the London solicitors, if necessary. Then, I need you to come with me to Danforth & Brierly, the pharmacists in the high street."

"Very well," said Mason. "Is it worth me asking why?"

Carr smiled, almost conspiratorially. "It will be easier to learn what I need to if I have a police presence with me."

"And what is it that you need to learn?"

"About arsenic and disinheritance, of course, inspector."

"And you want to do this now?"

"The sooner, the better, I think. Don't you?"

"By all means," said Mason, but he doubted a reply had been necessary or that Carr had expected one.

A telephone call to the Norwich solicitors had secured an emergency appointment with Mr Temple, who greeted them with an aloof but courteous professionalism. His frame was massive, so large that it was impossible not to consider it imposing, but it was contrasted with unusually small feet, which seemed hardly capable of supporting the bulk of what loomed above them. He was dressed formally, in a black jacket and waistcoat, with grey mourning trousers, which seemed to emphasise the funereal speed with which he walked. His head was almost bald, save for a fine fringe of white around the base of his skull, and the features must once have been keenly aquiline before age and excess had taken their toll. And yet, the eyes, peering over the incongruously delicate *pince-nez* which were perched on the angular nose, retained a piercing gaze of obvious intelligence. He indicated the two client chairs on one side of the desk, before settling himself in a sturdy, high-backed chair on the other. He offered them coffee, which was accepted, and when it arrived, Carr was pleased to find that it was strong and bitter.

"Terrible news about our late client," said Mr Temple. The voice was deep and melodic, marred only slightly by the faint trace of wheezing breaths. "I had expected you to come and see me, of course, inspector, although I confess that I had expected the visit to be from our local constabulary."

"It was Mr Kettering, sir, who requested that Scotland Yard deal with the matter."

Temple nodded. "Ah, yes, that would be something Ivor would do. May I ask, what your position in this is, sir?" The question was directed to Carr, and it was asked politely but without any trace of amiability.

Carr beamed at him. "I am a spectator only."

Mason felt compelled to explain. "Mr Carr was present when the tragedy occurred. I have known him for many years, and he has once or twice been of some assistance to me and my colleagues."

Temple seemed less than impressed. "What the popular novelists call an amateur sleuth, as I understand it. I don't read mystery thrillers myself."

"Nor do I," said Carr with a civility that was only close to being overplayed, "but then nor am I an amateur sleuth. Merely a retired criminal judge."

"Indeed?" If Temple still felt resentment towards Carr's presence in his office on official business, it was perhaps now a little less hostile. "Even so, I expected only to discuss my late client's affairs with the police."

Carr smiled. "I have no wish to offend. I shall be happy to wait outside."

Mason laid a hand on his arm. "It is quite all right, Mr Temple. Whatever you tell me, I shall confide in Mr Carr in any case, so it would save time and my breath if we simply got on with the matter in hand."

The rebuke, although delivered with official courtesy, was only too obvious, and Temple recognised it still for what it was. "Very well, we shall proceed. You wish to know the terms of Rowena Kettering's will, is that correct?"

"Just the salient points, Mr Temple," warned Mason.

"They can be briefly summarised. Save for a legacy to Miss Josephine Kettering, the whole of her estate goes to her husband."

Carr leaned forward. "This is the latest copy of the will?"

"It is."

"Her London solicitors, Galbraith, Simmonds & Ford, also have a copy, of course?"

"Yes, indeed."

"Had she telephoned you recently, perhaps with regard to changing the contents of her will?"

"Certainly not."

Carr's dark eyes gleamed. "The legacy to Miss Josephine, may I ask if it is substantial?"

Temple shifted his bulk uneasily in his chair. "It is a sum which ought to set up any young lady in today's world."

"How much?" asked Mason, with blunt authority.

"Ten thousand pounds." Temple said the words with neither preamble nor pretence, and this prosaic delivery of his answer seemed somehow to magnify its effect on his visitors. Mason gave a short whistle, and when he looked over to Everett Carr, he saw those dark eyes, fixed intently on the solicitor, glimmer with a fascinated intensity. Temple nodded gently. "A sizeable sum."

"Did Miss Josephine know about it?" asked Carr.

"No. That is to say, I think she was aware that her mother had provided for her in the will, but she had no idea of the precise details."

"Did Mrs Kettering have her own copy of the will?"

"Yes, she was provided with a copy, of course."

Carr nodded. "Would it surprise you to learn that she burned it?"

The news seemed to disturb the solicitor, and those keen, intelligent eyes narrowed in confusion. "It would indeed."

"Can you imagine any reason for her doing so?"

Temple shook his head. "None."

"None?"

"Unless you're suggesting that she was planning to disinherit someone." Temple leaned forward. "That could only be her daughter or her husband. But why?"

"There is, you see, Mr Temple," said Carr, his attitude now grave but commanding, "the possibility that Mrs Kettering destroyed her will for the purpose you suggest and that she planned to telephone you to explain that she was planning to change her will, but she was killed before she did so."

Temple saw at once the possibility. "This is dreadful. I can assure you, we had no such instructions from her."

Carr asked, "If her London solicitors had received those instructions, would you expect them to telephone you?"

"I should, indeed. As a professional courtesy, if nothing else, but also to ensure that our mutual client's instructions were consistent."

"And you have received no such telephone call?"

"No." An idea then struck the solicitor. "But I thought the inquest had delivered a verdict of murder against somebody outside the family."

"It did," said Mason, "but you can still see the significance of these enquiries."

Carr was turning his cane between his fingers. "Mr Temple, if your late client had intended to disinherit either of her legatees, who would you suggest she was most likely to strike from the will?"

Temple gave the matter some thought. "I would hardly have guessed she would want to disinherit either. She was devoted to her daughter, and she loved her husband."

"It is known that Mr Kettering wished to leave her," said Carr. "What if her daughter had also somehow betrayed her?"

Temple shrugged his huge shoulders. "I really cannot say. Rowena was a fiery woman, impetuous and impulsive, and certainly not someone to accept any kind of betrayal without some form of retaliation. She might well have taken steps to disinherit either if she felt strongly that they deserved it."

"Would you say that her husband wishing to leave her for another woman would prompt such a response?" asked Carr.

"Very much so."

Carr nodded. "Were there any other conditions of Mrs Kettering's will?"

Temple held up a finger, as if in recollection of something long-forgotten, and shifted his weight in his chair, a prelude to extracting his bulk from its confines. Crossing the room, he pulled at one side of his watch chain and, from the waistcoat pocket, produced a small key attached to the chain. This he used to open one of the filing cabinets, which lined one wall of the office. Temple took out a folder, shuffled the papers inside, and extracted an envelope. The folder was replaced, the cabinet locked, and the solicitor ambled back to his desk. Mason watched the performance closely, but Everett Carr paid no attention to it. Instead, his dark eyes were fixed on the sheen of his shoes and the silver ferrule of his cane against the dull, claret-coloured pattern of the carpet beneath his feet.

Temple, back in his place at the desk, pushed the envelope towards Mason. "This was given to me by Mrs Rowena Kettering a little over a week ago. A copy is also with her London solicitors, I believe."

The envelope was sealed, its colour the blue of the most delicate duck egg, and the handwriting across it elegant if slightly flamboyant. Carr was struck by how characteristic of the woman it was, as if the dynamics of the loops and the decorative quality of the slopes were as indicative of her nature as any acquaintance or dialogue with her might have been. So striking was the handwriting that it almost seemed as if the words spoke themselves aloud in that commanding and theatrical voice that the dead woman had possessed, a fanciful notion that made the dull, business-like function of the words themselves seem all the more perfunctory.

> *For Ivor,*
>> *To be passed to him in the event of my death*

Carr had a sudden sense of portentous disaster. He looked up at Mason, who seemed to view the envelope only with an objective curiosity. There was nothing in his expression that suggested that he had experienced a similar sense of foreboding which had descended over Carr's mind, like the rolling clouds of an impending thunderstorm over the sands of a holiday beach.

Mason looked at Temple. "You don't know what it says?"

The solicitor shook his head. "No."

"Mrs Kettering didn't tell you?"

"No."

Mason turned the envelope over in his hands. "This may be evidence, Mr Temple. Do you have any objection to my opening it now, in front of you?"

It was Everett Carr who protested. "It is addressed to her husband. He should be the one to open it."

"Ordinarily, I would agree," said Mason, "but this is a murder investigation."

"The letter is private, from a wife to a husband," insisted Carr.

"Murder destroys all privacy," Mason argued. "You know that."

But Carr was relentless. "Inspector, that envelope is one of the last wishes of a dead woman. You can be there when her husband opens it and, if it is evidence, I have no doubt he will surrender it to you. But he should have the right to read it first. She wished it to be so, and he deserves it to be so. Anything else would be a sacrilege."

Mason frowned. "You seem very sure about it."

"I am."

Mr Temple leaned forward in his chair, his eyes fixed on Carr. "If it weren't impossible, I'd think you had some way of knowing what is in that envelope."

Everett Carr did not look back into the solicitor's eyes, nor did he look at Inspector Mason. His attention was reserved absolutely for that pale blue envelope. "That is just my point, Mr Temple. I think I do know what is inside it. And that is why I am so insistent that Rowena Kettering's wish is carried out to the letter."

Chapter Thirty-Four

If Mr Temple was a man of considerable bulk, Mr Danforth was remarkable for his gaunt appearance. His face, though amiable and accommodating, was cadaverous, the cheeks prominent and the ocular sockets so pronounced that the pale blue eyes within them seemed unhealthily sunken and deep-set, behind the lenses of the half-moon spectacles perched on the long, prominent nose. The lips were little more than a fine crease across the lower part of the skull, and the ears seemed larger than they were against the frail slenderness of the face. The skin, pale and delicate, was like some sort of ancient parchment stretched tightly across the prominence of the bones. The fingers were long and skeletal, and the veins in the hands themselves stood out like blue cords, providing the only trace of colour against the paleness of the skin. The hair, thinning and white, was brushed back across a large, domed forehead, but swept up towards the crown away from the protruding ears. And yet, despite this appearance of withered emaciation, he seemed filled with energy and cordiality, and he greeted them with an affable eagerness that would have shamed a much younger man.

"Gentlemen, what can I do for you?" The question was both an offer of service and an obvious statement of intended desire to be able to perform his work.

The shop was small, but it gave an immediate impression of efficiency, which was perhaps conveyed most vividly by the tidiness and organisation of the stock. The walls were each filled with fitted shelves, stretching from floor to ceiling, and each crammed with bottles and containers of varying sizes and shapes. The furnishings were of varnished wood, whose deep brown colour extended to the counter behind which Danforth stood, and the various glass-fronted display cases which were scattered around the shop, and whose lower portions were adorned with labelled drawers. The counter itself held a jar of hard-boiled sweets, boxes of cigars, pouches of tobacco, a pair of measuring scales, and various other mundane domestic items. There was a faint aroma of chemicals, although Carr was not sufficiently scientifically minded to identify them, although he wondered whether he had detected the odour of ammonia. Whatever the smells left behind from the various preparations that were concocted in the back rooms of the shop, it struck Carr at once that it was darkly incongruous for such an ordered and respectable place to contain so many methods of dispatching a man to his final rest.

He and Mason had not discussed the letter given to them by Mr Temple, other than a brief exchange between them as they had left the solicitor's office, and that conversation had been little more than a tentative enquiry from Mason as to what Carr believed was in the letter, and a courteous but emphatic snub of the question in reply. Mason had known Carr long enough to appreciate that further enquiry would probably be useless, but he had felt it only fair to plead to Carr's kinder emotions. But when he had asked only for an idea, at least, Carr had shaken his head gravely. Fearing a total absence of explanation, Mason had continued to walk, but then Carr had spoken, the words carefully and seriously delivered. Carr had said, "I fear that the envelope contains perhaps the worst news of all." The cadence of his voice suggested that elaboration was unlikely and any further enquiry redundant, and Mason had been compliant.

This sombre mood had stayed with them as they journeyed back to Longhampton from Norwich, and Mason had still felt it when they had approached the pharmacists' shop. But now, in the wake of Mr Danforth's gaunt but affable face, and when confronted by his amenable if slightly sycophantic manner, it seemed almost churlish to continue to nurture such dark thoughts or, for that matter, to question Mr Danforth about matters of poisons and murder.

As he had been able to read Mason's mind, it was Everett Carr who spoke. "Good day, sir, and I do hope you can help us. I would be very grateful if you would let me have a brief look through your poison register."

The request was as unexpected as it was disconcerting. Mr Danforth's kindly face instantly darkened, not with suspicion but with regret that he was unlikely to be able to comply with a customer's wishes. He adjusted the half-moon spectacles, and the blue eyes registered his apologetic remorse. "May I ask why, sir?"

Mason stepped forward and produced his official identification. "I'm afraid it is a matter of murder, sir."

Mr Danforth, less perturbed by the presence of the police in his shop than why only one of these apparent detectives had bothered to show him any formal credentials, peered keenly at Mason's warrant card and then suspiciously in the direction of Everett Carr.

Mason both sensed and understood the hesitation. "Anything you feel you can say to me, sir, as an officer of Scotland Yard, you can say to the gentleman with me. I can assure you of that."

Danforth's attention remained on Carr, who smiled warmly. The chemist, taking a moment to consider his position, finally returned the smile and offered a brief but profuse word of apology.

"I am sorry, gentlemen," he said, "please do forgive me, but one cannot be too careful. The poison register is so very important that one mustn't treat any enquiry about it lightly."

"Indeed not, sir," said Mason with a smile that he hoped would provide some official commendation for the pharmacist's caution.

Danforth now reached under the counter and produced a large leather volume, which he prised open, revealing the faintly ruled lines of the ledgers inside. Carr saw the various names, addresses, and quantities of the respective purchases, and he thought at once that this was perhaps a larger and more onerous task than he had imagined. It was foolish to assume that he would be able to identify a single name so easily among these masses of details of identification. He showed no sign of his sudden quiver of anxiety, and instead leaned forward and began to glance down the ledgers.

His mind was already narrowing down the possibilities. Having decided to use arsenic to kill Rowena, this supposed poisoner would wish to purchase it swiftly and execute their plan as soon as possible. Similarly, Carr thought, they would not want to risk the poison being discovered in their possession. They would use it as soon as they dared, and a week was perhaps long enough to permit the culprit time to summon the courage for the deed and to find a suitable opportunity to carry it out. It was speculation, but it was not outside the parameters of intelligent credibility, and Carr proceeded to examine only those purchases from a week before Rowena died. At last, he gave a small exclamation of success. His finger rested now against an entry in the poison register.

"What can you tell me, Mr Danforth," he said with a smile, "about a customer by the name of Margaret Anders?" Carr ushered him over to look at the ledger. "You see, Mr Danforth? This lady bought two ounces of arsenic trioxide on 16 October, a little over a week ago."

Danforth looked at the entry indicated by Carr's forefinger: *arsenic trioxide; 2oz; Miss Margaret Anders; 10/16/1935.* The pharmacist shook his head, forcing his memory to recall the details. Carr was patient, his smile amiable and his expression politely reassuring, but he spoke no words of encouragement. Mason, standing beside Carr now, peered over his shoulder at the entry concerned. It told him nothing. The date seemed unimportant, the name was unknown, and the purchase entirely legal.

Danforth now began to nod his head. "Now, yes, I think I do recall the lady. She was the lady with the wide-brimmed hat, if I remember correctly."

"Wide-brimmed hat?" Carr's voice was only mildly curious.

"Yes, it struck me as rather elaborate for daily shopping requirements. She wore it low over her eyes, too."

"Could you see anything of her face?"

The pharmacist pondered the question. "Only an impression of pale skin, and a wisp of blonde hair."

Mason frowned. The description, though vague, was not of Daphne Clements, whose hair was dark. The blonde hair that Danforth had noted might have been a wig, of course, but if it was not, Carr had been correct, and there were two killers at Marsden Grange. Someone who had killed with morphine and someone who had plotted to kill with arsenic, someone who had pale skin and platinum blonde hair. The face of Josephine Kettering seemed to materialise before him, as if conjured out of the atmosphere by some sort of spell cast by suspicion and deceit. He looked at Carr but saw nothing in the placid and genial expression which suggested that a similar thought had seized hold of his mind.

"Do you remember anything else about her?" Carr asked. "Her voice, perhaps?"

Danforth shook his head. "She didn't say very much, certainly nothing which struck me as unusual."

"Had you ever seen her before?"

"Not that I can remember."

"Have you, by any chance, seen her since?"

Danforth shook his head. "No, I am sure of that."

Mason asked a question of his own. "Do you know the people from Marsden Grange?"

"Oh, yes," smiled Danforth. "The Kettering family has long been a customer of ours, through several generations."

"And you know them all by sight?"

Danforth seemed less sure than Mason might have assumed. "Well, not quite. I haven't seen the children for some years, for example."

"Felix and Josephine," Carr said.

Danforth nodded. "Yes, indeed. Josephine was only a child when I last saw her, and I haven't seen Felix since he was a schoolboy. No, it is Ivor Kettering and his wife whom I know best." His use of the present tense struck him suddenly. "Oh dear, perhaps I should say that I *knew* Mrs Kettering. Poor lady, such a tragedy." And then, a sudden realisation widened his eyes, and the gaunt cheeks paled with horror. "The arsenic I sold… it wasn't used to…?"

Carr gave a gentle word of reassurance. "You need have no fear on that point, Mr Danforth, rest assured."

"It is a relief to hear it, thank you, sir. The thought that one might have assisted in taking another person's life, however unwittingly, is too terrible to contemplate."

Carr offered a further word of empathy at Danforth's fears, and then pointed once more to the entry in the ledger. "Tell me, Mr Danforth, is this your handwriting?"

"The substance and amount are in my hand, sir, but the customer always signs and dates the purchase personally. That way, we can be sure that the correct dosage is recorded and we can be sure of who has purchased what."

Carr smiled in appreciation and gave a nod of his head. "A sound system, Mr Danforth, a sound system. That, I think, is all we require. Thank you for your time and your kind assistance. Good day."

"Pleased to be of service, gentlemen," said the pharmacist. He closed the ledger and replaced it under the counter. As he watched Carr and Mason close the door behind them, Danforth thought about how excited the grandchildren would be when he told them of the role he had played in the detection of a murderer.

Outside the shop, such boastful considerations were far from the mind either of Mason or Everett Carr. They walked in silence for a few moments, the inspector chewing on a fingernail, and Carr's eyes turned down to the pavement in serious consideration.

"So, there were two killers at Marsden Grange," said Mason. "Someone else was planning to kill Rowena Kettering with arsenic at the same time Daphne Clements was plotting to kill her with a morphine injection."

"Quite so," said Carr.

"And it looks as if Josephine Kettering was that potential killer. The description is vague, but it's close enough to put her under suspicion."

Carr did not reply. "It certainly clarifies some points, but there is more to be learned." Carr's mind was back in Rowena Kettering's bedroom, recalling in detail those newspaper clippings that he had discovered. "Tell me, inspector, does the name Salvatore Ferrara mean anything to you?"

"I wouldn't be much of a detective if I didn't."

Carr smiled. "Would your colleagues at Scotland Yard be able to find out as much as they can about his assassination and this witness who vanished?"

CHAPTER THIRTY-FOUR

Mason stopped walking, prompting Carr to do likewise. "Probably, but why?"

Carr's dark eyes glowed with amusement. "He is the final piece in at least part of this fascinating little puzzle."

"What can the death of a Mafia kingpin an ocean away have to do with matters at Marsden Grange?"

"You call it an ocean, inspector," said Everett Carr, "but if looked at in a certain light, it is merely a stretch of water."

He smiled and continued to walk. For a moment only, Mason watched him in stunned silence, the words still echoing in his mind. As a worthwhile answer to Mason's question, Carr's words struck the inspector as being next to useless.

Chapter Thirty-Five

When they arrived back at Marsden Grange, Dr Edwin Jarratt was quick to confront them. In truth, he had hoped to speak to either Carr or Mason as soon as he had heard the news about Daphne Clements' attempt on her life, and he was frustrated if not surprised by their absence from the house. He had paced the drawing room, the hallway, and the external grounds of the grange in his impatient wait for their return. It had been only a matter of hours, but to Jarratt, it had seemed like a lifetime, one drenched in confusion, internal conflict, and cigarette smoke. How many of the things he had consumed was impossible to say, but they seemed now to be all he could taste in his mouth.

The news about Daphne's solitary dance with death had reached the house in the early morning. Ivor Kettering had been devastated by the news, which Jarratt had been able to understand, even if Kettering's own son could not. Felix had received the news with aloof disdain, showing as little sympathy or compassion as if he had been told that one of the staff had been dismissed.

"You can hardly expect any of us to shed a tear over it, after what she has done," he had said at the breakfast table. "It's a pity they cut her down. It would have saved the country the cost of a trial, the hangman a job, and all of us the stress and indignity of reliving everything that has happened all over again in the witness box."

His half-sister, as Jarratt might have expected, had been rather more dignified in her response. "Do you have to be so crude all the time, Felix? At least think about Daddy, and keep your thoughts to yourself."

"I don't need you to lecture me about how to deal with my own father, thank you, Josephine." Felix may have hoped that the response had sounded belligerent, even dominant, but to Jarratt, it had seemed to be nothing less than petulant.

"I'm not lecturing you," Josephine had said. "I'm just asking you to keep some of your thoughts private. Besides, isn't it a matter of common decency?"

"Isn't what a matter of common decency?" Felix had demanded.

"Feeling just a little sorry for Daphne," Josephine had replied. "God knows, after what she's done to this family, I can't pretend to like the woman either, but I wouldn't wish this on her."

"Why not?" Adele Mills had asked. "She was going to die anyway if found guilty, which she surely would have been. Felix is right. If she'd succeeded in doing it herself, she would have spared us all a lot of time and trouble."

It had been Tilly Royce who had said the words which ended the conversation. "Can you hear yourself when you speak, Felix, or are you deaf to your own stupidity? None of us had reason to like Daphne Clements, but Josephine is right. The way you're talking is monstrous. The public hangman would have undertaken his work as the climax of a legal process that is fundamental to our system of justice, such as it is. It would be a hanging which meant something. What Daphne Clements did last night is something else entirely. It is an act of cowardice, arising only from her inability to confront her punishment and that very process I've mentioned. Short of anything else, it is an expression of guilt. But that doesn't stop what you're suggesting, Felix, from being both ignorant and offensive."

Felix had flushed and seemed ready to retaliate, but Jarratt had spoken before he had the opportunity. "You think it is a consequence of her guilty conscience, Miss Royce?"

She had looked at him plainly, without emotion. "Don't you, doctor?"

Now, staring out of the drawing room window, the question had come back to him. Did he think Daphne's attempt at suicide was a symptom of a guilty conscience? Knowing what he did, how could he? It was surely more accurate to say that Daphne's attempt on her own life was a cry for help, an act of fatalistic desperation, a moment of madness brought on by her predicament. That, at least, Jarratt could understand. There had been moments when he had thought he would have to face that dreadful loop of hemp at the end of that long, foreboding corridor he had always imagined and feared. He had never come as close as Daphne Clements, thankfully, but it had not been an unrealistic terror. It was certainly the fate Rowena Kettering had felt he deserved.

Suddenly, the memory of Florence Kendall came into his mind. It was strange how spasmodic his thoughts of her were. They came at the strangest moments, like now, or they stayed away for long, unexplained periods of time. The dream had haunted him more frequently over the last couple of days, no doubt encouraged by the macabre events of the weekend, his nights stained with the scarlet of blood and a young girl's cries of agony. Rowena had known about Florence Kendall and what Jarratt had done to her, and he recalled now with sudden vividness the confrontation in his consulting rooms, not long before Rowena's death, when she had used Florence as a reason to deny Jarratt the possibility of marriage to Josephine, and, he felt sure, for other more nefarious purposes. After all, was it not obvious that Rowena had intended to ruin him with his past, or at least allow him to know that she could do so? But then she had died, and with that happy coincidence, the fear of exposure and damnation had died too.

These thoughts were flowing uneasily through his mind when he saw Everett Carr and Inspector Mason walking up the driveway to the house. Jarratt ran for the drawing room door, pulling it open with an almost manic urgency, and similarly treating the front door. His movements were so quick, charged with such emotion, that both Carr and Mason were startled by it.

"Is it true?" asked Jarratt. "Has Daphne tried to kill herself?"

It was Carr who replied. "I'm afraid so, Dr Jarratt. She is in the hospital now, under police guard."

"How is she?"

"As well as you'd expect," said Mason, stepping over the threshold with Carr close behind.

Jarratt stared closely at both of them. "Are you taking it as a sign of guilt or desperation?"

"Both."

Jarratt frowned and shook his head. "I just don't understand it. I don't understand at all."

Carr frowned, but Mason shrugged his shoulders. "Nothing much to understand, sir. She killed her lover's wife and has now tried to kill herself."

"It doesn't make any sense, Inspector," murmured Jarratt.

"What doesn't make sense, Dr Jarratt?" asked Carr softly, his dark eyes narrowed in concentration.

"Why she'd kill herself." Jarratt spoke to himself rather than to anyone else.

Mason shrugged. "Guilt, conscience, cowardice. Call it what you like."

Jarratt nodded, but something about his dark expression suggested that he hadn't heard. Without another word, he walked away, inhaling deeply on his cigarette. Mason watched him open the front door again and step onto the exterior steps, closing the door behind him.

"He seems to be a troubled man," said Carr.

"Shock, I'd say." Mason adjusted his tie and straightened his jacket. "Whatever it is will wait. For now, we need to speak to Ivor Kettering about the letter that old Temple gave us. I can't say I'm looking forward to this."

Carr nodded vaguely, his attention still on the closed front door and his mind still on Edwin Jarratt beyond it. Almost mechanically, he replied to Mason's fears with a paraphrase. "Your mean task would be as heavy to you as odious."

Mason recognised the style. "Shakespeare?"

But Carr did not reply.

Chapter Thirty-Six

A brief enquiry with the butler revealed that Ivor Kettering was in his study. He received them warmly, but his expression could hardly be said to be congenial. It seemed to Carr as if the man had aged with unnatural speed over the last few hours. The eyes behind the spectacles were heavy, due as much to the weight of grief as to lack of sleep, and the cheeks seemed thinner than usual, as if the skin could barely now cover the bones. It was an illusion, brought about by exhaustion and stress, but it seemed no less real or disturbing for that. His manner, too, was distracted, and when he showed them to their seats, it was with a disturbed abstraction of mind. For a moment, both Carr and Mason could have sworn that Ivor had no idea who either of them were or, if he did, that their identities had barely registered with him. As Carr sat down, stretching out the damaged leg, he felt an acute sadness that, if his own conclusions about this letter from Rowena were accurate, the forthcoming interview could only add to Ivor's distress.

Mason handed the envelope across the desk. "Your wife's local solicitors have provided us with this."

Ivor took the envelope almost without recognising it for what it was. "This is Rowena's handwriting. I don't understand." He looked at the two of them with something approaching accusation in his eyes. "What's the meaning of this?"

"I think it would be best if you read it, Mr Kettering," said Carr gently, "and perhaps then we can deal with the matter."

"Why did the solicitors give this to you and not directly to me?"

Mason shifted in his seat. "It may be evidence in the murder investigation, Mr Kettering. Your solicitors acted quite properly. You can see that we have not opened the letter. We have delivered it to you, and you are to be the first to read it. To that extent, we have complied with your wife's wishes."

If Ivor retained any offence in the course of events, he kept it to himself. He picked up a slim stiletto of a letter opener and sliced it expertly across the top of the envelope. It was the practised hand of a professional man used to dealing with important correspondence on his own terms. Carr watched carefully as Ivor slipped the two folded pieces of paper from the envelope and adjusted his spectacles in order to read. Slowly, almost imperceptibly, Carr reached across the desk and took the open envelope in his hands. He sniffed at it gently and, in that moment, his worst suspicions were confirmed. He felt a physical surge of sadness swell within him, and gently placed the envelope back on the desk and closed his eyes.

For his part, Mason was also watching Ivor closely, and he saw now the minister's expression begin to change. The eyes began to widen, and their glimmer of confusion turned to flames of disbelief, and ultimately horror. The lips tightened in a silent refusal to believe what the letter told him, and his breath snorted from his nostrils in an almost animalistic fury. At last, he slammed the letter down on the desk, voicing a foul curse, and darted from his chair.

"It's a forgery," he declared. "I don't believe a word of it."

Mason looked at him. "May I ask what it says, sir?"

"It says nothing but lies. I don't know what sort of hellish game you think this is, inspector, but it ends now."

"I'm afraid you shall have to explain matters to me, sir."

Everett Carr rose gently to his feet and approached Ivor. "Why do you say it is a forgery, Mr Kettering?"

"Because there is no way it could be true, for one thing," hissed Ivor, "and, for another, it is typed. Rowena would never have typed a letter like that. She detested the machines. She'd never use one to type something like this letter, even assuming the contents were true. She would have handwritten it. It would have seemed to her more personal."

Mason had picked up the letter, but before he had begun to read, Carr had made a gesture to stop him. He limped over to the desk once more and carefully took the letter from Mason's hands and placed it back inside the envelope.

"There will be time for an official examination of it later, inspector," he said.

Mason glared up at him. "You know what it says, don't you?"

"I have an intuition."

Ivor turned to face him. "How could you know?"

"It was something Miss Royce said," replied Carr. "She told me that your wife had stopped blaming you for your son's death and that Mrs Kettering had accepted that it was her fault altogether."

"Tilly said that?" Ivor seemed grateful for this news, at least. "Tilly would know, of course. Rowena would never have told me as much. Far better that she thought we shared the blame."

"But you still do not believe this letter?"

"No."

Carr watched Mason, no longer willing to be kept in the dark, take the letter from the envelope, but he spoke only to Ivor. "Why then would your wife confess to the murder of your son?"

Mason's hands stopped fumbling with the letter as soon as the words were said. It was as if they had seized hold of his senses and his physical movements, so that he was incapacitated with shock and confusion. Carr now held his gaze and gave a short nod of his head. Mason broke free from his paralysis and pulled the letter from the envelope. He read it quickly. Somehow, its meaning mattered more than the actual words, but snippets of the confession screamed at him from the page: *"...no longer felt my life was my own...he would not stop crying, nothing would console him, and the sound seemed to get louder and louder...hated him in that one moment... just wanted the noise to stop... before I knew it...water over my hands and his head...now, no noise at all...nothing..."*

Disjointed phrases, but the tale they told was altogether too complete.

Mason felt suddenly in desperate need of a drink. His mouth was dry, his tongue stuck to its roof, and he craved a glass of cold water, except the thought of it conjured up the image of a desperate woman with her child's head in her hands, the spluttering of a dying boy, and the sounds of the river washing over pebbles and stones.

Ivor had not answered Carr's earlier question. Perhaps there was no answer for him to give, and Carr neither encouraged nor insisted on one. Instead, he asked another.

"Had your wife ever shown any evidence of feeling that she could not cope with motherhood?"

Ivor shook his head. "No. I tell you, Mr Carr, this is not true. That letter is a vile and malicious work of fiction."

"You say so purely because the letter is typed?"

"Yes."

"But the envelope is in her handwriting."

Ivor shrugged. "Then someone found that envelope and used it for their own purposes."

"Forgive me," said Carr with a gentle smile, "but what motive would there be for such a cruel trick?"

"I cannot say."

"Assuming what you say is true," Carr persisted, "how would the letter end up with your wife's solicitors? She must have intended to give them a letter, since she delivered it to them. And she must have intended it to be delivered in the envelope we have here. Otherwise, she surely would have noticed something was amiss."

Ivor was growing impatient. "Perhaps someone substituted whatever letter she intended to write with this filth, and Rowena didn't notice."

Mason rose from his chair and walked over to Ivor. "I am bound to say, sir, that I think this letter needs more attention than you may want to give it."

"You're entitled to your opinion, inspector."

The reply, brusque and obstructive, did not unsettle so seasoned an officer as Mason. "Do you really expect us to believe that this is a forgery and that its intention is little more than a vindictive practical joke?"

Ivor shrugged. "I don't care what you believe, inspector. I may have fallen in love with another woman, but I knew my wife. And she would not have typed that letter. Beyond that, I can be certain of nothing."

"Why would anybody wish to harm you so much as to perpetrate this disturbing and offensive hoax on you?"

Ivor considered the inspector's face. "Perhaps the malice was against Rowena. It is her reputation that suffers the most from this alleged confession, after all. And think of the slashed portrait of her. Someone clearly had a malevolent tendency towards her, even if that person couldn't bring themselves to kill her."

Mason smiled. "But the painting could not possibly have hurt *you*. This letter surely does. The painting being vandalised only suggests malice against your wife."

"If anything, inspector," said Ivor, "this vile letter encourages sympathy for me, wouldn't you say? No, no. Rowena was the target of someone's hatred, and this repulsive communication is another example of it."

"And your son's death?" asked Everett Carr.

Ivor glared at him. "An accident, as has always been the case. From an official perspective, and a personal one. Now, gentlemen, perhaps you would allow me some privacy."

Mason seemed about to say more, but Carr laid his hand on the inspector's sleeve and gave a subtle gesture of denial. A brief word of thanks was offered, which Ivor accepted with a bow of his head, and they left him in peaceful isolation.

"Do you believe him?" asked Mason, once they were in the hallway.

"In a sense," admitted Carr. "I can accept that he cannot bring himself to admit what Rowena Kettering did."

"You think the confession is true?"

Carr nodded. "As do you, my friend. But Mr Kettering is a man much afflicted by tragedy. His wife has been murdered, his lover accused and almost dead by her own hand, and now we tell him that his first-born child might also have been murdered by that same wife. How much death and suffering can a human soul take before it begins to reject the possibility of any further trauma?"

As a question, it seemed to Carr to be a monumental one, but Mason, ever practical, took it in his stride. "He's had some bad luck, that's for sure."

Carr ignored the insensitivity. "One thing I do believe, inspector, is that Mrs Kettering didn't use a typewriter."

"Why do you say that?"

"The envelope in which the letter was sealed was of a particular shade of duck egg blue. I saw envelopes of that shade in Mrs Kettering's room, as I am sure you did yourself. But what I didn't see in that room was a typewriter."

"That doesn't mean she didn't use one elsewhere."

"Why should she type a letter somewhere else and then use an envelope from her bedroom here? It is much more likely that she would write the letter and use an envelope she had to hand."

"Unless the typewriter is at the Campden Hill Square residence and she has the same envelopes there."

"A possibility," conceded Carr, "and it would be an easy one to confirm. Perhaps you would get one of your officers to check."

"If Rowena Kettering didn't write it, who did? And why? I mean, why should anyone wish to forge such a letter?"

Carr smiled. "If you consider the peculiar nature of the envelope itself, inspector, I think the answer to that particular puzzle will be very clear to you."

Several hours later, Mason was back in London pursuing various enquiries of his own, but the thought he had given to the envelope and the letter in the intervening period had provided none of those answers which Everett Carr had predicted with such confidence. And, to make matters worse, a report from his subordinate detectives informed Mason that there was no typewriter at the Campden Hill Square residence.

Chapter Thirty-Seven

The library had been unlocked and opened once more to the household. The scientific and forensic examinations of a murder investigation had come to their end. Fingerprints, photographs, and various other traces had been taken for analysis, the results of which would no doubt confirm the verdict of the coroner's court. The library was no longer an active scene of crime. It was simply a room filled with furniture, books, and memories. And yet, the more recent memories would inevitably erase the older ones, and neither the furniture nor the books could ever be looked at or admired again unless it was through the prism of murder. The indelible stain of violent death seemed to smear the contents of the room far more profoundly than fingerprint powder and the smell of forensic examination. Eventually, Ivor Kettering would order that the room be cleaned thoroughly, and the staff would be pleased to carry out the command, but even afterwards, the psychological traces of murder would linger, and for a period of time which it was impossible to determine.

Tilly Royce stood in the centre of the room, staring blankly at the ruins of it. The police's search had been thorough, but their attempts to restore the room to its former peace had been the opposite. The fingerprint powder still dusted the furnishings, like the first fall of a Christmas snow, and she found herself wondering whether some of the spines of the older books would ever survive the invasion of official investigation. She looked at the chair in which Rowena had died and saw the same frosting of scientific investigation on the wooden arms. The sight of it prompted an irrational and futile outrage. The necessary procedure of police investigation had soiled the specific location of Rowena's death, so that even the place of her death could no longer be sacrosanct, as if the process of investigation and justice was somehow more offensive than Rowena's demise.

Tilly was surprised to find that she was crying. Not wrenching sobs, such hysteria was not in her nature, but there were the traces of gentle, silent weeping on her cheeks which she wiped away with the cuff of her dress. The tears irritated her, seeming as they did to her to be signs of weakness, and she scrubbed at her cheeks as much in admonishment of herself as in embarrassment of her display of emotion. She let out an involuntary gasp of air, which showed that she had been holding her breath without knowing it, and she wondered now how long her lungs had been deprived of air. As an effect of what she assumed was grief, this mild but unconscious suffocation seemed strange to her. She began to breathe deeply, as if in compensation for it, and slowly, matters seemed to return to a semblance of normality. She could not say that they were normal. Nothing would seem normal ever again.

Slowly, as her reason returned, she became aware that she was no longer alone in the room. She had not heard him enter, and her sudden alertness to his presence made her gasp. He said nothing, but he had the grace to display some discomfort at interrupting what had obviously been a solitary moment of reflection, one which she supposed he might have felt was more appropriate to a church than a recently vacated scene of murder. If such a thought had occurred to him, he did not shape it into words. Instead, he stood in the doorway with his head bowed, one hand on the silver handle of the ubiquitous cane, and the other held ceremoniously behind his back.

"You startled me, Mr Carr," said Tilly, with a relieved smile.

Everett Carr shook his head. "It was not my intention, dear lady. You came in here to remember your friend?"

Tilly shrugged, as if she dared not admit the accuracy of his statement. "Just to have a quiet moment of peace."

"I am sorry for interrupting it." The words were genuine, but he made no effort to leave.

She looked at him closely. The dark eyes were as inscrutable as ever, and the whiteness of the hair and prominent moustache was now so familiar to her as to be almost comforting, but there was something foreboding about the way in which the heavy brows were drawn darkly over the eyes. Tilly, not usually a woman to display care or concern for strangers, could not help but feel some apprehension for him.

"You don't look quite yourself, Mr Carr," she said. "Is everything all right?"

He gave a short shake of the head. "It is useless to deny that something is preying on my mind, dear lady."

"Concerning me?" She watched the head now nod, but just as shortly. "And that is why you came to find me? It isn't a coincidence that you came in here?"

Another shake of the head. "Now that this room was opened, I thought you might come in here to have a moment of remembrance."

Tilly swallowed hard, but she fought against her instinctive reaction of surprise. "And what made you think that?"

Now, the dark eyes seemed as if they looked through her, with an intensity that was both remarkable and alarming. "Would you do something for me, dear lady?"

"If I can."

"It will require much courage."

Tilly laughed at this almost melodramatic demeanour of seriousness. "What is it?"

But Everett Carr did not laugh. If anything, his glare and his eyes deepened their gravity. "Will you tell me the truth?"

Whatever Tilly might have thought she expected him to say, it was not those words. For a moment, it seemed to her that she had misunderstood him. She recognised the words, and she knew what they meant, but their meaning seemed to have eluded her completely. She wondered if her expression was as foolish as she felt it must be. She was conscious of her mouth fighting to form words, but succeeding only in making incoherent shapes and sounds; she was aware, too, that her eyes flickered madly, as if the fluttering of her lashes could brush away the intensity of his question and what she felt would be his insistence on an answer. During her frantic grasping for a reply, Everett Carr remained motionless, his head bowed, but his eyes remained fixed on her with a dark insistence that she comply.

"Tell you the truth about what?"

Carr smiled gently. "You and Mrs Kettering, and what a poet once called *'the love that dare not speak its name?'*"

The quotation was clearly known to Tilly. She gave a small smile, less embarrassed than wry, and looked at him closely. "Perhaps, Mr Carr, it would be better if you told me what you think you know about it, and let me confirm it or not."

"Very well," he conceded, "but I must ask you again, dear lady, to tell me the truth. You will find, I'm sure, that I am not prone to indiscretion."

Tilly lit a cigarette and sat down in one of the reading chairs. She slung one leg over the other, a display of cool arrogance, to which Carr offered no reaction. He remained standing, leaning heavily on the cane, and idly stroking the Imperial beard.

At last, he spoke, the voice hushed and the delivery slow. "*It will make you feel totally alone if you love someone who can't love you back.*"

Tilly frowned. "I beg your pardon?"

"It was something Mrs Kettering told Miss Josephine. She was talking about her daughter and Edwin Jarratt, of course, but the words struck me as curious."

"In what way? They seem to me to constitute a very sensible warning."

"*Can't love,*" said Carr. "Does that seem natural to you? It implies a lack of ability rather than a question of choice. And surely, it is the wrong way around. Dr Jarratt *could* love Miss Josephine, and he did so, but she didn't feel the same. It was she who *could not love him.* Mrs Kettering's words are futile as a warning against Dr Jarratt."

"I'm afraid I can't help you with that."

Carr continued. "And yet, it seems obvious that Mrs Kettering's warning was about the perils of falling in love with the wrong person."

Tilly inhaled deeply on her cigarette. "Again, it seems like sensible advice."

"*'Someone who can't love you back.'* Someone incapable of feeling the way you do, perhaps. Someone whose nature, whose tastes, whose attractions do not match your own." Carr paused. "Mrs Kettering was talking about you, Miss Royce. Is that not so?"

She did not reply, preferring instead to smoke heavily. Carr watched her in silence for a long moment, willing her to speak, before finally abandoning the hope. When he spoke again, his disappointment was evident in his voice.

"You were in love with Rowena Kettering, Miss Royce," he said. "Her warning to Miss Josephine was a summary of the situation between you and Mrs Kettering. She could never return your feelings. There may have been times when she wished she could, I don't know, but the reality was that it could never happen. She simply did not feel the way you do. I can only imagine the pain that it must have caused you, and I can only marvel at your ability to remain so close to her despite it."

Tilly glared at him, her eyes alive with indignation. "Do you know what you're suggesting, Mr Carr? You're saying I'm something unnatural, something abhorrent to society, something illegal."

"I'm saying you are a woman in love, my child."

"A love which dare not speak its name?" Her voice was cynical.

Carr bowed his head sadly. "For the present, yes."

"The words I used just now were those of my father, Mr Carr. He was a drunk, a bigot, and a bully. I hated him as much as he hated what I am."

Carr shook his head sadly. "You remember when I said you had been seen staring at Rowena's portrait and had been heard to utter a derogatory term?"

"Yes."

"The word you used was *bitch*." He said it as if it caused him physical pain to utter such a term. "It was understood you were saying it about Rowena herself, but I see now that this was not the case."

"Really?"

"The bitch was Daphne Clements, and you thought of her as such on account of the suffering she had caused to the woman you loved. Is that not so?"

"No."

He seemed genuinely saddened. "We must have the truth. In my professional life, dear lady, I have seen humanity in all its forms. Wicked, depraved, vindictive, deceitful, and downright evil. But I have also seen it humbled, broken, ashamed, and remorseful. I don't see you as your father did, nor as our society and laws see you. I see you as a human being, someone who has faced adversity and prejudice and handled them with defiance. I see you as a woman in love. I see you as a loyal friend. I see you as a person with dignity and honour. You are not defined by any caprice of nature, dear lady. You are defined by yourself."

The speech, delivered with a quiet authority as much as emotive empathy, had its effect. Perhaps it was the words, or perhaps it was the compassion that moved her, or perhaps it was a mixture of both. Whatever the cause, Tilly could not prevent the dams of her resolve from breaking and the tears from flooding through. They were not gentle sobs, but forceful cries of anguish. To Carr, it seemed as if the years of suppression of her true emotions, her natural instincts, and her genuine desires were now released, and the magnitude of her relief was almost physical in its intensity. Carr moved to place a reassuring hand on her shoulder, but he resisted the impulse. It seemed to have neither meaning nor purpose. Instead, he stood in reverential silence as her tears fell. Eventually, Tilly rose to her feet, took a handkerchief from her sleeve, and dabbed at her eyes. Her voice, when it came, was hoarse.

"I'm sorry, Mr Carr. I didn't mean for you to see that."

"You need not apologise, dear lady."

"So few people understand. They know what I am, of course, but they either see it as a perversion or an illness. Felix Kettering, for example. He is incapable of accepting that my feelings for Rowena could ever be honest." She looked into Carr's dark eyes. "But you understand, don't you? You can believe it, Mr Carr."

He nodded. "Love is love, however it dares to speak its name."

She smiled and gave a brief laugh. "What a rare man you are, Mr Carr."

If it had been intended as a compliment, he did not acknowledge it. "Did Mrs Kettering know of your feelings for her?"

"I was foolish enough to show her how I felt, more than once. She was somewhat taken aback, to put it mildly. Only a few days ago, I repeated the offence. She was polite about it, but I knew it was unwelcome." She laughed, but there was no mirth in it, only an embarrassed regret. "One gets used to rejection."

He offered only a brief smile. "And yet she was close to you?"

"She was closest to Ivor and Josephine, of course, but outside of her family, yes, I flatter myself that we were close friends."

"And you were content with that?"

"No." The honesty was so naked that it was almost shocking. "I don't know if I can explain this, Mr Carr, but even if she couldn't reciprocate what I felt, it still meant the world to me to have her confidence, to be by her side, to be in her company. I suppose that makes me sound dreadfully possessive, not to say pathetic."

"I wouldn't say so," murmured Everett Carr.

"I suppose sometimes you have to settle for second best. If I couldn't be her lover, I could at least be her confidant."

"I might venture to say that it is a measure of your love for her that it was able to survive on mere crumbs of friendship."

"I never thought of it in those terms." She looked into his eyes. "I would have done anything for her, Mr Carr."

Carr smiled briefly. "Josephine Kettering did overhear you that day, as she told me."

Tilly nodded. "I was looking at the portrait of Rowena, wishing I could do something to alleviate her suffering at the hands of her husband and that damned Clements woman. I felt so powerless. I did call Daphne a bitch. It cannot come as a surprise to you, knowing what you do."

"No."

"But I didn't vandalise the painting and I didn't murder Rowena."

Carr shook his head. "I don't for a moment think you did. Tell me, how much did Rowena confide in you?"

"As much as she did in anybody. More so, perhaps."

"Did she tell you about the death of her son?"

CHAPTER THIRTY-SEVEN

"You know she did," said Tilly. "You've already asked me about it."

Carr smiled. "I mean, did she tell you the truth?"

Tilly stared at him, her eyes wide with shock and a slight but definite trace of fear. Her lips had parted, and Carr had the sudden impression of a vulnerable beauty about the aristocratic features. The arched eyebrows now suggested horror rather than cynicism, and the almond eyes betrayed a sense of dangerous anxiety rather than any feline arrogance. Most of all, it was the silence that struck him. The full lips, opened as if to speak, made no sound, and it seemed for a moment as if time had frozen in that single moment of her understanding.

"My God," she whispered, "you know about it."

Carr nodded slowly. "She did tell you?"

"Only a week or so ago. I couldn't believe what she was saying, quite frankly. I had never imagined her capable of it."

"But you understood why she had done it?"

Tilly nodded. "I like to think so. Once she told me, and the shock had subsided, there was a terrible silence. I don't think I have ever known a more dreadful and complete quiet. My mind must have rebelled against it because it started to conjure familiar sounds to compensate. I remember thinking I had heard a floorboard squeaking, and then I seemed to wait for a knock on the door, which never came, and voices in the corridor outside, but there was nothing. Just this weight of guilt and shame, and Rowena's desperate pleas for me not to abandon her." Tilly smiled. "As if I ever could."

"The mind can play tricks on us so easily, my child."

She looked at him and smiled. Despite herself, she now found him a soothing presence, and she was strangely glad of his company.

"Rowena had written a letter to Ivor, a confession," she said.

Carr nodded. "She'd sent it to her solicitors, both in London and locally, to be given to him after her death."

A sudden realisation hit Tilly. "Has he seen it?"

"I'm afraid so."

Tilly shook her head, as if to displace some thoughts which she did not wish to consider. "I've never liked Ivor. I've always been jealous of him, I suppose, but I would never wish this on him."

"Did anybody else know about the death of Peter Kettering?"

Another shake of her head. "Only me."

Carr allowed a moment to pass. "Why did Rowena wait so long before telling the truth about what she'd done?"

"I don't know."

"She didn't explain?"

"I asked her. All she said was that it was time the truth had its day."

"You know of no reason why she would suddenly think she needed to confess?"

"None."

"And you didn't press her on the point?"

She looked at him with something approaching resentment. "Of course not. If she wanted to tell me, she would have. I had no right to force her confidence."

"She did not confide in you about everything, then?"

"Nobody is an open book to another person, Mr Carr."

He bowed his head in compliance. "I mean only that you and she were so close that she would tell you everything."

"Most things, not everything. Some matters must always remain private."

"But she swore you to secrecy about the letter and what it revealed?"

"Yes. And if you hadn't already found out about it, I wouldn't have told you."

Carr nodded. "I understand that. Did you see the letter?"

Tilly shook her head and lit a cigarette. Carr watched the trails of delicate blue smoke drift to the ceiling. "She had already sent it to the solicitors when she told me about it."

"Would you be surprised to learn that she had typed it?"

She glanced at him, retaining control of her expression for long enough for him to wonder whether he had imagined the brief and instinctive flicker of confusion that had passed across her face. "Does it make any difference?"

"Mr Kettering says Rowena hated typewriters. He doesn't believe the letter is genuine."

"Because it is typed?" She watched Carr nod. "I'm afraid Ivor's deluded. The contents of the letter are certainly genuine."

"You can swear to it?"

Tilly smiled. "I knew Rowena better than she knew herself. She was a great actress, Mr Carr, but she wasn't giving a performance when she broke down confessing what she had done. Those tears were real. That hysteria was genuine. And that guilt was entirely sincere. Why she decided to type it, I can't say, but if it says she killed Peter in a moment of madness, it is true."

After a long moment, Carr smiled and nodded. "Yes, I rather believe it is genuine myself."

Tilly finished her cigarette. "She never recovered from Peter's death, not really. I said her guilt was sincere, but it was also profound. It sounds as if I am making excuses for her. I'm not. What I'm saying is that nobody needs to think she didn't pay for it, because she did. Her protectiveness of Josephine was a symptom of her guilt. The truth was, perhaps, that she had Peter too young. She suffered after the birth, mentally and physically, so she told me. And in that one moment of desperation, it was all over."

Carr was not surprised by Tilly's attempts to justify the death of the child, but he saw no reason why he had to agree with it. However heavy it may have rested on her conscience, Rowena Kettering had taken the life of her son. Whatever punishment she had delivered onto herself, it was not the punishment which the law demanded, nor the justice which Peter Kettering had deserved, nor was it the answer to the problems and difficulties which Rowena had faced as a new, young mother. Carr's capacity for empathy and compassion was wide, but it was not without boundaries. He could find sympathy for a distraught mother who felt she had no other choice, of course, but he found that he could not help but have a greater sympathy for the baby who was drowned after only a brief moment of life. Peter Kettering had deserved to live his life to its natural end, and his mother had robbed him of it. By the same token, however much he might abhor her crime, Rowena Kettering held the same right to life, and someone had taken it away from her, too. It was a universal entitlement, one shared by all of humanity, from the most innocent to the most wicked.

Like so many human conundrums, Carr felt it deserved serious contemplation, and he pondered it long after his conversation with Tilly Royce had ended. As he sat in silence in that room which had been visited and tainted by violent death, he felt certain that the notions of the death of the innocent at the hand of the guilty lay at the heart of the secrets of Marsden Grange, and he had a curious instinct that it was only now a matter of time before he could properly bring those secrets into the light.

Chapter Thirty-Eight

It was in the dying embers of the late afternoon that the paths of Everett Carr and Edwin Jarratt crossed once more. Despite the season, the skies had been blue for much of the day, but they had now turned to a dull orange, as if the moisture in the air had caused the cold blue of their steel to rust. The breeze was unusually warm, and the fields that extended beyond Marsden Grange seemed to glow in the early evening shimmer of dusk. The grounds of the house and its immediate surroundings seemed like an unreal and lusciously romantic version of country life, depicted on a natural canvas and painted by the very greatest artistic creator of all.

Carr had dressed for dinner early, staring out of the window of his room at the mists and mellow fruitfulness of the autumnal evening, and it had occurred to him that a small walk around the terrace would be a pleasant way to pass a few moments before the customary cocktails before dinner. Glancing at his watch, he found that there was plenty of time, and he felt that the evening air would be soothing. He saw nobody as he walked down the main staircase, and he had no sense of regret at the solitude. Everett Carr was a man accustomed to his own company. As it was, however, the idea of a pre-prandial walk around the grounds had not been one to have occurred to him alone.

He found Edwin Jarratt standing alone, gazing out over the fields at the back of the house, smoking in silence. For a moment, Carr hesitated to approach, but he saw it as less of an intrusion than a necessity. There were things that needed to be said, and they would be more easily dealt with if he could discuss them quietly with Jarratt and without having to force an opportunity for privacy. Carr lit one of his Balkan Sobranie cigarettes, his preferred choice of evening cigarette, and walked slowly and silently to the doctor's side.

"A beautiful evening," he said, once their initial nods of greeting had been acknowledged. "Skies such as this one make me wonder whether an atheist might be as well to change his mind."

"Are you a religious man yourself, Mr Carr?"

Carr smiled at the old vexed question that he had so often asked of himself since Miranda's death. "A wise man once said that proof of God was to be found in the flowers since their colour and smell are an embellishment of life, rather than a condition of it."

"It seems rather a leap," said Jarratt, ignoring Carr's evasion of his question.

"Perhaps we can all take some comfort from an ideal," replied Carr, "especially if the alternative is so bleak as to be unthinkable."

"A universe ruled by chance." Jarratt inhaled deeply on his cigarette. "Is that any more terrifying than knowing you are walking a path to your own destruction and there isn't a damned thing you can do about it?"

Carr examined the glowing tip of his cigarette. "If there is no God, does that make it easier for mankind to act like Him, or pretend to be Him?"

Jarratt glanced darkly at him. "I'm not sure I understand your point, Mr Carr."

Carr shrugged. "I mean only that if God does not exist, does it mean that human beings can act in His place? Could we, perhaps, determine who lives and who dies?"

Jarrett turned to face him. "Are you talking about murder?"

Carr gave a second shrug of the shoulders. "Of murder, yes, or of any other means by which a life might be taken."

Jarratt's eyes had narrowed, and his voice had taken on a quality not unlike the blade of a knife. "What is it you're driving at, Mr Carr?"

The dark eyes which turned to Jarratt were serious, at odds with the customarily affable smile beneath the white moustache and Imperial beard. "People might take a life for reasons which morally would not be criticised, but which our laws would still say was murder. Assisting a loved one to die in order to prevent continual and unbearable pain, for example."

"As a doctor, you can hardly expect me to agree with you," said Jarratt, his expression still laced with anger. "We take an oath for a reason."

Carr's smile now vanished. "And have you always adhered to what you swore, Dr Jarratt?"

The words seemed to have a startling effect. For a moment, Carr was not sure whether it was anger, fear, or guilt which raged in the doctor's wide eyes, and it took him a moment to realise that it was perhaps a tormented cocktail of all three. Jarratt did not physically stumble, but Carr's instinct was still to hold him upright, although he made no effort to do so. It wasn't necessary. Jarratt retained his balance, however tenuously, even if he did place one hand on the balustrade of the veranda. Perhaps, Carr thought, he did not have as much faith in his composure as he might have done. Nevertheless, it was clear that the effect of Carr's words had been a psychological one rather than a physical one. Jarratt lit another cigarette, the embers of the previous one barely extinguished, and the sudden stimulation of the nicotine into his body seemed somehow to calm his nerves.

"You know, don't you?" he asked at last, looking cautiously into the eyes of Everett Carr. "You know what I did."

Carr smiled gently. "I have made an educated guess."

"I suspect it's a correct one."

"How did Rowena Kettering discover it?"

"There are gossip and rumours even in Harley Street, Mr Carr. Fortunately, they didn't extend to Scotland Yard or Fleet Street." Jarratt offered a smile, but there was no humour behind it. "May I ask what gave me away?"

Carr inhaled slowly on his cigarette and blew a gentle stream of smoke into the atmosphere. "A number of things. Rowena's possessiveness over Josephine, her refusal to allow you or Lewis Davenport to marry her daughter, and Ivor Kettering told me that Rowena had seen her daughter almost as a second chance, a gift from God."

"Is that all?"

Carr shook his head sadly. "No. There was also her insistence that you were a murderer. At that fateful dinner on the night she died, she talked about you in particular, having strong views on life and death, that you would know what it means to commit murder. Between this belief that you were a killer, the loss of her baby, and your profession as a medical man, there lay the idea of a link between death and children. And then I remembered what you said to me when I asked you about the time and cause of Rowena's death. Do you recall it yourself?"

Jarratt nodded, lowering his gaze. His voice was that of an admonished boy caught out in a lie. "I said I was a gynaecologist, not a pathologist."

Carr nodded slowly. "A gynaecologist, a frantic allegation of murder, and an obsession over the death of a child. Is it such a leap of intuition to imagine a terminated pregnancy?"

Jarratt shook his head. "Call it what it was, Mr Carr. Perhaps Rowena was right after all. I killed an unborn baby."

Carr said nothing for a moment. "What happened?"

Jarratt closed his eyes. It was as if he was forcing himself to remember, but it might equally have been an effort to try to forget. "Florence Kendall was fifteen years old, the daughter of one of my patients. She was brought in by her mother. Florence had been assaulted by three men, whom she thought had been soldiers. They had taken turns, Mr Carr, two holding her down and the third…" A shake of the head was all that was required. "Florence's mother was certain she was pregnant, and a test confirmed it. Not long after that result, Florence broke down, mentally. I had no hesitation in carrying out the procedure. I didn't think about the legality of it. Abortion is, as you will know, Mr Carr, illegal."

Carr's voice was judicial in tone. "Unless there is a danger to the mother's life. Arguably, perhaps, also if there is the possibility of the mother's physical health worsening so much during the pregnancy that she would be past assistance once danger to life was confirmed."

Jarratt seemed not to have heard. "I have heard some doctors talk theoretically about it. One said he would never perform the procedure in case the woman in question was carrying a future prime minister. Worse, I have heard several of my colleagues suggest that it is always the girl's fault and she must bear the consequences."

Carr shook his head slowly and in disgust. "On occasion, I wonder whether I am made of the same fibres as other men."

Jarratt nodded. "I had no such qualms. I didn't think twice. What life would Florence Kendall have had, carrying and giving birth to a child she did not want, a product of something so monstrous, and never knowing which of the animals responsible was the father." He wiped away more than a single silent tear, before looking into Carr's eyes. "I did it. I did it gladly. Florence's life *was* in danger. Perhaps not physically, but morally. It was in danger of stigma, prejudice, contempt, and of a complete denial of opportunity and hope."

Carr placed a hand on the doctor's shoulder. "I can understand those feelings, my boy, and I can fully understand why you did what you felt was necessary."

Now, there was a flash of bitter fury in Jarratt's eyes. "Can you, Mr Carr? Would you have directed a jury to acquit me if I had been brought up on a charge of murder?"

Carr gave the moment only a brief consideration. The question was unfair, demanding an emotional response rather than a legally balanced one. Carr had not heard evidence from both sides, after all, but it had been his experience that a judge must rely not only on the law but on his own instincts. And of those, Carr was in full command.

"There is the girl's age," he said, "the dangers of bearing a child before physical maturity, the mental effects of the original crime itself. Those must be taken into account. Would a surgeon delay removing an infected appendix in order to save life before it perforates and bursts? It seems to me, Dr Jarratt, that those factors I mention are sufficient grounds for assuming that delivery of the child would cause physical harm to this girl."

"You believe so?" Jarratt seemed unable to accept it.

Carr nodded. "If a doctor has reasonable grounds to believe that a continuance of the pregnancy will cause damage or harm to the woman, physically or mentally, a jury would be entitled to conclude that the doctor is operating to preserve the life of the mother. I would like to think that would have been my judicial direction."

Jarratt gave a sudden, sneering laugh. "Rowena Kettering would disagree with you."

And now here it was, thought Carr, the moment for this particular truth to be told. "Perhaps, but she was not approaching the matter with a clear mind."

"What do you mean?"

"I mean that Rowena Kettering's perspective was distorted by guilt. Guilt, which she attempted to smother by transferring it to you."

Jarratt frowned heavily. It seemed for a moment that he did not understand, but Carr offered no further explanation. Instead, the dark eyes locked with Jarratt's and seemed to transmit a slowly dawning realisation in the doctor's mind. Jarratt ran a hand down his face, as if trying to erase the expression of initial bemusement and eventual comprehension from his face.

"Peter? Her son?" Jarratt's voice was so low that Carr almost did not hear the words. "My God…"

Carr nodded slowly. "Rowena's guilt twisted her mind. She was searching for a way of sharing that burden of guilt, but she found it nowhere until she met you. You were a perfect target for her paranoia."

Jarratt was nodding. "Yes, I can see that. Now, it makes sense. I understand everything now."

It seemed for a moment as if he might say more, but no further words came. Carr extinguished his cigarette and inhaled a mouthful of the fresh evening air. "Now, doctor, I wonder if I can ask you something else."

"Of course."

Carr glared at him. "What were you doing in the library at the time Rowena Kettering was murdered?"

Jarratt stared blankly at him, the question seeming to knock the wind out of him like a physical blow to his stomach. "I wasn't. I was outside on the terrace. I got locked out. You were there when I was let back into the house."

"That was after the event, doctor." Carr's voice was grave. "I'm talking about in the moments before Mrs Kettering was killed. You were in the library, and I would like to know why."

The pause which followed was long, but unconvincing. Jarratt made a show of feeling the cold and looked back to the house. "I'm afraid you're wrong, Mr Carr. I wasn't in the library that night."

Carr watched him walk back to the house. Jarratt did not look back towards him, and perhaps Carr did not expect him to do so. All the same, he felt the slivers of ice of instinct freeze his spine, not because he knew that Jarratt's answer had been a lie, perhaps, but rather because he had seen in Jarratt's eyes a glimmer of something that might have been defiance but which seemed altogether dangerously close to malevolence.

Chapter Thirty-Nine

The attack came back to him in broken images of memory. It was not simply the sensation of darkness descending, nor of the feeling of vicious fists against his face and head which flashed across his numbed mind, but also the more minute details of his suffering: the specks of spittle across his cheeks and the hissing breaths escaping through flared nostrils and gritting teeth, both products of his assailant's exertions, and the iron taste of blood in his mouth. And he could remember snippets of his thoughts of regret, guilt, and shame. Now, sitting on his bed, his lips and eyes swollen in the aftermath, he wished he had never started on his dangerous course of action, and he wished devoutly that his love had not turned to dark obsession.

Should he go to hospital? He doubted it. There was no pain in his ribs, and he doubted any other bones were broken. He could feel no loose teeth, and touching his cheekbones, though painful, suggested that there were no fractures to his skull. The bruises, though currently livid and savage, would fade over time. The assault had been the frenzied work of an amateur. For that, at least, he could be grateful. Besides, a doctor might pry into the background of the beating he had endured, and he had no wish to talk of it. It could not change what had happened, and to divulge the reason for it could bring him neither sympathy nor redemption. He was content to allow the matter to end, and end it had. He could no longer continue in his professional position, nor could he dare to indulge any hope that his personal affairs could result in happiness now. When he felt able, he would travel, and bury himself in a foreign city, where nobody would know him, and where nobody would be able to use his past against him. He had no family to consider, and there was nothing of any importance to keep him in England. Paris, perhaps. He would not be the first to live in exile in that city, but perhaps it was rather too close to London to serve his purpose. Rome, another possibility, or possibly even further afield than the continent. America, maybe.

Anywhere, he thought with a silent curse. Just anywhere but England.

The knock at the door surprised him. He felt the sudden intake of breath pass through his broken lips, just as he felt his instinctive desire to ignore the request for entry. His fingers seized the bedsheets, and he closed his inflamed eyes, willing whoever it was to leave him in peace. A second knock showed that the wish was futile, but his silence lingered.

Then, the familiar voice from behind the door. "Mr Davenport?"

Lewis lowered his head painfully. Somehow, it came as no surprise that his visitor, of all people, should be Everett Carr. Now that Lewis knew who it was behind the door, there seemed to be an almost cruel inevitability about it that had not occurred to him previously.

"If you don't mind, Mr Carr, I think I would prefer to be alone," he said.

"I understand that, of course, Mr Davenport," came the politely insistent reply, "but I rather think it cannot be avoided. If it is not me, it will certainly be the police. I hope you will appreciate that I am rather easier to get along with than them."

It seemed to take a long moment for Lewis to give the command that he knew he was always going to have to give. "Come in."

The little man stepped carefully into the room, closing the door with an almost reverential care. Lewis, still sitting on his bed, did not rise. When Carr looked at him, there was a modest flicker of reaction within the dark eyes, which perhaps suggested that the injuries were more severe than he had anticipated, but he did not comment on it. Instead, he indicated a small chair in the corner of the room, nodded appreciation at Lewis' agreement to its use, and pulled it slowly into the centre of the room. He sat down facing Lewis, a slight hiss of pain escaping from his lips as he stretched out the shattered leg, and he offered a small smile of gratitude for the chair.

"If you have come to ask me to name the person responsible for this, Mr Carr, I'm afraid I won't oblige," said Lewis. The words came with difficulty, the breaths between them uneasily delivered. "Nor will I—what would Inspector Mason say?—press charges against that person."

Carr nodded slowly. "Dare I say that if you did wish to do either of those things, I would try to convince you otherwise?"

Lewis smiled. "You think I deserve this?"

"No." Carr's voice was solemn. "But perhaps you think so."

"You might be right about that." Lewis looked into Carr's eyes. "If that's not why you're here, what do you want?"

Carr allowed a moment to pass before responding. "Mr Davenport, I have asked you on more than one occasion whether you were blackmailing Rowena Kettering, and you have refused to give me an honest answer, or any answer at all. Now, I shall give the answer myself, unless you wish to break your previous reticence. In light of what has occurred," he added, pointing briefly to Lewis' injuries.

"I have nothing to say, Mr Carr."

Carr's dismay was evident in this expression, which betrayed both frustration and annoyance. "Who do you imagine you are protecting now, Mr Davenport?"

"Perhaps the one person who still matters."

"Josephine Kettering?" Carr was recalling his conversation with the girl in question after the inquest. "Did she give you any definite answer to your proposal of marriage?"

"No."

Carr was relieved rather than surprised. If Josephine had thought her mind was decided on Lewis Davenport, but she had not yet accepted him, it perhaps meant that Carr's gentle warnings in *The Black Boar* had found their mark.

"Then what good is this nobility of yours now?" he asked. "You cannot possibly think she will marry you when she finds out why her father attacked you last night?"

Lewis stared in horror. "How do you know it was Ivor?"

Carr waved aside the question with impatience. "Because I know you, Mr Davenport. At least, I know your kind."

"You are going to have to explain that to me, Mr Carr."

"Very well," Carr snapped with a stern determination. "I shall tell you what I know, Mr Davenport, and we shall see how matters lie afterwards."

He took a moment to gather his thoughts before speaking once more. In the silence, Lewis Davenport wondered how much this foolish little man, with his game leg, his elaborate moustache, and gaudy lilac handkerchief and necktie, could possibly know about him. Perhaps, he thought, there was nothing to worry about after all. Surely it was simply a case of letting this stranger, as Lewis still saw him, say what he felt he needed to say and then denying any absurd accusation that was made. If the thoughts were designed to give Lewis confidence, they were not altogether successful. They might have been, were it not for those dark eyes of Carr's, which glared at him with an intense condemnation that Lewis found truly unsettling.

"Until this moment, Mr Davenport," said Carr, "I suspected you of blackmailing Rowena Kettering. I can assure you that I no longer suspect it."

"I should think not."

Carr's eyes became dangerous. "No, my boy, now I *know* it. I have encountered blackmailers in the past. They are never pleasant men, as you may imagine, but their motives are almost always very simple. In your case, the purpose of your blackmail was not to extort money, however, but to trap Josephine Kettering into marriage."

Even under the swollen lids, Carr could see the flash of anger in Davenport's eyes. "That is a monstrous thing to say."

"No, my boy, it was a monstrous thing to *do*." Carr slammed his cane against the floor, emphasising the change in perspective. His eyes were hard with rage. "You had discovered that Rowena's first child, Peter, had not drowned in an accident, but that Rowena had killed him in a moment of mental torture. Rather than show her any compassion, you chose to use the knowledge to your own ends."

"You're lying!"

Carr ignored the plea from the defendant. "Being the woman she was, of course, Rowena would not give her daughter to you. Her guilt over Peter had instilled in her a possessive desire to protect Josephine, which would never permit her to sacrifice her living child to a devious man like you. She thought, quite naturally, that you were interested only in Josephine's money, so she made plans to disinherit her daughter. She had no time to contact her solicitors before she was killed, but that was almost certainly her intention."

"Why? If she was so protective of Josephine, why leave her penniless?"

Carr shook his head. "Wills are changed very easily, my boy. Once you were gone, Rowena would have changed the will back again, and matters would be right. But," he added with a solemn conviction, "this was never about the money. Your blackmail was only ever designed to give you Josephine. But then, Rowena was killed."

"And you think I did that, too? In revenge, perhaps, because the blackmail hadn't worked?"

Carr shook his head slowly. "Whatever else you might be, you are not a killer, Mr Davenport. No, when Rowena was killed, you simply switched victims. If Josephine's mother would not give you what you desired, perhaps her father would. But he didn't. Instead, he gave you this." He waved his hand towards the bruises. "Ivor Kettering has been hurt and tormented most by the tragedies in this house. Your demand for his daughter's hand in marriage was more than he was willing to accept."

Lewis Davenport rose slowly from the bed and turned his back on Carr. He walked slowly towards the window and glared out through the pane, as if looking towards his now uncertain and broken future. "

"I don't ask for sympathy, Mr Carr," he said, "but what I did has cost me everything. I have been dismissed from my employment, of course, and once it comes out, Josephine will never speak to me again. Physical wounds don't seem to matter so much."

Carr was unmoved. "You don't deserve consideration, Mr Davenport. Your conduct has been beyond wickedness."

"I know that." This, at least, was the truth. "How did you know about me?"

"I told you that I had overheard your argument with Rowena Kettering," said Carr, "where she openly accused you of blackmail. My concern, as you know, was what reason she had to say it. When I learned that her son had not died in the manner everybody believed, it seemed a logical conclusion to draw. And then there was the fact that Rowena Kettering disliked typewriters."

The declaration seemed strangely irrelevant, and Lewis Davenport turned to face him, his brows furrowed in confusion. "I don't understand."

Carr smiled. "Very likely not, my boy, but the point is very simple. Rowena wrote a confession to her husband about Peter's death. She had confided in nobody but Tilly Royce about it. She had written it by hand and sealed it in an envelope, which she then addressed by hand, before handing it over to her solicitors. However," he continued, rising to his feet and walking towards Lewis, "the letter which those solicitors gave to Inspector Mason, and which he then gave to Ivor Kettering, was typed. For this reason, and given Rowena's hatred of the machines, he believes it to be a forgery. But it struck me that there might be another explanation."

"Go on," said Lewis, knowing what would now be said.

"Not a forgery, of course, but *a copy*. I have said that only Tilly Royce knew about the letter, but I think you had overheard that conversation. She mentioned hearing a floorboard squeak, although she thought she had imagined it. She hadn't: it was you."

"It was the merest chance that I heard them talking, and I took advantage of it." Lewis did not sound proud of it.

"You steamed open the letter, made a copy of it, and kept the original," said Carr. "You had to keep the original, of course, to prove its authenticity, or else the blackmail would be meaningless. When Ivor Kettering dismissed the letter, I happened to study the envelope. It contained a very faint odour of glue on the seal, suggesting that it had been re-sealed. When you showed Ivor the original letter, his doubts about what Rowena had done were gone. In his rage, he attacked you."

"I deserved it. You don't have to stand in judgement of me."

"I do not do so," said Carr. "Just as nobody will stand in judgement of Ivor Kettering for the assault. There will be no charges brought. He is a man more sinned against than sinning, Mr Davenport, and his sin does not begin to equal yours."

Lewis merely bowed his head. "I know."

"You do," said Carr without pause. "But, as I said, I know you, Mr Davenport, and I know what you are. Your conscience will be your punishment."

There was more to be said, but Carr was not vindictive enough to give the words a voice. Lewis Davenport would live with the knowledge and disgrace of what he had done. Josephine would demand an explanation of why her father had attacked the man she had decided to marry and only the truth about Lewis Davenport would be sufficient explanation. To Carr's mind, just as Ivor Kettering had suffered enough, this battered and wicked man had done likewise. There was no reason for him to know the cruellest irony of all, that the girl he so dangerously loved had chosen him and had decided to accept him as her husband. Making it known, Carr thought, could only bring more harm, and, despite his disgust, he was not a man to inflict meaningless pain on another human being. There was enough mindless harm in the world without any addition from him. And so, with a courteous bow, he left the young man alone to contemplate what future he might have and to confront whatever feelings of guilt or shame that might descend upon him.

Once he heard the door close, Lewis Davenport stood in silence for a long moment, before his swollen and brutalised eyes began to weep the tears which embodied those sad emotions which Everett Carr had predicted.

Chapter Forty

It was an interview for which Carr had no taste, but one which was so necessary that his personal feelings in the matter could hold no relevance. He felt certain now that he knew the truth about the death of Rowena Kettering, but there were still some questions that needed answers, even if the overall picture was now clear to him. However, it seemed to him that the solution to this riddle was of lesser importance than its effects on the people at the centre of it and the impact on those lives tainted now by some direct human wickedness. And now, at this interview, which he approached with trepidation, some of those consequences were painfully evident.

Ivor Kettering sat at his study desk, his head in his hands, and the quiet gasps of gentle sobbing escaping from his tightened lips, the efforts of which made his shoulders shake. He had declared his remorse so many times that it was in danger of becoming meaningless. Carr thought little of this apologetic repetition. To him, it was a sign of genuine regret, and he, for one, was pleased to hear it come from Ivor's mouth.

"It was just one more cruel injustice," Ivor said, the words barely audible beneath the tears. "First Rowena's murder, then Daphne's arrest, and now this bloody upstart claiming my daughter as if she were some sort of lot at an auction. I just lost control. Can you understand that?"

"Oh yes," said Carr without hesitation. "I doubt anyone would be incapable of understanding what you did. I have told Mr Davenport that there is no question of charges being brought against you. Quite apart from the fact that he would have to explain the reason for the attack on him, which would open him to perhaps graver charges than he brought against you, he understands that prosecuting you would be unwise. I have made him fully aware of his position. For what it is worth," he added with a shrug of the shoulders, "he is consumed by guilt about what he has done."

"Good," spat Ivor. Then, in a more measured tone of voice. "Good."

"As, I know, are you," said Carr.

Ivor looked into his eyes. "Do you know that? It's more than I know."

Carr nodded. "When the dust has settled, my friend, you will realise it without reluctance. For now, there is one more difficult task to perform."

"Josephine?"

"You must tell her before she sees Davenport's face. Her sympathy must be for you, not for him."

Ivor understood. How could he not? Even in the wake of his brutality, he could recognise the demands of logic, but it made the prospect of the confession required from him no easier to contemplate. But Carr was correct about where Josephine's sympathies should lie, and Ivor knew it. Slowly, he got to his feet and rang the bell, which was set into the small fireplace in the chimney breast wall of the study. Within moments, the lean and solemn butler had arrived.

"Bates, fetch my daughter, would you?" said Ivor. "Tell her it is urgent."

"Very good, sir."

As the butler began to execute the command, Carr stopped him. "I wonder if I might be impertinent, Mr Kettering, and ask a question."

"Of course."

The butler turned his attention to Carr. "How may I assist, sir?"

"You lock this house every evening, I think I am right in saying."

"Yes, sir. I go around each evening, ensuring the windows and doors are locked and bolted."

"Starting with the front door?"

"Indeed, sir."

"At what time is that?"

"Midnight, each evening, sir."

And there, thought Carr, was proof of a lie which he had long suspected had been told. "On the night of Mrs Kettering's death, when you were performing this duty, did you see anybody in the hallway at all?"

"No, sir."

Carr, satisfied, offered a word of gratitude, and the butler departed. He and Ivor waited in silence for Josephine to arrive. It was neither awkward nor companionable. It was merely the quiet of two men with little more to say to each other, but in whose company there was mutual support for the interview to come.

At last, however, Ivor broke that silence. "Did Davenport kill my wife?"

"No."

"Did Daphne kill my wife?"

This time, Carr did not answer with such speed or assurance. Instead, he lifted his dark eyes and looked at Ivor with a searching intensity. He was on the verge of responding when there was a knock at the door, and, without invitation, it opened. Josephine stepped into the room.

"Bates said you wanted to speak to me, Daddy." She saw Everett Carr and was at once surprised and disconcerted. "What are you doing here, Mr Carr?"

But it was Ivor who replied. "It is on Mr Carr's advice that I sent for you, darling."

"What's happened? Is this to do with Mummy's death?"

Her father shook his head. "I have something I must confess to you, darling, and I need you to sit down and listen."

"Daddy, you're frightening me." Josephine looked up at Carr as she sat down. She saw him smile warmly, a gesture which might have been solidarity, comradeship, or reassurance, possibly a combination of all three.

"There's no need to be afraid," said Ivor. He had now perched himself on the edge of the desk so that he was looking down at his daughter, seated in one of the chairs in front of him. "This is difficult to say and to hear, so please let me finish and don't interrupt."

When Ivor Kettering began his confession, Everett Carr turned his back on the discourse and stared out of the window of the study. He knew the story; he did not have to listen to it again.

He had not known what reaction to expect from Josephine Kettering, and he was too experienced in life to attempt to predict any human reaction to horrifying news. Shock was capable of causing various and diverse responses to such matters. He would not have been surprised at tears, nor would he have been amazed at anger, and he knew that he could not wager on either, but those were the two extremes that he might have reasonably expected. What he could not have foreseen, however, was the demeanour of apparent indifference which came across Josephine's expression as her father explained the depths of Davenport's betrayal and its violent aftermath. The eyes widened and the lips parted in mild incomprehension, as if she understood the words being said but neither their meaning nor their context. Carr would realise later that it was at this moment that Josephine began to change from a naïve and innocent girl to a woman who is aware that the world contains wickedness and danger. With this realisation, there came the understanding that Josephine's reaction of disinterest had been the product of this sudden education of herself. That was the shock and the surprise: not Davenport's betrayal, but what it represented in a wider context, and its effect was what had stunned Josephine into quiet disbelief.

"How could she do it?" she asked at last. "To a baby... How could she...?"

Ivor shook his head. "I am still trying to understand that myself. She wasn't well. The stress of giving birth, the demands it required, and the toll it took were all too much for her. Perhaps we were too young to have a family. Perhaps the reality of it was a shock to your mother. Maybe she thought it would be sun and roses. She was an actress, after all, and her view of the world was often romantic, not to say melodramatic."

"Is that an excuse for murder?" snapped Josephine.

"No," said Ivor gently, "but perhaps it is an explanation for it."

Josephine glared at him. "Can you forgive her?"

"I don't know. She took one child from me, but she gave me you. I have you, here and now. Maybe the past should be left to itself."

Josephine had started to cry, but she barely noticed the tears. "She's not the woman I knew, Daddy, not anymore. She's a stranger."

"You mustn't say that."

"It's how I feel." She wiped away a tear with the ball of her palm. It seemed strangely indignant, almost adolescent.

"Your mother loved you," said Ivor. "You must remember that."

"Was it love? Or was I just a way of suppressing her guilt?" She wiped away another tear. "And Lewis used that guilt to try to imprison me in marriage. It's frightening, inhuman."

Ivor nodded. "I know."

"I never thought love could be so monstrous."

"It can be cruel," said Ivor.

Carr turned back from the window, his eyes blazing with defiance. "But it can be pure, and it can be fulfilling. Not all love is represented by Lewis Davenport."

Josephine looked up at him. "No, not all love. Just the love that seems to find me. A blackmailer on the one hand, and a killer on the other."

"Your mother misjudged Dr Jarratt," said Everett Carr.

"Why do you say that?"

This was not the time for any explanation about the question of Edwin Jarratt. Instead, Carr limped slowly to the desk.

"The point for now is Lewis Davenport, not Dr Jarratt," he said.

Ivor nodded. "I wanted you to hear what had happened from me, not him. I'm not proud of what I've done, but I don't regret it either. I wanted you to understand."

Josephine took a long moment to respond. When she did so, she rose slowly and placed her arms around her father's neck. Into his ear, she whispered simply, "I do understand", and she held him tightly for an even longer moment. To Everett Carr, it seemed perversely like a moment of normality amid the confusion and deceit of the last few days. Here, in this close embrace, there was the personification of parental protection, of a father's love for his daughter, of comprehensible human emotions. What had prompted them seemed to Carr to matter less than the act of the embrace and its insistence that there was still order amid the chaos caused by violent and sudden death. It seemed strange to admit it, but Carr found it reassuring, even touching, that such solidarity between parent and child could rise so strongly from the ashes of Lewis Davenport's malice.

Josephine, ending the embrace, looked at Everett Carr. "That afternoon, after the inquest, in the pub, you were trying to warn me about Lewis then, weren't you? I'd told you I had decided to marry him, and you knew it was wrong. All that talk about love and being loved, that was your way of telling me that Lewis didn't really love me."

Carr nodded slowly. "I tried to dissuade you without hurting you."

"But how did you know?"

Carr was not eager to explain the argument between Rowena Kettering and Lewis Davenport. Reference to it would raise too many secondary questions. "An intuition, dear lady, nothing more."

She had more questions, he knew, but she did not ask them. Perhaps his expression was sufficient to discourage her. She looked back at her father. "I never want to see Lewis again."

Ivor shook his head. "You never have to. I have dismissed him, of course. He shall leave this house today."

"I wonder where he will go."

"I don't know," said Ivor, and then, with more malice, he added, "and nor do I care."

She looked at Carr. "But I do want to see Edwin Jarratt."

Carr frowned. "Why?"

"Because if today is a day of wicked revelations, I may as well find out from him why my mother thought he was a killer, and whether his idea of loving me was any better than Lewis'." The words, spoken with a strength of voice that had never before been present, were impossible to deny, and Carr again felt the growth of experience within her rise to the surface.

"If you wish it," said Carr, "I doubt either your father or I could prevent it."

Josephine held his gaze. "And are you going to let me speak to him without any idea of what he might say? Because you know, Mr Carr. You know what my mother meant by saying he was a murderer."

Carr nodded. "Yes, my child, yes, I do."

"Then tell me, please."

"It is better that he tells you himself." He took a step closer to her. "But, if you permit it, I shall come with you. Then, if he does not wish to speak, perhaps we can persuade him together to do so." And he smiled.

She did not return it with her lips, but her eyes sparkled with gratitude. "Thank you." She leaned forward and kissed her father on his cheek. Ivor's hands closed around her arms, his knuckles whitening. "I love you, Daddy."

"I love you, too," Ivor said, and it seemed to him as if he had never said the words to her before. "I love you so very much."

As he left the study with Josephine, Everett Carr thought that one relationship at least would survive and perhaps even strengthen because of the horrors of Marsden Grange.

Chapter Forty-One

Jarratt had abandoned his attempts to eat breakfast and had left the dining room, offering a curt farewell to Felix and Adele, who continued to eat their respective rashers and eggs and toast and marmalade. For Jarratt, the thought of food was repugnant, and he had satisfied himself only with coffee. The smell of bacon, eggs, and toast had permeated the room and, although usually he would have savoured its effects, it had seemed to him to be nothing less than suffocating. Sitting opposite Felix, whose appetite seemed keener than ever, Jarratt had watched forkful after forkful of food and mouthful after mouthful of coffee be consumed with hearty enjoyment. It had made him feel nauseous, and he had made his excuses and left, craving fresh air and, conversely, cigarette smoke.

He knew the cause of this lack of desire for food, of course, although he likewise knew that it was not confined to one cause. His talk with Everett Carr had disturbed him, and its details lingered in his mind, but their consequences also loomed in the shadows at the back of his conscience. It had felt strangely therapeutic to discuss Florence Kendall's tragedy, and the part he had played in it, certainly not because he took any delight in it, but because he had never spoken about it with anyone. He didn't count his talks with Rowena Kettering: those were threats and accusations, not intelligent discussions. With Carr, there had been empathy and perhaps an element of personal justification, and Jarratt had been grateful for it.

Which made the other problem that had seized hold of Jarratt's mind all the more difficult to solve. He knew that he should confess to Carr, not least because it seemed Carr knew everything anyway. Continued deception, in the wake of that realisation, seemed pointless. Furthermore, Jarratt now felt he owed Carr the confession, as payment in kind for the empathy which he had shown regarding Jarratt's past. What held Jarratt's tongue was the knowledge that once the confession was made, and once the whole truth was known, there would be no returning to the seemingly preferable sanctity of secrecy. People were brought up to believe that the truth mattered above all other things. It had certainly been Jarratt's parents' point of view, but they had never been able to explain why the truth was sometimes so difficult to tell, and why it was better to be told if it meant misery and disaster for someone who had no need to know the truth or could receive no benefit from knowing it.

Jarratt smoked heavily. Inhaling the smoke deeply into his lungs seemed somehow to purify his thoughts. There was more to be considered than one person's misery. The truth Jarratt could tell, the one which he knew that he should tell, would save a life. There was no escaping the fact, but nor was there any use in denying that in order to save one life, Jarratt would have to condemn another. He thought back to Florence Kendall. Then, he had suffered no such crisis of conscience. He had never thought any other course of action might be appropriate. As terrible as her assault and its sequel had been, Jarratt had known what he must do. In the case of the death of Rowena Kettering and its aftermath, he could find no road of certainty through the chaotic woods of indecision.

"Edwin?"

The voice intruded on his thoughts like rolling thunder on humid summer evenings. It was so startling that he almost gasped at it. Josephine was standing behind him, with Everett Carr at her side. He looked from one to the other of them, momentarily confused, although his senses were growing cautious. He finished his cigarette and flicked the end across the lawns.

"Can we speak?" asked Josephine.

"What about?" Jarratt's eyes were narrowed, but their attention was fixed on Everett Carr.

"She needs to hear the truth, my boy." Carr's voice was low, but its tone was gentle, like a priest advising a troubled parishioner. "Something very wicked has happened, and Miss Kettering needs to be reminded that there is goodness still in the world."

"What has happened?"

"Tell her the truth," urged Carr.

Jarratt looked at him with mild disbelief. "As proof of goodness?"

"Goodness, courage, moral judgement, call it what you will."

Carr's expression and his manner were so seriously supplicatory that Jarratt was alarmed by them. "What has happened?"

Carr seemed about to speak, but Josephine stepped forward. "I'll tell him, Mr Carr. It's only right that it comes from me, and perhaps then, Edwin, you will be able to be frank with me in return."

Jarratt, not at all sure that he could keep the promise, nodded his head. Carr stepped away, resting himself against the balustrade of the veranda, and began to rub his broken knee gently. The conversation which would now ensue would need no interruption or contribution from him. He watched them closely, however, willing each to listen to the other, and he slowly closed his eyes. Somewhere in the distance, birds were singing.

Josephine spoke first. Her voice was uncertain and, on occasion, it broke, but not sufficiently so for the story to be halted or for actual tears to flow. As she relayed the events surrounding her betrayal, she seemed strangely detached from them, except when the reality of them seized hold of her voice and attempted to strangle it. When she had finished, she simply fell silent. She looked neither into Jarratt's eyes nor at Everett Carr, her gaze concentrating only on her own feet and the flagged veranda beneath them.

Jarratt had listened without interruption, although there were times when he had struggled to remain silent. He had wanted to take hold of Josephine's hands during those moments when her voice failed her, but his anger had been so fervent that he had feared that he would squeeze them too hard, that he might shatter her bones. Instead, his fingers had closed in on themselves with fury, forming white-knuckled fists of fierce hatred. When Josephine told him about the revenge taken by her father, Jarratt nodded his head, and only at that moment did those fists relax and melt from instruments of retribution into the slender and nimble instruments of a healer.

"Thank you for telling me," he said. "I know it took courage. I have never liked Lewis Davenport, God knows, but even if I had known nothing of him, I would hate him now. I cannot say I think your father was wrong." He looked to Everett Carr. "Do you say he was, sir?"

Gently, Carr opened his eyes. "I have made my feelings known to Mr Kettering and, perhaps more importantly, to Mr Davenport."

If the answer was evasive, it seemed to Jarratt that it had lost none of its meaning. Somehow, even without saying so, Jarratt knew that Carr had answered his question, and he was in no doubt about how that answer lay. Jarratt looked into Josephine's eyes. The breeze had blown a strand of her hair across one eye, and he gently smoothed it back into place. Her eyes lifted to meet his when he did so, as if his hand had somehow controlled their movement.

"I'm so sorry, Josephine. You don't deserve any of it." He looked at Carr. "And Rowena did it? She killed her son?"

Carr nodded. "Mr Kettering, I think, understands why. He was right to say she wasn't well, and I think he may well be right about her mental state being an explanation, if not an excuse, for what she did."

Jarratt looked at Josephine. "I have heard of it. New mothers, faced with the responsibility, the demands, and the dependency of a child, they simply can't face it."

"They don't all drown their babies, though," said Josephine.

"No," said Jarratt. "But I have heard of them smothering them with pillows, shaking them so violently that they die, or even ignoring their demands for food so that they starve."

"Really?" It was news she had never thought could be delivered. "People feel like that?"

"Some."

Josephine tried to appear unmoved, but it was evident that Jarratt's words had made a severe impression on her. She seemed to struggle to find further words to say and, for a moment, she made a series of low, almost inaudible noises of indecision, and she nodded her head slowly several times, her eyes flicking between her clasped hands and Jarratt's concerned and caring eyes.

Here, she thought, was the bedside manner, the professional medical man's expression of consideration and sympathy, so far removed from what she had previously considered to be a demeanour of cool arrogance.

At last, Josephine found some words. "You're saying I shouldn't judge Mummy too harshly."

It was Carr who responded. "You have learned some terrible things in a short space of time, my child. It is best to allow those matters to settle and deal with them at length. Make no instinctive judgements."

"Easier said than done, Mr Carr," she said.

He nodded. "It certainly is, dear lady, but you must try to allow time to heal."

Josephine shook her head. "I'm not sure I can do that. On the one hand, I feel sorry for my mother and how she must have felt, but on the other, I can't bring myself to understand or forgive her for what she did. You tell me she was ill, but I never saw it in her. I can't recognise the woman I loved as my mother as being a sick woman. Physically, or mentally," she added, the final word not coming easily to her.

"No, said Carr, gently, "but it is the truth."

Jarratt took hold of Josephine's hands, so gently as to be almost hesitantly, but she made no effort to resist. "And bearing it in mind may help you to understand about me."

"How?" She had stiffened slightly, in apprehension.

Jarratt looked at Carr, who offered an encouraging nod of his head. Jarratt took a breath and looked directly into Josephine's eyes. "You have told me the truth, so it is time for me to do you the same courtesy."

Now, she did release her hands from his grasp, and she stepped slowly away from him, coming to rest beside Carr's side. Jarratt could not complain, and nor would it have done any good to try it. He looked at them, trying hard not to feel like a man facing an interrogation, but the feeling would not dissipate. Whether it was an effort to delay the inevitable or simply a matter of an addict's need, Jarratt couldn't say, but he lit a cigarette and inhaled deeply and gratefully on it.

He tried to convince himself that telling the story of Florence Kendall for the second time would be easier, but he found that this time it seemed even harder. Confiding in Everett Carr, a man who had seemed to know the worst of it before Jarratt had begun to speak, was one thing; explaining it all to this girl whom he had loved for so long, but who had never liked him on account of her mother's prejudices, seemed impossible. He felt as if he had more chance of turning back the clock so that Florence's attack had never happened at all than of telling her story and explaining his part in it, all over again. The cigarette offered no comfort or escape, nor did the second one, and he doubted the third would fare any better.

He was not conscious of speaking. He could hear a voice coming from far away, and he thought it could be recognised as his, but he wasn't sure. The words sounded as if they were being spoken through water, muffled and distorted, as if their meaning was trying to lose itself by design. Time was measured in the decreasing size of the cigarette he was smoking and in the repetitive movement of his feet as he paced in front of them across the veranda and back again. It was all happening to someone else, someone far away, someone who had lived a tragedy that had nothing to do with him, other than he had been asked to tell it.

And then, those barely comprehensible words stopped, and Jarratt became aware of a deep silence. He blinked furiously, as if waking suddenly from a disturbing dream, and he seemed momentarily to be unsure of his surroundings. Slowly, the house behind him and the lawns ahead of him came into focus, and he seemed to see for the first time the two people in front of him. With this strange return to reality came the obvious knowledge that the disjointed words had been his, that the terrible history that had been told had involved him, and that there was never any escape from it. He looked down at the remnants of whichever cigarette he held, and slowly he finished it.

"And there you have it," he said, not knowing really what any of it meant.

Jarratt looked at Everett Carr, and he saw the gentle assurance that all would be well. Daring to believe it, he looked at Josephine, whose expression initially convinced him of the opposite. Her eyes were awash with tears, her expression contorted with anguish, and her whole frame rocked with emotion. She pushed herself off the balustrade and ran towards him, her arms locking him in an embrace of conflicting emotions: pity, sympathy, anger, horror, possibly far more than either of them could count.

"She was wrong," Josephine whispered into his ear. "She was wrong about you. You're no killer."

Jarratt held her tightly now, closing his eyes tightly in relief, his breathing somewhere between a wail of agony and a laugh of liberation. He opened his eyes and looked at Carr. Despite the blurring of his vision, the cause of which he was too relieved to acknowledge, Jarratt could see Carr's expression of benediction. There was a smile beneath the impressive moustache, and the dark eyes glittered with something which Jarratt could not quite define.

Josephine looked into Jarratt's eyes. "All that time, I thought you were a monster, when all you did was save a girl's life."

"I'm not sure I see it as simply as that," Jarratt felt compelled to say.

"This girl, Florence, her life would have been ruined, as far as I can see, if she had survived the birth at all."

"And the baby?"

"Would he or she have had any life at all?"

Jarratt had no answer. "Don't think what I did was noble, Josephine. It was necessary, in my view, and on some level, it was justified. But I can't ever see it as heroic." The word sounded foolish to his ears.

"Life isn't black and white," said Josephine. "I see that now. We have to make the best of it." She looked over at Carr. "And Mother thought it was murder because of what she'd done. Because of Peter."

Carr nodded. "Her view of the world, of life and death, was tainted because of her guilt. But in the imagined future you conjure for poor Florence Kendall, my child, try to see something of what your mother felt she was suffering with her own first child."

Josephine had no reply to give, but her eyes narrowed in consideration, and the pale brows creased with mild alarm. Carr was content to allow the idea to settle in her mind. In time, perhaps she would come to understand and even, if she were brave enough to allow it, to forgive. To that extent, at least, he felt as if good had been done.

"Now, my children," he said, "I must try to find Inspector Mason. There is a piece of information which I have asked him to discover for me, and he should have it by now."

Jarratt released himself from Josephine's arms and walked over to him. "Before you go, Mr Carr, I would like a brief word."

"There is nothing more for you to say, my boy," assured Carr. "You have done well. And you may yet reap some reward for your courage."

Jarratt seemed pained by the words. "I don't mean any of that. After the kindness you've shown me, it seems grossly unfair of me to have to say this, but I lied to you. And I think it's time I made one last confession."

Carr smiled and placed a hand on the doctor's shoulder. "You need to say no more."

"No, you don't understand."

"You're wrong, doctor." Carr's eyes had hardened. "I understand everything about what happened in this house on that night."

There was something about those dark eyes and their intensity that made it impossible for Jarratt to disbelieve him. "In that case, I think you'd better have this. You will know what to do with it."

Reaching into his pocket, Jarratt took out a crumpled white handkerchief. Carr handled it gently, his lips smiling with a cool understanding. Somehow, he had known what it was that Jarratt was going to give him, and, with equal certainty, he knew why it was in Jarratt's possession. So sure was he, that Everett Carr did not need to register in his mind either the handkerchief or the flamboyant "RK" monogram stitched into one corner of it.

Chapter Forty-Two

There was one final piece of information that Carr felt was necessary before the whole truth could be known, but he was entirely reliant on the speed with which Inspector Mason was able to furnish it. Carr had no doubt that the resources of Scotland Yard would be able to discover what Carr needed to know, but the time it took was a matter beyond anybody's immediate control. Carr was not an impatient man, nor was he an unreasonable one, but he awaited Mason's report with increasing irritation. Idleness, he knew, would only serve to prolong his impatience, and so he busied himself as best he could.

First, he paid a visit to Daphne Clements in the hospital. The officer on guard was reluctant to allow him near the prisoner, however, and it took all of Carr's persuasive ability, not to say an excessive assurance that he was closely connected with Inspector Mason, to bend the will of uniformed officialdom. Even then, it required a telephone call to the local station for approval from the officer's superiors. When he allowed Carr to pass, there remained a glint of suspicion in the young man's keen eyes, which Carr returned with his politest bow and an almost unctuous word of gratitude.

Daphne Clements lay in her bed, her head turned away from Carr, facing the window, so that her neck was largely exposed to him. He saw the livid contusions around it, like a terrible necklace of bruises, and he was reminded of the similar abrasions around Lewis Davenport's eyes. The similarity was only superficial. For Davenport, Carr held nothing but contempt, but for Daphne Clements, he felt nothing but sympathy. It was perhaps this profound empathy that made his insides recoil in horror and disgust at the handcuffs that shackled her by one wrist to the bed. They struck him simultaneously as inhumane and unnecessary. She could hardly be expected to escape past the devoted policeman who guarded her, especially in what he assumed to be a drugged state, and even if she could manage to elude the guard, the doctors would hardly allow her to leave without some degree of resistance. And, he thought sadly, if she had been so far into a spiral of despair that her own death was the only visible solution to her, it was surely foolish to suspect that she would have either the energy or the mental capacity to consider flight. He understood the procedural logic of the manacles, but they raged against every aspect of his compassion for humanity.

Slowly, he moved around the bed and pulled a chair towards it, into which he lowered himself. He saw now that her eyes were closed, but they fluttered open at the sound of his arrival. He smiled gently and apologised in a low, avuncular voice for the disturbance. Daphne stared at him, but he had the idea that she barely saw him. She seemed to look through him, as if he were a figment of her imagination, if she was aware of him being there at all, in whatever form. It was to be expected, of course, given the sedatives she would have been given, but Carr could not shake the feeling that this vacant stare that she gave him had as much to do with her own depression as with any medical treatment. At last, however, there seemed to be some flicker of recognition and a smile hovered over her lips, but could not properly materialise.

"Mr Carr?" The voice was weak and hoarse.

"I am here, my child," he said, placing a hand on the side of the bed, a show of kindly solidarity. "I am sorry for disturbing you."

"What a kind face you have," she said.

He offered only a smile in response. "I come with news, dear lady. Matters are coming to a close. This nightmare will soon be over."

If he had expected any reaction of hope or delight, she was to disappoint him. "It should have been over before they brought me here."

"You must not say such things, my child."

Her free hand went to her neck, almost involuntarily. "A few more minutes was all I needed."

Carr slowly raised his hand to hers and brought it back away from her neck. "You are innocent, dear lady, and I not only know it, but I can demonstrate it. You must trust me."

She opened her eyes once more and looked at him with the expression of a woman who had been absent from goodness for too long and who could no longer properly recognise it when she saw it. "How can you be so sure?"

"Because I know who killed Rowena Kettering and I know why. And it was not you."

She frowned. "Then everything I have suffered, everything which has happened, has been for nothing?"

There were moments, Carr thought, when the triumph of truth over deceit did not come in blazes of glory and heroism. Sometimes, like now, it came with a painful acknowledgment that sorrow and despair could have been avoided if matters somehow could have been made to work differently. On those occasions, there was no inclination to rejoice, only to regret.

He struggled to find some words of comfort. "You have survived the ordeal, my child, and you will survive its memory."

"I wish I shared your optimism, Mr Carr." She smiled gently. "Once, I felt like that, as if the world was full of love and opportunity, and that it was a place where people could be happy. I don't feel it so much now."

Carr thought about Josephine Kettering. "You are not alone in those feelings, my child. I can only repeat what I have said. You are young. You will mend."

She stared at him for a long moment, as if trying to find some physical trace of the truth in his face or some confirmation from his expression that she might dare to hope again. "How is Ivor?"

Carr allowed a moment to pass before responding. He searched for the right words, perhaps for a way of evading the truth, but he decided against it. Daphne Clements had suffered too much from lies and deceit already. She now needed the truth to be told, however difficult it might be to hear.

"He is a much-troubled man," said Carr. "His concern for you, above all else."

"Things will never be the same between me and him now, will they?"

Carr knew the answer, but he did not say it. "For now, you must think only of the present, my child. Leave tomorrow to look after itself."

She smiled. "May I ask you a question, Mr Carr?"

"Of course."

"Have you always thought I was innocent?"

He leaned forward and placed his hand on her once again. "I have always considered it a possibility, yes."

She stared into his eyes, desperate to understand. "Why?"

Carr shook his head. "Now is not the time to discuss it. Tomorrow, I shall be able to make everything clear to you. For now, you must rest. I came only to tell you that you have nothing more to fear. Put your faith in me, my child, and I shall not let you down."

"I believe you, Mr Carr." The eyes now seemed more alive than before. "Thank you."

He bowed politely, then raised a finger. "But there are just a few things I wish to ask you before I leave. Firstly, this note you say came from Lewis Davenport. It almost certainly did not."

"It was signed in his name."

"Perhaps, but he did not write it. And you, I think, did not recognise the handwriting?"

"No, I'd never seen it before."

That was consistent, thought Carr, with a smile. "There was no reason why you would recognise it, my child. No reason at all."

"You know who wrote it?"

"Oh yes." He stroked the elaborate moustache carefully. "Now, tell me again about the hypodermic needle and the phial of morphine. Why did you pick them up?"

Her eyes rolled. "I've told you this already."

His smile broadened. "Forgive an old man's lapse of memory."

"I didn't want anybody to stand on them when they went into the library. It was instinct."

His dark eyes glittered. "Quite so. Did you notice that the morphine was the one stolen from your bag?"

"No. I mean, looking back, I know it must have been. But not at the time, no. I was too shocked by seeing Rowena."

"Of course," said Carr softly, as if apologetic for asking the question at all. "Did you see anything else of any importance or anything which struck you as odd?"

"No."

"Nothing which you might expect to see but didn't?"

She frowned. "No. Such as what?"

Carr shrugged. "These questions occur to me sometimes. They may mean nothing at all. Did you notice the French windows?"

She shook her head. "No. I couldn't see anything except Rowena in the chair. Just her, dead…"

Carr patted her arm gently. "Rest now, my child. Think no more of it. You have given me what I need. Tomorrow, your fears and confusion will be gone."

She held onto his hand for longer than he had anticipated, as if the security of feeling it in hers was too precious to abandon. Gently, almost paternally, he stroked her hair, and she closed her eyes. He remained where he was, holding her hand and stroking her hair until sleep overcame her. Then, softly, he released himself and limped silently away. When she awoke an hour or so later, it was as if he had never been there at all.

For his part, Carr was standing outside the entrance to the hospital, gathering his thoughts, when Inspector Mason called out his name. If the interview with Daphne Clements had been successful in terms of clarifying those issues that seemed to Carr vital for his case, it could hardly be classed as such for those discussions that had been less evidential and more personal in context. It saddened him to think that the lives of two young girls should be so adversely affected by the events at Marsden Grange that their future outlook on life was now considerably darker than it had been before. Such catastrophes never passed without leaving some scars, of course, but Carr was a man who relished the hope and ambition of the young, in its wide-eyed glory at the world and its opportunities, and when that youthful optimism was darkened by tragedy, it saddened him deeply. It was another symptom of this increasingly oppressive guilt that he felt at being the one left behind. He had survived the attempt on his life, and Miranda had not, and those children they might have had were never given the opportunity to live, but he still lived himself. How was it fair? He thought again about the man he had known, who had survived the war when his brother had not, but who had ended his own life in the bath, with a razor and a bottle of whisky. Carr had no such compulsions for self-destruction, but he felt he could understand them in others.

Into these melancholy thoughts, Mason suddenly intruded. He had evidently been running, for he was slightly out of breath and there were beads of sweat around his forehead and temples. Carr greeted him with an amiable smile and a word of friendship, patting him on the shoulder. Amid his recent musings, Carr found the inspector's face as good a tonic as any medicine in the building outside which they stood.

"You need to take a moment to recover yourself, my friend," said Carr.

"I called into the local station, quite by chance, and they told me you were here." Mason indicated a file of papers in his hand. "These are only preliminary notes, and we're waiting on a fuller report, but it is a reply from New York about the Salvatore Ferrara assassination."

Carr's eyes twinkled with excitement. "Ah, yes! And?"

"Ferrara was shot in front of one of his girlfriends, a dancer in one of his nightclubs." Mason's nose twitched with distaste. "Hardly the sort of place we'd be likely to visit."

"And the motive?"

Mason shrugged. "Some sort of retribution by a rival gangster."

"What the Americans will call 'a hit', I believe."

If Mason was amused by Carr's use of the vernacular, he did not show it. "The girl was to be the lead witness for the prosecution, but days before the trial, she vanished. Nobody seems to know why, but everyone's guess seems to be as near as damn it the same."

"She was scared away?"

"Pressure put on her, threats against her, anything from serious sexual assault to murder. You can imagine the details."

"Only too vividly."

Carr thought for a moment. "Do we know where she is now?"

Mason gave a wry smile. "I think you do, you old dog, but officially, no. Again, it's all rumours. There have been reported sightings from Mexico to Madrid, but none confirmed. Given your interest, Mr Carr, I'd say she was rather closer to home."

Carr gave an enigmatic smile. "And the name of this dancer, inspector?"

Mason consulted the notes. "Margot Adler."

Carr gave a curious chuckle of delight. "How very quaint."

"Is it?"

"In its own way, yes, inspector. From a psychological perspective, perhaps."

Mason shook his head. "Look, Mr Carr, I don't mind digging up all this information, but what point is there? It can have nothing to do with Marsden Grange, and even if it is connected, it's of no relevance." He pointed with his folder to the hospital. "The killer of Rowena Kettering is in there. And she has been since she tried to kill herself out of guilt."

To the inspector's surprise, Carr's eyes flashed with anger, and he struck his cane fiercely against the pavement. "No, Inspector! I warned you against running in the wrong direction, and you continue to do so. You must look more closely at the personalities concerned."

"My case is complete."

"It is far from complete. It leaves too many questions unanswered. Why should Daphne Clements buy arsenic if she meant to murder Rowena Kettering with morphine? Why buy arsenic at all, when as a nurse, she would be able to lay her hands on so many poisons? For that matter, how do you know that it was not Tilly Royce, also a nurse, who did not obtain such a poison?"

"There's no evidence of that," argued Mason.

Carr was not listening. "Who tried to run over Mrs Kettering, since Daphne Clements cannot drive a car? Who slashed the portrait of the dead woman? Most crucially of all, why were the French windows unlocked, and why was Daphne Clements holding that hypodermic needle and phial? You will say that these matters are incidental, but you know as well as I do that they must be explained if a defence barrister is not to use them to tear your theories into rags."

"And you can explain them all?"

"Oh, yes, inspector. Everything now is clear to me." Carr's anger seemed to have passed, and he patted his friend once more on the shoulder. "Come, and I shall explain everything to you over a little glass of something. You will need some sort of stimulant when you hear the truth of the matter."

Mason, never a man to refuse such an invitation, nodded his approval and allowed himself to be escorted to the nearest public house. In his mind, however, he remained satisfied with his assessment of the murder of Rowena Kettering, but he felt able to indulge Everett Carr for an hour or so. As matters transpired, in a little over half that time, his certainties about the case exploded, and his confidence in his conclusions was shattered. What was left behind in the wreckage of those erroneous theories and misinterpreted evidence was the cold, unfiltered facts of the matter. When Everett Carr set it out to him, Inspector Mason found that he was staring the truth in its face at last, and it glared back at him with all its hateful, wicked malevolence.

Chapter Forty-Three

Everett Carr stood in front of the mantelpiece, his head bowed, as the guests of Marsden Grange filed into the library.

He looked at his audience, wondering once again why he felt the compulsion to have these final confrontations, which some would undoubtedly call theatrical displays. Carr thought he knew the reason, of course. They were little more than the summary of evidence he would give at the end of every trial: a recapitulation of the facts of the case in question, a review of evidence from both prosecution and defence, before the final command was given for the jury's deliberations to commence. To Carr, they were second nature, but in this present case, against the theatrical background of Rowena Kettering's life, it seemed particularly apt.

He saw them all now, filing into the room and taking their seats, forming a semi-circle of suspicion and deceit. There were muttered exchanges of disgust when Lewis Davenport entered the room, the full extent of his blackmail and betrayal having been announced by Josephine Kettering earlier that evening. If she had taken a macabre delight in telling the story of it, nobody blamed her, particularly not Lewis. He had tried to talk to her in private, but she had refused, and he had not blamed her for that either. He had taken cocktails and dinner with them, but his presence had been largely ignored and tolerated only as a matter of good manners, rather than from any display of forgiveness.

Carr fixed his attention on each of them, as his eyes glanced around the room. Their expressions ranged from the anxious to the fascinated. Only Edwin Jarratt seemed close to appearing comfortable with the proceedings, his eyes fixed on Carr but with a smile hovering across the lips, a faded grin of support and understanding. Carr did not acknowledge it. Instead, his eyes passed on from Jarratt to Daphne Clements, sitting at the back of the room, her hands still clamped in irons, and a uniformed officer standing behind her, like some sort of midnight blue omen. Like Jarratt, she stared at Carr, but there was no vague smile across her lips and no expression of a queer sort of solidarity. In her eyes, Carr read fear and, on her lips, he imagined he saw a silent, breathless prayer of hope.

There was a silence, during which the final cigarettes were lit, the final drinks poured, and the final attempts to ensure comfort were made. Carr allowed it to pass before he began to speak.

"It was fitting, I thought, for us to meet here." He gave a slow but majestic sweep of his arm across the room. "This library was where the mystery of the death of Rowena Kettering began, and it is appropriate, I think, that it is in here that it ends."

"I thought it ended with the inquest's findings," said Felix Kettering, looking over his shoulder at Daphne. "No doubt about it, surely?"

"Yes, that's right," said Adele. "Why are we having to sit through this nonsense?"

Carr smiled gently. "You think this case is so simple, Miss Mills?"

"Open and shut, I would have said."

Carr's smile widened. "No doubt, but you are like my friend, Inspector Mason, who also believed this case to be as simple as it appeared. Daphne Clements was seen by all of us, standing over the body of Rowena Kettering, holding the very weapons used to kill her. And there were the words she said to Ivor Kettering, which you all seemed to think were so damning that they could have put the noose around her neck by themselves."

Felix scoffed. "Well, aren't they? What was it she said? *She's dead, and we're free of her at last.* Practically a confession. We're not going to pretend she didn't say it, are we?"

"No, Mr Kettering," said Carr.

"Then you agree with me?"

"No, Mr Kettering," repeated Carr with a more dangerous emphasis. "We shall come onto those words in due course, and I am pleased that you remember them so well because I want you to bear them in mind very carefully when I return to them.

"For now, let me take you through the events of that night and my own impressions of them. From the beginning, I have been conscious of the danger of taking matters as they appeared. Perhaps it was the influence of Mrs Kettering herself, the famed actress, whose Lady Macbeth I had so admired and enjoyed. But theatre is all about deception and deceit: swords and knives with blunted edges, or manufactured from wood but made to look like steel, revolvers with blank charges, painted canvases made to look like city streets, people pretending to be other people. Pretence, fabrication, and misdirection. I had that sensation throughout the progress of this whole affair, the idea that something was not quite how it seemed.

"You may dismiss what I say as being the product of instinct, of a suspicious mind, perhaps, and I might agree, were it not for two facts: the first, the speed with which morphine poisoning takes effect, and the second that Daphne Clements said that she picked up the phial and hypodermic needle so that people would not stand on them.

"As to the first, as Dr Jarratt confirmed to me, morphine takes between five or ten minutes to kill, if injected. A question which struck me immediately, but which seems not to have occurred to anyone else, including the good inspector and your local coroner, is why Daphne Clements, after murdering Rowena Kettering, should stand for five to ten minutes whilst her victim died, still holding the incriminating hypodermic needle and phial, and then scream so loudly that it brought the whole household to her side. What could possibly make her behave in such a way? As a murderess, would she not have committed her crime and crept silently back to bed in those five or ten minutes?"

It was Josephine Kettering who offered an explanation. "She might have wanted to make sure that the poison had worked."

Carr held up a cautionary finger. "But she is a nurse. She would know the precise amount required to kill and how long it would take to do so. Why should she need to make sure of it?"

Josephine thought for a moment, before conceding defeat. "It does seem odd."

"Odd indeed," said Carr, "and it concerned me. As, too, did this question of picking up the hypodermic needle and phial. Again, if Miss Clements was the killer, why would she need to pick up the hypodermic needle at all? She would have brought it with her, and she would surely have taken it away with her, once the deed was done. What she certainly would not have done would be to put it on the floor, pick it up again, and then stand with it awaiting discovery."

"You're assuming she's telling the truth about it being on the floor in the first place," challenged Felix.

Carr shook his head. "Why should she lie about it? She told the truth about the morphine being stolen from her bag. In fact, it was she who offered that piece of information of her own accord. Why lie about one point regarding the phial but be honest about another? You must accept, Mr Kettering, that if she is lying, then you have to account for her actions as I have set them out, and I repeat my previous objection on that point, that they simply do not make sense in those terms."

"And if she's telling the truth?" said Felix.

Carr bowed. "Then I think things begin to make a little more sense. Consider her precise words to me. She was afraid that someone might step on the hypodermic needle and the phial *as they entered the room*. Does that not suggest something to you? To me, it suggests that the hypodermic needle and the phial were *closer to the door than to the chair in which Rowena Kettering lay dead*. If they were by the chair, anyone entering the room would have time to register them and avoid standing on them, so Daphne Clements would have had no cause to fear that might happen. For her to think it possible at all, the hypodermic needle and phial must surely be so close to the point of entry that it might seem unavoidable."

"But what does it matter?" asked Josephine.

Carr turned to face her. "Because, my child, it suggests that they were left there deliberately, does it not? Miss Clements was meant to see them, and she was meant to pick them up. They had been carefully placed so that, psychologically, she would act on instinct and in exactly the manner she described. The culprit needed Daphne to pick up the hypodermic needle and phial before she sensed anything was wrong in the room. Had her suspicions been aroused, by seeing the body sooner, for instance, she might have taken more care not to touch anything. The hypodermic needle and phial must seem to have been dropped by accident, thereby creating no such suspicion, and compelling her to pick up the incriminating objects in all innocence."

"It seems rather a risk for someone to take," argued Tilly Royce.

"A calculated one, I think," said Carr.

Jarratt interrupted. "I know where you want this to go, Mr Carr. You want to say that Miss Clements was framed for the murder of Rowena Kettering. But anyone might have come into the library and found the body."

Josephine nodded. "And how did the killer know that Daphne would be in the library at all?"

Carr smiled. "Because she had been sent a note asking her to go to the library at one o'clock that morning. You will all be aware of this mysterious communication because it was dealt with at the inquest. It apparently came from Lewis Davenport, although he denied writing it. It alleged that there was some professional scandal attached to Ivor Kettering, which was in imminent danger of being exposed."

"There is no such scandal," declared Ivor.

Carr calmed him with a nod of his head. "The truth or otherwise of the allegation matters less than its effect. Daphne Clements had no way of knowing that the scandal was not genuine. She took it at face value. Why should she not? All she knew, in the moment, was that there was some danger threatening you, and the fact that it was your private secretary alerting her to the fact made it seem all the more genuine."

Mason nodded. "And Miss Clements didn't know Lewis Davenport's handwriting, so she had no reason to suspect it was fake."

Carr bowed in agreement. "The note's only purpose was to ensure that Daphne would be in the library at the time of Rowena's death. And now, you see the importance of those five or ten minutes which so confused me. Of course, Miss Clements did not stand there for that length of time, watching Mrs Kettering die. She had been told to be there for one o'clock, the very time Dr Jarratt and the police pathologist estimated was the time of death, which could only mean that Rowena Kettering had been injected with the morphine *five or ten minutes before that time*. And during those crucial minutes, the trap which had been laid for Miss Clements was set. But by whom and why?"

Carr began to pace the length of the hearth rug. "As to why, that is very easily explained. She was in love with Rowena's husband, and Rowena had refused a divorce. There had been a public argument between the two of them over dinner that night. For a killer wanting to murder Mrs Kettering for his or her own reasons, Daphne Clements was the perfect alibi."

Josephine looked over at Daphne with eyes that betrayed more sorrow and sympathy. "How awful."

Carr noticed the moment which had passed between them but simply continued with his analysis. "Having assured myself that Daphne Clements was being framed for the murder of Rowena Kettering, those seemingly incriminating words seemed to me now to be nothing of the kind. Mr Kettering," he turned his attention to Felix. "Your memory of them serves you well. What were they?"

Felix, taken aback by the sudden attention fixed on him, muttered the words once more. "*'She's dead, and we're free of her at last.'*"

Carr's eyes glittered. "Once I accepted in my mind that Daphne Clements was innocent, those words seemed to me to become nothing more than a statement of fact. Rowena was dead, and the question of granting a divorce no longer mattered. Ivor and Daphne were free to marry."

There were muted gasps of realisation. Eyes turned to face Daphne, down whose cheeks tears had begun to fall. Her attention remained on Everett Carr, and she realised now for certain that there were some people left in the world on whom one could rely and in whom one could place one's trust. He smiled at her, as if acknowledging her understanding, and he gave a small bow of gratitude.

"If Daphne Clements was innocent, however," Carr continued, "someone else in this house was guilty."

There was a murmur of hushed protest, the noise of shimmering silk as positions were shifted in respective chairs. Low voices made indeterminate sounds of disapproval, and eyes flickered over the faces of those sitting closest to each other.

"There had been previous attempts on Rowena Kettering's life," Carr was saying. "An attempt to run her down in Campden Hill Square and a glass of water filled with arsenic."

Jarratt's attention was seized, and he sat up in his chair. "Arsenic? Rowena was poisoned with morphine."

Carr nodded. "Nevertheless, in a glass of water standing on Rowena's bedside cabinet, the police found traces of arsenic. These two failed murder attempts convinced me that Daphne Clements was innocent of the crime. On the one hand, she could not possibly have attempted to drive a car into Mrs Kettering; on the other, why should she bother with the morphine if she had already poisoned Rowena's bedside water with arsenic?"

Jarratt was nodding his head. "So, you thought more than one person was plotting to kill Rowena: whoever drove that car, whoever poisoned the glass with arsenic, and whoever used the morphine."

Felix Kettering gave a snarling laugh of derision. "Three different murderers? It's preposterous."

"I did not say that there were three different murderers," said Carr calmly, "only that there was potentially more than one, none of which was Daphne Clements. Who then? Only by considering the people concerned could I hope to find the answer, and it soon became clear that everyone in this room had reason to wish Mrs Kettering dead.

"Her husband and Daphne Clements shared a motive, of course, in her refusal to grant him a divorce. Her daughter also had a motive, having learned that she was about to be disinherited, a strategy devised by Rowena Kettering to attempt to dissuade both Lewis Davenport and Dr Edwin Jarratt from marrying her. In both cases, it is fair to say that she underestimated both men. Dr Jarratt, of course, had an additional motive to silence Rowena, in that her continued accusations that he had committed murder might eventually lead him into serious trouble. As it is, for reasons which I shall explain later with the good doctor's permission, those threats were entirely misconceived."

Tilly Royce raised her hand. "It is quite clear where this part of the charade is heading, Mr Carr. Might I be permitted to explain for myself what you will no doubt say is my apparent motive for murder?"

Carr stared at her for a moment. "I am at your service, dear lady."

She rose to her feet. "I suspect everyone already knows, or at least suspects it. Ivor, I suspect you have always known."

Ivor glared at her. "You can hardly have assumed it was a secret, Tilly."

"Known what?" asked Josephine.

Tilly looked into the girl's eyes. "I was in love with Rowena. It was not reciprocated; I should make that very clear. She wasn't that type of woman."

Josephine stared at Everett Carr, pleading for him to disprove it. His eyes were heavy with regret, and he nodded his head slowly. "Remember, my child, your mother's warning about loving someone who cannot love you back?"

Josephine looked at Tilly. "She meant you?"

"I'm sorry, Josephine." Tilly looked around at the remaining faces. Their shock, their disapproval, their empathy, if any, meant nothing to her. Their feelings, their prejudices, and their opinions had no effect on her. They simply could never comprehend what had existed in her heart for the woman who was now dead. "I have nothing more to say," she hissed and sat down once more, with a potent mixture of haughty indifference and noble dignity.

Felix gave a cackle of amusement. "Unrequited love, the oldest motive in the book."

Carr turned to face him. "And what of your motive, Mr Kettering? Or that of Miss Mills?"

Adele glared at him. "I don't have any motive."

"Nor have I," said Felix. "Rowena didn't suspect me of being a murderer, she hadn't disinherited me, I obviously didn't want to marry Josephine, I wasn't secretly in love with my stepmother, and she wasn't able to prevent me from marrying Adele. By the standards of your possible motives, Mr Carr, I'm afraid the game is over."

Carr shook his head, the dark eyes hardened with determination. "The game is far from over. The pair of you have motive enough. You are a most devoted couple, is that not so? If one of you had a secret, the other would strive to keep it. Yes?"

Felix was on his feet. "I think you'd better say what it is you think I'm hiding from everyone, Mr Carr. Let me say first that I have a very good solicitor."

Carr smiled. "If you think you need to send for him, Mr Kettering, please do so."

"If you're going to accuse me of murder, perhaps I shall."

Adele put a hand on Felix's arm, coaxing him back into his chair. "Let the man talk, darling. He can't know or prove anything about you."

Carr looked at her and smiled warmly. "Very sensible words, dear lady, but I have nothing to prove against Mr Kettering. It is against you that I have proof, Miss Mills, and it is your secret which Felix Kettering is keeping, rather than the other way around."

Adele's eyes cut into him like the blades of an executioner's axe. "I don't know what you're talking about."

Felix took her hand. "Come along, darling. We don't have to listen to any more of this."

"There is nowhere to run to, Miss Mills," said Carr. "You certainly cannot return to America, can you?"

The words, spoken with an amiable innocence, seemed to stop time. Felix glared at Carr, his eyes glimmering with an astonished malice, which Carr had no difficulty in dismissing. His attention was fixed on Adele, who glared at him now not with blades but with brimming tears of fear. Carr nodded slowly.

"You have nothing to fear from me," he said. Glancing at Felix, he added, "Either of you."

Felix, in a final desperate effort to escape, pulled on Adele's arm. "Let's go, darling."

But she was unable to move. Whether it was her own fear or Carr's kindly eyes, Adele Mills could not help but remain motionless, as if she were up to her ankles in quicksand and any sudden movement would be fatal.

"How much do you know?" she asked.

"Everything," said Carr.

"How?" Her fear seemed to rob the question of any of its power.

"A few details, in themselves nothing of importance, but collectively, they were fascinating." He turned to Felix. "When I asked you, Mr Kettering, whether you had ever been to America, you said no. It was a lie. If you recall, I suggested to you early on that Daphne Clements might have been framed for the murder of your step-mother. You referred to her then as *a patsy*, a famously American turn of phrase. Again, just now, Miss Mills referred to this whole business being an *open and shut* case, another phrase of American origin."

"That means nothing," argued Felix.

"Not in itself," agreed Carr, "but there was the curious statement from Rowena Kettering herself about the attempt on her life in Campden Hill Square. Miss Royce was kind enough to tell me that Mrs Kettering had said that the vehicle had come at her *in the wrong direction*. What that meant was not clear, but it seems clear now that she meant that the car had come at her from the *right-hand side of the road*. You will be aware that the Americans drive on that side, as opposed to the left, as we do in this country."

Slowly, he allowed the meaning of his words to settle on the room. Then, slowly, Carr reached into his inside pocket and produced a newspaper clipping.

"The real proofs began to fall into place when I discovered that Rowena kept various souvenirs of her time abroad in touring productions," he said. "I found a selection of this type of clipping from various editions of the *New York Times*. There were various stories, anything from politics to criminal cases. This particular one," he added, holding the clipping above his head, "concerns the assassination of a Mafia crime boss, a certain Salvatore Ferrara. In particular, it concerns a witness to the crime who subsequently fled before the trial of Ferrara's killer. This witness was a nightclub dancer, by the name of Margot Adler."

Adele's eyes had closed, and her cheeks had lost their colour. Felix held onto her, glaring defiantly at the gathered throng, as if the whole company was now out for her blood. Josephine had let out a gasp of comprehension.

"Mummy said you'd been a dancer," she hissed.

Felix sneered. "Be quiet, Josephine."

Carr was nodding. "When I first met you, Miss Mills, you talked about how it was sometimes safer to bury yourself away in the countryside."

"Damn," she hissed to herself.

"A curious phrase to use," said Carr. "Why say it was safer to do so? Safer than what? Remaining where you were, back in America? Emphasising that you were buried away in the countryside suggested a desire for concealment."

"You're a very clever man, Mr Carr," purred Adele.

Carr bowed. "On our first meeting, Miss Mills, I had noticed a faint accent in your pattern of speech, although you have covered it very well."

"Thank you." Her native drawl was now more apparent, either by accident or design.

Carr smiled. "Finally, of course, there is the coincidence of your initials. A simple but effective inversion. One which I had seen elsewhere, in Mr Danforth's poison book, when you used the name Margaret Anders."

Mason was shaking his head, cursing his own blindness. "Margot Adler, Margaret Anders, Adele Mills."

Carr smiled at him. "If you cast your mind back, inspector, you will recall that Margaret Anders bought two ounces of arsenic trioxide."

Jarratt rose to his feet. "The arsenic!"

Felix glared at him. "These fancy bloody word games don't prove a thing."

"No," said Carr, "but perhaps the date on which the arsenic was bought does. It was purchased on 16 October 1935."

"So what?" asked Felix.

Mason was quick to reply. "In Danforth's records, the date is written numerically, and it gives the month before the day."

CHAPTER FORTY-THREE

Carr looked down at Adele Mills. "Another American character trait."

Adele had succumbed. Her shoulders shook with her sobs, and Felix held her tighter than ever. His eyes now were less defiant and confrontational, and they looked at Carr with a desperate plea for clemency. Jarratt had run over to the drinks table and poured a stiff measure of brandy, which he now forced under Adele's nose. She retched at it, but Felix took it with gratitude and gently eased the stimulant past her lips.

Carr spoke. "Margot Adler witnessed the murder of Salvatore Ferrara. She had been promised protection by the New York police, but she lost her nerve."

Adele was staring at him, but there was no venom in her eyes, only defeat. "Only because of the terrible things they said they'd do to me. Do you know what they were, Mr Carr?"

"I do." His voice was low, subdued by disgust and regret.

Felix took her hand in his. "One night, Margot appeared on the doorstep of my apartment in Manhattan. She told me that we had to leave that minute. They knew that she was appearing as a witness for the prosecution. How they knew, I don't know. Crooked cops, maybe. Anyway," he added after a grim pause, "there were threats, as you said. If Margot testified, they made it clear that they'd find her, torture her, rape her, and kill her. They threatened the most unspeakable things."

Carr closed his eyes in a painful memory. "When gangsters take revenge, they show no mercy."

Adele, her eyes now stained with tears, looked up at him over the top of the brandy glass she cradled close to her lips. In his dark eyes, she saw something of an understanding of her fears. How he could have known, she could not tell, but she felt certain that he did, and that the experience had been personal.

Felix was still talking. "So, we packed up and came home. We changed Margot's name, of course."

Carr was looking at Adele. "In my experience, people who use an alias often cannot deviate from their birth name entirely. In your case, dear lady, you felt compelled to keep your true initials, albeit reversed."

Felix nodded. "For a while, we thought we were safe. Nobody in America, none of our friends over there, knew very much about my life here. Then, without any warning, Rowena made it clear that she knew something about Adele's past. She was subtle about it, of course, but there was no doubt. I didn't know she had collected those clippings. I suppose something in one of them stirred a memory or aroused a suspicion."

Mason nodded. "She would have been able to get copies of past editions of the newspapers. It may even have been reported over here."

Carr nodded. "At some point, a photograph of the missing witness, this nightclub dancer, will have appeared, and Rowena must have seen it."

Felix sighed. "She threatened to expose Margot. I said she was beyond evil, and the world would be a better place if she just died."

Carr looked to Josephine. "That was the argument you witnessed, my child, as you told me when we first met."

Mason was glaring at Felix. "So, you thought you had better silence her."

Jarratt took the now-empty brandy glass from Adele's shaking fingers. "You tried to run her down, first."

Adele looked at him. "A moment of madness."

"And then you decided on poison?" Jarratt allowed the silence to speak for itself before he walked away to replace the brandy glass.

"This makes you serious suspects for the murder," said Mason. "You realise that, don't you?"

Felix got to his feet. "We bought and used the arsenic, I confess that. But she wasn't killed by that, was she? And like Mr Carr says, why kill her with morphine if we had already poisoned her drinking water?"

Ivor had walked over to his son, his eyes burning with rage. "If you murdered Rowena, say so."

"Father, the morphine had nothing to do with us, I swear. And we didn't actively plot to incriminate Daphne, or anyone else for that matter."

Josephine was crying now, and Jarratt was beside her, his arms around her. "I don't understand any of this," she was whispering. "I just don't understand."

Everett Carr stepped over to Ivor. "Your son and his fiancée planned murder, sir, but the fact remains that your wife did not die from arsenical poisoning."

Ivor looked into those dark, compassionate eyes. "But if they didn't do it, who the Hell did?"

"In order to answer that," said Carr, "we shall have to understand *why* your wife died. You see, Mr Kettering, the motive for your wife's death lies in the past. More particularly, it lies in *your own past.*"

Ivor stared blankly at him. "What are you suggesting?"

Josephine was suddenly breathless with fear. "Daddy…?"

Everett Carr allowed no time for any further reply. "The key to this mystery, Mr Kettering, and the clue to the only person who could have killed your wife is *the death of your first child, Peter.*"

Chapter Forty-Four

For a long moment, there was silence. Josephine's sobs had caught in her throat, and she stared now in horror at Everett Carr. Felix's fear was frozen in his lungs. Lewis Davenport rose to his feet, his heart hammering against his chest. Ivor's hands had clasped themselves into fists, and the air snorted from his nostrils like the fierce and predatory breaths of an animal.

"How dare you?" he hissed. "How *dare* you?"

Everett Carr stared at him with a dark compassion. "The central point to this whole mystery is the afternoon that your wife drowned your baby son."

Jarratt had risen to his feet, and now he gently placed his hands on Ivor's shoulders. "Perhaps we should let Mr Carr speak for a moment longer, sir."

Ivor allowed himself to be seated once more, but his eyes remained on Carr, burning with indignation. "Are you suggesting I killed my wife, Mr Carr, because she killed our son? I didn't know about that until you delivered that awful letter to me, for God's sake."

Carr shook his head. "I do not accuse you, Mr Kettering. Whoever killed your wife wrote that note to Daphne Clements, and she would surely have recognised your handwriting."

"And Daphne didn't know the handwriting," said Josephine.

"The killer must also have known about the effects of morphine poisoning, just as he or she must have been able to use a hypodermic needle," continued Carr. "The killer was also someone who despised Daphne Clements as well as Rowena Kettering. To frame one human being for the murder of another is to commit two murders. Who would hate those two people so much?" His eyes scanned the room, before finally coming to rest on the face of one of them. "A spurned lover, perhaps?"

Tilly Royce glared at him. "Don't be ridiculous."

Carr shook his head. "You wrote that note to Miss Clements, with the sole purpose of getting her into the library at that specific time. Of all the people in this house, you were one of the few whose handwriting Miss Clements would not have known."

"But only one of them," scoffed Tilly.

Carr ignored the objection. "You were in love with Rowena Kettering, by your own admission, and how you hated Daphne Clements for the pain she was causing the woman you loved. You were a nurse. Morphine and its effects would be well known to you."

Ivor leaned forward in his chair. "If she loved Rowena, she'd hardly kill her, would she? She'd kill Daphne or…me."

"Gladly, Ivor," Tilly smiled, but her eyes remained on Carr. "Do you have an answer for that?"

"Yes, but I would prefer you to supply it."

Tilly's eyes were hardened, but her smile was sardonically arrogant. "You can't have it all ways, Mr Carr. Ivor makes a good point, and I will add to it, just to show how ridiculous you are."

Despite the insult, Carr bowed politely. "Please do, dear lady."

Tilly was unperturbed. "You said that Peter Kettering's death was at the heart of the mystery. That was before I'd met Rowena. It certainly has no bearing on my feelings for her."

Felix was on his feet. "She's right, Mr Carr. It doesn't make any sense."

Carr held up a hand, commanding silence. "Did I not tell you that this is the world of the theatre, of smoke and mirrors, of things not being how they appear to be?"

Felix shook his head. "I don't understand."

Carr turned to face him. "The reason it makes no sense to say Tilly Royce is the killer is her apparent lack of motive. But what if the motive for Rowena Kettering's death was someone else's, and Miss Royce is merely an accomplice?"

"An accomplice?" gasped Josephine.

Carr nodded. "Miss Royce wrote that note to Miss Clements. She slashed the portrait. She planted the hypodermic needle and the phial of morphine. She did it all, but it was done to carry out a malicious plan to incriminate Daphne Clements and have her hanged."

"Whose plan?" asked Josephine, her voice shrill with anxiety and confusion.

Carr stared into her eyes. "Someone who wanted Rowena Kettering dead because of what she'd done to her son, Peter. Someone who hated Daphne Clements so passionately that her execution for murder would serve as a fitting revenge for stealing Ivor Kettering's heart. Someone who lost everything because of that relationship. Someone who had the opportunity to steal the phial of morphine from Daphne's nursing bag. Someone who said that Miss Clements and Mr Kettering would be together only over Rowena's dead body. Someone whom Miss Royce would help carry out such a plot without question or compunction." Carr posed each of the questions with an increasingly accusatory tone until, finally, he answered them with a triumphant flourish.

"The person who desired Rowena Kettering's death more than anyone else was Rowena Kettering herself."

The reaction was a curious blend of shock, ridicule, and surprise. Gasps of hesitant laughter hovered in the atmosphere, and the eyes that stared at Carr were collectively wide with disbelief. Josephine was shaking her head, tears forming in her eyes, and Jarratt wrapped his arms around her, soothing her with hushed assurances. Ivor seemed to deflate, as if the shock of the statement had been like a pin to his soul. Daphne's attention was reserved for Everett Carr, and she glared at him as if incapable of understanding what she had heard. Only Lewis Davenport seemed to understand the logic of Carr's indictment.

Only Carr had words to say. "The fact that Mrs Kettering was not in her bedroom at one o'clock, thereby allowing Josephine Kettering to search it, showed that she was already in the library at that time. But why? There had never been any suggestion of Rowena being summoned there. Why should Rowena be there at that particular time, unless she knew what was about to happen? Rowena Kettering dictated the note from Lewis Davenport to Miss Clements, two people whose handwriting her victim could not possibly have recognised."

Josephine was shaking her head. "I can't believe it."

Carr looked down at her. "She felt she had no reason to live, my child, and she planned her own death. As a final act of revenge, her killing was designed to implicate Miss Clements and see her hanged for murder."

Ivor was glaring at Tilly. "And you helped her?"

Tilly did not reply. If Ivor expected any response, he did not display his disappointment. Felix walked over to Carr.

"It seems so melodramatic," he said.

Carr nodded. "Did you not all complain that Rowena was prone to melodrama? You accused her of it at dinner on that night yourself, Mr Kettering. And your father complained that he considered it melodramatic that Rowena could not bear to see his first wife alive in you, so desperately wanted a child of her own."

"That is true," said Ivor.

Josephine screamed through her grief. "It isn't true. She didn't kill herself. Why should she?"

Carr limped over to her and looked down into her eyes. His were filled with warmth and sympathy. "She saw no way out, my child. As I said to Mr Kettering, life had treated his wife most cruelly. Her eyesight was failing badly—within two years, she would have been totally blind. The prospect was horrifying to her."

"But she would have managed," protested Josephine. "We would have helped."

Carr continued. "She was suffering so much, my child. She had lost your father to Miss Clements. Lewis Davenport knew the truth about the drowning of her son. She would lose your father to that secret as much as to Daphne Clements. All your mother's pain and grief, about her past and her present, converged, and her will to live abandoned her. And so, she decided she should die, but that it would be on her own terms."

"But she had lived with what she had done to Peter all this time," argued Ivor. "Why would it be a consideration for her now?"

Carr looked at Edwin Jarratt. "In an argument with the doctor here about Florence Kendall, Dr Jarratt asked her how she could be so pious and whether she had never done anything of which she was ashamed. Doctor, how did she respond?"

Jarratt spoke softly. "She stared at me as if I were the Devil incarnate."

"Precisely, because her guilt, which she had so desperately subdued for all these years, came back to her in that moment." He turned to look at Lewis Davenport. "Not long afterwards, she was threatened with blackmail because of it."

Josephine broke down in tears but offered no reply. Ivor came to her side and took her in his arms, rocking her as if she were a baby. Jarratt looked on, his eyes heavy with impotent grief and despair.

Carr spoke softly now. "The idea to kill herself must have already occurred to her when she accepted the invitation to tea at Daphne Clements' house. That was when she took the morphine from Miss Clements' bag. Whether the plot to condemn Miss Clements for murder was in her mind then, I cannot say. Only Mr and Mrs Kettering, and Miss Clements herself, could possibly have come into contact with that medical bag."

"So, Mrs Kettering had to be considered a suspect, at least in the framing of Daphne Clements," said Mason, with a shake of his head.

Carr smiled. "And if she was a suspect in that, she must be considered a suspect in her own murder."

Ivor had walked to the drinks table and poured himself a glass of courage. "It is all so bewildering."

Carr looked across at him. "As bewildering as I found the French windows."

"The French windows?" said Ivor, confused.

"From the beginning," said Carr, "I was puzzled by the fact that the French windows of this room were unlocked on the night of Rowena's death. Why should they be? There was no suggestion that Daphne Clements had entered or left by those windows, nor would she have any reason to do so. But why else would they be unlocked if not to allow someone to pass through them? It was raining that night, you will recall. If either Rowena Kettering or Daphne Clements had come through those windows, they would have shown traces of it. And why should they go out in their nightwear in any event? It made no sense, and yet there was nobody else in the room. Therefore, if nobody had entered through those windows, *someone must have left by them.*

"Only Dr Jarratt was outside this house when the death was discovered. You will remember, Mr Kettering, that you had to get your keys to let him in, and that he was partially dressed and wet from the rain. He claimed to have been walking on the terrace, but to do so in such weather seemed unlikely. Furthermore, he told me that he went outside at half past midnight through the front door. Now, Bates, the butler, locks this house at midnight, as both he and Ivor Kettering told me. There was no way in which Dr Jarratt could have left through the front door at half past the hour without a key, which he did not possess.

"However, he could have left through the French windows. The key was still in the lock. It was simple enough for him to turn it and exit the library, run round to the front of the house, and begin to bang on the door for entry. He was wet, certainly, but not so much to suggest that he had been exposed to the rain for over half an hour."

Felix was shaking his head. "But why should he lie about it?"

"Because he was in the library, hiding behind the curtain which covers the French windows," said Carr, "and what he saw from there slowly convinced him of the truth."

Jarratt was staring at Tilly Royce. "It's true."

Josephine looked up imploringly at him. "You saw my mother kill herself?"

But it was Everett Carr who replied, brandishing the handkerchief once more. "No, my child, he did not see that, because she didn't kill herself. This, after all, was deliberate murder."

Josephine glared at him. "But you said she killed herself!"

Carr shook his head. "No, no. I said that she wanted to die, that life had become too much for her, and that the plot to implicate Miss Clements was hers. I did not say that she killed herself."

Ivor was beginning to understand, as his mind drifted into the past. "She once threatened to commit suicide. I told her she wouldn't have the courage to do it."

Carr bowed. "And you were correct. When the crucial moment came, she lacked the courage to go through with it. So, she turned to her old friend, who had been a nurse, and who loved her so deeply that she would do anything for her." He looked at Tilly. "You said as much yourself, dear lady, if you recall."

Tilly simply stared into his eyes. "I remember."

Carr's voice was now gentle. "You injected her with the morphine, then wiped your fingerprints from the hypodermic and the phial, using Rowena's own handkerchief, and you placed them carefully where Daphne Clements would be sure to pick them up. Then, you handed the handkerchief back to Rowena. There would be no suspicion aroused by her holding her own handkerchief. Finally, you climbed onto a chair and slashed the portrait. And that was how those five or ten minutes, which so confused me, were spent."

"Why slash the portrait at all?" asked Felix.

"To emphasise the fact of murder. There must be no suggestion of suicide, even Rowena's contemplation of it. If there were, the second part of the plan would fail, and Daphne Clements would not hang."

Felix lowered his head, then looked at Daphne, feeling pity for her for the first time. "Yes, I see."

Carr continued. "But the plan went wrong, did it not, Miss Royce? And the reason was one which you could not have predicted or planned against."

"What was the reason?" asked Ivor.

With a dramatic flourish, Carr produced the monogrammed handkerchief. "The initials on this handkerchief, 'RK', clearly identify it as belonging to Rowena Kettering."

"Where did you find that?" asked Ivor. "It wasn't on Rowena's body."

"No," said Carr, "but that is where it was found, was it not, Dr Jarratt?"

Jarratt nodded, flushing slightly under the pressure of the eyes which now turned to him. "I found it on the floor by Rowena's chair. She must have dropped it when the poison took effect."

Tilly's eyes closed in their final defeat. "My God…"

Carr bowed his head. "Continue, if you please, doctor."

Jarratt stood up. "I was in the drawing room, having been unable to sleep. I decided to try again, and I was on my way across the hall to the stairs, when I saw the light in here was on. I came in to see who it was, and I found Rowena dead. Like Daphne, I saw the hypodermic needle and the phial, but my instincts were quicker than hers. I stepped over them. It was obvious something strange had happened, and I suspected murder. But the handkerchief puzzled me. I couldn't understand why a killer would leave it behind."

"And you wondered whether Rowena might have taken her own life?" asked Carr.

Jarratt nodded. "I thought it was a suicide, but I couldn't see any reason for it. Murder, perhaps, but not suicide."

"You said as much when Inspector Mason broke the news of Daphne's suicide attempt," said Carr. "Those were your exact words. At the time, both the inspector and I thought you were talking about Miss Clements, but in fact, you were talking about Rowena Kettering."

Jarratt seemed not to remember. "Then you told me about Peter's death, Mr Carr, and about blackmail, and it began to make more sense."

Carr nodded. "*Everything makes sense now.*' Again, doctor, your words to the inspector and me. You had not quite understood what you had seen from those curtains, Dr Jarratt, but now, I think, you do."

Jarratt nodded. "I no longer thought it was murder, so I didn't think it would matter if I touched anything. I picked up the handkerchief and would probably have picked up the needle and phial, too, but I heard someone coming. I know now that it was Daphne."

Carr patted him on the shoulder. "Yes, she was approaching the library, thinking she was about to meet Lewis Davenport. If she saw you there, you would be in a very tight spot, so you hid in the only available place, behind the curtains."

"I realised at once that I was in even more danger there," said Jarratt. "Not only was I in the room of a suspicious death, but I was hiding. I knew how it would look. So, as you say, I let myself out of the French windows. I knew that the front door would be locked, but there was nothing I could do about it. I thought I could just lie about the time and hope it was overlooked."

Carr nodded and smiled. He turned to face the whole assembly. "That, my friends, is the truth surrounding the death of Rowena Kettering. It was murder, yes, committed by Miss Royce, but it was a murder committed at the behest of the victim. The mastermind behind it was Rowena Kettering herself, the motive for it was Rowena Kettering's, and the plan to frame Daphne Clements for it was Rowena Kettering's."

He looked at Tilly Royce, hoping that there might be some trace of regret or remorse in her eyes. To his sadness, he saw neither. He saw only a glimmer of pride or, at least, something that might be mistaken for it, and he thought he was unable to understand it. But slowly, as realisation of what it was which he saw in those eyes struck him, he saw something altogether more malicious and more disturbing staring back at him. He saw love.

But not the love which he so desperately cherished in himself for Miranda, nor the love whose joys he so fervently wished on those people for whom life was just beginning, and nor the love which convinced him so often that there was goodness in the world. The love he saw in Tilly Royce's eyes was something quite different: unfiltered, passionate, unrepentant, and darkly absolute. Her words, which had evoked sympathy in him when he had first heard them, now struck horror into his heart: *I would have done anything for her, Mr Carr.*

And as they led her away, Tilly Royce smiled coldly at him, and Everett Carr seemed to feel some part of his soul fracture beyond repair.

Chapter Forty-Five

Their last meeting took place where they had met for the first time, but it was not the same for either of them.

Before, there had been ignorance; now there was knowledge. There had been lies, where now there was truth; and there had been confusion, where now there was explanation. But was anybody, Josephine Kettering thought, better off for it? She did not pose the question to Everett Carr, but she had the growing suspicion that he knew she had asked it of herself. And perhaps Carr had asked it, too, and not for the first time. Certainly, he did not feel better. Those feelings of guilt over Miranda's death, of which he had become so aware over recent months, had not subsided because of his enquiries into Rowena Kettering's murder. If anything, he feared that the guilt had intensified, as if every secret he had unveiled at Marsden Grange had tainted him and become a part of him. And when he looked at Josephine Kettering, Carr seemed to detect something of those fears reflected in her eyes. He saw a girl who had matured and on whose brow the wickedness of the world had left its mark, like that of Cain.

"I'm going away," said Josephine. "Abroad, I mean. Too many memories here."

"Will you return?"

She shrugged. "I haven't decided. Possibly."

"Where will you go, my child?"

"I thought about America. They say it is the land of opportunity." Petulantly, she kicked a stone with the toe of her shoe. "But then Felix and Adele said they were going back there to try to put things right for themselves, so perhaps I won't go there after all."

"Miss Mills is going to testify?"

"Funny, isn't it?" she said with a bitter smile. "How we can't bring ourselves to call her Margot or Miss Adler." Josephine's smile faded. "I can't see what good her testimony can do now. When she vanished, the case was dropped."

"It can be reopened," said Carr. "Where will you go, if not America?"

"Edwin suggested the continent. Florence, perhaps, Geneva, somewhere like that. Perhaps I'll take him up on it."

"He will go with you?"

She shook her head. "I want time alone."

"And if you return?"

She smiled faintly. "Perhaps there is a chance for us. If he behaves himself."

Carr returned the smile. "He loves you. He always has, I think."

"I haven't heard anything from Lewis," she said. "He has gone back to his parents in the North. It was good of you to help Daddy convince the police not to charge him for the blackmail."

"His conscience will be his punishment," said Carr. It had been Ivor Kettering who had expressed the matter best: *We don't want the time and trouble of a prosecution. We want to forget him and have him out of our lives.*

Josephine gave a short shiver. It was growing colder. "Daphne and Daddy have ended their relationship."

"I am sorry to hear it."

There was a twist in his tone of voice which unsettled her. "But you're not surprised?"

Carr shrugged his shoulders. "Perhaps it is too soon to wish for any happy endings, my child. There must be a period of healing for everyone."

She looked at his damaged leg and the sadness in his eyes. "Even for you?"

He nodded slowly. "If I can allow it for myself."

A moment passed between them, and at some point during it, she had begun to cry.

"It's so unfair," she said. "After everything that's happened, the only person who can say they truly loved anybody seems to be Tilly Royce, and that just doesn't seem right."

"It is not right, Miss Kettering, by which I meant it is not correct." Carr turned to face her. "Do not judge the quality of love by Miss Royce's feelings for your mother or by your mother's manipulation of those feelings for her own purposes."

"I can't help it."

"You *must*." Carr's eyes glittered. "You have learned things about your mother, about others you care about, and it has shaken your belief in the world. That is natural, and you must not let it taint you. You must allow yourself to flourish. You must see love for what it truly is, and you can only do that through the future and the living, not through the past and the dead."

"How can you be so optimistic after everything that has happened?"

"I believe in goodness, my child. And so must you." He took hold of her arms. "Because if you do not, you may never love again."

She looked into his dark eyes. "You still believe that love can mean something, Mr Carr?"

He nodded. "Oh, yes, I do. It can and it must. I have said to you before that you have survived this ordeal, and you will survive its memory."

"Perhaps some time away will prove you right."

Carr smiled. "And if it does, you will meet with me and tell me so?"

She laughed and nodded. She stared at him for a long time and then wrapped her arms around his neck. Into his scarf, she muffled a word of gratitude, and then she began to sob gently. For a short time, Carr held her in his arms and strove to keep tears from stinging his eyes.

At last, they separated, and he brushed a final tear from her cheek with his gloved hand. "Go now, my child, and live your life."

She kissed him once more and left him in peace. He never did see her again, but he received letters spasmodically over the next few years, the last of which said that he had been right. Love did matter to her once more, and to prove it, she was engaged. She had enclosed a photograph of her with the man in question. It was not Edwin Jarratt. Josephine Kettering had travelled to Florence after all, and she had found love once again with a successful painter. Carr spared a thought for Jarratt, but for the doctor, too, time would heal. It was only Everett Carr who remained incapable of forgetting his pain. He had learned to live with it, but he was learning that he might never be able to escape from it. He had kept Josephine's photograph on his mantelpiece for several weeks, before deciding that there was a better home for it elsewhere. The decision made, he made the customary journey from the Albany to the cemetery. In the distance, the trees whistled in the breeze, and birds sang happily in the early afternoon sky. Carr was kneeling at Miranda's grave, laying fresh flowers, his eyes glancing frequently to her name and the dedication on the stone. Beside the flowers, he placed the photograph of Josephine Kettering and her artistic fiancé. Had things been different, he thought, it might have been a photograph of his own daughter on the brink of marital happiness. It was a sentimental gesture, perhaps, but Carr made no apology for it. Instead, he preferred to treat it as a reminder of that assurance that he had given to Josephine, one which he knew that Miranda would have shared.

"Love must always mean something," Everett Carr said, placing his fingers on the gravestone. "Mustn't it, my darling?"

About the Author

Matthew Booth is the author of the Everett Carr mysteries, novels inspired by the famous Golden Age of detective fiction, and the noir thriller, *The House of Skulls*, featuring private eye, Alex Priest. Matthew has appeared at numerous events, discussing topics such as Sherlock Holmes, crime and supernatural fiction, film noir, and Jack the Ripper. A member of the Crime Writers Association, he is the current Editor of its monthly magazine, *Red Herrings*, and the co-host of the film noir podcast, *Mean Streets.* He lives with his wife in Manchester, England.

AUTHOR WEBSITE:
  https://www.levelbestbooks.us/matthew-booth.html

SOCIAL MEDIA HANDLES:
  Twitter: @HolmesBooth
  Instagram: matthewboothauthor
  Threads: matthewboothauthor

Also by Matthew Booth

<u>The Everett Carr Mysteries</u>
A Talent for Murder (Level Best Books)
The Dangers of this Night (Level Best Books)
A Killing Amongst the Dead (Level Best Books)
The Serpent's Fang (Level Best Books)

<u>Other Crime Fiction</u>
The House of Skulls (Pegasus Mackenzie Publishing)
When Anthony Rathe Investigates (Sparkling Books)
The Further Exploits of Sherlock Holmes (Sparkling Books)
Sherlock Holmes & the Giant's Hand (Breese Books)